BAA BAA BLACK DEATH

Best Wishes

Bev Rodman

Aug/07

BAA BAA BLACK DEATH

A Novel

Beverley Armstrong-Rodman

iUniverse, Inc.

New York Lincoln Shanghai

BAA BAA BLACK DEATH

iUniverse books may be ordered through booksellers or by contacting:

iUniverse
2021 Pine Lake Road, Suite 100
Lincoln, NE 68512
www.iuniverse.com
1-800-Authors (1-800-288-4677)

This is a work of fiction. All of the characters, names, incidents, organizations, and dialogue in this novel are either the products of the author's imagination or are used fictitiously.

ISBN: 978-0-595-44879-1 (pbk)
ISBN: 978-0-595-89203-7 (ebk)

Printed in the United States of America

Acknowledgements

— Several people have helped and encouraged me along the way

— My husband Ward, who not only keeps me focused, but is always there for me

— My daughter Heather, and son Greg, whose wit, wisdom, and technical help, keep me on my toes

— My sister Jean Archer, whose unfailing enthusiasm cheers me

— My life-long friend and kindred spirit, Marilyn Sutherland, who has travelled the path with me

— My close friend Judith Kennedy, whose elegant hand appears on the cover, and who had fun doing the research

— My buddy Carson Martin, who also did the leg work with great enthusiasm

— My artistic friend Faith Amadio, who once again managed to translate my ideas into a great cover.

Many thanks to each and every one of you

Alphabetical List of Characters

The Black Sheep — looking for love in all the wrong places
Dr. Drew Carson — a moody plastic surgeon
Cleo Chandler — happy-go-lucky boutique clerk
Steffie Chapman — beautiful part owner of boutique with Kitty
Eva Conrad — one of the Black Sheep's early victims
Vickie Craig — Cassie's close friend
Mitch Donaldson — successful mystery writer
Peter Dunlop — realtor with eyes on Steffie
Ginny — Cattery employee with sad past
Barry Johnson — bad tempered male nurse
Lacey — Kitty's sister
Lana, aka Pat Danvers — another Black Sheep victim
Bud Lang — affable detective/partner of Jack Willinger
Scott Matheson — unpredictable, womanizing fireman
Cassie Meredith — heiress who loves two men
Dave Meredith — Cassie's absent husband
Sheridan Monteith — Mitch's society girlfriend
Nick — ex con with bad gambling habit
Adrian Simpson — handsome airline pilot
Dr. Keith Spenser — flirtatious doctor who loves the ladies
Josh Tuttle — carpenter with an attitude
Jack Willinger — detective with a secret love
Kitty Winfield — attractive part owner of boutique
Marg and Harry Winfield — Kitty's parents
Petie and Rosie Winfield — Kitty's cat companions

CHAPTER 1

▼

She hadn't had time to scream. He had been quick and efficient, wasting no time, no excess energy. Funny how he always managed to take them by surprise. They were usually so damn trusting, so pathetically confident in his friendship and his goodness.

He hummed quietly to himself, as he arranged the body. Actually, as he examined her from all angles, he was satisfied that she looked as good as could be expected. Too bad their eyes bugged out so ridiculously when they were strangled — rather like cartoon characters. At least her thick mane of coppery red hair was beautiful against the pale green bedspread.

"Eva, Eva, Eva," he chided, shaking his head, as he straightened her legs, and smoothed the long denim skirt. "Why did you have to be such a bimbo? What made you such a fickle bitch?" The questions of course, were rhetorical. Eva was past giving explanations in this world.

Her tank top had pulled up during the struggle, so he took pains to tuck it carefully under the braided gold belt. The arms were next. He placed her left arm gently along her side, not too tight to the body, he cautioned himself. He was humming again as he worked. She had to look relaxed and peaceful. He couldn't stand disarray. Bending her right arm gently at the elbow, he placed it palm up. Now for his little surprise.

Facetiously telling her to stay there, and that he would be right back, he walked quietly and purposefully to the front hall, and retrieved his briefcase. Removing a plastic bag from one of its inner pockets, he carefully unwrapped a small, tissue-covered item. Back in the bedroom, he placed it in her right palm, and gently folded her fingers around it.

There she was — a once pretty young woman, lying on top of her bed, holding a little ceramic black sheep. In life, she had been a lovely, fun loving, vivacious woman. In death, she looked ghoulish, with bulging eyes, petechial hemorrhaging, cyanotic lips, and ugly reddish purple bruises starting to appear on her neck.

An errant thought intruded, as he gazed at his handiwork. What if he were to use poison next time, instead of strangulation? He was quite sure that there would be a next time, although the thought made him somewhat uneasy. There were plenty of easy access, over-the-counter drugs he could use. Something like that would be almost impossible to trace. It could be difficult though, forcing someone to swallow a handful of pills.

He stared into space, momentarily distracted from the job at hand. How about an injection? He gave fleeting headroom to that possibility, then discarded it. True, their faces wouldn't look so monstrous if he didn't strangle them, but what the hell. It served them right to look horrible in death, if they had acted horribly in life. There was a certain poetic balance in that, which made him smile. No, he had started with strangling, so to keep things well ordered, he had to continue with that modus operandi. This was serious business, much more than just a cheap thrill. He did it because it had to be done, and it had to be done correctly.

Anyway, why was he even thinking along these stupid lines? He shook his head in disgust. Strangling was so 'up close and personal'. He could look into their eyes, and make them understand why he had to do it. Occasionally, he whispered to them very softly, as his fingers closed around their slender necks. Strangling made a statement the way poison pills or needles couldn't. He wouldn't even consider guns or knives. They had their place, but they were so barbaric.

He had been over the pros and cons of various killing methods many times. It was a game he enjoyed — a little mental exercise. Some people did crossword puzzles, some played trivia. He spent his time studying different ways to commit murder. Well, to each his own. His conclusion was always the same. Strangling was the method of choice. Now, however, he had more serious business.

Slowly he sat down in the white rocking chair, and methodically searched the room with his eyes, for any clues, any mistakes he might have made. It was a very restful and pleasing room, with the moss green carpet, the gold and green geometric pattern on the drapes, and the white and gold French Provincial furniture. Eva had good taste. Too bad she hadn't had the morals to go with it.

The adrenaline rush was gone as quickly as it had come. Now he was just tired. He needed a drink as badly as a mosquito needs blood. Yes, he wanted a good drink and his own bed, along with the peaceful oblivion which sleep would bring. Strangely, he never had nightmares after these "episodes." He always slept the sleep of the pure in heart. The thought made him chuckle.

No wonder he was so tired tonight. Eva had put up much more of a fight than he had expected. The others had been easier, no doubt of that. He should have taken into account that she jogged and did push-ups every day. She had been very proud of her figure, and had worked out regularly to maintain all the curves in the right places. His carelessness could have been a fatal error. She had actually almost managed to get away, after she kicked him so hard on his kneecap. Shoot, her legs had been like pistons. He was lucky that she had missed the family jewels. He was sure that's where little Eva had been aiming.

Although the knee ached, and he felt exhausted, he had to be thorough. He mustn't get complacent and make any mistakes. He was performing an important task, a necessary evil. Someone had to rid the world of the oh-so-easy ones, the fickle ones. Each woman was so different, yet they were all the same. Every woman he had ever known was gullible and trusting, yet deceptive and cunning. Well, they didn't know what cunning was until they met him — the Black Sheep. He was the smart one, the bad one, and, much as he loved women, his mission was to rid the world of the tramps. What a task! It seemed never-ending.

His mother had always told him that he was the black sheep of the family. If she could only see him now, she would know that he had lived up to her expectations, her predictions. He WAS the Black Sheep par excellence, and no one suspected. No one had any idea. His mother might have guessed, but he had taken care of her. Actually, she was his first. It had been a thrill placing the little black sheep into her unresisting hand. "Your predictions came true, ma, and I'm giving this back to you. I'm the Black Sheep now, and I'm king of the world. What do you think of that?" he had asked with a sardonic smile, as her sightless eyes had stared back at him.

As he rocked in the little white chair, he remembered his mother with dispassion. After the death of his father, she had become a different person. She had always been a bit on the cruel side, and totally insensitive, but in a way things got even worse after his father had finally succumbed to his interminable illness.

The good thing was that she became too tied up in her own affairs to bother with the beatings, which she had given him for as long as he could remember. He could never understand why his twin brother Mike, had escaped unscathed from her wrath. In her eyes, Mike was the good twin, he was the bad one. After his father's death, however, she had lost interest in both of them. All he knew for sure was that she went for a nose job, got her boobs enlarged, dieted herself down to the size of a stick, and started chasing after every guy who came within the radius of those coquettish eyes. Hell, she was cheating on his father, even while the poor man was lying on his deathbed.

She sickened him, and he had finally taken care of her. She had been so surprised, that she hadn't put up any resistance. He could still see her buggy eyes staring at him in disbelief, as he squeezed his hands around her scrawny neck. In her last moments, he made her pay for the beatings, and for every night he had lain awake, listening to her sighing and giggling with some stranger in the next room, while his poor dad lay dying. If sometime in the future he was finally caught — not very likely — some pompous psychiatrist would probably testify that every time he killed, he was in essence re-killing his mother. What psychobabble horseshit that was. Still, he shrugged mentally, it was likely true, at least in part.

The next trauma in his life was when his wife left him. That devastating bit of drama had almost driven him off the cliff, so to speak, but he had managed to keep himself together somehow. It took him weeks to wrap the knowledge around his brain. Marcy had actually had the nerve to leave him. It was almost impossible to grasp. The horrible indignity of it was that she had run off with another man — a Mexican artisan named Eduardo, who made jewellery. She made jewellery too, and they had met at a convention. He had been good to her in his own way, they had fun together, at least he thought they did, and the realization that she had left him, had struck him like a bolt of lightning.

He had wished them both dead, and that was exactly what had happened. They had been killed in a three-car pileup, before they even made it to Mexico. That was when things started to unravel. The guilt was a living thing, snapping and snarling at his heels continuously, until he finally convinced himself that they really had deserved to die.

His life had just started balancing itself out again, when suddenly his twin brother Mike had committed suicide, and something had snapped. He had felt a sharp pain in his head, as if something had actually broken or come loose. He and Mike had been so close, even though Mike was the favoured twin. When Mike killed himself because of a woman, he just couldn't take it. Of course, knowing that he had played a large part in the suicide didn't help any.

Mike's adorable wife Ginny, with the big eyes and the tinkling laugh, had been caught cheating on him, or so it had seemed at the time. On hearing the dreadful news about his beloved wife, Mike had locked himself in the garage, turned on the car, and sucked in the carbon monoxide. He, the Black Sheep, had been the one to tell his brother about Ginny, and he had been the one to find Mike dead. After that, punishing flirtatious and unfaithful women had become a crusade. It was a crusade which would end when he finally killed Ginny.

CHAPTER 2

▼

Damn, his knee hurt. Eva had really landed a good one. He'd have to put ice on it when he got home.

Slowly he made his way to the blue and yellow bathroom. Everything seemed in order. There was nothing here to give him away. He grinned at himself in the mirror, handsome devil. Why would any right thinking woman leave him for another man? It made no sense. He had so much to offer, and yet eventually they always did leave him. His friends described him as genial, fun loving, charming. They knew he was intelligent. They knew he was charming. They just didn't know he was a killer.

He had studied a lot about serial killers, and had come to the conclusion that he was nothing like any of them. He had a good job. He functioned well in society. He had many friends — good friends, who liked him, and trusted him. He was the last person in the world anyone would suspect of being a killer. No one knew he had ever been married. He played the swinging bachelor part so well.

Straightening the fluffy towels on the rack, he went back into the bedroom. One final inspection of the body, a quick repositioning of the rocking chair, and he was almost done. The stereo was still playing her favourite cd — some twaddle about everlasting love. It was set to play over and over, and he decided not to touch it. It would keep poor Eva company.

He had felt the anger building up all week, until he thought he might explode. It was like an oil gusher, waiting to burst upon the world. It became difficult to concentrate on his work. He had seen her kissing and hugging another man, even though she was supposed to be his girl. That meant that she just had to be punished.

He had moved to Niagara Falls to make a fresh start, and Eva was the first woman here he had dated for any length of time. As usual, he had been careful not to be seen in public with her — just in case. He had been pretty sure that she might be the right woman for him, but something always made him hold back a bit. Fleeting suspicions made him cautious. A man could never be too careful. There was always that possibility that she would be like the others, so he had taken no chances. He took her to out of the way places for movies and dinners, and he made sure that she didn't meet any of his new friends. Telling her that he wanted to keep her to himself for a little while, had worked as it always did. Women were so trusting.

She reminded him of his sister-in-law Ginny — fickle to the core. She just couldn't be trusted, and that knowledge had fuelled the fires of his rage.

Thinking of Ginny now, he had to sit down again. His feelings about her were so damn ambiguous. There were times when she was on his mental hit list, but there were other times when he just wanted to love her, and eventually marry her. He knew this was crazy, but he couldn't help it. It seemed that he had always loved Ginny.

He understood now that she really had not been unfaithful to his twin brother Mike. It had all been a terrible misunderstanding. She had been telling the truth when she claimed that the man in uniform was her brother. How was he supposed to know that? Wouldn't anyone have jumped to the same wrong conclusion? The thing was, he knew positively that it was his fault for running to Mike with the wrong information, but it was Mike's fault too, for believing him, instead of his wife. At this point, he wasn't sure just whose fault it really was, and it was gnawing away at his soul, if, indeed, he even had a soul.

There were times late at night, when he lay in bed, staring at the ceiling, and trying to put all the blame on Ginny. Those were the times he made up his mind that she had to be killed. Meanwhile, he took out his rage and confusion on other cheating women, or women he perceived to be unfaithful. As far as Ginny was concerned, well, he would make his decision about her soon enough. Sometimes he could picture them happily married, the past all forgotten. Occasionally, however, he could very clearly picture her dead. It was literally driving him crazy.

Suddenly he stiffened — jarred from his memories. He listened with the intensity of a cat, when it suspects the presence of danger. The sound of the siren was getting louder. Was it police, fire, ambulance? He stood like a marble statue, concentrating on the approaching sound, holding his breath. His mind raced, as he considered the possibilities. No one could have heard the scuffle. Eva hadn't had time to scream. No, the sirens weren't for him. Shaking his head ruefully at his own foolishness, he got back to the job at hand.

Working quickly but efficiently, he took the small digital camera from the briefcase, and walked back to the bedroom. Finally taking off the rubber gloves, he took three pictures from three different angles.

They were excellent, and eventually they would go into the album — the Black Sheep Album, which he planned to put together. For now, though, he would make prints, and they would go loosely into the steel filing box, which was locked away in his bedroom closet.

His briefcase was still on the dining room table. Putting the camera back into the case, he removed a pair of very sharp scissors. He cut the rubber gloves into the tiniest of pieces, then carefully and methodically, he flushed them down the toilet, a few at a time. There was no way anyone would ever get fingerprints off those gloves, he thought, with a satisfied smirk.

He stood quietly in the pretty bathroom, taking another good look around. You couldn't be too careful at a time like this. It was the little things, the stupid, seemingly unimportant things, which could give you away.

It was late, and he was sure that no one had seen him arrive. He was also just as sure that no one would see him leave. If they did, however, he would be unrecognizable. He grinned to himself, as he pulled on a curly wig, and placed a pair of dark-rimmed glasses on his nose. They were just clear glass, but they changed his appearance dramatically. He then turned his light coloured reversible jacket inside out, so that he was now wearing a black jacket. It would be next to impossible in the dark for anyone to see him leaving, and certainly no one could identify him, if it ever came to that. He smiled as he inspected his appearance in the foyer mirror.

After one last thorough check of the living room, he took a hanky from his pocket, and carefully used it over his hand, to turn off the lights and open the door.

He walked quickly, and tried to look casual.

In the distance he could hear thunder. Because it was so late, all law-abiding citizens were safely tucked into their beds, or at least they should be. He hoped the storm wouldn't hit before he got home. It had been a long night, but there was one less sleazy woman in the world. Although his knee hurt, and he was very tired, he still felt great. He was humming again softly as he headed for his car.

CHAPTER 3

▼

Kitty Winfield shook the rain from her colourful umbrella, as she fumbled with the key to the gift shop. It was a charcoal grey morning, dull and dreary. Rain was falling in gentle spurts. Thunder boomed threateningly, but the rain seemed dispirited, as if it just didn't have the heart for any torrential displays. It had been raining off and on all week, and Kitty told herself that it would soon be sunny and beautiful again. After all, how much more rain could there be left up there? The gloom matched her mood, which was a little depressed, and a lot angry. The morning phone call had taken her by surprise, and she still couldn't believe he had been bold enough to contact her, and act as if nothing bad had happened between them.

She kicked a paper cup out of the way, and watched it roll aimlessly across the pavement. If she had the time, she would cheerfully and vengefully kick it around the block, pretending it was the handsome and oh so loathsome head of one cheating, back-stabbing, lying, Scott Matheson. Then she grinned at her foolishness, as she stooped to pick up the offending cup. She and Steffie were conscientious about keeping the front of their boutique impeccably clean, and free of trash.

Unlocking the door, she walked through the gift shop toward the office in back. For once she didn't stop to admire the shelves of crystal miniatures, which were placed to face the morning sun. There was no sun this morning, to make beautiful rainbow prisms on the walls. She took no particular notice of the shelves of pretty pens and extravagant writing paper. The display of Scandinavian whatnots was totally ignored.

She did, however, stop to smile at the whimsical display of designer teddy bears. She always imagined them welcoming her with outstretched arms. She adjusted the velvet hat and pearl necklace on a honey coloured bear, with big blue glass eyes. Jiggling the foot of a large grumpy looking bear, wearing spectacles and a long scarf draped rakishly around his neck, she said "Hi, Charlie. What's up?" This was one of her favourite displays. The bears were like family — each with his or her own personality.

She moved on to the office, where she deposited the dripping umbrella in the sink of the tiny washroom. Unfastening her burgundy raincoat, she hung it up, and absent-mindedly ran her fingers through her shoulder length, honey blond hair, which was as damp as her mood. The dampness was causing little tendrils to curl around her oval shaped face. To her everlasting disappointment, her hair was not the tawny gold of a lion's mane, it was just plain yellow. She was sure people suspected that she bleached it, but unfortunately it was natural. She really envied her partner Steffie's beautiful, shiny, blue black tresses. She looked like a Tahitian princess — very exotic.

Putting her purse in a drawer, she started a pot of coffee.

She was here almost an hour early this morning. After waking up at the crack of dawn, she had showered, dressed, and fed the cats. Making a pot of tea, she toasted a bagel, and had just brought in the morning paper, when the phone rang. At this hour, it was either her partner Steffie, who was also her best friend, or her dad, who often called early to have a quick chat.

To her chagrin, it was Scott, her ex boyfriend, and the call left her feeling shaky and angry. He had been friendly and charming, and had the hubris to say that he would love to see her again, that he missed her, that no woman ever left him. He honestly couldn't seem to understand why she was so bummed. When he asked if she would go to dinner with him, she had almost choked.

"Scott, I'd rather stick bamboo shoots up my nose and set fire to them," she had answered, before slamming down the receiver. Now, of course, she could think of a dozen witty, cutting-edge retorts she could have made. Still, the bamboo shoots thing wasn't bad on short notice. She smiled at the picture it presented.

The call had fractured her calm to the point that she couldn't concentrate on the newspaper, so she had stuck it in her coat pocket, and set out for the shop. Kitty had a quick temper and a short fuse, and Scott had managed to push the right button. Anyone could see that she had reached her boiling point, judging by the steam coming out her ears.

Her partner, Steffie Chapman, would be here soon, but Kitty thought she might have time to read a bit of the news before Steffie arrived. Steffie was not a morning person. Actually she could be downright hostile first thing in the a.m. Once she had a couple of jolts of caffeine, however, she was a fun-loving, enthusiastic dynamo. Kitty always knew enough to keep silent, until good old Steff had drained the coffee pot. It was her artistic temperament which caused the mood swings. She loved to paint, and her watercolours and sketches sold very quickly. Like a pendulum, her moods swung from happy and high on life, to quiet and withdrawn, or even angry and aggressive. Kitty was never sure which Steffie would show up for work, but in spite of her moodiness, she was a very dear friend.

Before retrieving the slightly damp newspaper from her raincoat pocket, a series of unwelcome pictures began flashing in her head. They were memories, uncalled for and unwanted, but memories that seemed determined to march across her mind, like crazy home movies gone awry. The unwanted thoughts and feelings were bombarding her like stones hitting a tin roof.

Helplessly, she pictured herself snuggled in bed with Scott on the weekend, reading the newspapers, and eating toast and peanut butter. Then she saw them walking hand in hand on Clifton Hill, heading for the awesome cataracts. They had always loved to play at being tourists in this beautiful tourist city. They would go into the little souvenir shops, marvelling at the plethora of tacky items, which were supposed to depict Canada and the Mounties, and the world famous falls. They would stand at the brink of those incredibly powerful creations of nature, right down by Table Rock, and gaze at the roaring, tumultuous natural wonder, getting soaked by the spray, yet unable to tear their eyes away from the hypnotic scene. These pictures played over and over in Kitty's unwilling mind. The entire romance had come and gone so quickly, yet in retrospect, it played out in slow motion.

Why hadn't she been able to sense what a loser he was? Now was the time to collect all the memories from those seven whirlwind weeks, the good and the bad, lock them in a box, and pack them away somewhere deep in her subconscious, hopefully never to be thought of again.

Kitty was not one to dwell on bad luck, or bad times, or bad people. There were too many fun things to do, interesting people with whom to interact, and challenges to meet. Still, Scott had managed to get under her skin, and it really bugged her that he had treated her shabbily before she had a chance to dump him.

She opened the newspaper, and put her feet up on the ottoman. Concentration, however, seemed way beyond her grasp. More pictures were flashing in her head. It had been a day just like this when Scott Matheson first came into her life. He had been wearing his fireman's uniform, and he was good looking enough to be the poster boy for the department. She had kept her eyes on him, while she tried to look busy rearranging an entire shelf of ceramic flowerpots. Eventually, he had wandered over to the jewellery display, and had started examining the bracelets. She had asked if he needed any help, and his smile was dazzling, as he said that he definitely could use the expertise of a lovely lady.

Eventually, he bought a beautiful braided silver bracelet. He certainly had good taste, she thought to herself, as she gift-wrapped it for him, along with a couple of other small purchases. She couldn't help wondering about the lucky recipient, and what she was like.

Two days later, he had sauntered back into the shop, this time out of uniform. He was wearing stone washed jeans, and a cranberry coloured shirt, open at the collar. He was tall and slim, with a shock of dark brown hair, and brown eyes edged by long lashes more suitable for a woman. His smile was enough to melt the heart, and weaken the knees of the most hard hearted gal. As he spoke with Steffie, and looked at some little carved figurines, he kept glancing over her shoulder. He was actually watching Kitty, who was arranging silk flowers in a large Mexican pot.

"Hi there," he had said in a friendly voice, dazzling her again with his smile.

"Hi there," she had answered inanely. Oh what a clever reply, she groaned inwardly. She felt strangely tongue-tied, and had been unable to think of a single thing to say. This wasn't like Kitty at all. She had noticed Steffie rolling her eyes and grinning.

"How about a cup of coffee? Do you think your boss could spare you for a while?" he had asked in a conspiratorial whisper.

Kitty had laughed at that. "She isn't my boss, she's my partner," she had whispered back to him. What was the matter with her? Why was her stomach doing flip-flops? He was just a guy — better looking than most, but still just a guy. He likely put his pants on one leg at a time, the same as every other guy she had ever known. Still — there was something about him which was tantalizing and exciting.

He just laughed, and said that if she was the owner, she could definitely take a break for half an hour. She could tell by his assured manner that he wouldn't be good at taking rejection.

To her own surprise, she had acquiesced. They went down to the corner, and sat in a Tim Horton's doughnut shop, drinking coffee, and talking for almost an hour. Kitty had lost all sense of time. That had been the beginning, but she hadn't realized just how soon the end would come.

"Get a grip, girl" she muttered to herself, as she tried to refocus on the newspaper. She had to forgive herself for falling into the "Scott trap." She knew she wasn't the first who had fallen under his spell, and she certainly wouldn't be the last, but it embarrassed her to have been one of his gullible victims. She had to shut down those movies in her mind. The figures, mostly herself and Scott, kept appearing as if in some weird diorama, standing and moving awkwardly at her command. This time she willed them to disappear, as she took a sip of her coffee, and read the startling headline, "Second Niagara Woman Strangled."

CHAPTER 4

▼

The story in the morning newspaper had few details, but Kitty read every word with interest. The young woman, Eva Conrad, had been found dead in her little rented house. It seemed that Eva was a dealer at the Niagara Falls-view Casino. According to friends, she had come here from Northern Ontario, just a few months ago. When she didn't show up for her early shift at the casino, one of her co-workers had called her home several times, leaving messages on the answering machine. After work, she had driven to Eva's house, and had become nervous at seeing the car in the carport, but no sign of Eva. The worried friend had finally called the police, and watched, weak with fear, while they broke in, and found Eva dead on her bed.

The interesting thing about the article, was that the police said this killing had much in common with one which had occurred two months previously. They said that the killer had left a calling card of sorts, identical to one left after the first murder, but, of course, they could not divulge the nature of this important clue. They would be working round the clock to catch this bold and dangerous killer.

How lame, Kitty thought. This crime would likely go unsolved, just as the other one had. What could the killer have left at the scene, she wondered, as she searched the paper for more stories concerning the crime. She remem-bered reading a murder mystery in which the killer always left a playing card in the victim's hand. She thought it had been a jack of diamonds, but wasn't sure. In another book, the killer left one line of an old song at each murder scene, sticking the paper in unusual places on the victim's body. It made her shudder to think about it. What was the calling card this killer had left?

When Steffie came crashing through the door, exclaiming loudly that some jerk had splashed her from top to bottom with his car, Kitty reluctantly put the newspaper down, and got up to help her partner clean off her shoes and coat, which were liberally spattered with mud. There were even a few splotches on her face, but Kitty didn't dare laugh.

"What a shitty way to start the day," complained Steffie, looking at her clothes in dismay. "It was a young punk driving a red corvette. Why is it that so many rich kids have no manners, and so many of them drive red sport cars? He just looked and laughed, and kept on going. I hope all four wheels fall off that damned car, and I hope all his teeth turn green by the end of the day! Look at me. I look like a Dalmatian, or a spotted lizard!"

"Well, you do look a bit uh — speckled," commented Kitty with a grin. "I think we can get it all off though," she added helpfully, wetting one end of a towel.

As the two friends worked to clean Steffie's clothes and her face, Steffie took a good look at Kitty, and remarked, "What's up with you? You look wilted or something."

"Yah, I guess that just about sums it up," said Kitty, laughing ruefully. "Scott had the nerve to call me this morning and try to make nice. He was just as sweet as a li'l ole sugar pie," she added with a Southern drawl. "It just irks me no end that he made such a fool of me. Why didn't I see it coming? I hate being caught in a common old cliché, and that's exactly what our entire relationship was — just a bad cliché. I still can't believe that I fell for him so quickly and completely. I should have listened to you, because you didn't like him from the start."

Steffie had heard it all before, and she was truly tired of it, but, being a stalwart friend, she was always willing to listen and give advice. "That's for damned sure that I didn't like him. It was because he reminded me so much of my ever-lovin' ex. He was such a charmer too, that it took me three years to catch on. You were lucky, you only wasted seven weeks out of your life."

"I hate being made a fool of, but somehow I let him wine me, dine me, and then decline me, and I never saw it coming. Man was I stupid! Well, believe me, never again. I know I've said it before, but it bears repeating. From now on, I'm the ice queen. I'll be charming and elegant, but no guy will ever melt my heart. Sounds like something from a dime novel, doesn't it?" she laughed. Her mood was already improving. Kitty could never stay angry or sulky for very long.

"I would hazard a guess that you'll be Miss Ice Queen for just about as long as it takes until the next heartthrob walks through the front door," grinned Steffie. "Anyway, what about Drew? Where does he fit into this picture?" She asked this as she peered at herself in the mirror. Fortunately her curly black hair seemed to have missed most of the mud spatters.

Dr. Drew Carson had been dating Kitty for three weeks now, and she seemed to like him well enough, although Steffie couldn't really tell. Coincidentally, Kitty had also met him in their shop, when he had come in looking for a gift for his sister. Steffie hoped sincerely that the new relationship her friend had started with Drew, wouldn't turn out as badly as the one with Scott. Kitty had been very quiet about her dates with Drew, and Steffie wasn't sure just what the situation was.

"Oh, Drew's just a friend," said Kitty casually. "He's okay, but there are no sparks there. He's generous though, and he's good for a laugh, but he's a bit too sulky for my liking."

That was the end of the conversation. Steffie knew when to back off, so, before Kitty went to unlock the front door, and open the shop for business, Steffie said, "Hey, here's one for you. Who starred in "Meet Danny Wilson?"

This was a game the two friends played often, and they were both good at it. They loved to test each other with old movies and movie stars.

Kitty frowned and stared into space before saying, "That's an easy one. I can think of three. How about Frank Sinatra, Shelley Winters and Raymond Burr?"

"Ah, you're such a smarty," laughed Steffie, shaking her head in disgust. Gulping down another half cup of coffee, she took one more look at herself in the mirror, decided she was quite presentable again, and followed Kitty out into the boutique.

The day hadn't started well for either one of them, but it went by quickly and smoothly. As it often does in Niagara Falls, the rain stopped, the clouds disappeared, and the sun came out, shiny and golden. There was a surprising amount of business, due to a series of tour buses, which had deposited their passengers at the many new hotels in the city. "Aunt Aggie's Attic" was listed as a "must see" on several of the tour brochures, and during tourist season, business was brisk — sometimes appallingly so.

As customers came and went, Kitty often thought that this boutique provided a parade of life's little vignettes. Some of them they got to know much better than others, but all of the customers were interesting in their own way.

Kitty and Steffie now regretted naming their boutique "Aunt Aggie's Attic." They wished they had held out for a more imaginative and colourful name, because more and more often they heard people refer to it fondly as "The Triple A," which sounded really tacky. Somehow, it sounded like a gas station. There was nothing they could do about it now, however, and as long as the money kept rolling in, who really cared?

Whenever there was a lull in business, the two friends speculated about the gruesome murder. Was the perpetrator someone who lived in Niagara Falls, or was he a transient just passing through? It was more likely that it was someone who lived here in the tourist city, because of the similar murder here two months ago. Could it possibly be someone they knew, or a customer who had been in their shop?

Sometime during the afternoon, Steffie suddenly gasped and looked at Kitty. "You know who it could be, don't you?"

Kitty nodded her head. "I know what you're thinking. I've just been thinking the same thing. It could be that creepy guy with the sunken eyes and the bad breath."

"Tha-at's ri — ight" cooed Steffie in a sing-song voice. "He's pushy and foul mouthed. Remember the time he asked me out, and when I refused, he called me an uptight bitch who thought I was too good for him."

"What I do remember is you saying that those odd patches of hair on his mainly bald head, looked like tarantulas clinging to a large egg." Here Kitty started to laugh, and soon Steffie joined in.

When they had calmed down, Steffie said, "He couldn't be the one, could he? I mean, he dresses well, and he has nice taste in gift items, but could you picture him as a killer?"

"Yes, I really think I could," answered her friend. "Man, I hope he doesn't come back."

"Well, if he does return, let's play it really cool. Be polite, but not too friendly. We don't want to set him off, or give him any reason to want to hurt us," Steffie added grimly.

"You know, we've talked about it before, but we never do anything about it. Do you think maybe we should be putting some sort of an alarm system in here? We're doing pretty well these days, and someone might think about robbing us, or this strangler might come in here and attack us. Do you think it would be a wise investment?" Kitty was frowning, as she twiddled one of her curls and looked at Steffie.

"It's stupid that we keep talking about it and then don't do anything. Why don't we call some companies next week and get some rates?"

"Sounds like a plan," agreed Kitty, as she went to wait on a tall, thin, grim faced woman, who wanted to see some antique rings for a man. It will take more than a ring for her to catch a man with that sour face, Kitty thought uncharitably, as she walked the woman over to the showcase.

It was soon time to lock up and head back to their respective homes. Although they often stayed to enjoy a quiet glass of wine after work, today they were both anxious to pack it in. Laughingly, they admitted that they were eager to get home, and watch the local television news for more info about the crime.

"Go straight home now, and lock all your doors and windows," counselled Steffie, as they parted in the small lot behind the shop. "This is one time I'm happy to have such a compact apartment. I wish you weren't in that big house all alone."

Steffie liked to say that her little apartment was cosily intimate. In Kitty's mind it was just too friggin' small. She was helping her friend look for something larger, but nice condos in a good area, with a great view, and a reasonable price, were seemingly impossible to find.

"I'll be fine in that big house all alone," retorted Kitty. She had heard this same lament several times, and was tired of it. "Just give me a call before you go to bed, and don't open the door to anyone, unless, of course, he's handsome, and has a bag full of money under his arm."

They both laughed happily as they went their separate ways.

CHAPTER 5

▼

As Kitty drove home along Morrison, then up Dorchester to Thorold Stone, and into Rolling Acres, she kept thinking about the strangler. Was it the victim's ex husband who had killed her? Not likely, since another woman had been killed two months earlier. Was there really a serial killer loose in town? What had the poor woman's last moments been like? How long did it take to die when you were being strangled? Finally, as she turned onto her street, her mind went back to Scott, and she began scolding herself again for having wasted time falling for him. He had proved to be a grade A, giant sized rat, whiskers and all. Still, it had been fun while it lasted.

As usual, she left the car in the driveway, rather than bothering to put it in the garage. She liked it sitting there, so that people knew she was home, and that it wasn't an empty house waiting to be robbed.

She waved to her next door neighbour, who was out watering her geraniums. The neighbour's little dog Maxie, raced to greet her, and Kitty had to stop and pet him. Maxie was an undetermined breed, but he was a friendly little fellow, who went into spasms of joy, as she rubbed his ears, and told him he was handsome. She would have to wash her hands well before her two cats smelled them. They always inspected her hands and ankles very carefully, and if they smelled Maxie on her, they would walk away haughtily, and punish her for her disloyalty, with the silent treatment, as only a cat can give it. It would take the sound of the can opener to coax them to forgive her.

Just then, she looked up at her front window, and saw that her two cats were sitting on the back of the chesterfield, watching her as she petted and played with Maxie. "Oh shoot, I'm busted," she muttered. Their beautiful feline faces were staring out the window, turned to the sunshine like flowers. They didn't look happy at what they saw.

Tears suddenly sprang to her eyes. She loved these two trusting little creatures with all her heart, and she knew the love was returned. She was sorry they had seen her petting Maxie, but they would soon forgive her.

Before she could go inside, she heard Adrian, who was her neighbour on the other side of her house, calling her name. Adrian Simpson was a commercial airline pilot, and there were times when he was a bit too friendly. He was unmarried, and seemed to have a very busy social life when he was here. Because of the nature of his work, he was away for days at a time. Kitty enjoyed his company, and they often shared a cup of coffee or a glass of wine, but she was in a bit of a hurry tonight. She sighed as she watched him hurry across her lawn.

"Hi Kitty. I was hoping I could catch you. How about dinner tomorrow night and maybe a movie?"

He was very attractive, and in his pilot's uniform, he was a knock-out. She had enough trouble in her life though, and didn't want to get involved with this happy-go-lucky woman chaser.

"Sorry, Adrian," she grinned. "I've told you before. You're too hot blooded and exotic for my simple tastes. I'm just a plain old stay-at-home type. Go find yourself one of your Barbie-bimbos."

He laughed at this, and shook his head. "I'll get you one of these days, Miss Kitty. You're going to go out with me yet. I don't give up easily."

They kidded and bantered for a few minutes, before he sauntered back across the lawn.

She unlocked the door, and put Adrian out of her mind, as unwelcome thoughts of Scott popped into her head again. She kept asking herself what signs she might have missed, signs that would have told her she was a moth getting too close to the flame. Now that she could see things more clearly, without the blinkers of love, or lust, or whatever she wanted to call it, she realized that there had been many signs along the path, signs which she had simply ignored.

That darn early morning phone call had really stirred up a lot of muck. How in heck could she have given her heart to that heartless individual? How could she have been so deliriously happy for seven whole weeks, before the bottom fell out, and she had crashed, bruised and broken. Well, maybe she was being a wee bit melodramatic. She tended to self-dramatization, and enjoyed the colourful paths down which her imagination often led her. She shook her head, and grinned at her poetic flights of fancy. Still, it had been pretty traumatic, and it had really shaken her faith in her ability to judge character. She certainly wasn't going to make the same mistake with Drew, or anyone else who might come along.

By now she had almost forgotten all about the local murder. As she hung up her raincoat, and put her umbrella away, she called to Miss Rosie and Sir Peter. The delicate little calico, and the big orange tabby, were so happy to have her home, that they wound round and round her legs, purring with pleasure. They sniffed her ankles, but didn't seem too concerned with any doggie aroma from Maxie. It was a long slow trip to the kitchen, as she tried to avoid stepping on eight little paws and two fluffy tails.

"Well, guess what it's going to be tonight, gang?" she asked them, as she deftly changed two water bowls, and filled two plates with roast turkey slices from the deli. She knew that she spoiled them shamelessly, but they were her family here in Niagara Falls, and she loved them with all her heart. They were funny and wise, and they were wonderful companions.

After they had been fed, and were sitting cleaning themselves, before cuddling down for their evening nap, Kitty made herself some macaroni and cheese. Putting her plate on a tray, along with half a bottle of red wine, she guiltily added a Twinkie. This was a "no-no" dinner, full of cholesterol and calories. Probably the healthiest thing on the tray was the red wine, but she didn't care. She thought of it as "comfort food," but Steff would definitely call it "mean cuisine."

She carried it into the living room, placed the wine bottle within reach on an end table, turned on the television, and curled up on the sofa. The cats were right with her, one on her stomach, and one on her feet. They missed her when she was gone all day, and they were like two clinging barnacles when she was home.

Sipping her wine, and listening for more coverage of the murder, she lost herself again in the happy life she had been enjoying with Scott. What a difference one month could bring, she thought ruefully, as she rubbed Miss Rosie's ears.

Kitty Winfield was a beautiful girl. She had high cheekbones, big blue eyes, and naturally blond hair, which curled softly in the rain. She was tall and leggy, and had an aristocratic air about her. Anytime she looked in a mirror, she fleetingly thanked the complexion gods for her soft, creamy skin, with not a freckle in sight. It seemed so much more difficult to take a freckled person seriously.

Although she was a blond, she was as far from the dumb blond image as anyone could get. After the break-up, however, she had felt less than beautiful, less than attractive, less than intelligent. She had felt like a darn fool. She had been temporarily rendered "hors de combat," but had bounced back quickly. She was too smart, and had too much self-respect, to let someone like Scott get the best of her. Still, his treachery had been a shock, and that nervy call this morning had stirred up all the memories.

Enjoying every mouthful of the macaroni and cheese, and sipping her wine slowly, she allowed her mind to drift back. She had to pinpoint all the warning signs which she had missed during the relationship, so that she would never again have such a disastrous experience. She closed her eyes, but kept one ear tuned to the TV, in case there was any more info about the strangled woman.

The announcer's voice faded, as Kitty concentrated on Scott and their hot affair.

Scott had known all the right moves. The first time they showered together, he soaped her gently and slowly. It did feel good, so good that she didn't have the heart to tell him that she never used soap on her sensitive skin. She had put up with dry, itchy skin for the next few days, but at the time, the feel of his big sensuous hands on her body had seemed worth it. Thinking about it now, she had to laugh. What an idiot she had been. It was as if she had "sucker" written on her forehead. She could see now that he had been way too smooth, too polished. "That should have been a big warning sign, guys," she said to the two cats, who couldn't have cared less.

Being a fireman, Scott worked strange hours and shifts. She never understood the rhythm of his work schedule, and he seemed hopeless at explaining it, so she just made herself available whenever he was free. "Oh boy, was that ever a glaring danger signal," she mumbled, frowning at the memories. "He knew damn well what his schedule was. He just didn't want me to know. Why couldn't I see how evasive he was? He was likely dating that redhead the very same time that he was dating me." She grimaced at the disgusting idea.

Sir Peter, aka Petie Pie, really wasn't interested, so he jumped down, and began to stretch first one hind leg, then the other. Yawning, then licking a patch of fur on his chest, he sauntered over to a chair, jumped up on its back, and gazed out into the dark night.

The break-up with Scott had come suddenly. She had been seriously thinking about dumping him, but hadn't quite made up her mind. It rankled that he had inadvertently made the decision for them. She had returned a day early from a visit with her parents in Toronto, and was delighted to see Scott's car in the driveway. He had promised to come in each day to feed the cats.

She could still remember so clearly, placing her purse and the grocery bags on the deacon's bench in the hall, then running up the stairs to surprise him. Well, she had surprised him all right. The shades were drawn, and there were candles burning on the dresser and bedside tables. It was just light enough to make out Scott entwined in the arms of someone with a lot of red hair. Strange how she had noticed the red hair and the silver braided bracelet, which he had bought in the boutique the first day she met him.

Kitty had a quick temper, and she had thrown the first thing handy. Unfortunately, it was her gramma's silver hairbrush. She had aimed it right at Scott, but it had missed, and hit the headboard, and now the lovely brush had a big dent in it. It was an ugly reminder of an ugly scene. Anyway, what happened next had been bizarre to say the least. She had fled down the stairs, and out the front door. Once it slammed behind her, she realized that she had locked herself out of her own home! What an idiot!

She had sat on her front steps in shock, not knowing whether to laugh at her own stupidity, or to cry at Scott's infidelity. She ended up doing a bit of both. It was so ridiculous and humiliating, to be locked out on the street, while the ice cream was melting in the hall!

She couldn't believe his nerve at bringing a dolly to her home, while she was out of town. It was so demeaning, so ignorant, tasteless and heartless.

She had begun to wonder whether she would have to ring the bell, and ask to be let in, when the two miscreants came out. The redhead rushed past her quickly, as if expecting to get a bullet in her behind — which Kitty was happy to see was rather wide! Scott looked sheepish, and told her that they had to talk. She had the presence of mind to demand her key from him, before slamming into the house with as much dignity as she could summon. He had tried to call her during the next few weeks, but had finally given up. Maybe that was why his call this morning, acting as if nothing was wrong, had upset her so.

"Stop it you idiot," she told herself, as she put her dishes in the dishwasher. "You aren't going to waste another moment on that loser. He was morally and emotionally challenged, and he isn't worth another minute of your time." Having spoken these words, she busied herself putting out some crunchies for the cats, checking the back door, turning out the kitchen light, and heading up the stairs. Her two little companions soon followed.

Taking a quick shower, she felt strangely uneasy. Thoughts of the poor strangled woman, who had been alive at this time just a couple of days ago, kept intruding. How had the killer entered her home? Was he someone the woman had been dating, or was he a total stranger? Was he out prowling the neighbourhood tonight, looking for another easy victim?

Kitty was not usually a nervous person. She had no time for that. She was usually very pragmatic, except for her occasional flights of poetic fancy. Tonight, however, she felt strangely nervous with all these speculations. Realizing that she wasn't going to sleep comfortably, she went back downstairs, and checked all the doors and windows again, before calling Steffie.

"Are you all tucked in safely?" she asked her friend.

"You bet. I've made myself damn jittery thinking about the strangler. I've checked my door and the windows several times," admitted Steffie, who lived in an apartment on the sixth floor.

"I'm sure you're a lot safer than I am," said Kitty with a grin. She didn't really believe that there was any danger. Still, Eva Conrad had likely not suspected that she was in any danger either.

"Listen. Let's go to the movies tomorrow night. There are at least three good ones on at Niagara Square, and we deserve a night out. We haven't done that for ages. We could have a bite at Boston Pizza, and then catch the early show. What do you think?"

"Sounds great to me," replied Kitty, sitting on the edge of the bed, and kicking a little silver ball for Sir Petie, who was ready to play. Unfortunately, she hadn't been able to teach him to retrieve the little ball. Once he chased it, he just sat beside it, waiting for Kitty to throw it again. She always got a lot more exercise than he did when they played.

"Okay then kiddo, sleep tight, and I'll see you in the morning."

Gathering the cats onto the bed with her, she was tempted to leave a light on, but scolded herself for being so silly. Still, there seemed to be more noises than usual in the house, as she tossed and turned and tried to get comfortable. It was going to be a long night.

CHAPTER 6

▼

Kitty Winfield lived in a big house in the Rolling Acres area of Niagara Falls. It had been left to her by her grandmother, two years earlier. How lucky could a girl get? Grandma Winfield knew that Kitty loved the house, and that eventually she hoped to make Niagara Falls her permanent home. When she was a teenager living in Toronto, she had loved coming over to Niagara, to visit her grandmother on weekends. She adored the beautiful city, and had made up her mind that she would live there some day.

Now her life seemed just about perfect. She lived in her grandma's elegant home, except that now it was her home. She had the gift shop of her dreams, and she had the best partner and friend in the world, with whom to share the fun and hard work in the shop. At this point in her life, she was just where she wanted to be. Scott Matheson was simply a few bad chapters in an otherwise perfect story.

As a little girl in Toronto, Kitty had desperately wanted to be called Madison. She had a friend at school who was called Madison Saunders, and to Kitty, that was a perfect name. Surprisingly, her mom and dad had seemed to agree that from now on, if they could remember, she would be called Madison. Joke! She should have known that they were too smart for her. All the following week they called her Matilda, or Millicent, or Miranda, or even the old fashioned Mabel, but never Madison. They innocently claimed that they were quite willing to go along with her request, but just couldn't remember that unfamiliar name. Finally, when even some of her friends began calling her Mabel, after hearing her mom call her that, she gave up in disgust.

Now Kitty looked back and laughed at that period in her life. She had wanted to be Madison so badly. Now, she really liked the name Kitty. She had grown into it over the years. She even liked it when her dad called her Kit Kat or Kitty Kat, or Miss Kitty. Somehow the affectionate names suited her. She still thought, though, that if she ever had a little girl of her own, she would call her Madison.

A big redwood deck was being added to the back of Kitty's house. Sliding patio doors would open right off the kitchen, and the new deck would be large enough for an umbrella table and chairs, plus several loungers. She could already envision the big pots of colourful flowers she would add, and the hummingbird feeders, which would hopefully attract the feisty little hummers. When he finished the deck, she was planning to have the workman, Josh Tuttle, build her a screened-in gazebo in the large yard. The cats would then be able to sit out there with her, and enjoy the fresh air and the birds, from a safe vantage point.

Kitty was used to dealing with people. She had a gift for being able to appear friendly and interested, without letting the person get into her space. She liked Josh Tuttle, and appreciated the excellent work he was doing. He was a charming fellow, with a quick wit, and soulful eyes. He had a bit of a cockeyed smile, which was almost irresistible. The only thing which caused her some concern, was that it seemed every time she looked out to see how he was doing, she caught him looking in at her. She didn't want to encourage him, but it was difficult to curb her natural enthusiasm and friendliness. She just didn't like the feeling that he might be a Peeping Tom.

Josh was tall and fair, with rippling muscles and very large hands. Today he was wearing a leather tool belt, and was bare chested. It was difficult not to admire his fine physique. Although he owned his own company, he said that he still liked to get out and work with his hands once in a while, rather than being stuck in the office all day. He was intelligent, and had travelled to many countries, so that he was a great conversationalist. He was also a flirt. Well, come to think of it, what man wasn't? That didn't bother her though. She was willing to fend off his advances, as long as he continued to do such beautiful work.

As usual, he had arrived this morning just before she left for the boutique, and after talking to him momentarily, she made sure to lock the kitchen door on her way out. Although she liked him, and admired his very professional work, she felt that there was something a bit too pushy about him, and she didn't want him to have access to her house when she wasn't there.

As she walked to her car in the driveway, she marvelled at what a glorious morning it was. How could anything bad ever happen in the world on a morning like this, she mused. She could hear the plaintive crying of a pair of mourning doves, and she felt Josh's eyes upon her. She turned and waved to him, before getting into the vehicle.

She and Steffie were kept busy until mid morning, at which time Steffie grabbed a duster, and began methodically cleaning the shelves, while Kitty did the same at the other side of the shop. They did this routinely in their spare moments, so as to keep the boutique sparkling and attractive at all times. Dusters were hastily hidden any time a customer walked in. They often laughed at the fact that they kept the boutique much cleaner and neater than they did their own homes. They had one woman, Cleo Chandler, who worked for them four days a week. She was a great help in sorting and tidying, and keeping things in order.

Steffie and Kitty had met by chance in Toronto, at a night class for computer buffs. At the time, Kitty was working for a lecherous old lawyer, who couldn't keep his hands to himself. She was fed up, and knew that she had to get out of there before she decked the old coot. Anyway, she was ready to take the plunge, and pursue her dream of opening a trendy boutique, full of exotic items.

Amazingly, Steffie had ambitions along the same line, and they decided to become partners. Steffie had been married and divorced. During her marriage, she had worked as the accountant and bookkeeper in a dress shop in Toronto. Since Kitty had just inherited the house from her grandma, the time was right for a move, and she easily persuaded Steffie that Niagara Falls would be a great place for their venture.

It hadn't taken them too long to find the perfect building in a perfect location. It had been a flower shop in its former life, and was bigger than they originally wanted, but it turned out to be ideal. They had never worked so hard in their lives. They painted and papered, went to craft shows, and visited every gift shop in the Niagara peninsula, shamelessly stealing ideas. They surreptitiously took notes on what worked and what didn't, what was attractive and what was clumsy in other boutiques. It was an exhilarating time for both of them. Their youth and enthusiasm, (Kitty was 28 and Steffie was 30), carried them through the first two years, while they learned by trial and error.

Now out of the red, and making a very nice profit, the trendy boutique was the "in place" to shop for unique gifts. They had a solid base of regular local customers, as well as a busy and exciting walk-in trade. They were particularly popular with the tourists, who came to town on package deals to golf, gamble and shop.

"You seem a bit dispirited this morning, Kit. Is everything okay?" Steffie looked concerned, as she touched her friend on the arm.

"Oh I'm fine I guess. Now don't you dare laugh, but I was really nervous in the house last night at bedtime, and I hate that feeling. I don't want to be afraid in my own home. It's ridiculous."

"Did anything happen to scare you?"

"No, just all the talk about the strangler. Actually I kept remembering a stupid book I read last year. I can't recall the title, but it was about some woman in an old plantation house. She didn't realize it, but there was a false wall in her closet, and it led to a tunnel, which led to the basement. It was a huge old house, and she kept having the feeling that she could hear someone breathing in the dark bedroom at night. Well, she was right. It was a psychopath who came and went at will through the tunnel, and he used to watch her sleeping. It was spooky, and I couldn't get it out of my head. I felt so stupid, but I got up and pounded all the walls in the closet, just to be sure that they are solid, and don't open into any dark tunnels. Now in the light of day it seems absurd." She shook her head in disgust.

"Shoot, you big baby. You let your imagination run away with you at times. You've got to be tough, kiddo," laughed Steffie, punching her lightly on the arm. "Now, having said that, do you want me to come and sleep over tonight after the movies?"

"No thanks, Steff. You are totally right. I can't let myself give in to such nonsense. I'll be fine, but I must admit that I closed the closet door, and put a chair under the knob, so that it couldn't be opened from the inside."

They both laughed as they got back to work. Steffie started tidying the greeting cards, and Kitty headed for the cat display. She loved this section of the shop, where everything was geared to the true cat lover. There were ceramic, wooden, and stuffed cats in all shapes, sizes and colours. There were mugs, hats, sweatshirts, parasols, tote bags, tea cosies, oven mitts, books, and cards. Kitty's favourites were the woven wallhangings in autumn shades of brown, orange, and cream. She had one hanging in her family room, and she enjoyed looking at it, with its variety of felines. It added a certain aesthetically pleasing and comforting ambiance to the room.

The morning seemed to drag along at a snail's pace. Customers were all demanding and cheap. They were looking, but not buying. It seemed as if the entire world was in a bad mood.

Things didn't improve any when Mrs. Brody, and her bratty five-year old Johnny, entered the shop. Although Kitty loved children, her heart always sank when Johnny and his mother appeared. Mrs. Brody didn't know how to say "no" to the little monster, and he always left a chaotic trail of destruction behind him. They raised their eyebrows at each other, groaned silently, and gritted their teeth, as the disastrous duo approached.

When Steffie saw Johnny put a tea cosy on his head, and open one of the cat parasols, she raced to stop him, but not in time. Whirling around, he managed to knock two cat mugs off the shelf, before she grabbed him, and said through clenched teeth, "You little beast. This is the last time you're coming in here, making a nuisance of yourself, and breaking things. We've told you before, Johnny, you are not to touch one single thing in this store."

Steffie's dark eyes were blazing, and her cheeks were very pink. At that moment, any man in his right mind would have found her absolutely gorgeous. Johnny, however, was not aware of her potential charms. The brat was trying to kick her, the tea cosy perched at a rakish angle on his head. It was a ridiculous scene. She yanked at the cosy, and snatched the parasol from him, as he began to kick in earnest, all the while yelling "You're not my mother. You're not my mother."

"Well, thank the Lord for small mercies," said Steffie, fiercely. "If you touch anything else, I shall pick you up and throw you out into the street. Now stop that kicking or I'll kick you right back." This threat was delivered with a murderous glare, just as his mother approached.

"Oh dear, it was an accident. He's just a baby. You can't speak to him like that. You'll frighten him and break his spirit."

"Well, he frightens me, and I'd love to break his so-called spirit," declared Steffie. She was quickly losing control. "He breaks things every time you come in here, and you never discipline him, and you never pay for the breakage. He's a little monster, and we don't want him in the store. As a matter of fact, we can't afford him."

"I never heard of anything so outrageous," exclaimed Mrs. Brody, grabbing the back of Johnny's shirt, as he tried to reach for a large ceramic cat. "If that's the way you treat a little harmless child, I shall never bring my business here again."

"Is that a promise?" Steffie was beyond caring that she had just lost them a customer with more money than brains. The aggravation simply wasn't worth it.

"I have a good mind to sue you for child abuse," sputtered the angry mother.

"You don't have a good mind at all, or you would know that this little —," Here Steffie was about to say "brat", but changed her mind and said "fellow". "You would know that this little fellow needs some serious discipline. He's a lovely looking boy, and I'm sure you'd like to be proud of him," she added lamely, trying belatedly to smooth out the situation. "He really needs to be taught how to behave in a store. I'm sure you can understand that," she couldn't help adding. She noticed that Kitty was standing with an amazed look on her face, as her friend did battle with Mrs. Brody.

The woman stared at Steffie appraisingly for a moment, then surprised them both by laughing. "You know, that's exactly what my husband keeps telling me. We adopted Johnny two years ago, and he's just so adorable that I can't say 'no' to him. Then she surprised them by adding, "I really appreciate that you've been honest with me. I'll be back, because I love this boutique, but I won't bring Dennis the Menace with me next time. I'll leave him at home, and let my husband deal with him." She then gave Steffie what seemed to be a genuine smile, took Johnny by the hand, just as he tried to lift a large ceramic pot off the shelf, and hurried out the door.

She had barely disappeared, before Kitty said dryly, "Well, it works for me. I specially like your exquisite sense of diplomacy." Then she started to laugh. "You do have a way with words, Steffie old girl. That little monster deserves a good whacking, but I would never have had the nerve to speak up to the mother the way you did. You can be damn tough when you want to be. Did you see the look on her face? I thought she was going to stomp on your tongue, when you said that if he kicked you, you'd kick him back. She just couldn't believe what you were saying."

Steffie was beginning to look a bit sheepish, and Kitty had to grin. They busied themselves picking up the pieces of the broken mugs, as they talked.

"I guess I did get carried away. Forgive me for losing us a paying customer?"

"Au contraire, I don't think you've lost us a customer at all. She did such a quick about-face, that I'm sure she knew you were right. That little hellion does need some discipline, and if she comes back without him, I'd say you performed a good service for us. Heck, you may look like a babe, but you've got the disposition of a pit bull. I thought I was going to have to restrain you," she laughed. "It looked as if you might really throw him out bodily, and then, of course, his mother would have attacked you. We could have had a real brouha. Just imagine the headlines, 'Shopkeeper throws child into street. Shop closed permanently.'"

They both giggled, and shook their heads, as Kitty continued. "It really had quite a surprising and happy ending, didn't it? Somehow you've made a friend. Only you could have pulled it off, Steff," she added fondly.

Steffie sighed. "I know I completely lost control and made a fool of myself, but I can feel my blood pressure go up every time they walk into our lovely boutique. Maybe I should have a valium handy for any time they come in."

"Better still, I'll lock you in the office next time," grinned Kitty. "Actually, I doubt that we'll ever see the reprehensible little toad in here again. I like kids, but I can do without that one. You did a good deed today, Steff, so don't beat yourself up about it."

CHAPTER 7

▼

It seemed to be the kind of day which brought out the crazies. They had just tidied up the devastation caused by little Johnny, when a strange looking man entered the shop. Both women immediately went on the alert. He was giving off strange vibes, and they searched his face, and watched his hands.

"Methinks his gut runneth over," whispered Steffie, looking at his enormous pot belly. He looked like a beach ball with legs. "You help him, and I'll stay near the phone," she muttered.

The rotund little chap was mumbling to himself, as he wandered around the store. Kitty asked if he needed any help, but he ignored her, and kept going round and round the aisles, picking up items, peering at them, and replacing them with great care. Well, at least he wasn't another Johnny Brody, she thought. He had doused himself in some kind of pungent after-shave lotion, and its noxious fumes wafted behind him like a vapour trail. Kitty's nose was beginning to itch, and she was afraid she was about to have a sneezing attack.

After twenty minutes, the little man smiled broadly, and asked if they were the owners. He had a high pitched, droning sort of voice, and Kitty thought he sounded like a Louisiana locust. She had read the phrase once in some book, and had loved it. She didn't know whether there was such a critter, but if there was one, it would definitely make a noise just like this little guy.

When they affirmed that they were indeed the owners, he asked eagerly whether they wanted to sell the shop. They laughed, thinking it was some kind of joke, but he was very serious. He asked them to think about it, and said that he would be back.

After he left, Kitty and Steffie just stared at each other in disbelief. "He looked a bit like Rumpelstiltskin," chortled Steffie.

"He was as flaky as granny's pie crust," said Kitty with a grin. "I don't think he's the Black Sheep, though, do you?" she joked.

"No, he's too short. He'd have to stand on a stool to get his hands around anyone's neck," replied Steffie. "Honestly, they sometimes come out of the woodwork, don't they?"

Kitty was thinking how attractive Steffie looked today, in her lavender coloured cotton dress, with a little crocheted lavender jacket over it. Steffie was so striking in appearance, that it was amazing some guy hadn't snapped her up by now. She, however, was very edgy, and usually gave off obviously "hands off" vibes, when any man began to look at her with interest. Kitty hoped that she would soon start dating again, but in the meantime, she seemed quite happy with her life.

They were still laughing about the weird little man, when the door opened, and a tall, good looking chap, with an interesting scar along his jaw line, walked into the store. He was accompanied by a bear of a man, who looked rather like the infamous bull in the china shop. Steffie shuddered at the damage he could do, if he accidentally backed into one of the display cases, or tripped over one of the vases, placed so artfully around the premises. After just getting rid of Johnny and the little roly-poly, they certainly didn't need this big bear lumbering through the aisles.

The two men walked casually through the store, obviously waiting for something or someone. As soon as the last customer left, the handsome one with the scar, approached Steffie, and asked if she was the owner. When she said that she was co-owner with Kitty, the two men showed their badges. They were detectives with the Niagara Regional Police. They looked familiar to Kitty, but she couldn't imagine where she had seen them.

"I'm Bud Lang, and this is my partner, Jack Willinger," said the big man with the crinkly laugh lines around his eyes. They were a deep chocolate brown, and somehow he looked as if he laughed a lot. Both women liked him immediately. They also felt that Jack Willinger was one of the most attractive fellows who had crossed their threshold in many a day. You could tell that he was fully aware of the affect he had on women, but he didn't act conceited, just very sure of himself.

"Surely you're not here to arrest us for child abuse," laughed Kitty. "We just threw a woman and her undisciplined brat out half an hour ago, after he broke a few things."

"No," grinned the big one named Bud Lang. "We'll give you a pass on that." Then, pausing a moment, and looking around the shop, he continued. "As you know, we've had a strangling in the city this week, and we're working on the case. We're covering all the gift shops and boutiques in the Region, looking for a certain item, which the killer likes to leave at the scene. It's difficult, because we're trying to keep the nature of the object secret, but we have to find out where it was purchased."

"Actually, two identical items have been left at the two murder sites in the past two months," added Detective Willinger. "Now, we're going to have to tell you what it is we're looking for, but we're asking for your full co-operation in not talking about it with anyone, until you read about it in the paper, or see it on television. We know it's a losing cause, but even a couple of days will give us a head start on this guy. Once the papers get hold of the info, it's ballgame over. All the crazies will be coming out of the woodwork, confessing to the crimes, and reciting all the facts which they've read. Can we count on you to keep silent for a while?" This last was asked in a deep voice, as he looked from one to the other, with his Paul Newman blue eyes. Detective Lang was wandering around the shop, obviously looking for something in particular.

"Of course you can count on us," Steffie answered eagerly. "We'll co-operate in any way we can, and we certainly won't tell anyone." They were both wondering whether the objects had in fact been purchased here, and if so, which one of them had actually dealt with the killer. The thought made little shivers run down their backs, and they looked at each other in dismay.

Both detectives eyed the women carefully, then seemed to come to some decision. "Okay, what we're looking for is a small black ceramic sheep about this big," said Detective Willinger, indicating the size with his hands. "Have you ever sold anything like that?" Kitty and Steffie could tell by the tone of voice, that the detective didn't have much hope that they had such an item in the store. Boy was he in for a surprise!

They gulped, as they glanced at each other, and nodded their heads. They had indeed sold at least four of the little sheep, and there were a couple more in the boutique.

"Is this what you're looking for?" asked Kitty, walking over to a display case, and returning with one of the unique little figurines.

"That's it!" exclaimed Detective Lang jubilantly. "This is the first shop we've found that sells them. Now, do you keep a list of the customers and their purchases?" he asked hopefully, knowing full well that things were never that easy in a murder investigation.

"No we don't," said Steffie regretfully. "Quite a few of our customers pay cash, which means that there is no record of the person's name. They simply get a cash register receipt for return purposes. For those who pay by credit card or cheque though, we would have a record. We've been selling these sheep since before Christmas, so we'd have to go through months of paper work."

Just then, two women entered the store, and started browsing. Kitty stayed to keep an eye on them, and to help them if need be, while Steffie took the two detectives into the office, to continue the conversation. Kitty didn't want to miss anything, and hoped that she could get rid of the customers quickly. This was exciting, as well as a little frightening. Could they really have sold one or two black sheep to the killer? It was certainly not a happy thought.

Unfortunately, the two customers wanted to browse, and took forever to make their selections. By the time they were ready to pay, the detectives were ready to leave. Cautioning Kitty and Steffie again not to say anything to anyone, they thanked them, and said they would be back later.

"What else did they say, Steff? Are we going to have to go through all those records for them? That could take forever."

"Yes, but they're coming back to help us. They asked if they could come tonight about 7:30, and I said sure. Hope that's okay, Kit. I know we were going to go to the movies, but this is much more important, and we can do the movie thing tomorrow night. Detective Lang said that they have been to three shops already, and not one of them carries these. They need the name and address of our distributor, as well as a look at all the records. Just imagine, we may have actually talked to the killer, and had him right here in the store. It's scary isn't it?"

"Damn right. I hope some other store carries them, and that's where he got them. I wouldn't want to think that we were connected in any way to those killings. I'm trying to remember something about the ones that I sold. I think I've only sold two, and I'm sure that one was to somebody I know. Oh darn, I can practically see myself wrapping one up in a gift package. Who the heck was it?" She was frowning as she went to the cash register to help another customer.

The rest of the day went by quickly, and Kitty asked Steffie to come home with her for a quick dinner. She had to feed the cats, before coming back to the shop for their appointment with the police. They went in Kitty's car, and chatted non-stop about the events of the afternoon.

Both women agreed that the two detectives were quite charming, to say the least. Jack Willinger, in particular, was interesting. He had a laid back, quiet energy about him, and he exuded such a male presence, that women probably just fell at his feet. You could tell he was aware of his affect on women, but he didn't push it. Bud Lang, on the other hand, seemed full of mischief. He seemed the type who would love to play practical jokes, yet he looked to be kind, and likely sensitive. Both men were intriguing.

Halfway through the evening, Steffie made coffee, and brought out some cookies, which they always kept on hand to provide a little energy during the day. There were some days when they didn't have time to stop for lunch.

The search was disappointing. It appeared that only one black sheep had been purchased by credit card, and the buyer was a little old lady they both knew from church. She sure as heck couldn't be the strangler. The detectives took her name and address anyway, knowing that she might have a husband or son or grandson for whom the sheep had been purchased. That didn't make any sense to Kitty and Steffie, since there were supposedly two black sheep involved, but they refrained from asking too many questions.

They promised to keep trying to remember to whom they had sold the other sheep. It wasn't very likely, considering the amount of merchandise they sold every day, but they would do their best. They liked both of these men, and by the end of the evening, working in such close quarters, they were calling each other by their first names. Unfortunately, both men had made casual mention of their wives. Darn it, thought Steffie ruefully, all the good ones are taken. Even though she had no interest in getting involved in a relationship at this point in her life, she still liked to look.

The detectives admonished them again to please keep silent about the black sheep. The longer they could keep the media from finding out, the better chance they had of catching the guy. They knew, however, that it was a losing battle. Sooner or later, likely sooner, the press would find out, and broadcast it to the world. The longer it could be kept secret, the less likely it was that the killer would get rid of any other little black sheep he had on hand.

Kitty and Steffie stayed in the office a little longer, after the detectives had left. They were all keyed up and excited about the search, and very disappointed that they hadn't been able to be of much help. They were sure that little old Mrs. DeMarco from the church, wasn't going to be a good lead. She was such a sweet old thing, that it was unlikely she would know any potential killers, or be one herself.

It was spooky in the parking lot. Their cars seemed to be hunkered down, staring glumly at them. They wasted no time locking the vehicle doors, and taking off, honking good-bye, as they went their separate ways. Neither one noticed a tall figure lurking in the shadows.

Steffie wakened about four, in a cold sweat. She was shaking, as she turned on the bedside lamp. It must have been all the talk about the killer and the black sheep, which had caused the nightmare. As she got up to get herself a glass of water, she tried to recapture the frightening scenes. In the dream, Kitty was involved, and the killer had been stalking her. He was dancing with her, twirling her round and round, as his fiendish grin grew wider and wider.

Steffie couldn't see his face clearly. She just knew that he was the killer, and she watched with horror, as a little black sheep flew from his pocket, and landed on the floor. The sheep seemed to come to life, and began walking deliberately toward Kitty. Then the music stopped, and the killer's hands were suddenly around Kitty's neck. Steffie was running, but she was running in molasses. Each step took an eternity, and she knew that she could never reach her friend in time. She was trying to call out for someone to help her, but no one could hear her. The only sound was the baa baa baaing of the little black sheep. It was at this point that she had wakened, heart pounding and hands shaking. She rarely dreamt at all, and even during the worst days of her marriage, she had never had nightmares.

She drank her water, and stared at her pale face in the mirror. Her wild mane of curly black hair was even wilder than usual. She must have been tossing her head on the pillow, as she dreamed of trying to run.

Splashing cold water on her face, she turned out the bathroom light, and returned to her bed. She lay for a long time, trying to calm herself by rationalizing the dream. The killer had been the last thing she thought of before going to bed, so it wasn't surprising that she might dream about him. She had never met any detectives, so of course they had made an impression on her, and got her thinking about the murders. The thought of possibly having sold the black sheep to the killer was awful. It somehow made her feel guilty. It made the shop seem guilty. No wonder it had all carried over into a scary dream.

She thought momentarily of calling Kitty, to be sure that she was safe, but she told herself that she was being paranoid. Kitty wouldn't appreciate being wakened.

Turning out the light, she found that sleep was impossible. She tossed and turned and fussed with the bed clothes. The first chirping of the morning birds was a welcome sound. Finally, abandoning all hope of sleep, she got up to have a soothing shower, locking the bathroom door firmly behind her.

CHAPTER 8

▼

He could feel the pressure growing every day, all the signs were there. He had a queasy feeling in the pit of his stomach. There was a dull thudding in his head — not an ache, just a heavy, full feeling. He was antsy and hyper, and the tips of his fingers felt tingly, as if they could feel themselves wrapped around a pretty neck.

The first time it had happened was just before he had killed his mother. He hadn't known what was happening to him then, and he had been frightened. The relief which came after he had killed her, was unbelievable, and unexpected. The rush of adrenaline, as he squeezed her scrawny neck, had been incredible. Immediately after that unprecedented act, he had been suffused with a great sense of tranquility. There was no more thudding in his head, no queasy stomach, no feeling of anxiety. His fingers had felt fine. He remembered standing looking at them, and waggling them in amazement. No more tingling.

Placing the little black sheep in his mother's hand, had been a spur of the moment touch of genius. It was a toy which he had carried with him since he was a little boy. Actually, his mother had given it to him, and in his mind, it was a special charm which would someday kick in, and bring him good luck. His mother had called him the black sheep of the family, and had sworn that he would never amount to anything. He and his twin brother Mike had been so alike, yet in his mother's eyes, he was the black sheep. How unfair was that? Well, he had shown her. The day he killed her, he placed the black sheep in her open palm. "You were right, ma, and I'm giving this back to you," he had whispered. "You've finally done something good for me. You've made me feel great. Your little Black Sheep feels like the king of the world."

When the feelings began to build up again, he kept himself as busy as possible. Today he was cleaning out his closet, and he was sweating. He had been working faster and faster, almost with maniacal speed, as if to outrun the thoughts and feelings which were dropping and bouncing in his head, like rotten apples falling from a tree.

He knew he was going to do it again, yet he didn't really want to. He knew it was wrong, yet it felt so good, and seemed to be the only way he could get relief from the pounding and tingling. He kept telling himself that they had deserved it. Each woman he had strangled had been a tramp. The silly thing was that he loved women, and all he really wanted was to find one who would be totally his, one whom he could trust one hundred percent. He needed one who wouldn't tempt and tease and flirt with other men, the way his mother had.

When he was functioning normally, doing his job, and doing it very well, he understood that he was sick, that he needed help. When the feelings started building up though, he was able to justify his actions. They made sense to him, regretful though they might be. It was all so damn confusing. No point in trying to figure it out, although it really was absurd. He was likely the only serial killer around, who still had a bit of a conscience.

He would do one more, and then he would try to quit. He had to kill Ginny, much as he loved her. She should have been his, but she had married Mike instead. That was bad enough, but when he had seen her walking into a hotel with a big guy in some kind of uniform, he had to tell his brother.

Mike tended to fall into heavy bouts of depression, but who would have guessed that the silly fool would kill himself. Somehow, he tried to believe that it was all Ginny's fault, but he knew that wasn't true. She had been meeting her brother, who had come into town unexpectedly to see her, before being sent to Afghanistan. He shouldn't have gone running to his brother with false accusations, before getting the true story. It was Mike's fault too though. Why did he have to be such a hot head, and run and suck up those exhaust fumes? The entire thing had been a dreadful screw-up.

There had been four killings so far, all within eighteen months. His mother was the first, and at that time he hadn't realized there would be any more. It had just felt so good, so right. Placing that little black sheep in her hand had made him feel wonderful. He laughed every time he thought about it. The police in his hometown hadn't put much energy into trying to solve the case. She was no one important — just the town bimbo. He hadn't lived at home for years, so he wasn't even a suspect. The police had certainly slipped up on that one.

The second strangling had really been an accident. He had been in Toronto, just driving around, wondering what was wrong with him. He had felt so nervous, so angry. The prostitute wasn't young — likely in her forties. He had watched her strut back and forth near the corner — the pink boa around her neck, matching the pink shorts, which were so tight that they looked as if they had been sprayed on her flabby butt. He had driven around the corner three times before he made his decision to pick her up.

It had enraged him that she got in the car so willingly. Didn't she realize how dangerous that could be? When she started talking suggestively, he became more angry. Were all women this disgusting? What in hell was he doing here? He felt as if he was watching himself from a distance. The anger became so intense that his fingers gripping the steering wheel were white. There was sweat on his forehead, and his hands were slippery by the time they got to a remote area. Once he stopped the car, he didn't waste any time. Before she knew what was happening, his hands were around her neck, and he was squeezing.

In her frantic struggles and flailing, she had grazed his shin bone with the spiked heel of her fancy hooker shoes. She had actually torn his pant leg with the damn heel. That enraged him so much, that he wound the pink boa round and round her neck, tying it in a knot. He had dumped her into the Don Valley ravine, and taken off.

Driving back to Niagara Falls, he had cursed himself for not having been prepared. He hadn't brought a little black sheep with him. Part of him wanted people to know that it was the Black Sheep who was doing it, but the other part of him knew that was really stupid. Why leave a trail for the police? This murder would be of very little significance. It would be just one less prostitute in the world. Still, he wished he'd had a black sheep to put in her hand. It was his signature, and he realized that subconsciously he had known all along that there would be more killings.

He was going to have to buy some black sheep, and it took him weeks before he was able to find a shop which sold them. Although they were bigger, and looked different to the little plastic one he had carried as a child, they would have to do. What he really regretted was that he didn't have his camera with him. From that day on, there was always a camera in the car.

That had been number two, but the police, of course, had never made the connection. The third one was also a prostitute, but that time he had picked her up right off the street in Niagara Falls. He had gone out cruising that night, with a little black sheep in his pocket. Knowing what he was going to do was exciting and frightening. It was really dangerous, because it would have been so easy for someone to recognize him.

He had gone back to her messy, stuffy little room with her, and it had made him cringe. He was fastidious, and he couldn't breathe in its stinking, cloying atmosphere. She had a collection of Barbie dolls all around the room, and he felt like smashing them, with their perfectly formed bodies, meant to tease and titillate. He did actually tear the heads off a couple of them, after he had strangled her. Then he realized how foolish he was being, and he got himself back under control.

The calmness settled over him, as he placed the little black sheep in her hand. Two of her long false nails had torn off in the brief struggle, and he noticed with disgust, that her own nails were chewed down to the quick. He took three pictures from three different angles. They turned out well, and would look good in the album.

As he made his way home that night, he realized that killing prostitutes was a useless and hopeless task. It was like trying to drain the ocean with a strainer. From now on he would only kill a woman if she really deserved it. No, that was wrong. He wouldn't kill at all. He could control himself.

He wasn't angry now, and in his calm and peaceful mood, he couldn't even imagine why he had done these terrible things. There would be no more stranglings. He was lucky that he had escaped punishment so far, and he wouldn't push his luck. He was an intelligent, handsome person. People liked him. He had lots of friends. He was like Ted Bundy, who had not been your typical psychopath or sociopath. No one had suspected Ted for a long time. It was just a random piece of luck that he had been caught. Well, no one suspected the Black Sheep either. He performed an important function in society, but it was time to quit. He could control himself. He muttered this over and over like a mantra, as he washed up and went to bed.

Even though he had tried to convince himself that he would never do it again, he began looking for somewhere else to buy a few more black sheep.

He knew it was wrong, and there was absolutely no reason to have any more of them in his possession, yet he couldn't stop looking for them.

He had eventually found a distributor in Vancouver, who carried them. He had gone to very elaborate means to order some, along with several other items, and to have them mailed to a post box in Toronto. This he had rented under a false name, and had cancelled it after his purchase had arrived safely. He was sure that he had covered his tracks well. He paid cash for everything. Even if the police ever did find the Vancouver source, and even if they had a record of the sheep being purchased in the midst of a large order of all kinds of junk, the postal box in a false name would be a dead end for them.

Eve had happened two months later, and he had promised himself that she was the last. He had really liked Eve, thought that maybe she was the one for him. She had reminded him of Ginny. He had seen her kissing and holding hands with some guy though, when they were supposed to be seeing each other exclusively. It was humiliating, and he couldn't let her get away with it.

Now the feelings were building up again. He felt as if his head was going to explode. The latest object of his affections obviously liked men, and was dating someone else at the moment. Right now though, he mustn't let himself think about her. When he had these feelings, no one was safe. She was a lovely girl, and he was sure that they would be a perfect couple. He just had to be careful, and take his time with her.

CHAPTER 9

▼

Two afternoons a month, Kitty did volunteer work at the Greater Niagara General Hospital. She liked to work in the children's ward, where she could play games, read books, and tell stories to the sick kids, when their parents couldn't be with them. She enjoyed cuddling and rocking the little ones, who would cling like koala bears in her arms.

Steffie, on the other hand, didn't have much patience with children. She found them too demanding and ill behaved. In her mind, they were all like little Johnny Brody — the kid from hell. She did, however, get along well with elderly people, so she spent her volunteer afternoons twice a month in the geriatric ward. She enjoyed reading to them, or writing notes for them, or even sitting quietly listening to music with them. The old people loved this tall, exuberant gal with the wild mane of curly black hair, and her irrepressible sense of humour, and joie de vivre.

It was actually while working at the hospital, that Kitty had first met Dr. Drew Carson. They had literally bumped into each other while rounding a corner, coming from different directions. It was a couple of weeks later, when he had walked into her shop, and they had recognized each other. He made some inquiries about her at the hospital, and the day after meeting her at the boutique, he stuck his head into the pediatric ward at the end of her shift, asking her to have coffee with him in the hospital cafeteria.

He was a plastic surgeon, and reputedly a very good one. He kept his private life very private, and was a bit of a man of mystery around the hospital. Dr. Drew Carson was tall and skinny, with an untidy shock of fair hair, and deep green eyes behind John Lennon glasses. Because no one knew too much about him, and because he and Dr. Keith Spenser had reputations as swingers, there were many nurses who were just waiting for the chance to date him.

Over their coffee, he told Kitty that his wife had died, and since he was on his own, it had been easy to close up his practice in Nova Scotia, and move to Ontario to start all over. There were women everywhere who wanted to fix their tits and asses, he had remarked quite candidly. He had gone on to say that face lifts, bum tucks and breast enhancements weren't exactly what he had in mind when he first went into medicine, but that was where the money could be found.

Kitty thought that was a very cynical remark, and got the feeling that he didn't have much respect for women. She found that he had a great sense of humour, though, and had a laugh which she found appealing. When he asked if she would like to go to dinner and a movie, she hadn't hesitated. It was time to start dating again after the Scott fiasco.

Their first date had been interesting to say the least. They had gone to a restaurant in one of the high rise hotels overlooking the falls, and it was a breathtaking view. She soon discovered, however, that he had a habit which was extremely annoying. She didn't know whether it was nerves or what, but he kept toying with the silverware, lining it up perfectly, one inch from the edge of the table. He also kept realigning his water glass and wine glass.

In order to tease and test him a bit, Kitty deliberately placed her silverware and glasses askew — doing it in a very casual and surreptitious way. She could see that it really bothered him. How strange! She decided that he must be an obsessive compulsive type, or at the very least, a perfectionist. That was likely what made him a good surgeon.

She realized that he really wasn't her cup of tea. There seemed to be no chemistry there, but in many ways he was a funny and decent guy. We all have some little idiocyncrasies, she told herself, so, somehow, she kept accepting his calls to take her here or there. He wasn't a romantic possibility, but he was turning into a friend, at least in her point of view.

Today was Thursday, and the boutique had been constantly busy. When the phone rang, Steffie answered it, and handed the receiver to Kitty, muttering "Think it's the great doctor calling." She was happy that Kitty was dating again, but after the way Scott had hurt her, Steffie felt very protective of her friend. She knew that all the nurses seemed to think Dr. Carson was a catch, but she had also heard that he and his friend Dr. Keith Spenser were quite the wild bachelors.

"Kitty, how do you feel about sand, water, beach volleyball and a barbecue?" he asked in a business-like fashion.

"What are you talking about?" she laughed, as she kept her eyes on two customers who had just entered the shop, and were browsing with their backs to her. After their first year, she and Steffie were always aware of possible shoplifters. That year they had lost an inordinate amount of merchandise, because of being too trusting. They were actually considering installing a video camera and some mirrors to protect themselves, but hadn't done anything about it yet.

"Well, Keith Spenser has just rented a cottage up on Lake Erie, and he's having a barbecue party this Sunday. Your friend Cleo will be there with some guy from the hospital, and Keith is planning to ask Steffie. He's had his eye on her around the hospital, and he thinks she's quite a babe.

It should be a great day. All we have to bring is some wine and a dessert. I'll bring the wine, but are you any good at desserts?" he asked hopefully.

"Sure. I'll whip up something yummy." She rolled her eyes at Steffie, as she pretended more enthusiasm than she felt. "What time is this little do?"

"I'll pick you up at two. Be sure to wear something pink."

"What? Why pink?"

"Because I know you'd look sensational in pink with your blond hair. Don't disappoint me now. I'll see you Sunday." With that, the phone connection was broken. Drew was not one to waste time on small talk.

Kitty sighed and looked over at Steffie. "Well, that's a change. He usually likes to take me to out of the way places, where we won't meet anyone we know. He says he can't stand running into his patients when he's out socializing. Anyway, I'm going to need some help here, kiddo. There's a barbecue on Sunday at the cottage Keith Spenser is renting. Apparently Keith is going to call you to invite you, and Drew wants me to wear pink. What do you think about a man who tells you what to wear?"

"I think that I would tell him to go stuff it," replied Steffie, as she rearranged a couple of knick-knacks.

"The trouble is, I know that I do look good in pink. It's a great colour for me. My inclination is to wear anything but pink, just to show him that no one tells me what to do, but then I'm only hurting myself, and being stubborn. Actually, I've been thinking for quite a while that I'd like a new pink bikini this summer. Shoot, now I'm in a real quandary." She was chagrined that Drew had put her in this position. "I don't think I have anything that's suitable for a barbecue, though. How about you?"

"Well, I'll wait and see whether he calls or not. I don't even know the great Dr. Spenser, except by reputation. We've said hello a couple of times at the hospital, and I had coffee with him one day, but that's it. The only reason I'd consider going, is because it's supposed to be a beautiful day on Sunday, and it would be terrific to get up to the lake. Anyway, it's a great excuse to go shopping. Why don't we go after work? They have some good sales on at the Pen Centre. We wouldn't want to disappoint the good doctors now would we?"

Before the day was finished, Keith Spenser had called and invited Steffie. Things were working out well.

Sunday turned out to be one of those glorious Niagara Falls days, with clear blue cloudless skies, bright sunshine, and just a whisper of a breeze from the west. The air was pure and clean, no hint of smog. It had rained during the night, and the lawns and trees appeared to be a shimmering emerald green. Kitty was sure that Niagara Falls was one of the most beautiful places in Canada. The acres of fruit lands were peaceful and aesthetically pleasing to the eye. There was a certain tranquility and grace about them.

In the spring, the pink cherry blossoms and the white apple blossoms, transformed the area into a fairyland. The bright pink Japanese cherry blossoms and the raspberry coloured flowering crabs were Kitty's favourites. Steffie, however, loved the lilac gardens at the School of Horticulture. She liked to walk through the gardens, inhaling the sweet perfumed air. She sometimes thought that when she died, she would miss these fragrant, beautiful flowers, and the peaceful surroundings, more than anything else. It seemed that every season in Niagara had its own charm, and the two friends felt that it was no wonder the tourists came in droves. They often told each other how lucky they were to live in this paradise.

"Now you guys be good while I'm gone, no tearing the house apart," Kitty admonished the cats, as they lazed around in the sunny kitchen. The felines, however, didn't seem too interested in what she had to say. Miss Rosie was washing her tail with great concentration, and Petie Pie was lying on his back, all four feet in the air, enjoying the warmth of the sunshine.

The two friends had gone to church first, and were being picked up around two. Kitty was surprised and a little annoyed that Josh Tuttle was there working, when she arrived home after church. What carpenters ever worked on a Sunday morning? Josh explained that he was going out of town for a couple of days, and was just trying to get a bit ahead with his work today. Kitty decided it was very nice of him to make the effort. When she told him, however, that she would be out the rest of the day, he had frowned and looked cross. What's his problem, she wondered, as she locked the sliding doors, and went to the front hall to watch for Drew.

He laughed in delight when she appeared in a shocking pink halter top, and a long pink and cream flowered skirt. "You look amazing," he exclaimed, as he took the dessert plate from her, and placed it carefully on the floor in the back. You ain't seen nothing yet, she grinned to herself, as she thought of the new pink bikini, which was snuggled in the beach bag, along with a change of clothes, and a fluffy beach towel.

Kitty couldn't remember when she had enjoyed herself so much. Keith Spenser's cottage was an absolute delight, but it was certainly no cottage. It was very old — built back in 1894, and was an Adirondack or shingle style house, which had obviously seen better days. Kitty, however, could easily imagine it in all its glory. It was huge, with seven bedrooms upstairs, and an entire top floor, which had been the servants' quarters.

Since Keith was a carefree bachelor, Kitty wondered why in the world he had rented such an enormous place. Still, she recalled that he had a reputation as quite a swinger, so maybe he needed lots of room in which to chase and romance the ladies, — a place in which to "swing," so to speak. He would certainly have all the privacy he wanted, and he could really have some fabulous parties there. This barbecue was likely the first of many.

She loved the living room, which was at least forty feet long, and which had a huge stone fireplace as its centerpiece. She was sure that the large living room windows with the tiny square panes on top, were what they called the 'arts and crafts style.' What was so interesting, was that the windows ran around three sides of the living room, and they all had wide window seats, which would be fabulous for storage. They would also be wonderful places on which cats could rest, and look out at the world.

Steffie was also intrigued with the old place, and, with Keith as her guide, spent almost an hour wandering around the three floors, exclaiming at, and admiring all the old furniture. Some of it was just old, but some of the pieces were real antiques, and likely very valuable. There were two pianos. The baby grand in the living room was in dreadful condition, but the upright in the oversized dining room, was playable. Steffie found some great old music in the piano bench, and hoped that Kitty might play the piano later on, and they could have an old fashioned sing-song before the night was over.

The highlight of the dining room was the wooden table, (she wasn't sure what kind of wood it was), which would easily seat twenty or more people. There were several candelabra placed at intervals on it, and an old sideboard was filled with china treasures. Imagine letting a stranger actually rent this place!

By the time they made their way up to the servants' quarters on the top floor, they were quite comfortable with each other. "Keith, there must be so much history in these rooms. I can just picture some young Irish girl named Nora or Eileen, living up here. She would have been small and wiry, with a pale complexion, rosy cheeks and black curly hair. She would have been the nanny, or more likely, the chambermaid, and she was likely straight off the boat from Ireland.

When her days' duties were done, she would have gazed out these windows at the beach and the water, and she would have been thinking that she had found a bit of paradise, but she would have also been very homesick for Ireland. I wonder whether they just had the one servant, or whether they had two or more sharing these quarters. There was likely a robust nanny with chubby cheeks, to take care of the children, and maybe there was even a gardener. There's a lot of lawn out there. What a shame that there aren't any diaries or photos of the families who have lived here over the years."

"You've got quite an imagination, Stephanie. I've never really given much thought to what the original families would have been like, or how many servants they had. You know, I haven't had a chance to explore all the cupboards and closets yet. No telling what I might find. If you are interested though, maybe you'd like to come up again, and help me go through some of the old trunks in the basement. I'm sure the owners wouldn't care. Besides, I'm thinking seriously of putting in an offer. I think it would be a fabulous place to own and to fix up."

Steffie was taken aback at his suggestion that she come up with him to go through some of the old trunks, but she agreed that it would be fun. Truthfully, she didn't think she would be very comfortable up here at the lake alone with Keith. His reputation had preceded him. Still, it would be interesting. Keith was a bit of a mystery man. One minute he was serious and a bit pompous, the way so many doctors can be, and the next minute he was flirting and teasing outrageously. He was just average height, and he had a sort of squared off jaw which gave him a rugged look. He walked with his feet splayed out, and seemed more like a cowboy than a doctor. He dressed really well though, and seemed fastidious about his appearance.

She wondered what his patients thought of him. She also wondered about the old house. She felt that it had a lot of buried secrets which she would love to uncover.

CHAPTER 10

▼

When they finally emerged from the dark mansion into the bright sunlight, Steffie saw that Kitty was happily engrossed in a wild game of volleyball. Drew, however, was glaring down at Kitty from a chair on the overly large deck. When he saw her look up at him, he quickly got up, and went down to the beach. Kitty sighed inwardly. What had she done now? He would likely sulk the rest of the day, but did she really care? She wasn't sure. She returned to the volleyball game, and refrained from looking at any of the men as much as possible. There was no point in aggravating Drew unnecessarily.

Cleo plopped herself down beside Kitty when the game was finished. She was medium height, but really well put together, and she obviously spent a lot of money on clothes. She had an open, honest face, with big green eyes and thick curly eyelashes, and there was something about her which men seemed to find very attractive. It might have been her fine features and smooth skin, or her brown curly hair and big boobs, or it could have been the cute little sprinkling of freckles across her nose. Kitty, however, suspected it was the aura of fun and laughter which she exuded. It was difficult not to laugh and have fun when Cleo was around.

"What a great party," she exclaimed, as she kicked off her sandals, and squeezed her toes in the sand.

"Yes, it is. Listen, you secretive girl. I didn't know you were dating Barry Johnson. He's a nurse isn't he? I'm sure I've run into him at the hospital. Where did you meet him?"

"Oh, he looked after my dad when he was in hospital," Cleo shrugged. "He's okay, but I know I can do better. I like Keith Spenser, and he's a bachelor too. You're lucky though with Drew. He's interesting. There's something about him which is very appealing. I'd like to know what goes on behind those little John Lennon glasses."

Kitty laughed, and looked over at Drew. He really was interesting, and she did enjoy his company, when he wasn't being childish. Was she too critical of him? Was she giving him a fair chance? She pondered these questions, as she idly ran sand through her fingers. Then, as if coming to a decision, she said, "We're just friends, Cleo. It's nice to have someone to take you to dinner and a movie once in a while."

"Really?" cried Cleo with excitement. "You mean you wouldn't care if I dated him?"

Kitty was quite taken aback. Cleo was ridiculous. All she thought about was men, and how she could get them to ask her out. She wasn't sure just how she would feel about Cleo dating Drew. She didn't think Cleo would be his type, but who knew? She liked Drew as a friend, and had fun with him, but there was no spark there, so she decided it would be fine if Cleo could get her clutches into him. She was pretty sure that it wouldn't happen, so she graciously said, "No, of course I wouldn't mind. Give it your best shot and see what happens." Then she felt strangely grumpy, and walked over to speak with someone else. Cleo with all her scheming ways, was becoming tiresome.

Somehow, over the hamburgers and hot dogs, the subject of the strangler came up. Everyone had an opinion, and there was great speculation as to what it was that the killer left at the scene. One know-it-all type said that she had heard from a very reliable source, that he left a silk scarf wrapped around the victim's neck. It was difficult for Kitty and Steffie to keep their mouths shut, and not tell them what they knew. They wondered how long it would be before the truth about the Black Sheep hit the papers. They also wondered why they hadn't heard anything more from the detectives. They had liked both of them, especially Jack Willinger, who was a very attractive guy.

Steffie came home in the car with Drew and Kitty. Keith was staying at the cottage overnight. She was thankful that he hadn't asked her to stay. He was fun, but Steffie had sent out plenty of signals that she wasn't interested in any kind of a relationship.

Drew was quiet on the drive back from the beach. Steffie wondered whether he was mad that she was hitching a ride with them. Maybe he had wanted Kitty all to himself. Kitty couldn't tell whether he was sulking over something, or just tired. In any case, she wasn't in the mood to placate him.

He refused an invitation to come in for coffee, and leaning over to give her a quick peck on the cheek, he left both women to scramble out of the car, and gather their belongings. Then, apparently having a quick change of heart, he leaped out of the car, and caught up with Kitty on the doorstep. "You looked sensational today, Kitty. I was proud of you. Thanks for wearing the pink. I was right — it's a great colour for you." Giving her a hug and a quick kiss, along with a wave to Steffie, he was gone.

They stood there a moment looking after him, and shaking their heads. His moods were mercurial to say the least.

They fed the cats, and sat down to have a glass of wine, before Kitty drove Steffie back to her apartment.

"Did you see that guy with Cleo? He couldn't keep his eyes off her, and she pretty well ignored him. He wasn't too happy."

"I know, and Keith kept ogling her too. She looked great in her teeny weeny bikini. I suspect though, that she has a crush on Drew. She seemed to be talking to him every time I turned around, and she thinks he's 'interesting.' Oh, and I couldn't keep a straight face when that Viola Pritchard claimed that she knows for a fact that the strangler is leaving a silk scarf at each crime site! I really had to bite my tongue not to tell them the real story."

"Me too. So what do you think of Drew, now that you've spent an entire day with him? How does he measure up?"

"You know, I like Drew, but there's no spark there, certainly not like there was with Scott. I'd like to have him as a friend, but that's all."

Steffie heaved a huge sigh. "Oh, for heaven's sake. You're still suffering from 'Scottitis'," she grumbled. "You know darn well that he was no good, but he was exciting, and he got your juices flowing. He was suffering from testosterone poisoning. Just remember how it turned out! My ex was a lot like Scott — good looking, charming, fast on his feet, and a real stinker. You'd better give Drew a chance. Don't throw him away just because there aren't any sparks yet. With Scott there were too many sparks, and you crashed and burned."

Kitty laughed ruefully. "You're right, I'm sure. You always tell it like it is. It's just that I think Drew might be the jealous type. He seems so moody too. I don't like moody people, — with the exception of you, of course." Here she gave her friend a playful nudge.

"Maybe I should invite him over for dinner one night, and see how the cats react to him. Remember when I was going with Scott, the cats really didn't like him. That should have been a warning sign for me. Cats are very intuitive about people. When he came over, Rosy always disappeared into one of her favourite hiding places. Petie Pie liked to sit on the couch behind his head, and yowl in his ear. Then, when Scott would chase him down off the couch, (which always annoyed me), Petie would sit on the floor in front of Scott, and start licking his other end, with one leg stuck straight up in the air. I think it was Petie's way of giving him the finger."

They both laughed, then Steffie said, "I wonder where the strangler is tonight, and whether he has any more black sheep? Shoot, I hope they catch him soon. Now I find myself staring at hands all the time. Men all seem to have such big hands."

"All the better to strangle you, my dear," said Kitty. "Please, no more talk about the strangler. I'll never sleep. I'm already nervous in my own home, and that's ridiculous. I'm afraid I'll have nightmares."

Steffie was thinking about the nightmare she had experienced concerning Kitty. She was glad that she hadn't told her about it.

They were just getting into Kitty's car, when Steffie squawked, "Kitty, have you seen my purse?"

"No, did you leave it in the house?"

"I must have. Sorry. Give me the key, and I'll run and get it."

Kitty waited while Steffie went back in. Moments later she returned, a worried look on her face. "I've either left it in Drew's car, or I left it up at the lake house. Let's go back in and call Drew first. Shoot, I hope it isn't way back at the lake."

They called Drew, and waited while he went out and looked through his car. "No, sorry, it's definitely not there. You must have left it at Keith's place."

"Damn it, Kitty. What do we do now? That purse has my keys to the boutique, and to my apartment, and to the car, and it has my bank books and credit cards in it. I've got to get it. Do you have the phone number up at the lake house?"

"No I don't. I'll call Drew again and see if he has it."

Unfortunately Drew did not have it, and had no idea who might have it. "You'll just have to wait and contact Keith tomorrow, when he gets back to town," he said in a rather annoyed tone.

It ended up that Steffie had to stay overnight with Kitty. She was really worried about her purse, and could hardly sleep. She called Keith's home the next morning, and was just about to hang up in frustration, when he answered.

He sounded gruff, and in a hurry.

"Keith, it's Steffie, and I've done something really stupid. I left my purse up at the cottage yesterday, and it has all my keys in it."

There was silence on the line for a moment, and then Keith said, "Shit. How did you manage to do that? I thought women always had their purses glued to their hands or shoulders. If you had called me up there I could have brought it back for you. As it is, I'm just on my way to a couple of meetings in Toronto, and I won't be back till tomorrow, so I can't go looking for it," he said rather ungraciously. "Tell you what, if you really need it right away, I'll leave the keys to the cottage in my mailbox here. Come pick them up, and then you can drive up to the lake yourself and get the damned thing. Just be sure to lock up well before you leave."

Where was the gracious host of yesterday? Today Keith sounded like an old bear with a sore paw. Anyway, that seemed the only solution, so Steffie thanked him and hung up.

They both had to get to the boutique, so they decided that they would drive up to the cottage right after work.

CHAPTER 11

▼

Kitty and Steffie raced home to feed the cats and turn on the lights, because they knew it would be dark before they got back from the lake. Little did they know just what lay ahead.

Setting out, they made a quick stop at Harveys, to get themselves some hamburgers and coffee. Steffie hated junk food, but agreed that there was no choice this time. She never liked to buy salads at the fast food places, in case they weren't washed properly. For such a carefree, fun loving person, Steff could be very uptight about food.

There were very dark clouds in the sky, as they hit the Queen Elizabeth Way, (known to all as the QEW), to Fort Erie.

"Gosh, I hope it isn't going to rain. Did you hear a forecast at all today?" asked Kitty, glancing up at the overcast skies above them.

"No, I never did turn the radio on at the shop. We were just too busy. There were some good customers today. I can't believe we sold three of those lovely cat afghans."

"Yes, and I sold that big brass box, which was taking up so darn much space. I think we've got some shipments coming in tomorrow, so it's a good thing we made some room today."

Traffic wasn't too heavy on the highway, but they had only gone a few miles, before the heavens opened, and they were caught in a real deluge.

"Shoot, this is awful. I hope it doesn't rain all the way. Look how dark it's getting," grumbled Steffie. "I still can't believe that I came away without my purse. I've never done that before. Hey, wait a minute. Weren't we supposed to turn at that corner back there?" she asked.

"Oh no, were we? I can't see the signs in this damn rain, and to tell you the truth, I wasn't paying that much attention when Drew drove up yesterday. I'll turn around up here."

They turned around in a gas station, went back to the corner, turned again, and were soon hopelessly lost.

"What the heck is the name of the road we're looking for?" asked Kitty grimly, as she peered through the rain and mist.

"I've no idea. I just assumed that you would know where we were going. I do remember Keith saying something about turning at the Holiday Inn."

"You're right. That does sound familiar. Okay, let's retrace our steps to where we got off the highway, and start again. I'm pretty sure that Keith told me it's called the Stockton House, after the wealthy American doctor from Buffalo who built it, and it's in the area called Rosehill, so we'll ask someone if we have to.

Keith really did give me a lot of historical background for the place, but I wasn't paying very close attention. I felt a little awkward being alone in that big house with him, — specially upstairs. I think he said, though, that someone called Ezra Rose owned acres and acres of land along the lake front, and he eventually sold it off in small parcels to wealthy people from Buffalo. I guess that's why the area where Keith's cottage is located, is called Rosehill. It's funny that they call it a cottage though. It's a real summer house, not a cottage. That place was a mansion in its prime."

At one point, it was raining so hard that they had to pull over to the side of the road and wait it out. Eventually, however, they found their way to the old lake house, which lurked, dark and foreboding. A vicious wind had come up, and seemed to be whipping the rain in circles.

"Yikes, this feels like a hurricane," complained Steffie, as they parked the car, and bolted up the stairs. The house was definitely unwelcoming, and they felt quite spooked, as they struggled with the key. The lock was old, and unwilling to open, and they were both totally soaked by the time they finally heard a reluctant click, and pushed each other inside.

It felt as if the old place was saying, "I put up with you yesterday, but you're not welcome here tonight."

"Whew, is this the same place where the sun was shining, and crowds of people were running around in their bathing suits?" whispered Kitty. Somehow it didn't seem right to be talking in a normal voice. It was as if, subconsciously, they didn't want to waken any dormant spirits.

"Let's just get my purse, and get the heck out of here. Come up with me, Kitty. I'm sure I left it in the bedroom where we all changed, but I don't want to go up there alone."

It was pitch dark now, and not being familiar with the layout, they had difficulty finding any light switches. Finally, however, they found a switch for the stairs, and headed up to the second floor. It wasn't just their imaginations running wild, the old place was definitely not as welcoming on this dark, stormy night.

They couldn't remember which bedroom had been used as a change room, so they started at one end, and began checking each room. As there were seven bedrooms upstairs, it took a while. Finally they came to the lovely corner room which overlooked the lake, and sure enough, there sat Steffie's purse, where she had placed it on the dresser.

"Thank goodness. I feel as if I've just found an old friend," she laughed, picking it up and clutching it to her chest.

On their way across the massive hall, Kitty said, "Steff, did you notice this beautiful old chair? Isn't it something?" She pulled it out a bit from the wall in order to have a better look.

"Looks in pretty bad shape to me, but I guess it was nice in its time," replied Steffie, who wasn't interested in looking at antiques tonight.

"Phooey on you, you old grouch," laughed Kitty, as she carefully pushed the chair back against the wall. It was so old, that she was afraid she might damage it.

As they clumped back downstairs, they looked at each other, and thought the same thing. "You know, we're going to be frozen if we drive back in these wet clothes. What if we build a fire in that gorgeous stone fireplace, and try to dry our things a bit first?"

"Steff, that's a great idea. By then it will have stopped storming, and it will be much safer to drive. Let's see if we can find any matches, and we'll get that fire going. Do you think that Keith would mind?"

At this point, they really didn't care whether Keith would mind or not. They were cold and wet, and a fire sounded like a terrific idea.

Once the fireplace was lit, the old mansion seemed much more friendly. They turned on every light they could find, and put matches right beside the many candles, just in case the power went out.

"If I had driven up here by myself, I wouldn't have had the courage to go upstairs," laughed Steffie. "Of course, I had no way of coming up here by myself, since my spare car key is in the apartment, and the keys for the apartment are right here in my purse. Thank goodness you were willing to drive me up, Kit."

"Hey, this is an adventure. I wouldn't have come up here by myself either, but we'll laugh about it tomorrow. Wait till we tell Keith that we had to light a fire and dry our clothes."

By the time they had sat there in companionable silence, the warm fire was making them sleepy.

"Listen. It's still raining really hard, the wind seems to be getting worse, and I'm sleepy as heck. Do you think we should sleep for a while, and then get up and go as soon as it stops raining?" Kitty was wondering how she could drive home, when her eyes wouldn't stay open.

Steffie nodded her head. "I've just been thinking the same thing. If we're going to stay the night, though, let's see if he's got any wine left from yesterday. We can replace it when we get back to town."

They found a nice bottle of burgundy, got a couple of glasses, and returned to their places in front of the fire. The more wine they drank, the less scary the house seemed. By the time they had finished, and made their way upstairs, everything seemed pretty funny. They had decided that they would just use one bedroom — neither was brave enough to sleep alone in this huge old dwelling, which seemed to belong to another era.

They chose a small, cosy room with twin beds, and a connecting door to a bathroom. Fortunately, all the beds in the place were made up, as if waiting for long overdue guests. There were extra blankets in a huge linen closet, which opened off the main hall. The hall itself was big enough to be divided into two more bedrooms.

Steffie could picture some thin little maid — just a girl really, in a black uniform, with a white apron and cap, loading her arms with fresh sheets from this closet, and doing the rounds, making up all seven bedrooms every time more family and guests arrived for lovely weekends. She could picture her so clearly, the same little Irish girl named Nora, or Eileen or Bridget, whom she had imagined upstairs in the servants' quarters yesterday. Actually, for one heart stopping moment, she thought that she could see her standing there in the hall, looking at them. She had curly black hair and rosy cheeks, and a pert little nose. She was standing perfectly still, staring with big black empty eyes. They weren't exactly unfriendly, but they certainly weren't welcoming.

Steffie shook her head quickly, realizing, or hoping, that the combination of wine, fatigue, and an overactive imagination, had begun playing tricks on her. Just as she opened her mouth to ask Kitty if she could see anything or anyone, the vision or spectre, or whatever it was, gradually disappeared. It just disintegrated.

"What's wrong with you? You look as if you've seen a ghost," teased Kitty, as she opened the bedroom door.

"I think I have," muttered Steffie, shutting the door, and placing a chair against it. Kitty whispered "good idea." She was now wishing that they had just returned to the car, and gone to the Holiday Inn up the road.

Neither one wanted to mention the dreaded word "mouse," but they both looked carefully for any telltale mouse droppings on the bed or in the bathroom.

As they finally snuggled into the two beds, they listened to the wind whining and sighing, and they prayed fervently that the old mansion wasn't haunted.

CHAPTER 12

▼

The rain continued to beat down with a tempo all its own, and the wind continued to howl. It seemed that the storm had no thought of abating in the near future. It was some time later, when Kitty awoke with a start. She lay there staring into the darkness, wondering what had disturbed her sleep. There were many unfamiliar sounds surrounding her. The old wooden floors creaked occasionally, as if being stepped on by some unknown and unwanted guest. The wind was howling in off the lake, and the waves were lapping angrily. The rain was still pelting down, as if the heavens had sprung a huge leak, and Kitty longed to be back in her own familiar bed, with the cats snuggled beside her.

Another thump made Kitty jump, and it wakened Steffie. "What was that?" she cried, sitting upright in her bed.

"I don't know, but I've been hearing all kinds of weird noises. I think that thump came from upstairs. You don't suppose there could be anybody up there, do you?" Kitty suggested, only partly in jest.

Steffie got out of bed, and felt for the light switch. She knew that they had left the bathroom light on, and the connecting door open, but it was now pitch dark.

"Shit, the power's off," she cried in dismay. "I don't think I like this place, Kitty. We should never have stayed."

Kitty had already come to the same conclusion, but it was too late now. She wasn't about to set out driving in this storm.

"Here, I'll light the candle," she said, feeling carefully in the dark. The welcome little flame instantly brought warmth and comfort to the room. Just then, however, a triple thump from above made Steffie jump, and clutch at Kitty's arm.

The women looked at each other. "Do we run, or do we go see what that is?" Steffie asked, trying to act lighthearted. She hated to admit that she felt very uneasy.

Kitty couldn't believe hearing herself say "Let's go see what it is, or we'll never get back to sleep." Instantly she wanted to take the words back, but it was too late. Steffie was moving the chair away from the door, in an empty gesture of courage.

"Come on, kiddo. There are two of us, and likely only one of them."

That didn't exactly instill confidence in Kitty, but she wasn't going to admit to her own trepidation.

Slowly they opened the door, and peered out into the vast hall. The candle, which Steffie was now holding, didn't throw its light very far, so the outer limits of the hall were in total darkness. Anyone could be hiding there. In bare feet, they padded across the floor, to the door which led upstairs to the servants' quarters.

"I wish we had a weapon," whispered Kitty, trying to stay as close as possible to Steffie, without actually crawling right up her back.

They mounted the stairs slowly and carefully, holding their breath, listening for any more threatening sounds. Kitty thought they would both turn and run if they did hear anything. Steffie would likely drop the candle and set the place on fire. Her imagination was getting ahead of her again.

They hesitated at the top of the stairs, and looked as far into the darkness as the lambent candlelight would allow. This was insane. What would they do if there was a man hiding up here? He would kill them before they had a chance to run or scream or fight back.

Apparently the place had been empty for a long time, so it was possible that some old broken down derelict or homeless person had taken up residence. He wouldn't be at all happy to have it rented now. He might even have begun thinking of it as his own place. Steffie shook her head, as if to get rid of the frightening possibilities. The worst one was the unwelcome thought that this could be where the Black Sheep had been hiding. That possibility was too dreadful to even consider.

They walked slowly around the enormous space, which was broken up into rooms without doors on them. That was odd. Weren't the servants allowed any privacy, or had the doors been removed more recently for some renovation project?

When the thumping came again, Kitty whirled and nearly knocked the candle out of Steffie's hand. They had been passing the window when the noise scared them, and both realized with relief, that it was a large tree branch being whipped against the window and the cedar siding, by the strong wind. They laughed as they realized how foolish they had been — acting like two scared little kids in a haunted house. Still, Steffie kept glancing over her shoulder, as they made their way carefully back towards the stairs. She felt that the house didn't want them there, and that the young Irish girl named Nora, who might have lived and worked here years ago, didn't want them there either. They weren't welcome in this old house, which seemed to have settled itself contentedly into the past.

For one insane moment, Kitty thought she saw a shadow moving in a far corner. She gasped and grabbed Steffie's arm. "Steff, do you see anything over there?" she whispered.

"Where?" Steffie asked anxiously.

"Right over there," said Kitty, pointing. "Look, didn't you see something move?"

Steffie stood totally still, and peered into the blackness. The candlelight didn't quite reach the corner, and for a second, she did think that maybe she had seen something move, but after staring for a moment, she shook her head.

"I think it's just the flickering of the candle, which is making shadows," she said doubtfully, as if trying to convince herself.

They turned and almost ran down the stairs, as if the devil himself was chasing them. They broke into a bit of hysterical laughter, as they reached the pseudo safety of the bedroom. They felt much braver now, yet Kitty noticed with approval, that Steffie was quick to put the chair back against the door.

"Wait a minute, Steff. Open the door again and let me look out into the hall."

"Why, for goodness sake? We're safe where we are, I think."

"I need to see something," persisted Kitty.

Taking the candle, she cautiously opened the door, and took a few steps out into the hall. Then she gave a little squawk of fear. "Steff, did you move that chair?" she asked hopefully.

"Now, when did I have any chance to move a chair," responded Steffie, coming out to see what Kitty was talking about.

Sure enough, the antique chair, which Kitty had pushed back so carefully, was now sitting out a bit from the wall.

"Please tell me you're just playing a joke on me," whispered Kitty, her voice wavering a bit.

"Honestly I'm not, Kitty. I didn't move that chair."

They stared at each other, then bolted back into the bedroom. "This place really is haunted," muttered Kitty. "What should we do?"

"I'm not going out there again till it's light," asserted Steffie. "I don't think they or it want to hurt us. They're just trying to scare us, because they don't want us here. We'll stay in here till light, then we'll get the heck out as fast as we can. You try to sleep first, and I'll stay awake, and keep the candles lit. Then, if you waken up, I'll take a turn snoozing while you keep watch. We'll be fine," she said without much conviction.

Of course, neither one could sleep. Pulling a blanket off the bed, Steffie wrapped it around herself, and sat on the chair, which was pushed against the door. Kitty sat up in bed, and tried to keep her heavy eyes from closing.

What a night! They talked in whispers, but then fell into a strained silence, as they both listened for noises in the seemingly unfriendly old house. Kitty realized that she was anxious to talk to Mitch, and tell him all about this adventure. Perhaps he could use it in his next book.

She sat there, leaning against the pillows, wondering what type of families had lived here over the years. Were they happy? Were there many little children playing hide and seek in the dark hallways, and making sand castles on the beach? Did anyone die here? Did they have fabulous parties? She could picture elegant soirees, where the ladies all wore long gowns, and the men were resplendent in tuxedos. They would have sat at that long dining room table, set with good china and crystal, and many candelabra. Or, maybe they had picnics and barbecues on that huge front deck, lighting the hurricane lamps at twilight, and watching the large freighters heading for the Welland canal.

Then she imagined some old couple, childless and friendless, living here alone, never walking the beach, never having friends for dinner or for party weekends, — just two lonely old people waiting to die. No, that wasn't part of the history of this marvellous old dwelling. This house was too full of life. It had a history, and she was sure that it was a good one. It was too perfect an old summer house to have anything but great memories in every nook and cranny. Steffie was just hoping that Nora, or whoever that ghostly figure had been, was gone for the night.

Kitty soon realized that Steffie, their self appointed guardian, was sound asleep, sitting upright in the chair, her head resting against the door. Good old Steffie. What an ideal, trustworthy friend she was.

For some reason, Kitty didn't feel scared any more, so, blowing out the candle, she closed her eyes, and finally slept. In her restless tossing and turning, she dreamt that she worked here as a housemaid, and had found stacks of money hidden under the linen in the hall closet. The dream was so real, that she had to take a peek the next morning, when the sun was shining brightly. Sadly, there were no stacks of money, only stacks of old towels and blankets. Oh well, it had been a nice dream.

They were both amazed and puzzled to see that the antique chair was once more positioned right against the wall. Had they imagined the entire episode last night? Had the flickering candlelight played tricks on them? Had they just had too much wine, and talked themselves into the scary stuff? Was it possible that booze, fatigue, and plain old fear, could have caused them to have the same hallucination? They didn't know, and in the lovely bright sunshine, they didn't care.

The lake was calming down, and the world looked fresh and green. They couldn't believe that they had been so utterly silly last night. The beautiful old house seemed charming and friendly in the light of day, and if they hadn't had to get to work, they would have enjoyed staying and exploring. It was amazing what a little sunshine could do to raise your spirits, and put a new light on things. They considered going back up to the servants' quarters to investigate, but decided against it. If indeed, the ghost of the little Irish servant girl Nora, or whatever her name might have been, was roaming around up there, they didn't want to know. They would leave her in peace, to guard her domain.

Kitty was happy to get home to the cats, and after a quick shower, a bite of breakfast, and a cuddle with each of them, she was off to the boutique. She had had quite enough adventure to do her for a long time, or so she thought, but she had forgotten that fate has a way of stepping in when one least expects it.

CHAPTER 13

▼

The shop had been a mad house all morning. It was a Friday, and several tour buses had arrived, bringing happy vacationers, who had come to town on golf and casino packages. These people were always ready to shop. One woman spent almost four hundred American dollars on gifts for her family and friends. She said that she was doing some early Christmas shopping, and had never found so many wonderful things in one store.

Since she had spent so much money, Steffie didn't like to refuse, when she requested that everything be gift-wrapped. Rolling their eyes at each other, they worked at top speed to get everything packaged nicely, in between waiting on other customers. They both wished that Cleo was here to help them, and decided that they would definitely hire her full time.

Kitty had forgotten to bring her lunch with her, so when the time came, she raced out to pick up some fast food. It was against Steffie's dietary principles, and she would undoubtedly scold Kitty for her bad eating habits, but on this busy day, there was no time for anything else.

Steffie was run off her feet while Kitty was out. "Thank goodness you're back. It'll likely quiet down now, but honestly I've been run ragged. Some poor old guy came in, and he had obviously had a stroke. His left arm was useless, and he reminded me of an old broken toy. The veins on his hands were so webbed that they looked like a map. He was a sweet old fellow, though, and I spent a lot of time with him."

"We all know that you are a pushover for old men," laughed Kitty. "The important question is, did he buy anything?"

"Sure he did. He spent over a hundred dollars on this and that," replied Steffie good-naturedly. "I wrapped everything for him too. What else could I do?"

Kitty smiled at her friend, and went to make a pot of tea. Steffie was so good with elderly people, but she was so bad with kids. "Just call me if you need me. I'll gobble this junk down as fast as I can."

Waiting for the kettle to boil, she put her feet up, and tried to relax, knowing that Steffie might call her at any moment. She was thinking about Drew, and wondering whether it was worth while dating him. He was intelligent and funny, but he lost points for being so moody, and because there was no spark in their relationship, no hot chemistry. She rather hoped that he would fall for Cleo's charms, and she wouldn't have to be the one to break off the friendship.

Kitty was quite happy living alone, and putting all her energies into the boutique. She figured, however, that eventually she would find the love of her life — someone with whom she could share everything, the elusive "perfect partner." She knew it was probably stupid, but she wanted someone who made her blood rush to her head, made her stomach do flip-flops, and made her toes tingle. Drew was more like a big brother with whom she could laugh and be at ease, but he wasn't her prince charming. Sighing at the complexities of life, she rinsed out the teapot and her cup. Putting on some lipstick, she quickly combed her hair, then headed back out into the fray.

The afternoon flew by, and they just had an hour to go, when Steffie looked up to see Cleo coming through the door. This was one of the days she didn't work, but she just couldn't seem to stay away from the shop.

She browsed and chatted with them, before deciding on a silver baby frame, and a baby treasure box, in which to keep baby's first tooth, first lock of hair, first shoes, etc. "My sister's had her baby, and I can't stop buying gifts for her," she admitted, as she paid for her purchases, receiving a nice employee discount. "This business of being an aunt is going to be onerous. I'm going to be godmother too and I'm very excited."

"How are things going with Barry?" asked Kitty, as she finished wrapping the parcels.

Cleo laughed. "He's okay, but nothing special. Keith Spenser asked me out, but I couldn't go. I still wish I had seen Drew first. There's something about him that I like."

Well, at least she's honest, thought Kitty.

Cleo continued with a grin, "I hope that Keith asks me out again. A doctor is a whole lot better than a male nurse."

Steffie just nodded, but she didn't think that Cleo had a hope with Keith Spenser. He certainly loved the ladies, but he was a confirmed bachelor. It was unlikely that he would ever settle down with just one woman. She wasn't the least disturbed that he had asked Cleo out. He really wasn't Steffie's type.

Cleo suddenly changed the subject. "You know I love working here, and I wish you'd hire me full time. The shop is so busy these days, that you know you could use me. Please think about it." Her big green eyes were pleading, as she gazed from one to the other.

"Actually, we have been thinking about it," admitted Steffie. "If you want to work five days a week, that's fine with us. When you come in on Monday we'll work out the details."

"Great," crowed Cleo, clasping her purchases to her chest. "I know you won't regret it. I truly love this boutique, and I have some good ideas to make it even better. See you Monday," she called, as she disappeared out the door, a happy smile on her face.

"Do you think we'll be able to stand her full time?" queried Steff with a grimace. "She's just so darn eager. We may be making a huge mistake. What does she mean by ideas to make it better? If it was any better we couldn't keep up. I like it just the way it is," she grumbled.

"I agree. We're certainly not going to let her come in and start changing things — the little twit. It won't be as much fun as the two of us being here alone, but we're getting awfully busy. You have to admit that she's a good worker, and she knows the merchandise well. We'll never get anyone better or more enthusiastic."

"I know you're right on one level," sighed Steffie, "but it's just, I don't know, three's a crowd and all that. You and I work so darn well together, and this shop is our baby. I guess I don't really want to share it full time with anyone else, but I know we need her. I just hope that she doesn't use it as a place to meet more men. We have a lot of good men customers, and I'd hate to see her flirting with all of them."

Kitty hadn't thought about that possibility, and she frowned as she pictured Cleo shining up to every male who walked through the doors. Maybe they should set down some ground rules right away.

There were no more customers after Cleo left, so before Kitty went out back to start unpacking a new order, she said, "Okay, smartie, tell me at least two of the stars in Knock On Any Door."

Steffie stopped what she was doing, and screwed her eyes shut. "Well, I know that John Derek was in it, but I can't think of anyone else. I give up."

"I don't remember any woman in it, but I think that Humphrey Bogart was the lawyer. I was hoping you'd be able to tell me some others."

"I'll think about it while I tidy up here," said Steff, as she headed for the gift cards, which didn't stay neat very long. "That's not fair though. You're supposed to know the answers before you ask the question, you dork."

Kitty just laughed, as she headed out to the back, leaving Steffie alone in the boutique.

In the weeks to come, she would go over and over in her mind what came next. No matter how she tried, however, she could not change the events which were to follow.

As she worked, Steffie was trying to think of a good old movie with which to stump her friend. She was annoyed with herself that she couldn't remember any of the other players in "Knock On Any Door."

Hearing the front door open, she turned, and gasped in disbelief and shock, when a man carrying a gun, came hurrying in, looking around furtively as he approached. He had the collar of his jacket turned up, and his hat pulled down over his forehead. He was wearing sunglasses, so it would be impossible to identify him.

"Shut up and don't move," he menaced, after looking quickly around for other customers.

"You've picked the wrong place to rob," said Steffie, in as loud a voice as possible. She wanted Kitty to hear her, and call 911. "The money's already gone to the bank, so the till is almost empty," she added, trying to look as truthful as possible, while her knees began shaking like castanets.

"Shut up I said," growled the thief. "Is there anyone out back?" He waved his gun toward the office door.

Steffie silently prayed that Kitty wouldn't make any noise, as she replied "No, I'm all alone." Maybe she should have said that there were several people out back, but she wasn't a very good liar, and her heart was pounding so savagely that she couldn't think. She had never seen the business end of a gun before, and it was damn scary. She couldn't believe this was happening to her.

Her adrenaline was flowing, but she felt glued to the spot, undecided on a course of action.

"Okay, now open the cash drawer, and hurry up," he gestured with his gun again. Then as an afterthought, he asked, "What's the most expensive stuff you've got here?"

"What do you mean?" asked Steffie numbly, not making any move toward the cash register. She had to play for time, and just hope that Kitty was aware of what was going on.

"I mean, what's the most expensive stuff you've got here," he answered crossly. "How about that jewellery? What's it worth?" Now he walked quickly to look at the jewellery case, pointing his gun at Steffie all the way.

"Well it depends on what you mean by expensive." Steffie couldn't believe she was having this conversation, while staring into the end of a gun. Her breath was coming in little gasps, but she was trying to stay calm and focused. She was also beginning to feel a bubble of anger rise in her throat. How dare he come into their perfect little world and threaten them? She'd like to hit him with something. What did they have that would do the trick? Surely she could outwit this guy, and maybe knock the gun right out of his hand. Think, Steff, think, she told herself.

"I mean, is there anything in there over a hundred dollars?" he asked.

"Well I guess so," said Steffie slowly. There was something familiar about him, and she wondered whether he had been in the store the previous day, checking things out. He seemed really nervous and unsure of himself. Maybe if she acted like a half-wit, he would take pity on her, and put the gun down. Then she could jump him and yell for Kitty.

"I don't usually work here. I'm just minding the store till the owner gets back from the bank," she added. The longer she kept him talking and distracted, the more time the police had to get here.

But what if Kitty hadn't called 911? What if Kitty didn't even know what was going on, and would appear any moment right into the line of fire? Maybe she was in the washroom, or maybe she had gone out the back door for some reason. Maybe Steffie was all alone with this gunman. Not a happy thought!

CHAPTER 14

▼

The would-be robber was agitated, and his jerky movements indicated that he was likely high on something. He was wired for sure. Steffie's thoughts were bumping and skittering in her head now, like frightened ants. There had to be a proper way to handle this situation. She and Kitty had often talked about what they would do, if they were ever robbed, but it had been more joking than anything. It had seemed such an unlikely possibility.

She thought bitterly of all the times they had discussed putting in an alarm system. Why hadn't they followed up on it? They deserved to be robbed just for being so stupid. It was very unprofessional and careless of them, and could prove to have been a big mistake. At the moment, she still had no idea of just what a big mistake it had been.

She was mentally beating herself up, as she tried to figure a way out of this mess. If only Kitty had been in the store with her when he came in, they might have been able to do something. Two heads were always better than one. No, maybe it was better that Kitty was in the back. At least there was a chance that she knew what was happening, and had already called the police. Steffie just had to stay calm.

Who was she kidding? She was just about as un-calm as she had ever been. She took a few deep breaths, as the robber stood nervously looking around the shop. What was he looking for? What was his plan? Would he use the gun? She was pretty sure that he was more nervous than she was. That wasn't necessarily a good thing.

Was it better to keep him talking, or should she just let him take what he wanted and go? They were well insured, so it wouldn't be a big loss. Still,

Steffie balked at the thought of letting this guy leave the store with any of their hard-earned money. Then common sense kicked in, and she decided that heroics would not be a good idea. He could take whatever he liked. She just wanted him out of the store.

"Look, just take what you want, and go. You're scaring me with that gun. Please put it down. I'll do what you say, so you don't need it. I can't think with you pointing it at me."

"You won't be able to think if I shoot you either," he snorted. "Just open the cash register, and put all the money in a bag. Step on it. No, wait a minute. Show me some of the good stuff in this case. Are those rings real?"

He was pointing now to some of the antique rings, which ranged up to five hundred dollars or so. Steffie loved those rings, and couldn't bear the thought of this bold young twerp stealing them, and pawning them.

"We keep the case locked, and I'm not sure where the owner hides the key," she said, slowly, as if she was stupid. Maybe he would believe her, and forget about the rings.

He had been talking tough, and maybe he really was tough, but Steffie sensed that he was as scared as she was. Hopefully, that should give her some kind of an advantage, because she knew that she was smarter. A friend of hers in Toronto had once told her that you should always assume you are smarter than anyone else in the room. That gives you a distinct edge. Still, who wanted a scared young gunman on drugs running loose in the store? It might not matter that she was smarter. After all, he was the one with the gun, and that damn thing looked mighty big at this point.

"Okay then, just get me the money, and hurry up." He was waving the gun again, as if looking for something or someone to shoot. He really was nervous, and that made Steffie nervous.

She walked as slowly as possible to the register. She didn't want to make any sudden moves. This little twerp was so tense and edgy, that he was like a firecracker ready to explode. She was wearing her long hair piled on top of her head today, with little tendrils around her face and neck. It made her look wild and carefree, but in reality, she was as frightened as she had ever been. She tried a watery smile, to show that she was harmless, and willing to co-operate, but it came out as a grimace. Where the hell was Kitty, and where were the police?

Kitty had been unpacking a very dusty box of garden ornaments. She had just come into the little office from the storage area at the back. She needed to wash her hands and blow her nose. The dust was making her feel sneezy. She was just about to turn on the tap, when she heard Steffie say, "You've picked the wrong place to rob." At first she thought that Steff was just kidding around with some friend, but she tiptoed to the door to make sure.

What she saw made her heart give a gigantic leap. They were being robbed at gunpoint! It wasn't possible. Who would be stupid enough to try to rob a shop on a busy street like Victoria Avenue? It could only be someone hopped up on drugs, she thought grimly. God, she hoped that Steffie wouldn't do anything crazy. She had a real stubborn streak, and wouldn't give up the money easily.

Kitty wasn't sure what to do. Should she rush out there? — and do what? He would either shoot her as she came through the door, or he might shoot Steff. Their only advantage was that he didn't know she was there in the back room. She hurried across the floor on silent feet, grabbed the phone, and tried to stretch the cord as far as it would go towards the little washroom. She mustn't let him hear her. The cord barely made it to the bathroom, but she was able to close the door partially. Whispering into the phone, she told the dispatcher that they were being robbed at gunpoint, and gave the address.

"Please speak up, I can't hear you," was the maddening reply.

Kitty couldn't speak up. She tried again, hissing the words into the phone. This time the dispatcher heard her, and promised that the police would be right there. "Leave the phone off the hook, and keep the line open," she commanded.

Kitty placed the phone carefully on the floor, then tiptoed back to the door. Peeking out, she saw that the robber was still waving his gun around, and Steffie was walking slowly over to the cash register. What should she do? There was no way that she was going to let this guy hurt Steff, but if she went hurtling out there, it might scare him into shooting. Still, it seemed cowardly to hide here in the safety of the office.

She realized that she was a witness to a crime in progress, and that she had better be able to give the police a darn good description of this meathead who was threatening Steffie. Damn, why hadn't they installed that video camera which they had discussed? Why hadn't they followed up on their idea of having an alarm system put in? Well, if they got out of this situation unharmed, she promised herself that they would be putting in a state of the art system as soon as possible, hopefully tomorrow.

Taking a deep breath, she tried to focus. He was just average height, and he had a black baseball cap pulled way down to meet his big sunglasses. Somehow, she knew that he was young. He wore scruffy jeans, with the requisite rips in both knees. His shirt was a dirty mustard yellow, with something about "eat shit" on it. How witty, she thought. This guy was a loser. There was a tattoo on his left hand, which might have been a snake or a lizard. His shoes were tattered, and looked ready for the garbage heap. She tried to fix the details in her mind.

Just then, the front door opened, and a little old couple walked in. At first they didn't see the gunman, but as he turned quickly and raised his gun, they both let out a squawk, and backed out of the door, nearly knocking each other down in the process. It was amazing that he didn't shoot them, but now he was really agitated. He seemed almost paralysed with indecision. He was obviously a novice at this line of work. Then, gesticulating wildly, and dancing from foot to foot, he shouted "Hurry up and put the money in a bag."

Kitty's nose was now really twitching from those dusty boxes. She hadn't had a chance to blow it, and she realized with horror that she was going to sneeze. Desperately, she held her finger under her nose, and covered her mouth with her hand, but she couldn't stop the loud sneeze, which reverberated throughout the shop. It was followed by four more. Kitty could never sneeze just once.

The surprised and frightened gunman whirled in her direction, and the gun went off. Whether it was deliberate or accidental, they would never know. Kitty would never forget the startled look on Steffie's face. She uttered a weird little squeak, as she clutched her left chest, and fell against the display shelves of crystal goblets. The shelves collapsed like dominoes, as Steffie, her face suddenly looking like old tissue paper, fell unceremoniously to the floor. The robber hesitated for a moment, then turned towards the door. He was going to run. The creep who had shot her dearest friend, was going to get away. This thought pierced her head, as she raced to Steffie's side.

"Oh God, Steff, hold on. You're okay. You're going to be fine. It's okay, it's okay." She was crooning the words, as she tried to staunch the flow of bright red arterial blood coming from Steffie's chest. First she put her hand over the wound, but that was useless, so she ran and grabbed one of the lovely cat afghans, and pressed it over the hole from which the blood was pumping steadily.

What would she do if the police didn't come? What if they were stuck in traffic? She had never felt so frightened in her life. She had to save her friend, but how? Steffie was trying to say something, which sounded like "get alar-rrmm," but her eyes looked glassy, and the words weren't coming out right.

"Hang on Steff. The ambulance has just pulled up." What did a little lie matter now? It might do some good. "Don't you dare give up. The paramedics are here. You're going to be fine."

She felt frantic, and it didn't help that her nose was running. It suddenly occurred to her that she had called for the police because they were being robbed. The police wouldn't necessarily bring an ambulance, or would they? This thought made her moan in terror, but just then the commotion at the door caught her attention. Taking her eyes from Steffie momentarily, Kitty saw that the beautiful boys in blue were here. Niagara's finest had arrived. The would-be robber, maybe killer, would not get too far, and miracle of miracles, here came the paramedics. She had never seen anyone who looked more beautiful than those young men. She had only called for the police, but they had brought the ambulance too. Kitty breathed a sigh of relief, and whispered a prayer of thanks. Now if they could just get Steffie to the hospital in time, there was room for hope.

CHAPTER 15

▼

Kitty knew that she would never fully recover from the trauma of that day. She went through it as if in a dream — no, not a dream, a nightmare, a sickening, terror-filled nightmare, from which there seemed no escape.

There was total pandemonium when the police arrived. By the time the gunman was carted away in handcuffs, and the paramedics were working on Steffie, several curious bystanders were trying to get into the shop, to see what was going on. The police did a good job of keeping them out, but they were crowded around the door and the windows, trying to get a peek. Kitty wanted to smash every one of those curious faces, — damn nosy looky-loos.

"Ghouls," she muttered savagely, as she sat on the floor beside Steffie, who was unconscious, and appeared dead. If she was breathing, they were very shallow breaths. Of course, with the big cat afghan, which Kitty was still pressing over the hole in her chest, it was difficult to tell.

Kitty had never been so terrified and heart sick. Because of a stupid sneeze, her friend had been shot, and maybe killed.

When the paramedics came in, one of them gently pushed Kitty aside. "What's her name?" he asked quietly.

"Steffie. Stephanie Jeanne Chapman," replied Kitty tersely.

"Okay, Steffie, open your eyes for me now. We're here to help you, and you're going to be fine. Just open your eyes." But Steffie didn't open her eyes.

All the while this young man was talking, he and his partner were working quickly and efficiently. It was a tremendous relief to see them working over her, and lifting her onto a stretcher. Kitty told herself hopefully that they wouldn't be working this hard, if Steff was already dead.

She barely remembered getting into the ambulance. They tried to keep her out, but she pushed the one attendant, who tried to hold her back, and, shaking her head, she jumped in beside her friend. They couldn't waste time arguing with her, so they sternly told her to keep out of their way, and the doors closed behind them.

The siren shrieked and wailed, as the ambulance rushed through the busy Friday afternoon traffic, but nothing would have been fast enough for Kitty. With a leaden heart, she watched, as the paramedics did their work with speed and efficiency. An intravenous line was deftly started in Steffie's seemingly lifeless arm. A big pressure bandage was applied to the bleeding chest. An oxygen mask was put over her face. A blood pressure monitor was in place. One paramedic was in constant communication with the hospital, telling them Steffie's condition from minute to minute. It seemed that everything possible was being done for her friend, yet Kitty suspected that it wasn't enough.

She stared in despair at Steffie. This just couldn't be happening. It was definitely a nightmare from which she would waken any minute. Please God let it be a nightmare. Steffie's glorious mane of black hair had come loose, and was cascading around her white face. The lovely yellow "kick-ass" jacket she was wearing, was now open, and covered with blood, so much blood. It was arterial, and it was pumping. How could she live with that much blood gone from that slim body? Kitty had watched scenes like this on television a thousand times. She liked medical drama, but nothing had prepared her for the real thing.

At the hospital, an emergency team was waiting for the ambulance. With a certain calm speed, Steffie was examined, and rushed away to the operating room. Again Kitty was pushed aside. This time she couldn't go with her friend. As she paced in circles, she realized with a start, that she hadn't locked the boutique. She wasn't even sure whether anyone had closed the front door. They would be robbed blind. Strangely, this was no cause for concern. Her whole being was concentrated on Steffie. Realizing that this was a time for some serious prayers, Kitty headed to the little chapel. This was the only way she could help her friend now.

The next few hours were the longest in her life. No one could or would, tell her anything about Steffie's condition. She didn't know whether her friend was alive or dead. Finally she took the time to try to clean herself up a bit. There was a lot of Steffie's blood drying all over the front of her long skirt and sweater. There wasn't anything she could do about that, but at least she was able to wash her face and hands, and run her fingers through her hair.

It was then that she realized she didn't have her purse. It must still be back at the shop, in the office. Taking a few deep breaths, she stared at herself in the mirror, and willed herself to calm down and think. Then, borrowing a quarter from one of the admitting clerks, she called Cleo, praying that she would be home. She told her what had happened, and asked her to pick up both purses, lock the boutique, and come to the hospital. She felt somewhat better after making herself take charge. Hysteria wouldn't do Steffie any good.

Borrowing more money from the admitting clerks, who were so kind and understanding, she called Cassie. Cass and Vickie had become important people in her life, and she knew that they would be horrified and devastated at the news. As it turned out, Vickie had just seen a news bulletin about the shooting, and they were just leaving for the hospital, wanting to help and give moral support if possible. Kitty felt somewhat better, knowing that they were coming to sit vigil with her.

Under normal circumstances, Kitty quite liked the Niagara General Hospital. It was much smaller than the huge ones in Toronto, and that made it seem more friendly. From doing her volunteer work here, she knew a great many of the staff in the coffee shop, the front desk, the gift shop, and, of course, the pediatric ward. She didn't, however, know anyone in the emergency department.

By now the newspaper and radio station had heard about the aborted robbery attempt, and the shooting, and had arrived at the hospital. Soon they were pushing mikes into her face. She didn't want to talk about it, and hated every one of these intrusive people. She bit her tongue, however, realizing that they were just doing their job. They might seem pushy and insensitive at times, but after all, the information which they got, was exactly what the readers and listeners and viewers wanted. The public soaked up every salacious tidbit, and begged for more. There was no point in getting cross with them. They had a job to do, and she did too. Her job was to be here for Steffie, and she mustn't lose sight of that. She didn't have energy to waste on anything else.

She noticed a reporter from the Hamilton television station, come running in, and realized that her parents might hear about the attempted robbery, and think that it was Kitty who had been shot. That thought galvanized her, and she quickly borrowed more coins, and went to call them in Toronto. It was while she was on the phone with them, that Drew suddenly appeared at her side. Finishing the call, she flew into his arms.

"Kit-Kat, I just heard it on the radio. They said that one of the owners had been shot, but they didn't say which one. I was afraid it was you. Are you okay?"

She nodded her head dumbly, as he held her close, and patted her comfortingly. "How's Steffie?"

"Oh Drew, I don't know. No one will tell me anything. She's really badly hurt though I think. She's lost so much blood." She had regained control of herself, and was determined that she wasn't going to cry. That wouldn't help Steff.

"Could you find out what's happening? They'll tell you the truth. Please go, Drew, and come back and tell me that's she's going to make it. I'll wait for you in the chapel."

Sitting in the peaceful atmosphere of the tiny chapel, Kitty began thinking of all the experiences they had shared — both good and bad. Since their friendship had begun, Steffie had always been there for her. She remembered the night that little Miss Rosie had eaten some of the Christmas poinsettia leaves. Kitty hadn't known that it was poisonous to cats, and Steffie had sat with her at the veterinarian's, while he worked on the little calico, to save her life.

She remembered the time she had found Scott in her bed with the red-headed floozy. Well, actually she was a very pretty gal, and possibly a nice one, but in Kitty's mind, she would always be a floozy. Her heart had been temporarily broken, and it was Steffie who had sat with her, hugging her, drinking wine with her, letting her vent all her anger and hurt. Steff had been wonderful. Now she was lying upstairs, fighting for her life, or maybe already dead. Kitty felt paralysed with anger at the stupid little twerp, wearing a shirt that said "Eat Shit." He had come into their lives, and ruined everything.

Eventually Cleo arrived at the hospital, and found Kitty sitting quietly in the chapel, her eyes closed, a sodden hanky clutched in her hand. Kitty was so glad to see Cleo, that she hugged her, and began to relate everything that had transpired. Cleo realized that the gunman must have come into the boutique just minutes after she had left. She was relieved that she hadn't been there, yet disappointed to have missed the excitement.

Cassie and Vickie arrived moments later, and they all sat in the chapel, talking quietly.

It seemed a long time before Drew reappeared, and they could tell by the look on his face, that the news wasn't good. The bullet had barely missed her heart, but had hit an artery, which had caused the massive hemorrhaging. They were giving her blood, but were having difficulty repairing the artery. Her blood pressure was critically low.

The four friends just stood there, staring at Drew, unwilling to accept what he was saying.

"You'd better prepare yourself, Kitty," he said softy. "She's pretty badly hurt. She may not make it."

"Don't say that," she snapped at him. "Don't you dare say that, Drew. You're a doctor, you know that miracles happen. Steffie's a fighter. She's young, and she's strong. She won't let an old bullet kill her without putting up one hell of a fight. Don't you ever say that again. We'll have faith, and we'll pray, and there's no way God will let anything so useless happen. She's too young to die, especially at the hands of an idiotic little twerp who's too lazy and too dumb to get a job." With that, Kitty turned her back on Drew, sat down, and began digging in her purse for another tissue. Her hands were shaking, but she appeared calm. The anger was gone as quickly as it had come.

Cassie said, "Let's all sit here and say a prayer for her. Maybe God will listen if we all talk at the same time."

Drew got them some coffee, and sat with them for a while, then he was off again to get the latest report. He felt awkward with these women who were so determined to think good thoughts, and who obviously expected a miracle. He didn't think there was going to be any miracle. The surgeons were doing all they could, but it didn't look good.

Cleo eventually left to go home, but Cassie, Vickie and Kitty sat there talking quietly, and praying. It was a long night.

Eventually Drew returned, and said that there was now cautious optimism. The hemorrhaging had stopped, and her blood pressure was gradually climbing. He seemed surprised at his own words. He really had thought that Steffie was a goner.

At this point, Drew insisted that he was going to take Kitty home. There was nothing she could do for Steffie tonight, and she had to get some rest, if she was going to be at the hospital all day tomorrow. Kitty however, wouldn't budge. She was going to stay right there until she knew that Steffie was going to pull through. Cassie and Vickie stayed right with her.

Towards morning, they finally got the good news for which they had prayed. Her blood pressure had stabilized, there was no more bleeding, and she was breathing on her own, without the help of a ventilator. It was then that they all had a good cry. The relief was wonderful. Their prayers had been answered. They had bombarded God with pleas and prayers and promises, and perhaps He had really listened. They chose to believe that He had, and they were ecstatically grateful.

Eventually, Drew took Kitty home, and Cassie and Vickie left as well. They all agreed to meet back at the hospital after having a few hours sleep.

Back at Kitty's house, Drew coaxed her to drink a small brandy, and then got her into a relaxing shower. He got in with her, just to be sure that she didn't faint from the brandy and her ordeal. When he realized that she had had nothing to eat since her hastily gobbled slice of pizza at lunchtime the day before, he made her a cup of tea, and some toast and jam. It would give her enough energy to see her through, while she slept.

Kitty was so emotionally drained, that she hardly knew what was going on, but she did know that Drew was being quite wonderful. She would have to remember to tell him that sometime. She was sure that she wouldn't be able to sleep, and felt like a traitor being here in her safe home, with Drew at her side, while Steffie was all alone in that scary hospital. He insisted, however, that she get into bed. Cuddling up beside her, he wrapped his strong arms around her, until she fell into a fretful sleep. He dozed on and off too, reluctant to move, for fear of disturbing her.

After he had finally slept for a couple of hours, he wakened to find both cats cuddled on the bed beside Kitty. They seemed to sense that she needed them, or maybe they had just found a cosy place to sleep. One never knew with cats. Drew got out of bed as quietly as he could. Rubbing toothpaste over his teeth, he washed his face, and frowned at the stubble. He would have to borrow one of Kitty's razors, and give himself a fast shave before going out.

His call to the hospital was reassuring. Steffie had made it through the night, and was doing as well as could be expected. She was now thought to be in pretty stable condition, and there was a good chance that she would recover. It was marvellous news. He knew very well just how much Steffie meant to Kitty. Although very different in temperament, they seemed to be closer than sisters. He thought fleetingly about the phenomenon that was friendship. Women seemed to have the market cornered on that one. Men were never that close, except, of course, for brothers.

When Kitty began to stir, he made a pot of tea, and toasted some English muffins. It felt strange working around in her kitchen, but he was thankful that he had been available to stay with her. When the two cats wandered into the kitchen, and sniffed his feet suspiciously, he found some food for them, then took a tray up to Kitty.

Her sleep, though short, had done her a world of good. She felt calm now, and had faith that Steffie would survive. Still, she was anxious to eat and dress and get back to the hospital, but Drew pointed out that she would only be able to visit for 5 minutes every hour, so there was no great rush. They decided that he would drive her to the boutique, where she could pick up her own car. She had already realized that the shop would have to stay closed, till she could get all the blood and broken shelves and glass cleaned up. It would be a mess, and she wasn't anxious to see it, but it had to be faced. She would hire a cleaning team to come in and do the dirty work.

Before they left for the hospital, Josh Tuttle arrived to begin working on the gazebo. He frowned, and looked sullen, when he saw Drew in the kitchen. He hadn't heard anything about the shooting, so Kitty filled in the details for him. He seemed genuinely relieved that Kitty hadn't been hurt, but he still acted sulky. Kitty didn't really notice, since her mind was at the hospital, but Drew was aware of his attitude, and thought that it was rather strange. Did this guy have the hots for Kitty, or was there anything going on between them? He scowled as he considered this possibility. The thought of Josh being alone there with Kitty, made him angry and uncomfortable. He'd have to find out just who this guy was, and what he was up to, if anything.

In the car on the way to the boutique, Drew tried to question Kitty about the carpenter. She, however, was not focusing on anything but getting to the hospital, to see for herself that Steffie was out of danger. Drew decided he'd have to question her later, when he had her full attention.

CHAPTER 16

▼

Cassandra Meredith smiled to herself, as she drove along the Niagara Parkway, towards the little village of Queenston. Her good friend Victoria Craig, was here visiting her from Vancouver, and would be staying for a month or longer. It had been almost two years since Cassie had inherited almost twenty-five million dollars, in a very bazaar series of events, which had left five people dead. When the dust had settled, and the bodies had been counted, it was clear that Cassie had certainly come out on top. She and Vickie were still alive, in spite of various attempts to kill them, and Cassie had inherited what she considered "an obscene pile of money".

Cassie and Vickie had been friends since kindergarten, and they were kindred spirits. When they were together, they were really together. Vickie, however, was much more spontaneous than Cassie, living on the theory that you jump first, and ask questions later. She could usually talk Cassie into going along with any of her crazy schemes, and over the years, they had found themselves in some tricky situations.

The fact that Cassie had inherited all that money, hadn't changed anything in their relationship. Cassie had generously and lovingly given Vickie a million dollars as a gift, so Vickie now had the money to do as she pleased. And, it pleased her to come to Niagara Falls each summer, to be with Cass.

With the newly acquired money, the old friends had taken a few great trips together, while their husbands "did their own thing." Cassie's husband Dave, still liked to travel, searching out new talent for his agency. He certainly didn't need the money now, but he loved the work. Vickie's husband Brian, was still writing books, and doing research in the British Isles. This summer Dave was in Greece, and Brian was up in Scotland, on the Isle of Skye.

Strangely, and perhaps sadly, their long absences lent more credence to the old adage "out of sight, out of mind," than it did to the idea "absence makes the heart grow fonder." Both husbands had taken their wives' newly found wealth with aplomb, and had simply continued on with their former life-styles. The women, on the other hand, had used their new financial situations to do any fun thing they could think of, keeping themselves too busy to really miss Dave and Brian. It was a strange turn of events, but it seemed to work for both couples.

Now Vickie was facing a new crisis, because Brian was making noises about maybe moving the family to Scotland permanently. He had totally fallen in love with the people and the country. He even liked all the sheep, finding them picturesque and pastoral. Vickie and their son and daughter were digging their heels in, and had no intention of leaving Canada, so at this point it was a Mexican stand-off.

Vickie had flown over to spend a week with Brian, two years ago. That was the infamous summer, when she and Cassie were both almost done in by Willy the Weasel, as well as by some of Cassie's unsavoury relatives. The trip to Scotland had not turned out well, however, for the irrepressible Vickie.

She had been driving Brian's rental car, and had somehow managed to go the wrong way on one of those Machiavellian 'round-abouts' so famous or infamous in Britain. She had been involved in a fair sized crash with two other cars, and miraculously, no one had been badly hurt. Vickie had escaped with only a broken collarbone, and various scrapes and bruises. In actual fact, her ego was bruised more than her body, and that was the end of Scotland, as far as Vickie was concerned. Exclaiming that they were all "quite mad" over there, she had been happy to get back to her home in Vancouver. The accident had happened two summers ago, and Vickie had now put it all behind her.

The two friends often talked about the events of "the summer that was," when so many bad things had happened. They always concluded, however, that things had turned out wonderfully for both of them.

At first Cassie had been traumatized with all that had happened, and she wasn't even sure that she wanted the money, considering its source. She soon talked herself out of that nonsense though. She had given a million dollars to Vickie, and had given away a good bit of the rest to various charities. Because of the interest which twenty-five million dollars accrued so quickly, there was still plenty in the pot. On this particular day, Cassie was driving toward what she considered her greatest achievement so far.

As she approached the fenced in compound, Cassie looked up at the large sign, which proclaimed that she was entering "Cassandra's Cattery", and in smaller letters, "a feline haven." Indeed, Cassie couldn't think of a lovelier haven for lost, abused and unwanted cats, than what she had created here.

From the time she was a little girl, she had talked about having a place where she could take in stray cats. No one had paid much attention to her, but the idea had simmered and bubbled in the back of her mind for years. Once she actually realized, and came to terms with the fact that she was a multi-millionaire, and could do whatever she wanted with the money, she worked to make her dream a reality.

The first step had been when she and Vickie flew to Key West, to visit Ernest Hemingway's home on the island. It had become world famous, because it was a safe harbour for the descendants of his first polydactyl (six-toed) cat. The friends had stayed a week on the island, spending a few hours every day at the Hemingway estate, talking to the staff, and taking copious notes and pictures. Of course they had left themselves plenty of time to visit Sloppy Joe's, which supposedly had been Hemingway's favourite watering hole. They also drank margaritas on the beach, and shopped in all the intriguing little boutiques. Their main objective, however, had been to learn all they could about how the sixty or so cats were managed, and how the whole operation worked.

Cassie had purchased the perfect piece of property just outside of Queenston. It was an old mansion sitting on over an acre of land. She still winced when she thought of what it had cost to make the changes necessary, and to build the tall fence, which surrounded the entire property. Thank goodness her husband Dave had never asked her what the final cost had been. He felt that it was her money, and she could spend it however she pleased. Good old Dave. He had been wonderfully supportive, as they entered this amazing new phase of their lives, with all the money anyone could ever possibly need. Her kids had been good too. They loved the idea of the cattery, and both worked there after school when they had the time.

Cassie drove slowly around to the back of the cattery, got out of the car, and stopped to pick up a lovely cream coloured female with long legs, whose name was Nicole. She had shamelessly copied many ideas from Hemingway's cat haven, one of them being, to give each cat the name of a famous movie star or author. This one was so pretty that she just had to be named for Nicole Kidman. She let the little cat down in the cool kitchen, as she greeted two of the staff, who were preparing the feeding dishes for dinner.

"Hi guys. How are things going?" she asked, looking around at the spotless kitchen.

"Everything's good," answered Annie Harper, a young girl who worked here every day after school. All of Cassie's staff were cat lovers, and she was constantly checking to be sure that she hadn't hired anyone who would hurt the cats or be careless with them. She had a full time veterinarian, who lived in a small house on the property. In addition, she had hired a very lovely young woman named Ginny, who was in charge of the staff, when Cassie wasn't there.

All the entrances had small swinging cat doors, so that the cats could come and go as they pleased. She had taken the idea of a large outdoor drinking fountain from Hemingway's estate, and had actually put several around on the property. The water was changed every day.

There were many large old trees surrounding the house, and dotted all over the property, so that the cats could climb all they wanted. Any trees too close to the fences, had been cut down, so that the cats couldn't climb a tree and leap over the fence. The cats, though, knew a good deal when they had one, and they all seemed very content with their safe and beautiful home. They came and went as they pleased inside the fence. They slept where they wanted, inside or out, ran and chased, and played games with the staff. All staff members were expected to participate in giving the cats plenty of exercise, so they threw little balls for them, dragged toy mice through the grass, and fluttered feathers on long sticks, to encourage them to jump.

A huge screened in porch with padded window seats, ran around two sides of the old house. It was everything Cassie had dreamed of when she was a kid, and she was out here almost every day, playing with the cats, and discussing things with the vet and the staff.

So far, there were fifty-one cats calling the cattery their home, but they were equipped to handle a hundred. She hoped they never went over that number, because it would break her heart to have to turn any away. The cats were up for adoption, but people were investigated thoroughly before being allowed to take a cat home. As yet, no polydactyls had arrived on the scene.

"We've got a new addition to the family," said Ginny, as she walked through the house with Cassie. "Someone dropped him off outside the gate this morning, and he just sat there crying. Luckily Dan heard him, and went out to bring him in. People are so stupid. Why wouldn't they call and bring him right to us, instead of dropping him off out there?"

"Who knows," replied Cass, shaking her head. "I've come to the conclusion that there isn't too much intelligent human life on this planet. Where is the little guy?"

"Dr. Joan took him in to examine him, and to clean out his ear mites. She says he seems fairly healthy, but he's thin. He's a friendly little fellow. Wait till you see him. He's black, with little white paws and a white collar. He's just adorable."

Ginny thought every cat there was "just adorable." Cassie really liked this gentle, intelligent girl, who was apparently coming out of a very bad domestic situation. Cassie didn't know what it was, and she didn't like to pry. She had heard rumours, however, that Ginny's husband had committed suicide. She hoped that eventually Ginny might confide in her. Coming to work at the cattery when it first opened, seemed to have been good therapy for her, and Cassie knew how lucky she was to have Ginny. She was totally reliable, and was like a mother hen to all the cats.

She went into the vet's office, to see the new addition. After cuddling the little fellow for a few minutes, she walked outside, and watched a staff member playing with the twin kittens Martin and Lewis. Then she headed back to Niagara Falls. She was on her way to the hospital, to see how Steffie was doing.

Cassie had first met Kitty, when she had come out to the cattery to adopt Sir Petie and little Miss Rosie. They found they had a lot in common, and had become friends, getting together occasionally for lunch. Cass was also quite taken with Steffie's art work, and had bought several of her sketches. The three women had become good friends, and when Vickie came to town, she made it a happy foursome.

Cassie was considering building a small gift shop on the property, and filling it with cat items, so she often dropped into the boutique to check out the merchandise. She had been appalled and frightened when Steffie was shot. Bad things like that just shouldn't, and usually didn't happen in Niagara Falls. Her own bad summer two years ago, had just been an aberration. She prayed that Steffie would survive, but knew that it was touch and go.

CHAPTER 17

▼

As Cassie drove along the Niagara Parkway, she enjoyed looking at the myste-rious green Niagara River, dotted with sailboats. The rejuvenating, cool ver-dant grass of the parkway, was juxtaposed beside the turbulent, foamy green water of the river. Somehow it was a peaceful combination.

Right across the river was Lewiston, New York. There were tourists having picnics at the many tables set out along the miles of parkway, which stretched between Niagara-on-the-Lake and Fort Erie. Now that she had so much money, she knew that she could live anywhere she wanted, but there was nowhere she would rather live than right here in the Niagara Peninsula. She and Dave were thinking seriously of buying one of the large homes along this stretch of parkway, but as yet, had not seen anything available which suited them. She was quite happy with the home she had, but it would be nice to have a much bigger library, and bigger bedrooms than those in her present house.

She was thinking about what it would be like to live right on the Niagara River, when a car pulled up beside her, and the driver motioned her to pull over. Not on your life, buddy, she thought, until she got a better look at the driver, and realized it was Jack!!!!

Cassie's heart started thumping, and she felt flustered, as she obediently pulled over, and got out of her Porsche. She was fleetingly grateful that she looked good in her lime green slacks and white lace top. In the months to come, Cassie often wondered what would have happened, if she hadn't stopped that fateful afternoon, to talk to this marvellous man, who had been such an important part of her life at one time. Because of stopping to talk to him, she became involved in the Black Sheep mystery, and it would become a tangled tale.

"Jack," she exclaimed with delight, as the tall handsome man, with the scar on his cheek, came toward her.

"Cassie," he muttered, as he took her in his arms, and gave her a lovely, heart stopping hug. "I couldn't believe it was you. It's been a long time," he said, pulling back and admiring her with those Paul Newman blue eyes, which she had always loved.

"Oh, Jack, it's wonderful to see you. What have you been up to, and why don't I ever run into you?"

"Well from what I hear, you've been doing a lot of travelling since our big adventure. How's it feel to have so much money, or is it vulgar to mention it?" He laughed when he asked this.

"Jack, it feels great. Honestly, I'm having so much fun. When the will was finally settled, there was almost twenty-five million in it. Can you believe it? You know Pru and Matt had won the twenty million lottery about three years ago, and they had invested it very wisely. They also had money before they won the big pot, and all the interest just built up very quickly."

Jack just shook his head at the thought of so much money. Man, wouldn't that be nice! "Well, I heard that you had been travelling a bit, and of course I've read all about the cat farm. Good for you, finally managing to put your dreams into reality. Not many people get a chance to do that. I can still remember you talking about having a place for stray pets, when you were just a kid."

"Well, it's been a wonderful experience. By the way, I saw Bud at the cattery about six months ago. I'm sure you know that he and his wife came out and adopted two darling little cats. Remember the day that my Muffy sat on his lap and covered his pants with fur? Actually I was hoping that you might have come to our opening," she added reproachfully.

"I thought about it, I really did, but then I decided it might not be such a good idea. Every time I see you, I feel as if I'm back in high school, and I want to run away with you." He shook his head at his own foolishness. "I'd love to have lunch with you someday though, just to catch up. What do you think? I promise I'll behave, or at least try to."

Cassie hesitated while she processed this idea. She was vaguely aware of the big orange tiger lilies in the ditch along the road, and the cars whizzing by. She was aware of how hot it was, and what a nice little breeze there was coming off the river. The few clouds were white swirls, like icing on a birthday cake.

These were all peripheral images though, registering somewhere on a sub-conscious level. Mainly, she was trying to concentrate on Jack. She would love to have lunch with him, but would it be a good idea? Unfortunately not, so she sighed and said, "You know, I'm really busy these days." Right away she saw the hurt look in his eyes, and before he could reply, she said, "Oh, what the hell. Of course I'd love to have lunch with you. Let's do it this week before Vickie makes me change my mind."

Cassie, Vickie, and Jack, had all grown up together in Sudbury, and Jack and Cassie had become lovers in their teens. Vickie and Jack never got along well. They always seemed to be fighting for Cassie's attention. When they were younger, Jack had been a terrible tease. A typical little boy, he had taken great pleasure in ruining their tea parties, in chasing them with frogs or snakes, and in throwing their dolls up into the trees. He had been a menace, and both little girls had hated him with a passion.

As they grew older, however, Jack turned into a heartthrob, and Cassie's passion became the grown-up kind. He was not only good looking in a rug-ged way, but he was very smart in school, and extremely popular. He had a wicked sense of humour, but he was charming and fun, and Cassie had fallen hopelessly in love with him. Vickie, however, just couldn't see his charms, and there had always been tension between them. Jack felt that Vickie was a bad influence on Cassie, leading her into too many scrapes and misadven-tures. Vickie, on the other hand, never really trusted Jack, always fearing that he was going to break Cassie's heart. They had clashed on many occasions, and Cassie had always been torn between them. That was a long time ago, though, and they were all older and wiser now.

Cassie suspected that she would regret it later, but right at this moment, lunch with this old friend and lover sounded just fine. It would be much bet-ter to do it before Vickie had a chance to give her a hard time, make her see reason, and talk her out of it.

Cassie found it amazing that people were so deferential to her now, just because she had money. In a way it was ridiculous, but it was also fun. She was always concerned, however, that the money might cause rifts between her and some of the people she loved. In this case, she was thinking of Jack, and she hoped that her money didn't make any difference to him. She hadn't seen him for almost two years, which was ridiculous when they both lived in the same city. Of course, they were both married, and had no legitimate reason to see each other, but that was beside the point. Although she loved David, who was kind and gentle, and very good to her, her heart beat wildly whenever she thought of Jack.

Standing on the side of the road, looking at him now, he still seemed to be her old Jack — full of fun, witty, intelligent, and so damn handsome. She wondered how a guy could have a big scar running right from his ear almost to his chin, and still be so attractive and desirable. She also noticed that he was as fit and trim as ever. His stomach was as flat as it had been in high school. She wondered whether he worked out a lot, or whether he just had good genes. What a hunk! How had she ever let this one get away!

Well, a lunch with just the two of them was likely foolish, but she hoped that she could spend time with Jack, without getting herself into trouble. He still made her knees weak, and her heart pound, but she assured herself that he was just a very dear friend, and that there was nothing wrong with having lunch with him. Part of her knew that this was ridiculous, that she was just fooling herself. Of course it was wrong to have lunch with him. The other part of her, however, couldn't wait to be alone with Jack, and damn the consequences.

In spite of knowing that they were playing with fire, they made their arrangements to meet at the Riverbend Inn the following day. It was a gracious and elegant inn situated on the parkway. Although the thought remained unspoken, they both hoped that the Riverbend was far enough out of the way from Niagara Falls, that they wouldn't see or be seen by anyone they knew.

Regretfully, they said their goodbyes, and Jack refrained from hugging her again, but did give her a kiss on the cheek. Cassie didn't know whether to be glad or sorry. She really wanted him to take her in his arms, and kiss her passionately, but she knew that was a road down which she mustn't go.

Cassie and Jack had experienced a torrid, passionate relationship when they were very young. Unfortunately, they had been driven apart by Cassie's mother, (actually her grandmother), but that was a whole other story. They had reluctantly gone their separate ways, and had met again totally by accident two years ago. That was when Cassie had been tangled in a murderous plot, in which she and Vickie were supposed to be the victims, along with several others.

Although she and Jack were both happily married to other people, they realized that there was still a very strong chemistry between them, and they both knew that it was better if they kept as far apart as possible. Fortunately, they had not run into each other for a long time, so the temptation hadn't been there.

Getting back into her car, Cass thought fleetingly that it was very handy that David was away in Greece at the moment. She wouldn't have to tell him anything about the date they had made. Besides, she was simply meeting an old friend for lunch. There was nothing wrong with that, was there? "There's plenty wrong with it, Cassie," she said out loud. Her guilty conscience was picking at her, and she wondered whether she should call Jack and cancel. "No, that would break his heart," she said, talking to herself again. "I'll go, and we'll have a lovely talk about old friends and old times. I'll be friendly but distant, and it will be quite harmless. Yah, right!"

The traffic was light, and she pondered the pros and cons of this impromptu luncheon the rest of the way home. She'd have to tell Vickie, or would she? Vickie would definitely not approve. Well, it wasn't really any of Vickie's business, was it? Cass and Vickie were such close friends though, and had been for so many years, that she knew she would tell her everything about the luncheon date — good or bad.

That settled, her thoughts turned to wondering what she would wear. In her mind's eye, she began at one end of her closet, choosing one outfit, then another, not finding anything that suited her. Then she remembered the new outfit she had just bought last week, and she began to smile. She was actually singing along with the radio by the time she turned into her driveway. She knew that Vickie wouldn't be home yet from the library, so she went into the house to tell Sugar Plum and Muffin all about her afternoon. As usual, the two cats didn't really seem to care.

CHAPTER 18

▼

When he woke up that morning, the Black Sheep had no idea that he was going to kill someone that night. He had been successfully warding off the wicked feelings for days now, and he told himself that he really had licked this whole killing thing. He wasn't going to do it anymore. He had been very lucky so far, but everyone's luck runs out eventually, so why take any more chances.

As the day progressed, however, one little annoyance after another began to fester in his mind. He gradually became frustrated, angry and nervous. By dinner time he had a real problem. He struggled with his feelings, but they were stronger than he was. The nervousness and pressure had been increasing all day, till he thought he might explode. He had become manic in everything he did. He realized that he was going to have to kill again, in order to get any relief.

He didn't have his plans worked out yet for Ginny. At one point he was definitely planning to kill her. Then he realized that he likely still loved her, so why kill her? He might just start dating her, and make her fall in love with him. She was the girl he had always wanted, but his brother Mike had won her. He still didn't understand how that had happened.

He thought sometimes of that day he had glimpsed her going into the hotel, arm in arm with the guy in uniform. It turned out she was telling the truth when she said he was her brother. Mike had killed himself for nothing. He finally had to admit to himself that Mike's death was all his fault. That idea rammed around in his head like lottery balls in a cage. He had been mistaken about Ginny. She hadn't been unfaithful. He should make it up to her, make her fall in love with him, marry her, give her a wonderful life. He gazed into space as he tried to picture that scenario. The sweat was beading on his forehead, and his hands were tingling. What should he do?

When he had killed his hated mother, he had been like a child with its first taste of chocolate. The feeling had been so delicious, that he wanted, indeed he needed, more. The unexpected thrill of his hands around her neck, squeezing, tightening, watching the changes in her face, had awakened something in him. It had prodded his previously unknown lust for killing, had opened an entire new world to him.

The fact that he was becoming less and less able to control these cravings for the power and release which killing brought him, not only frightened him, but tantalized him too. He was a high functioning member of society, doing a job, and doing it well. He was the kind of person about whom neighbours and friends would say, "He has always been such a lovely man, so friendly and easy-going, such a charmer. I can't believe he could do such a thing." He often pictured the scenario of the police finally catching him, and parading him past the television cameras. It was something which he couldn't and wouldn't allow. If he ever thought they were closing in, he would simply kill himself. He would never be able to stand the shame and the notoriety.

These were the thoughts with which he was struggling on this Friday night. He could have called someone for a date, dinner and a movie, or a drive along the river. He was far too agitated for that, however. He was fighting the feelings with everything he had, like a child saying 'no thank you' to a toy he really wants. He knew it was wrong, he knew it was dangerous, and he knew that he didn't want to do it ever again. That was what one part of his brain, or his conscience, or maybe his very soul, was telling him. On the other hand, he knew it was exciting, it was thrilling, it was all powerful and consuming. It also soothed him, and gave him the release he needed. It was the drug of choice. He had to do it, just this one more time.

The dichotomy was tearing him apart. Not for the first time, he wondered whether he was some type of strange split personality, a schizophrenic, or a bipolar. Perhaps the traumas of his childhood had warped and bent him, until his real self had been driven inward, and this other somewhat reluctant killing machine had come to life. No, that was ridiculous. He was a normal human being who had temptations which he simply had to overcome. He mustn't indulge his desires like a spoiled child.

As he was worrying at all these thoughts, like a little kid picking at a scab, he was trying to keep himself busy, by cleaning out the refrigerator, an odious task at the best of times. Bottles and jars were being emptied and thrown into a recycling box. Shelves were being rearranged and washed. He had a perfectly capable cleaning lady, who came once a week, but tonight this was something he had to do himself. It took energy and a bit of concentration, and one might have wondered whether he was trying to scrub the evil thoughts right out of his head.

By now he had a man-sized headache, something which was happening more and more frequently. Taking two Tylenol, and pouring himself a stiff drink, he flopped down on the sofa, like a worn out rag doll, and turned on the television. Flipping distractedly from channel to channel, he felt the inexorable unease and queasiness slowly turning to rage. Why should he have to endure these feelings? Why should he be sitting here like a sick fool on a Friday night, trying to keep himself under control like some crazed Dr. Jekyll and Mr. Hyde? Just one killing, just one rotten woman out of the way would do it. It would bring him the exhilaration and then the blessed release which he needed.

Suddenly, like a clap of thunder, his mind was made up. With a wicked grin, he headed to the bedroom to change. He sang a wordless tune while he showered. The decision had been made, and some of the tension was already released. Anticipation was a wonderful panacea.

He told himself that there would be no prostitutes tonight. There would be no Ginny either. He wanted to meet a sweet young thing, possibly a secretary or a nurse, or even a cop. Yes, a policewoman would be great. His pulse quickened, as he thought of the possibilities. He would buy her some drinks, dance with her, talk and exchange stories. Maybe they would go for a drive. Maybe she would be the one, his own true love, the one who would love him passionately for the rest of his life. Perhaps, finally, she would be the one who would never leave him, never look at another man. Maybe she would be the one to save him from himself. If he could just find the right woman, he would never kill again. Yes, tonight just might be the night.

Pulling on a pair of tight blue jeans and a dark turtleneck, he admired himself in the bathroom mirror. Should he or should he not? Yes, he would put on the moustache and the curly hair. He looked good in them, and just in case —. He let the thought trail off, as he concentrated on the moustache. He decided against the glasses this time. They made him look too dorky. Of course, if he met a girl he wanted to date again, how would he ever explain the disguise? He pondered that one while he brushed his teeth. Sure, he would say that he had done it on a dare, just for a joke. He would say that one of his buddies had suggested it. Everyone knew he loved to joke and kid around. He was charming enough that he could get away with just about anything. Women really liked him, and found him very believable. It was a knack he had.

Any bar in Niagara Falls would be too risky. There were too many people who might see him and recognize him, even with the false hair and moustache. St. Catharines would be better. It was only 15 miles away, but it was far less likely that he would meet anyone he knew. He was aware of the risk he was taking, but that only added to his excitement.

Carefully wrapping the little black sheep in tissue paper, he told himself that he was just being sensible, just covering all possibilities, just preparing for any eventuality. He stuffed it in his pocket, and promised himself that he really wouldn't use it, he would have no need of it. He could control himself. This would be some sort of test. Still — no harm in being prepared.

He had been to this particular bar before, and it was always crowded on a Friday or Saturday night. Perfect! That was exactly what he needed. There would be a great crop of women from which to choose. Also, because it was crowded, it would be much more difficult for anyone to remember him. Of course there would likely be no reason for anyone to have to remember him. He was just out for a good time. He kept telling himself this over and over, but part of him really didn't believe it. He knew he was looking for trouble, and the excitement was exquisite.

The unholy noise accosted his ears, as he made his way casually through the crowd. The place was packed, and the music was deafening.

They were standing double deep at the bar, which gave him a good chance to survey the room. Most, or perhaps all of the booths and tables were taken, but that was okay. He knew from experience that people came and went in a steady stream. There were so damn many lonely people looking for love and companionship. What was wrong with a society which produced so many unhappy and unconnected people? Women. That was what was wrong with society. There were far too many unfaithful tramps, full of flattery and empty promises, ready to break a man's heart.

He loved women, and he longed to have one of his very own. He just hadn't found any good ones yet. Kitty Winfield might be one of the good ones. He hadn't made up his mind about her, although, regretfully, he was leaning to the dark side. She was proving to be quite a gadabout, flitting from one man to another. He was playing the waiting game at the moment, but it didn't look too good for Miss Kitty.

An itinerant thought caught him off guard. Could he really be insane? Yes, probably, but what the hell. He was who he was — the Black Sheep. He was smarter than anyone in this bar, and tomorrow he would definitely try to change his ways. Perhaps this would be his swan song tonight.

Like a fat woman who is always going to start her diet "mañana," he promised himself that tomorrow he would turn over a new leaf. He would throw away the rest of the black sheep and the camera, and that would be the end of it. Well, maybe he would keep one sheep in case he needed it for Kitty. Downing his drink, he continued to survey the room.

It was a restless crowd, everyone looking for someone, but it seemed to be a relatively happy mix. People were actually talking to each other, hoping to make that special connection. He began to feel hot and light-headed, and was beginning to sweat. He could feel the dampness under his arms, behind his knees, and in his crotch.

He was soon watching an attractive redhead standing halfway down the bar, sipping a drink, and looking around hopefully. She was definitely a babe. He waited and watched, just to be sure that she was alone. She was wearing tight jeans and a form fitting yellow sweater, with a plunging neckline. Her breasts looked large, like two melons. He had just made up his mind to approach her, when some dipstick in tight pants and a shirt open almost to his navel, started talking to her. Well, that was an opportunity lost. She had looked like a good possibility. He had pictured himself talking with her in an easy, clever manner, holding her in his arms, as they tried to dance to the pounding music.

He was now on his second beer, and the antsy, uneasy feeling was growing. He didn't really like beer, but it appeared to be the drink of choice in this bar. He reasoned that if he ordered beer like almost everyone else here, there was less chance of the bartender remembering him. A gin and tonic might draw enough attention that the bartender would remember. Sometimes it was tiring having to think of all these little threads, but he must leave no clues. For safety's sake tonight, he needed to be the man who wasn't there.

There was a very nice looking woman sitting at the end of the bar, engaged in a heated discussion with a man whose hair was too long, and who was wearing a leather jacket. The bar was hot and stuffy, and the guy must have been sweating in that jacket. As the Black Sheep watched, the woman with the short brown hair, shook her head violently, and threw the remains of her drink into the man's face. He stood up, glared at her, wiped his face with his hand, and stomped right out the front door. The woman sat there looking close to tears, and the Black Sheep made his move.

Sitting down quickly beside her on the now empty stool, he grinned and said, "Good for you. I like a woman who has a bit of spirit."

She looked at him angrily, and then gave an aborted laugh. It came out more like a hiccup. "I don't know what came over me. He just makes me so angry sometimes." She closed her eyes, and clenched her fists for a moment. Then, like lightning, her mood seemed to change. Shaking her hair back from her face, she smiled at him, as she crossed her legs provocatively.

He bought her a drink, and suggested that they move to a booth, which had just become available. It was his good fortune that the bartender had been at the other end of the bar when the altercation took place. He would have no reason to remember the good looking man with the curly black hair and the moustache, sitting down beside her.

She was pretty in a hard sort of way, not the type of woman he usually dated, but tonight was special. Maybe he had been going after the wrong girls all these years. This one called herself "Lana". He doubted it was her real name anymore than his was Jerry. She claimed to be the manager of a sports shop in the mall. They talked and laughed and seemed to be having a good time. He told her that he was a sales rep for a big drug company.

He was cursing himself for having taken those two Tylenol along with the scotch, and now the beer. His head was feeling fuzzy, and he wasn't sure what the hell he was trying to do. He should just go home and get this stupid curly wig off, along with the damn moustache. They were driving him crazy. His head was itchy, and he needed to scratch. He didn't want to leave her, but he needed to pee, and he wanted to throw cold water on his face. She nodded agreeably when he said that he would be right back, and he made his way to the men's room slowly, and with great concentration. The floor seemed to be tilting a bit.

By the time he returned, she was chatting happily with a semi-bald, fat assed fool, who was seated across from her in the booth. The guy's head was shaped like a football, and he seemed to spit as he talked. Who did this peckerwood think he was? Anger flared in the Black Sheep's eyes, as he stormed up to them. He cautioned himself not to make a scene and draw attention to himself, but he could feel the bile boiling up inside.

Sliding into the booth, he put his arm around her in a proprietary manner, and whispered that they should go to a different bar, where the music was better. He glared at lard-ass, who got the hint, and left in a hurry. He felt calm and in control, as he watched the interloper head to the bar. What a wimp. When she readily agreed to go with him, he counted that as a strike against her. She must be a tramp, coming in with one guy, picking up a second one, and leaving with a third one. What was wrong with her? Didn't she understand about being faithful and steadfast, and sticking with one person? Was she stupid, or just a bimbo?

As they headed for his car, he decided that she definitely needed to be taught a lesson. She was a dumb, ignorant fool — just like the rest of them. He was riding an emotional elevator — angry and agitated one minute, calm and serene the next. Lana, however, didn't seem to notice. Lana had no idea that she wouldn't be going home tonight. Lana was riding into oblivion.

CHAPTER 19

▼

Lana cuddled up beside him in the car, her head on his shoulder. She was trying to be provocative, but how could she possibly know that this very action would annoy him? She was wearing a new perfume, and although it smelled nice to her, to him it was dreadful. He was very sensitive to odours. He had smelled that aroma before, and it made him feel nauseous. It was like rotting flowers, or broccoli cooked in vanilla.

She was very upset about the altercation in the bar with Georgie. It was just that he made her so mad at times. Tonight she wasn't feeling so hot, and should never have come out to the bar in the first place. Now she had to go home, and try to make it right with Georgie. Well, Georgie would just have to wait. This guy, (he had told her that his name was Jerry), was good looking, although that black curly hair didn't look real. She wondered whether it might be a wig. Was he really bald under all that hair? She didn't like that idea. Maybe she should try to run her fingers through it, to see how it felt.

He was driving erratically, and having one of his hot flashes. Now the perspiration was bursting out on his forehead, and the back of his neck. In one minute he was going to tear off this goddamned wig, and throw it out the window.

She kept jabbering away, talking about Georgie, the long-haired geek with whom she had arrived. He was sweet, he was loveable. She shouldn't have thrown her drink in his face. She needed to call him and apologize. The drivel just went on and on.

Did Jerry think that she should call Georgie and beg his forgiveness? Jerry thought that she should shut up before he pulled out her tongue. His heart was pounding now as badly as his head, as he pulled the car over on a deserted stretch of road along Lake Gibson.

He sat there, staring out the front window of the car, and not saying anything. It was spooky. What was wrong with this guy? She was beginning to feel a little nervous. It had been foolish to come out in the car with him. She didn't know him from Adam. What if he was a rapist? What if he was a murderer? What if he was going to beat her up? She didn't like any of those possible scenarios. Maybe she could get him to go back now. Yes, that's what she would do. She would tell him that she wasn't feeling well, and they would turn around.

She had just opened her mouth to tell him how sick she felt, and that was really the truth, when he turned to her with a strange smile on his face. There was enough moonlight that he could see her eyes, as she stared at him in fear. Somehow she knew, and that excited him.

She tried to reach for the door lock, but he was too quick for her. His hands were around her neck before she realized what was happening. She squirmed, and tried to fight, but the drinks she had consumed, and the element of surprise, were too much for her. "Jerry's" hands were strong and unrelenting, as he squeezed tighter and tighter.

Oh, Georgie, she thought. Where are you when I need you. I'm so sorry for fighting with you. Just come and find me, get me out of this horror.

He couldn't help lecturing a bit, as he gazed into her eyes. "You shouldn't have come with me so easily, Lana," he said in a scolding tone. "You're nothing but a flirtatious tramp. Why didn't you just go home with George? Don't you see that there are too many of you fickle, empty-headed bimbos in the world? You have to die because you do nothing but bring pain to others."

Suddenly he stopped, loosened his grip a little, and stared into her terrified eyes. What was he doing? Was he crazy? Who was this woman? She was nothing to him. He didn't need to kill her. Unfortunately, he had already gone too far. It was regrettable, but he had no choice now. Once again his hands tightened around her slender neck. Her face turned red, and her eyes began to bug out. He hated that part.

Racing around to the passenger side, he unfastened her seatbelt, and half carried, half dragged her along the road, to a small grove of bushes beside the lake. It wouldn't hide her for long, but that was okay. He wanted her to be found. Maybe it would warn other women not to be so damn trusting and fickle. Working quickly, he arranged her as neatly as possible in the bushes, then taking out the little black sheep, he placed it in her right hand. This was all wrong. Where was the release, the feeling of satisfaction? All he felt was agitated. He couldn't take the time to fix her as nicely as he would have liked, because there was too much risk of another vehicle coming along.

Hurrying back to the car, he grabbed the camera, and rushed back to the body. He could feel the sweat trickling down his neck, and his hands were so sweaty, that he dropped the little camera in the bushes. He had to get down on his hands and knees to find it, and in doing so, he cut his hand on a piece of broken glass. "Shit," he muttered, as he sucked on the bloody cut. This was not the way it was supposed to be. He needed to get out of here. Things were closing in around him, and his breath was coming in explosive little gasps. There was none of the usual pleasure in snapping the requisite three pictures. All he could think of was getting home safely, and never ever doing it again.

He forced himself to take some deep breaths and calm down, as he stood there in the dark. He wondered whether he might have dropped anything besides the camera. Making his way back to the car, he retrieved a flashlight. Quickly checking the area, he assured himself that nothing had been left to give them any clues. Just as he was straightening up, however, a car pulled up.

"Are you okay, buddy? Need some help?" asked an earnest young man of about twenty, as he quickly undid his seatbelt and got out of his car.

This was the worst possible luck. What should he do? There was no way he wanted to kill this guy too, yet it would be ballgame over, if this young fellow identified him. Thinking quickly, he staggered a bit, kept his head down, and muttered that he'd had too much to drink, and was just barfing in the bushes. "Thanks anyway," he said. "Thanks for stopping."

The young chap looked concerned, and replied "Oh, I know what that's like. Been there, done that." He laughed, and took a step closer to the strangler.

The Black Sheep quickly put his hand to his mouth, turned around, and headed back into the bushes, making gagging sounds, as if he was going to barf again. "Sorry," he shouted, keeping his head averted as much as possible. "You can go, I'll be fine now. That really sobered me up," he claimed. Then he bent over, pretending to clean vomit off his shoes, with a couple of leaves he had hastily pulled from a tree.

The good samaritan finally decided there was nothing he could do to help, so giving a half wave, he returned to his car. It was a couple of minutes, however, before he actually drove away. What was he doing? Why didn't he go? Was he calling the police?

Actually, the young man was trying to decide just what he should do. There was something not quite right about the guy in the bushes. Well, it was none of his business, so he'd better just move along and forget about it.

The Black Sheep kept bent over, glancing surreptitiously at the car. What should he do? If the guy was calling the police, he had to get out of here. Should he kill him? Could the young fellow identify him? Had he seen his license plate?

He had just decided that he had to kill the interfering little maggot, when the young man started up his car, and drove away. He had no way of knowing just how very close he had come to death on that lonely black road.

The Black Sheep heaved a huge sigh, as he hurriedly started up his car. Whew! That had been a close call. Had he managed to keep his face well hidden? Yes, he thought so. Well, nothing he could do about it now. This was the most panic he had ever felt, and he pounded the steering wheel in anger and despair. His adrenaline was really pumping. This wasn't the way it was supposed to be.

What had he proved? What had he accomplished — a big fat nothing. Did he feel any better? No. Maybe he shouldn't have left the sheep in her hand. He had been in too much of a hurry. What if he had dropped something there — a valuable clue for the police? What if he had left a drop of blood from the cut on his hand? He hadn't checked carefully enough. Should he go back?

Everything had happened too fast. He hadn't thought it out well. He hadn't even known for sure that he was going to do it. He had lost control, something he had promised himself would never happen. As far as he knew, this was the first time there had ever been a witness, and he had let him get away. That realization stunned him. What had he been thinking? He was overcome with panic. He had to get home before another car came along. He had to get home before the police arrived! That little do-gooder had likely called them.

This time there was no humming, no self-satisfaction, no feeling of release. He was just an agitated bundle of nerves. The saliva was thick in his mouth. Then it seemed to dry up, and he could barely swallow. That poor woman hadn't hurt him. She hadn't deserved to die. Now he was killing women for no good reason. He was consumed by self-loathing and fear. He was nothing but a twisted pervert. Perhaps the time had come to turn himself in, or better still, to do himself in. Somehow he wanted to be stopped. Tears of rage and frustration slowly made their way down his face, as he headed back to Niagara Falls. The night had been a fiasco, and he was eaten up with an overwhelming sense of dread. This time there had been a witness. Had his luck finally run out?

CHAPTER 20

▼

Steffie Chapman was kept in intensive care for almost a week, before being deemed well enough to be moved up to a bright room in the Brock unit of the hospital. Kitty's parents had driven over from Toronto, to help in any way they could. They liked Steffie, and appreciated what a good friend she was to their daughter. They were also very relieved and thankful, that Kitty had not been shot as well. Steffie was coming along better than anyone had anticipated, and was soon almost her old feisty self again. Nothing would hold her back for very long, at least that was what Kitty ferventley hoped.

The boutique was kept closed, while they cleaned up the mess, and repaired the damages. Kitty's parents helped, along with Cleo, and a cleaning crew. It was only a few days before things were pretty well back to normal. Of course nothing would be quite normal, until Steffie was back working side by side with Kitty.

The extensive coverage of the shooting, resulted in streams of customers flowing into the shop. Business was booming. Niagara Falls is a relatively quiet city, with very little serious crime. The attempted robbery during daylight hours, and the shooting, whether accidental or deliberate, were considered big news. For a few days at least, Aunt Aggie's Attic knocked stories about the Black Sheep right off the front page.

Cleo was run ragged, and even Kitty's mother was pressed into service, as Kitty raced back and forth from the boutique to the hospital. Steffie wanted to be kept informed as to everything that was going on. She laughed at Kitty's tales of customers pretending to shop, when all they really wanted was to glean some inside tidbits about that fateful afternoon. They were all concerned about Steffie, who was a great favourite with the regulars.

Kitty was surprised the first day that Steffie was moved into her private room, when Peter Dunlop came to visit the patient. He was a real estate broker, who had been helping Steffie shop for a condo. He was a tall, fun-loving chap with prematurely gray hair, and a lot of laugh lines around his eyes and mouth. He didn't seem to take life too seriously, and was always able to see the funny side of any situation.

The third time that Kitty walked into Steffie's room and saw Peter sitting there, laughing with Steff, Kitty heard faint alarm bells in her head. She wondered whether something was going on here. No casual acquaintance would be visiting that much, and bringing gifts every time he came. Kitty was anxious for her friend to find herself a nice companion, but this guy seemed too much like a "fly by night" party animal. Was he just flirting with Steffie in order to make a quick sale? The next time that she and Steff were alone, she broached the subject.

"Steff, what's going on here? That guy never leaves."

"Tell me about it. Every time I come out of the washroom, he's sitting here waiting for me, with a big grin on his face. I think he's just being nice though, because he wants to sell me a condo. Besides, not too many people get shot, you know. I guess I'm a bit of a celebrity at the moment. Now don't you dare try to make any more out of it than that."

"Stephanie Jeanne Chapman — you little vixen," cried Kitty. "While I'm worrying myself sick about you, here you are flirting from your hospital bed. Doesn't he ever work?"

"Lay off, Kitty. As usual, you're putting an exaggerated spin on things. He's been very nice, bringing me books and magazines and candy, and if it will help me get a good condo, then I'm all for it."

Kitty wasn't buying it. "Come on, Steff. What's up? You look all giddy, and you've never been able to lie to me. Besides, I don't think you put on that lipstick and mascara just for me." She was grinning now, and cocked her head at Steffie with a goofy look on her face.

Steffie sighed and laughed. "Kitty, you are pathetic. You're worse than a damn dog sniffing at a bone. Peter just happens to be a really nice guy, but I am not looking for romance. I've told you many times, now that I'm safely out of my marriage, I'm loving my independence. I have no intention of getting involved emotionally or physically with another guy for a long long time.

I do, however, appreciate the occasional male company, just for a dinner or a movie or a play at the Shaw. Guys can be great company, if there isn't too much testosterone in the air. Peter makes me laugh, even though he is starting to get on my nerves. Now, let me say it one more time. I am not looking for a romance, so lay off the match-making." She scowled at Kitty as she said this, then laughed and threw up her hands. "You're getting me all riled up, and that's not good for me, so let's talk about something else."

"Hey, don't hold back now. Just say what you really think," grinned Kitty, hands on hips. "I suspect that he got a glimpse of you in your hospital johnny, with your elegant bottom exposed to all and sundry. That's all any guy would need."

Steffie laughed, and crossed her eyes. She was sitting in a chair, wearing the emerald green quilted housecoat and slippers, which Kitty had brought for her. They had cost a lot, but Steff was so delighted with them, that they had been worth it. The green seemed to suit her shiny black hair, which at the moment was loose and tousled around her shoulders. Her colour was good now, and any man would find her very attractive, although hospital rooms weren't usually conducive to romance.

Kitty was disappointed that Steffie was so adamant about not wanting any involvements just now, but she respected her feelings. She would undoubtedly find herself the right guy eventually, so Kitty would just have to mind her own business. Besides, she didn't think that Peter would be the right one for Steffie. He was too flimsy somehow. Steffie deserved the very best the male population had to offer.

The plan was for Steffie to come and stay with Kitty for a week or longer, once she was out of the hospital. It would be a perfect arrangement. She would have the cats to keep her company while Kitty was working, and Kitty would be there at night, to cook dinner, and make sure that Steffie didn't get overtired.

The night before she was to be discharged, Kitty threw a little impromptu "getting out of the hospital" party for her. As she walked down the hall toward Steffie's room, she felt the ghosts of so many people walking with her. It was a weird feeling, and sent chills down her back. It was as if those who had died here, relinquishing their tenuous hold on life, were surrounding her, their vacant eyes staring at her. Were they friendly, or were they menacing? She didn't know, but she shuddered as the cold feeling swept over her, and was delighted when she looked up and saw Keith Spenser heading from the other direction. He was coming to Steffie's party too, and his appearance seemed to chase the spectres away.

Since Steffie was in a private room, they could close the door, and hopefully they wouldn't be too noisy. Kitty shook off the oppressive feeling which had come over her, and put on a big smile, as she entered Steffie's room.

The party was a great success. Cleo came, as did Drew, along with two nurses Steffie knew from the geriatric ward. They were sisters, and had the unlikely names of Robin and Sparrow. Apparently their mother, whose name was Birdy, had a twisted sense of humour. The girls had suffered many jibes and jokes over the years, but were both very nice. Barry Johnson, the male nurse, dropped around for a few minutes, and even the head nurse stuck her head in to wish Steffie good luck, and to admonish them to keep it quiet. Peter was there, and Kitty was interested to see that he got along well with everyone. She still felt uneasy about him hanging around so much, but if it was okay with Steff, it was okay with her. Of course Cassie and Vickie had also been invited, so the hospital room was overflowing.

Kitty had brought some silver balloons (no latex allowed in hospitals anymore), some champagne, and chips and dip. Steffie got a wonderful array of "going home" gifts. There was a basket of chocolates, cheeses, crackers, little jars of jam, and wine. This was from Kitty and her parents. Someone gave her gift certificates to Swiss Chalet, so that she could eat take-out chicken dinners and not have to cook. Someone else gave her two books by the popular mystery writer Mitch Donaldson. Pictures were taken amidst much laughter and clowning.

Kitty noticed that Cleo was flirting rather openly with Keith, and Barry, the male nurse, obviously didn't like it. He took off without saying goodbye to anyone. The last Kitty had heard, Cleo had a crush on Drew, but he was being very attentive to Kitty, so Cleo had apparently set her sights on Keith. She was a foolish, flighty little thing, and was playing with fire. Kitty just hoped she wouldn't get burned.

The head nurse finally had to come and shoo everyone out. It had been a great party, and Steffie seemed psyched about getting out the next morning, and going to Kitty's for a while. After everyone left, Kitty gathered up Steffie's things, and they chatted for a few moments.

"Did you see the way Cleo was flirting with Keith?" asked Steffie. "He seems totally enamoured doesn't he? Maybe she's the one who's going to hook him. I didn't like the way Barry was acting, though, when he slammed out of here." She was looking tired and droopy, as she took off her housecoat and slippers, and got back into bed.

"I hope she knows what she's doing," said Kitty, as she put everything into a couple of big shopping bags. "I'll take these things home with me tonight, and I'll be here around 11 tomorrow. I guess I should call first to be sure that you've been discharged. Anything else I can do before I leave?"

"Not a thing, thanks. You've been wonderful, Kitty. I don't know how I would have gotten through this without your love and support. What a friend! It was a great party, and Peter seemed to fit right in with everyone. Shoot! I hope he's not going to become a pest. Once I'm out of here, I'll have to discourage him, but he's been awfully good to me." She shook her head, as she looked at her friend. "I don't want to hurt his feelings, but he's not for me, and the sooner he knows it, the better."

"Well, he seems nice enough," said Kitty, in a noncommittal tone. Then, looking closely at Steffie, she saw to her surprise, that her friend looked distressed.

"What's the matter?" cried Kitty. She had a guilty feeling that maybe the party had been too much for the patient.

"I know I should be happy that I'm getting out of here, but I feel so scared. What if my shoulder and arm and chest never really heal? What if my arm remains all stiff and useless? What if that guy comes back and shoots me again?"

This was so unlike the strong-willed, positive thinking gal that Kitty knew, that she was really taken aback. Of course it was just one of Steff's strange moods. No wonder she was down in the dumps, with all the pills and shots she had been having.

"Well well, Miss Gilda Glum, look at you feeling all sorry for yourself. You're going to be fine, and you darn well know it. Look how lucky you are that the bullet didn't hit your heart. You twit, you wouldn't be sitting here talking to me now if it had. Once you start your intensive physio, you'll be back to normal in no time. The doctor said that you're going to be fine, so why look for trouble? You're just tired tonight. You'll feel better in the morning." She very carefully hugged her friend, and patted her back, as one would with a child. Steffie was a really complicated person — maybe that's what made her so interesting.

"Okay, time for a little quiz," said Kitty. She was determined to get Steffie's mind off her troubles.

"Who starred in Waterloo Bridge?"

"Shoot, that's too easy. Do you think I'm brain damaged?" demanded Steffie with a grin. "It was Vivian Leigh and Robert Taylor."

"Damn, you're good" laughed Kitty in mock admiration. "How about Battle Cry? Name three stars in that movie." She was now sitting at the foot of the hospital bed, watching Steffie carefully. She seemed to be perking up.

Steffie frowned, and patted her chest very lightly where it was still bandaged. "This area is starting to itch a bit. It must be healing. Okay, now, how about Aldo Ray and Dorothy Malone, and, um, oh shoot, I don't know. Give me some time and I'll get it."

"Fine. You can tell me tomorrow, but no cheating and asking the nurses."

"Get out of here," laughed Steffie, her momentary depression seemingly all gone.

Kitty left the hospital reluctantly. She wondered again whether having the little party had been too much excitement for the patient. Oh well, what's done was done. Steff would be much better physically, mentally, and emotionally, when she got her home.

Back at the house, Kitty's dad helped her carry Steffie's things up to the guest bedroom. Luckily there were four bedrooms in the house, so there was lots of room for company. Anyway, her parents were leaving for Toronto in the morning, and the friends would have the place to themselves. Kitty sighed, as she wondered whether she would be dealing with a lot of mood swings from Steffie.

Mrs. Winfield made them a cup of tea, and as they sat chatting, she brought up the subject of the Black Sheep. "I'm so glad that Steffie will be here with you for a while. I wish she'd move in permanently. I hate the idea of you being all alone while that strangler is roaming around out there," she said with a worried frown.

"Oh mom please don't start. We've been over this so many times. I'm perfectly capable of taking care of myself. There are good locks on all the doors and windows, and there's no way that I would let any stranger into the house, so what's the problem?" Kitty didn't want to get into another argument with her mother, who tended to be overly protective.

"The problem is that he has killed at least two people we know of, and maybe a whole lot more. The problem is that no one knows what he looks like, so it could be anyone. Maybe it's one of your regular customers. Maybe it's your dentist, or that carpenter working for you. Who knows? The problem is that you give your trust too easily. You think that everyone is as nice as you are. You just can't be too careful at a time like this." Mrs. Winfield sniffed with an aggrieved air.

"Come on now Margaret. Don't get yourself all upset. You know that Kitty is careful, and that sicko is likely miles away by now. There's no guaranty that he's still in the Niagara area." Kitty's dad always took her side, for which she was very grateful.

"I don't care. I won't get a good night's sleep till he's caught. Don't you go dating any strange men, or walking alone at night."

"Yes ma'm," grinned Kitty. "I promise I'll become a hermit and lock myself in the basement." They all laughed at that, and Kitty's dad asked if she would play them a couple of tunes before they went to bed.

Kitty could play the piano, not well, but adequately, and her parents loved to listen to her. Her dad always joked that after all the money they had spent on her lessons, they should get some pleasure out of it.

The stairs in this house curved up to an interesting minstrel balcony, which overlooked the living room. That was where the piano sat. Kitty obediently ran up the stairs, and began to play one of her dad's favourite tunes. Petie Pie suddenly appeared, and leapt onto the piano top, where he could feel the vibrations of the music. This caused him to purr loudly. Everyone laughed at his obvious enjoyment of the music.

Before going to bed, Kitty's dad drew her aside and said quietly. "I don't really care for that guy who's doing your deck and gazebo. He's a bit strange. He asked me an awful lot of questions about you, and he seemed evasive when I asked him anything about himself. Just watch it, Kit Kat. I don't want to scare you, but be sure you do keep the doors locked when he's around. Promise?"

Kitty sighed. "I promise. I just wish you wouldn't worry so much. Josh seems fine to me. He's doing a super job, and he's almost finished. That little gazebo is going to be wonderful. Next time you come over, we'll be able to sit out there and enjoy the garden, without any pesky mosquitoes bothering us." She kissed him on the cheek, and gave him a hug. She loved her parents dearly, but her mom in particular, could be a real pain. She wished they would give her a little more credit for being able to take care of herself.

CHAPTER 21

▼

Cassie dressed very carefully for the luncheon with Jack. Her mid-calf length skirt was a light filmy burgundy colour, with the uneven hemline so popular at the moment. She had put on a form fitting pink sleeveless top, and covered it with a little burgundy bolero. Her white spiked strappy sandals were very flattering to her long dancer's legs. As she checked herself one last time in the mirror, she wondered fleetingly how Jack's wife dressed. She had never seen the mysterious "Darla", but she understood from Jack's partner Bud, that Darla was a real "looker." "Well, you're not so bad yourself, Cassandra Meredith," she said to the mirror, as she picked up her little white purse, and headed for the car. She had butterflies in her stomach, and self-recriminations in her heart, but nothing was going to stop her from having this lunch with Jack.

She was glad that Dave was safely away in Greece, but felt horribly guilty at being glad! "Get a grip, girl," she muttered to herself, as she set out on this clandestine rendezvous. She knew it was stupid, but that wasn't going to stop her. She would do her "mea culpas" tomorrow.

Vickie had just shaken her head gloomily, when she heard what Cassie was planning to do. She hadn't tried to talk her out of it, though, for which Cass was extemely grateful.

As she drove along the Niagara Parkway, she couldn't help remembering the last time she and Jack had met for lunch. It had been almost two years ago, when she had called the police to tell them that she thought she was being stalked, and she and Vickie were sure that a murder had been commit-ted. The two detectives who showed up at her door were Jack Willinger and his partner Bud Lang. Jack and Cassie hadn't seen each other for many years, and they were both very shaken up by the unexpected encounter.

Dave had been in Europe at the time, and Jack was having marital problems with Darla. That had been the perfect opportunity to dive back into a passionate affair, but they both had too much class, too much integrity, and too many family ties, to do anything so dishonest and unfair. They had gone out for one luncheon, on the pretext that Jack had to talk to her about the murders. That one luncheon had been hot, but nothing had come of it. Neither one was ready or willing to compromise his or her marriage.

Cassie squirmed a bit, as she wondered what would happen today. She had to keep reminding herself that she was happily married, that Dave was a loveable, reliable, wonderful man, that she had a great life with him, and that she had no intention of rocking the marital boat, or tearing the fabric of her carefully orchestrated life.

She wondered though, for the millionth time, how or why a woman could love two men at the same time. Dave was caring and gentle, and they had made a good home and family together. Jack, on the other hand, was exciting, charismatic, intense. He could set her heart pounding just with a look or a touch. Life with him would be challenging, full of fire works, surprising. Life with Dave, on the other hand, was comfortable, secure, warm and safe. The two men couldn't be more different, yet she loved them both.

The gracious and stately Riverbend Inn gave the appearance of elegance, wealth and timelessness. The four white pillars made her think of Scarlett's beloved Tara. As she drove slowly up the long driveway, she appreciated the luscious green lawns, and graceful old shade trees. At one side of the inn was the patio, where guests could sit, enjoying a cold drink, and gazing out over the vineyards. It was an idyllic spot, which lent itself well to a romantic tryst. "Stop that, you idiot," she muttered, as she checked her face in the rear view mirror, locked the car, and sauntered toward the front door. She didn't want to appear too anxious, just in case Jack was watching her.

Although her mind was focused on Jack, she was still aware of the attractive lobby. A huge chandelier hung from the center of the ceiling. To the left was the registration desk, to the right, a small display case showing artifacts from the War of 1812. It contained shoe buckles, arrowheads, and coins, which had all been found during a dig in 2003. On either side of the lobby were stairs running up to the beautiful rooms. Cassie didn't want to think of those rooms just now. "Get thee behind me, Satan," she muttered, as she strode through the lobby, and into the dining room.

As before, when they had lunched at the Casa D'Oro in downtown Niagara Falls, Jack was already there, waiting at a table in the furthest corner. He was sitting quietly, looking around at the other patrons. He's always aware of his surroundings, Cassie thought. It's as if he's always on duty.

He was wearing a light gray summer turtleneck with short sleeves, and her knees turned to water as she walked towards him. He was a man who looked sexy in a turtleneck, and he knew it darn well. Cassie had always encouraged him to wear turtlenecks, when they had been together, and she knew that he was wearing this one just for her. He looked at her appraisingly. "Cass, you look terrific. I could take you in my arms and squeeze the life right out of you," he said with a chuckle, as he pulled out her chair.

"You silver-tongued devil," she laughed. "You could always weaken my knees with all your sweet talk, but I'm older and wiser now." That was what she said, but what she was thinking was that she could fall into bed with Jack that very minute, if he only said the word. She prayed he wouldn't suggest it, because she knew that for some reason today she had no resistance. She should never have come.

They bantered lightly for several minutes, before the waitress came to take their drink orders. Sipping their red wine, Jack finally became serious, and asked, "Does your husband still travel as much as he used to, and does he know you're here today?"

Dave had been away all during the summer two years ago, when Cassie and Vickie had been in such danger. Indeed, he hadn't known anything about all the frightening happenings, until Cassie took a surprise flight to Spain, and told him everything that had transpired. By that time, she had inherited the millions, and life as they knew it, had never been the same.

Dave still had his talent agency, and still liked to travel, leaving Cassie to enjoy her inheritance, and do with it as she wished. She had immediately put five million in his account, five million in trust for each of her two children, and kept the rest for doing good works and for having fun. Cassandra's Cattery was her first big project, but it wouldn't be her last.

After they had exhausted the subject of old school mates — they had both lost track of most of them, they went on to talk about the murders two years ago. From there they went to Vickie, and the great friendship between the two women. Jack and Vickie had never really liked each other too well, although they had arrived at a friendly truce after Vickie and Cassie saved Jack's life from the infamous Willy the Weasel. Finally they came to the subject du jour — the Black Sheep.

Jack, of course, couldn't divulge too many facts about the case, but he gave her enough little tidbits to whet her appetite for more.

"Jack, do you really think he might have bought the little black sheep at Kitty's boutique?" Cassandra was intrigued with the idea.

"There's a very good chance that he did," replied Jack, who looked as if he was talking about one thing, but thinking about something else. Cassandra had a pretty good idea of what he might be thinking, and she kept trying to steer the conversation to safer waters.

As they nibbled on their Caesar salads, and dunked the crusty Italian bread in olive oil and spices, Jack said, "Cass, when I'm with you, I feel as if I'm back at school, out on a date. Do you ever think about those times, and how crazy in love we were? Do you ever wonder where we would be today if your mother hadn't pried us apart?"

Cassie sighed, and wondered what to say. She thought of that old expression "the tension in the air was so thick that you could cut it with a knife." She had always thought it was just a foolish saying, but now she finally got it.

Taking a sip of wine, she gazed out the window, pondering how best to begin. Finally, putting down her glass, she said, "Jack, I'll be totally honest. Those were some of the happiest days of my life, and I often think of them. In spite of that, I'm happily married with a husband I love, and two great kids. I would never do anything to jeopardize what I have, but I do dream and speculate about what our lives would have been like together."

She paused there, and wondered whether to say any more, then, smiling at him, and giving him the benefit of her big blue eyes, she continued slowly. "When I'm near you, I can feel the chemistry, and there's an electricity which almost hurts. You are the most interesting, enchanting, desirable man I've ever known, but you aren't mine any more, and you never can be. If we can be friends, and if we can see each other once in a while, I think we should grab that, and hold onto it. We mustn't expect or try to have any more than that, because too many people would get hurt. I know that deep down you agree with me, so please don't make it any harder than it is."

Jack just sat there, looking at her, appraising her, trying to read between the lines. Finally he shook his head sadly and laughed. "You're right, of course. I wouldn't do anything to hurt Darla, but, oh my God, if we could just roll back the years. If only I hadn't let your mother chase me away, and if only you had stood up to her."

"Amen to that," she said, with an attempt at a grin. "Now let's stop feeling sorry for ourselves, and tell me some more about the Black Sheep. Do you think he's a local guy?"

Jack had a difficult time pulling himself away from his memories, but he made a good effort. Everyone now knew about the little black sheep, which the strangler left in each victim's hand, and little ceramic sheep had suddenly become very desirable collectibles. People could be ghoulish, and, of course, that made it much more difficult for the police to chase down the strangler. Little black sheep were in high demand.

"Now tell me about Willy the Weasel. Is he still in prison?"

"Yes, as far as I know. That was a terrible fiasco though. Some idiot judge let him out on bail, and he raped another woman, and then tried to get to Vancouver. They caught him in Sudbury, and he'll be in jail till he's too old to remember what it was he liked to do."

They went through more wine and two cups of coffee each, before they realized that there was no excuse for prolonging the luncheon. They had expressed their innermost thoughts to each other, and had had a wonderful time just talking and staring into each other's eyes. Now it was time to get back to their real lives. There was no reason to see each other again, except that neither one was ready to say goodbye on a permanent basis.

Cassie could hardly believe her own voice when she took his hand and said, "Jack, could we do this again in maybe three months? It was so wonderful just to sit and talk about old times. This luncheon will keep me going for weeks, but I know now that I need to see you again, even for such a little while."

He looked at her lovingly as he laughed, "Cass, you know I'd walk over hot coals for you. If you're game for another lunch, then so am I. I'll call you in October and we'll do it again. Meantime, be really careful, please. This Black Sheep is a very dangerous character. We think he may be a professional man, or someone who is well established in the community. He's clever and meticulous, and he must be a real charmer. Don't let any man into your house if you don't know him well, and if you haven't invited him. This guy never has to break and enter. He just seems to be invited or expected. Give my best to Vickie, and don't you dare try any sleuthing on this one."

Cass had no particular interest in the Black Sheep. It wasn't like two years ago, when her family had been involved so dramatically. It was easy, therefore, to promise not to go sleuthing.

The afternoon seemed to be winding down by the time the waitress brought the cheque. Jack glanced at it casually, then glanced at Cassie, who was looking out the window. He seemed to be considering something, and then said quietly, "Just charge it to my room please."

Cassie thought her heart would leap right out of her chest. Why would Jack have a room here at the Inn? There was only one possible reason. Her face flushed, and she stared at him. He tried to look insouciant and innocent, but instead, looked a bit sheepish, as he reached for her hands. "Shall we?" was all he said, as he led her toward the stairs.

Cassie was having trouble swallowing, and her feet and arms felt numb. Somehow she had always known that this day would come. In a detached state, she seemed unaware of the lovely Renoir paintings on the wall, and the two comfy looking armchairs in the hall outside Room 209. She had no control over the situation, as Jack unlocked the bedroom door, and nudged it shut with his foot.

Taking her in his arms, he nuzzled her neck just behind her ears, gently kissed her eyes, then found her mouth.

Cass couldn't breathe. She was eighteen years old again, and her whole life was ahead of her. Her arms went around his neck, as if he was her refuge from the storm. Then her fingers were gently tracing the scar, that ugly yet appealing scar, which hadn't been there when they were teenagers.

Who knew how long they stood like that, kissing, murmuring, touching. Cass wasn't allowing herself to think. She was simply going with her feelings, and it was heavenly.

Somehow they found themselves dancing to music only they could hear. Dancing had been one of their favourite pastimes so long ago, when they were young, and so very much in love.

There was total silence in the quaint bedroom of the old inn, as they danced and remembered the good times. The trance-like quality of the shared experience went on for some time. Then Jack stopped, and very slowly and deliberately, he began to undo the little bolero top, and pull it off her shoulders. Cass was helping him, but suddenly she felt a piercing pain in her heart. It might have been a metaphorical pain, but it hurt just as much as if it was the real thing. She stopped, drew back, and looked up into Jack's handsome face, once again running her fingers along that intriguing scar.

"Jack," she whispered, with tears in her lovely blue eyes. "You know we can't do this. We had our chance and we blew it. We're two different people now, and we're all grown up."

Jack stared at her with a stricken look on his face. He looked pathetic, and somehow comical, holding her little top in those big hands of his. He started to speak, then stopped. Finally he dropped his arms in defeat, and took a few steps back. "You're right, dammit. I can't do this to Darla, it would break her heart. Lord knows I've been dreaming about it, but you would likely come to hate me, and I know I'd hate myself.

I've loved you for so long, Cass. You've always been in my heart, even all those years we were separated. The thing is, you are absolutely right. Our time has come and gone. We had our chance and we blew it. Now we can't hurt others just to indulge ourselves." He sounded as if he was trying to convince himself.

Cassie stared up at him, trying to calm her racing pulse. "I could never hurt Dave that way, or my kids. You're a wonderful man, and I love you more than you'll ever know, but we made choices and promises a long time ago, and we have to abide by them. We made a huge mistake back then, but making another one today wouldn't help anyone. We'll always be friends, but we can't ever be lovers." Then, trying to lighten the mood, she laughed, "That sounds like a song title."

Jack laughed with her, and said, "I'm sorry I put this temptation in your path. I must have been crazy to think that it would work."

"It almost did," she grinned, as he folded his arms around her again. They stood there embracing for a long time. Then Jack said, "Come over here and sit down. I promise I won't touch you. Let's just think this through one more time." He wasn't about to give up too easily.

He sat in one of the chairs, hunching forward, while Cassie perched tentatively on the edge of the bed.

While they talked, she couldn't help noticing what a lovely, tasteful room it was. She was sitting on a Queen sized bed, with two large posts on the headboard. The painting over the bed was of a Victorian couple, with the man's head lying in the woman's lap. Oh, brother, thought Cass. Get me out of here, this is way too seductive.

There was a lovely gas fireplace in one corner. Cass could only imagine how sexy and cosy it would be to be lying in bed in each other's arms, gazing at that marble fireplace in the dark. It sent shivers of delight down her spine.

Placed against one wall, which was painted burgundy, was an elegant, small escritoire, over which hung another painting, this one of two women.

An inviting fruit basket sat on the coffee table. French doors opened onto a private balcony overlooking the vineyards. Across those vineyards, she could see the Peller Estate Winery. She noticed how much it looked like a French chateau. Jack certainly had picked an elegant and romantic spot for this would-be tryst. What a shame that it wasn't going to happen. She had to get out of here before her resolve crumbled like old cork. There was just too much pressure. She wanted to say "yes" so badly, but she knew in her heart that she had to say "no."

Eventually, with regret and determination, he helped her on with her little bolero top. She had to grin as she looked around the room one more time. Those windows had really been steamed up for a few lovely minutes. She would cherish the memory of this afternoon forever. She would take it out occasionally from her memory's treasure box, and handle it gently. It would keep her warm and bright on cold dark days. She felt like a martyr as she gave up what might have been.

As they walked together down the elegant staircase, Cass was again vaguely aware of many gilt-framed pictures on the walls, but her mind was in a fog. Had they done the right thing, or had they made another huge mistake?

Jack walked her to her car, and they were both very careful not to let their bodies touch. Then, putting his hands on her shoulders, he gave her a quick kiss, barely touching her lips, but Cassie impulsively threw her arms around him and kissed him long and hard, as if there was no tomorrow.

"Thank you for this afternoon," she whispered. "I'll cherish the memories, and just imagining what might have been, will keep me going for a long time. I love you Jack." Then, hurrying into her car, and blinking the tears from her eyes, she sped away without looking back. If she had, it would have broken her heart. Jack was standing watching her drive away, and he looked as forlorn as a man could be. He also looked like a man ready to kick himself around the block for just having made a very bad decision.

She was almost home before she realized that they hadn't made any definite plans to see each other again.

CHAPTER 22

▼

Steffie's first week out of the hospital was spent happily with Kitty, and it went quickly. She rested every day while Kitty was at work, and did all the exercises the physiotherapist recommended. That stupid kid who had shot her, likely hadn't meant to, but she wasn't going to let herself be his victim. The sooner she was functioning again one hundred percent, the happier she would be.

Every night when Kitty got home, they would order in chicken or pizza, or Kitty would throw together a big salad full of healthy veggies. One night she even made them macaroni and cheese over Steffie's protests. She just grinned and told her friend that this was providing the calcium which she needed. Steffie shuddered at all the junk food she was eating, but she was definitely improving every day, so Kitty felt confident that she was doing something right.

Peter came over one evening, and took Steffie for a nice car ride to Niagara-on-the-Lake. It felt so good to be out again, that it lifted her spirits immensely, and made her even more anxious to get back to work. After ten days of pampering, she went back to her own little apartment, and things seemed to be getting back to normal.

This particular Saturday, Kitty had been working in the back yard most of the day, and talking to Josh, who was putting the second coat of white paint on the gazebo. That would be the end of his job, and Kitty realized that she would miss seeing him out there working so hard, and she would miss their conversations. He was a very interesting man, who owned his own successful company, but enjoyed manual labour. He claimed that he loved the feel of the wood under his hands, and it gave him a sense of accomplishment to create something like the gazebo or the deck.

It was later that same afternoon, when she went in to make up a tray of iced tea and date squares, warmed in the micro. "Come and take a break, Josh," she called, as she placed the tray on the glass table, which was now sitting proudly on her beautiful new deck.

Josh had also installed a fancy green and white roll-back awning, so that there could be shade on the deck if so desired. He had done such an excellent job, that Kitty felt it was worth every penny it had cost her.

"This is great Kitty. I was really getting thirsty," Josh said, gulping down the cold tea. He would rather have had a cold beer, but what the heck, iced tea would have to do.

They chatted randomly for a bit, then Josh asked, "What do you think has happened to the Black Sheep? We haven't heard anything more about him. Do you think he's left town, or do you suppose that these jerky police around here have just given up? He's obviously way too smart for them."

"Oh, I don't agree at all, Josh. How can you say such a thing? He certainly seems to be a very crafty fellow, but they'll catch him. He'll make some mistakes, and they'll get him. I just hope it's sooner rather than later."

"Doesn't it scare you to be alone in this big house all the time? Do you ever lie awake at night, listening for him to come up those stairs? Imagine what it must feel like to have his hands around your neck, squeezing tighter and tighter." Josh was sweating profusely from his work in the sun, and he looked slightly demented as he asked these questions.

"Stop it Josh. You're just trying to scare me. What in the world are you talking about? Why would I ever imagine such a horrible thing?" Now that he had put it into words, Kitty really could imagine the strangler with his big hands going around her neck. Josh had big hands. She had noticed them the very first day. They were great hands for strangling, she thought giddily. She had to admit that lately, just like Steffie, she was noticing the hands of every man she saw. She was letting her imagination run away with her, but why would Josh be so stupid as to say something like that? Was he deliberately trying to frighten or intimidate her? She wished he would finish his tea break and get back to work. She was sorry now that she had been so nice to him. She just didn't want to talk to him anymore.

"Okay, sorry I mentioned it. I just worry about you all alone in this big place. It would be so easy to break in if someone wanted to."

"No it wouldn't," she denied angrily. "There are great locks on all the doors and windows, and I'm having an alarm system put in this week." Where had that come from, she wondered. She had no previous intention of installing an alarm system here at the house, but suddenly it sounded like a pretty good idea.

Quickly she changed the subject. "Where are you going to be working next?"

"I've got a job in St. Catharines, and it will likely last about three weeks," he replied, without much enthusiasm. "I've enjoyed working here, and I'm sorry that it's all finished. I definitely plan to see you again. How about dinner tonight?"

Kitty was taken aback at this suggestion. Somehow they had jumped from the strangler to a dinner invitation in one easy step. "Oh, I'm sorry but I'm busy tonight. Thanks anyway." She was thankful that she had a dinner date with Drew, and hadn't had to make up a lie.

Josh frowned and asked, "Are you still going out with that so-called doctor?"

"What do you mean — 'so-called'?" she asked crossly. "Drew is a bona fide medical doctor."

"Well, maybe he is, but I don't think much of his line of work. Women who want to enlarge their breasts and get liposuction on their flabby thighs, aren't exactly the most needy of people," he added sourly.

Kitty was aghast. She had to defend Drew, although in her private thoughts, she had often felt that his work wasn't very important. It was just a means of making a lot of money. He did more of the "tits and asses" type of work than he did with accident victims or birth deformities. She certainly wasn't about to admit that to Josh, though.

"That's a dreadful thing to say," she replied. "He takes care of all kinds of people. He certainly isn't limited to cosmetic surgery for vain women. Anyway, how would you know? You don't know him at all."

"Hey, calm down. Don't get your panties all in a knot," he laughed. "I do know that you and I would get along really well. You just have to give me a chance."

"I'm sorry, Josh. I appreciate the invitation, but,"

Josh jumped in before she could say anything more. "Don't go all high and mighty and holier than thou on me now. You know that you've been flirting with me for weeks. What are you — just some kind of a tease who thinks she's giving the hired help a treat? Don't kid yourself. I know that you like me, and I'm not going to take 'no' for an answer."

Kitty jumped up at this point. "Well, you'll have to. I certainly have not been flirting with you, and I'm very sorry if I gave you that impression. I was simply trying to be friendly. Actually you should get back to work. I'll get your cheque."

Kitty's voice had turned very cold, as she picked up the tray and hurried into the kitchen. With her hands full, she couldn't lock the door behind her. As she put the tray down on the counter, she felt his arms go around her, and he began nuzzling her neck.

"Stop it. What's gotten into you? Leave me alone, please." She tried to push him away, but his arms were strong.

"You're going to be damn sorry, Miss Fancy Pants. I could get any girl I want, and I happen to want you. Don't be too hasty now. I know exactly what you need, and I'm just the guy for the job."

If she hadn't been so surprised, she would have laughed. Obviously Josh had a big opinion of himself, and a big mouth to go with it. He could sing a duet by himself, she thought, with a grimace. His mouth is big enough for two people. What a loser. She managed to squirm loose, and slap him as hard as she could on the face. He replied by grabbing her arms, and holding them behind her back, as he kissed her roughly. She wanted to gag, but instead she held her breath and let herself go limp. For Josh it must have been like kissing a goldfish.

"You're disgusting," she squeaked when he let her go. "Here, take your cheque and get the hell out. I'm really disappointed in you, Josh. It's a good thing you're finished, or I'd fire you."

He stood staring at her for a minute, as if trying to make up his mind about something, then tipping his hand to his head in a sarcastic salute, he went out the back door. Kitty stood there, shaking with anger, then headed up the stairs to shower and get ready for her date with Drew. She wouldn't tell him what had happened. He wouldn't understand, and would likely suspect that she had led Josh on. Drew was definitely the jealous type. Lord save me from macho meatheads, she thought glumly, as she undressed.

The sharp needle-like rays of hot water were invigorating and somehow soothing, and Kitty soon calmed down, and started to laugh. The nerve of that twerp. Wait till she told Steffie. No, bad idea. Steffie didn't like her being alone in this big house, so she wouldn't tell her.

She was relieved that she wouldn't have to see Josh again. No way had she flirted with him or encouraged him — or had she? She tried to think back on all the times she had brought him a cup of coffee and a doughnut, or had sat and chatted with him for a few minutes. Surely he couldn't have mistaken that for flirting? She was just beginning to feel a bit guilty, when she thought she saw a shadow through the glass shower doors. Quickly turning off the water, she opened the door a crack, and stuck her head out. Her heart leaped into her throat.

Josh was standing in the bathroom, with a big grin on his face. "Don't panic. I just came back to tell you that you left the kitchen door unlocked. That's really careless. You have no idea who could wander in and hurt you."

Was that a threat? She tried to be calm, as she assessed the situation.

"How did you get in here?" she asked angrily.

"I just told you. You left the back door unlocked. That's incredibly stupid, with the Black Sheep loose out there."

"No, I mean how did you get in here to the bathroom?" She always locked the bathroom door when she took a shower. After all, wasn't that what every single girl had learned from the movie "Psycho?"

"This door was unlocked too. You are way too careless. That's exactly how women get killed. Here, let me hand you a towel." He grinned at her as he handed her the big fluffy bath towel off the rack.

"Josh, please go. This is very awkward, and you know that you shouldn't be here. I'll get dressed, and we can talk downstairs." Her mind was racing. She was positive that she had locked the bathroom door, but if so, how had he gotten in so easily? True, she had been upset when she came upstairs. Had she left it unlocked? She knew he was right about her not locking the kitchen door. That truly was stupid. Right now, though, she had to get rid of him. The things he had said about the strangler came back to her. Please God don't let him be the strangler, she thought, as she clutched the towel around her, and refused to step out of the shower stall.

"Hey, Kitty, I didn't mean to scare you, I just wanted to warn you. Lock up for safety sake. Don't trust anyone. There are a lot of kooks out there you know. I'm going now, so you can get out of the shower. Have a nice date with the doc, and I'll call you soon."

With that, he grinned at her again, and was gone. She came out of the shower stall, and quickly locked the door, looking carefully at the knob. It did seem a little loose. Could he have jiggled it to unlock it, or had it been unlocked all the time? She was weak with relief, as she leaned against the door, and prayed that he really was gone. Now she was undecided about leaving the bathroom, in case he was lurking somewhere in the house.

It was only when she heard little Miss Rosie crying and scratching at the door, that she had the courage to open it. She looked carefully around the bedroom, but of course he could be hiding in the closet or under the bed.

Unsure what to do, she grabbed her nail file off the dresser, and leaned over to peer under the bed. A nail file wouldn't be much help, but it would be better than nothing.

Well, thankfully, there was no one under the bed, — just a few dust bunnies. The closet was the real test. She had to open it to get at her clothes. There was no point in calling the police. She would look like a fool, and then maybe Drew and her parents would find out. That would be awful. They would never give her a moment's peace. No, she had to handle this herself.

Picking up Miss Rosie, and depositing her on the bed, she tiptoed to the closet door, nail file held high. She didn't know what good it would do, unless she could stick it right in his eye or up his nose. She listened there intently for what seemed ages, then, taking a deep breath, she turned the handle quickly with her left hand and jumped back. Silence.

She stood staring into the closet for a long time, listening for any sign of breathing. Finally she got up her courage to push the clothes aside and peer in. There was no one there. Heaving a sigh of relief, she dressed quickly, then hurried downstairs to check the back door. It was locked. So was the front door. Now feeling more brave, she walked through every room in the house. Suddenly she thought of Petie Pie. Where was he? What if Josh had let him out, or had hurt him?

She tried to remember every hiding place that the big orange cat liked, and Drew was ringing the front doorbell, when she realized with a laugh that Petie was trailing along behind her. How long had he been following her? What a little devil. Sighing with relief, she let Drew in, and went to check her hair, and get her purse.

Before they left, she told Drew that she thought she had heard a funny noise, and got him to check out the basement for her. No way was she going to tell him anything about Josh, and stir up a hornet's nest.

She was too wigged out to have any appetite, and Drew knew that something was wrong. He kept pressing her, but she tried to pretend that she was just tired. They ended up having a colourful fight, at least it was a fight on her part.

It was really Drew's fault. He should have realized that Kitty was on edge, and that it wasn't a good time to broach such an unexpected and off the wall idea. Unfortunately, he blundered along, and asked her whether she would move to the Bahamas with him, if he decided to give up his practice here. She stared at him in astonishment, assuming that he must be kidding, but she knew that Drew didn't have much of a sense of humour. If he was serious, he was being ridiculous. They had never discussed marriage or any kind of a future together. They barely knew each other. Treating it as a joke, she facetiously replied that she might consider it, as long as Petie and Miss Rosie could go with her. Drew foolishly and cavalierly answered, "Oh Kitty, you can't take those cats to the Bahamas with us. You can leave them here, and we'll get you one, if you want, when we get there."

Seeing the horrified look on her face, he stumbled along, digging himself in further. "We'll find them a good home, or they could go to the Cattery. What's the problem?"

Kitty couldn't believe her ears. He obviously had no understanding of how much she loved her two little friends. They were like family, and he was a big horse's ass. She stood up, glared at him as if he had just unzipped his pants, and exposed himself, and threw the remains of her wine right in his face. She had seen it done in the movies many times, and had always wondered whether she would have the nerve to do it. It felt great!

She stomped out of the restaurant, and called a taxi. She was furious with Drew, but proud of herself. It had been the right thing to do.

During the short taxi ride home, she told herself that Drew was an insensitive moron, with his outdated John Lennon glasses, and his ridiculous attitude. She forgot how kind he had been the night that Steffie was shot. She forgot the nice dinners they had shared. As far as Kitty was concerned, Dr. Drew Carson was toast.

It was on the way home that she realized this was one night that she really would have liked him to come in with her, just in case Josh had come back. She hated being nervous in her own home, but Josh had really caught her off guard, and she wasn't sure that she trusted him.

She tried to tell herself that he was harmless, that he would never hurt her, but she wasn't very convincing.

Besides her newfound doubts about Josh, she was absolutely furious with Drew. Any man who could totally and unfeelingly disregard her love for her pets, was not the man for her. Whether he had been kidding or not, the relationship was over.

Tears of frustration and disappointment welled in her eyes, as she realized that she had encountered two idiotic men on the same day. It wasn't a good record. She had a feeling that she wouldn't get much sleep tonight.

CHAPTER 23

▼

It was storming in Niagara Falls, one of those sudden summer storms, with great streaks of lightning flashing across the dark sky, thunder rumbling in the background, like a tiger with a sore tooth, and huge angry looking clouds sulking overhead. Kitty could feel a decided drop in temperature. She was curled up on the chesterfield, one cat on her lap, and one seemingly attached to her hip. It was definitely a night for cuddling. She knew she should go up to bed, but as it was just after 9 o'clock, it seemed too early. She was quite comfy right where she was, with a good book, and her two little friends.

With Steffie back in her own apartment now, Kitty and the cats missed her. She was usually ready with a laugh and a crazy story, and she and Kitty loved to talk about all the strange customers they had. They were having video surveillance cameras installed this week, and Kitty was contemplating having an alarm system installed in the house.

When the phone rang, breaking the stillness, Kitty didn't know whether to answer it or not. She didn't like to talk on the phone during a lightning storm. Miss Rosie jumped nervously, but there was no movement from Petie Pie, who was snuggled against her hip. She wondered how he could breathe under the pretty afghan she had thrown over her legs, but he seemed to like the warmth and the darkness.

Putting down her book, she reluctantly picked up the phone. If she saw any more lightning, she would hang up quickly, no matter who it was.

"Hi Kitty girl," came her father's welcome voice.

"Dad," she said in surprise. She had just talked to her parents two days ago. "What's up? Is everything okay? How's Mom?"

"Your mother's fine — no problems. I just called because I miss you, and because I want to ask my best girl a favour."

Kitty groaned inwardly, not knowing that this one favour would eventually change her life forever. Her dad could be a pest at times, but he was a good guy. "Okay, Dad, you don't need to butter me up. What do you need?" she laughed.

He laughed too, a deep chuckle which Kitty loved. "Well, honey, here's my problem. Let's get right to it. You know that I'm on the library board, and two nights ago we had a "meet the author" party, and I met Mitch Donaldson. You've read some of his books, haven't you?"

"You know I have," answered Kitty in delight. "He writes wonderful mysteries. What's he like?"

"I'm not really sure," her father hesitated. "He's very quiet and reserved, rather stern. He's nice enough though, I think. I quite liked him after the short time that we spoke. He's working on a new mystery, which is going to be set in Muskoka. Imagine that!"

Kitty knew her dad was leading up to something, but she couldn't think what it could be, so she said, "That's interesting."

"Yes, well, he was telling me that he wants to rent a small cottage up there for a week, to soak up the local colour and atmosphere etc. You know me, honey, I sometimes put my mouth in gear before my brain engages." He waited for her to laugh.

Kitty merely grinned and said "Sometimes?"

"Now now. Don't be disrespectful to your old father. Well, anyway, somehow, before I knew that I was going to do it, I jumped in, and suggested that he could rent our small cottage for a nominal fee, and have the use of the canoe to paddle around the lake. That way he could get the feel of the beauty and mystery of the area."

Kitty knew her dad was just stalling, before getting down to the favour he wanted. She squawked in dismay "You've never rented out our little bunky before, whatever made you do it?"

"I don't know, Kit. I guess maybe I was impressed talking to a big author, and he did seem very nice and quiet," he added lamely. He knew all too well how much Kitty loved the small cottage up the hill from the main one. She had always considered it hers, and she stayed in it when her parents were in the big one.

"Okay, what's the favour?" she asked suspiciously.

"Honey, I twisted my back quite badly last night, helping old Fred next door lift his air conditioner out of the window." Now was the time to play on her sympathies. "It hurts so much that I must have done something bad to it. There's no way I can drive, or even go up and down the stairs without help. Anyway, I'm having second thoughts about letting him have the place, and being up there all alone, so your mom and I were going to go up and spend the week in the main cottage, and keep an eye on things. Now that I've hurt my back and can't go, this is where you come in.

Kitty interrupted, "You want me to go up there for a week and show him how everything works and keep an eye on him?" She was incredulous at the idea. She was supposed to babysit the famous author Mitch Donaldson? Her dad must be getting senile.

"That's it, honey." He sounded relieved now that he had told her the tale of woe. "Do you think you could get away on such short notice? I hate to ask you, but we're in a bind here. Besides, you could use a little vacation after what you've been through." There was a pleading tone in his voice, and Kitty didn't know whether to laugh or be cross with him.

The idea of sitting on the dock, and watching some glorious Muskoka sunsets was very appealing. Those sunsets always seemed to sooth her soul. They gave such promise of a new clean day. She could get very poetic when she thought about those awe-inspiring sunsets.

After a moment's hesitation, she said, "Daddy, I'd love to. I've been wanting to get up there for some quiet time to myself, and who wouldn't want to meet Mitch Donaldson? Imagine a real author staying in our humble little cottage. This will be fun. If I can possibly manage it, I will. When is all this supposed to happen?"

"He's going up there this Saturday," her dad said hesitantly, waiting for her reaction.

"Yikes, so soon? Well, I'll have to check with Steffie, and see if she'll move back in here to look after the beasties. But Dad, what's with your back. How bad is it, and have you seen a doctor today?"

"I could barely move last night, and I've stayed very quiet all day. If it isn't any better by tomorrow, I'll call the doctor. Anyway, don't worry about my back. Just do this favour for me, and I'll love you forever."

"Phooey. You'd love me even if I had warts on my nose and drool on my chin," she kidded.

"No way, kiddo. I only love beautiful, talented girls who run fancy boutiques, and are very good to their decrepit old fathers."

"You'll never be decrepit, you old rascal. I feel as if I'm being conned here, but I don't care. I can't wait to get up to the lake. Thanks for pushing me into it. It's just what I need right now. I'll call you back in a while, after I talk to Steffie."

She was quite excited by the time she called Steffie. This was just the break she needed. It had been a very tough summer, what with Scott, the shooting, Josh, and then the fiasco with Drew.

She loved their two cottages in Muskoka. It had to be one of the most beautiful places on earth — even better than Niagara Falls. The granite outcroppings, the mix of deciduous and coniferous trees, the clean navy blue water, the slight mist in the morning, the mournful call of the loons, — all combined to form a certain kind of paradise in her mind.

The two cottages were located in a small bay, with a ravine on one side, and dense bush on the other. It was a perfect hideaway, providing almost total privacy. In spite of all the cottages on the lake, it was still relatively wild country. Foxes, raccoons, and even the occasional black bear, roamed freely. Sometimes they would see an old porcupine climb the oak tree outside the dining room window. Friendly little chipmunks scurried and hurried, gathering nuts, and hiding them with such nervous energy, that they looked like tiny Keystone Kops. Hummingbirds flocked to the feeders, and Kitty and her family had always enjoyed sitting for hours in the screened gazebo, watching the wildlife, and hiding from the mosquitoes. It was a peaceful, calm haven, an island of tranquility in an otherwise crazy world. She couldn't wait to get up there.

The big cottage was old, and it had certainly seen better days. It was getting shabby, and constantly needed work. She and the folks were always painting, repairing the dock, fixing the water pump, mending screens. Keeping it in shape was a never-ending chore, but because they all loved cottage country so much, it never seemed too big a deal. Now that her sister Lacey was living so far away in Thunder Bay, it fell to Kitty to help her parents with the cottages whenever she could.

The newer cottage or 'bunky' as they called it, was a little gem. It sat at the top of a slight hill, and was accessed by a winding path through thick trees. From its small cedar deck, they had a fantastic view of the lake. They called it "Treetops," and Kitty had always thought that it would make a perfect honeymoon cottage. There was a Muskoka stone fireplace in the living room, and a big picture window. The large bedroom had windows on two sides, looking into the woods. There was a pristine ensuite with a big shower enclosure, and a tiny kitchen well equipped with the necessities. It was totally self-contained, although it shared the septic tank and water pumps with the main cottage.

Being electrically heated and well insulated, the bunky was a cosy retreat, even in the coldest winter. The family sometimes went up for a winter week-end, to do some cross country skiing and skidooing. It was such a perfect lit-tle retreat, that Kitty was amazed and somewhat cross that her dad had offered to rent it out to a total stranger. Since that stranger was Mitchell Donaldson, however, her favourite author, it was easy to forgive him.

Things seemed to fall into place perfectly. It was as if Kitty was definitely meant to go. Steffie and Cleo could handle the shop with no trouble. Cleo was proving to be a gem. She was such a hard worker. Steffie would stay in Kitty's house to look after the cats. They got all the petting and cuddling they could handle when she was around, and she always had special treats for them. They would both be fat as little piggys by the time that Kitty returned.

Just once, shortly after Kitty got her two cats from Cassie's cattery, she decided to take them to the cottage with her. What a mistake! In fact it had been a total disaster. Because they were house cats, they had to be kept inside the cottage at all times. When the family went out in the boat, or sat down on the dock, the cats howled their displeasure at being abandoned. Their clarion calls could be heard all over the lake. Only the sounds of the boats and seadoos could drown them out. Even the birds seemed to stop singing, in order to listen to the Hallelujah chorus. At night, when the loons made their haunting calls, the cats answered with plaintive yowls, which were guaranteed to wake the dead.

One time, when a visitor didn't shut the door quickly enough, Petie Pie escaped into the wild unknown. They spent the afternoon searching and call-ing in frantic and pleading tones. They were tortured by mental pictures of him being attacked by a raccoon or a fox. After several hours of unadulterated terror, they heard a sheepish meowing, and looked up to see two wide green eyes peering down at them from the very highest branches of the oak tree. Petie Pie, in a moment of madness, had climbed the tree in delight, but had no idea how to get down. He had apparently watched their frenzied search all afternoon, too frightened, or possibly too embarrassed, to make a sound. Lit-tle Miss Rosie had stationed herself at the screen door, watching the activities, and howling at top volume all afternoon, as if begging them to find her companion.

Kitty's dad had to drag out the big ladder, and while she and two friends held it steady, he had climbed up and rescued a very subdued cat. Petie had clung to her dad's shoulder, as he climbed back down, but when he was safely back in the cottage, he stalked haughtily away, as if they had all made a huge fuss about nothing. The cats were never invited back to Muskoka.

Besides giving her a great chance to relax and enjoy the beauty of cottage country, Kitty realized that this would be an opportune time to distance herself from Drew. After the incident in the restaurant, he had called a couple of times, obviously expecting her to apologize. Kitty told him very clearly that she didn't see any future in their relationship. Drew wasn't willing to accept that. They had parted on unfortunate terms, and she felt badly about it. She now remembered how kind and reliable he had been the night Steffie was shot, and she would have liked to keep him for a friend.

The idea of meeting a well-known author — her very favourite author, was exhilarating and exciting. Grinning at her own foolishness, she planned to pack her copies of his books, hoping to have him autograph them. There was very little information about him on the dust jackets, except that he was an extremely private person. She pictured herself sitting having a drink with him on the dock or in the gazebo, and answering all his questions about cottage life and cottage country. Maybe he would want her to go in the canoe with him, to show him some of the beautiful spots. This was definitely going to be a week to remember.

CHAPTER 24

▼

In her brown shorts and yellow tank top, with gold sandals on her feet, Kitty looked and felt great, as she sang along with her cds on the four hour drive to the cottage. She set out at six in the morning, planning to be there long before Mitch Donaldson was due to arrive at noon. She would get his small cottage aired out and dusted, and have the bar frig turned on. She would put the two sun chairs out on the deck, and have the cottage look very welcoming for him. If she had time to pick them, she would put a nice bouquet of wild flowers on the table in the bunky. This was going to be such a fun week.

Her dad had given the mystery writer the keys, and a hand-drawn map, but Kitty wanted to be there first. That way, she could have the water turned on, and both cottages looking really good. After all, this guy was quite a celebrity. She would show him where everything was, and how things worked. Maybe he had never been to a cottage before. He might be a totally city-bred type of person. Maybe he didn't know that you had to shut the doors quickly, so that the nosy little chipmunks, and the voracious mosquitoes didn't get in. Perhaps he wouldn't realize that you couldn't leave any garbage around, for fear of attracting the black bears. On the other hand, maybe he knew all about cottage life, and perhaps it was just Muskoka that was new to him. Well, she would soon find out.

As she finally turned onto the half mile of cottage road, she was delighted as always with the profusion of wildflowers, which swayed and danced gently as the car drove by. She had never been sure of the distinction between weeds and wildflowers, she just knew that she loved them all. She sometimes envied the fact that Steffie could paint so beautifully. These flowers were definitely worth painting.

Kitty was thankful that she had never brought Scott up here. Of course that was more good luck than good management. They had dated in April and May, and that was black fly season in cottage country. Fighting off myriads of biting black flies would not have been conducive to a romantic interlude. On the other hand, Kitty thought with a grin, that she would have loved to see Scott bitten to a pulp.

After the lovely drive on this gorgeous summer morning, she was dismayed to see a strange car parked behind the main cottage. Shit!! Mitch Donaldson, the mysterious author of mystery books, was already here! What was he doing arriving so early? He had specifically told her dad that he would be there around noon. Now she felt cross. She had wanted to be unpacked and organized before he showed up. The cottage was supposed to be aired, blinds open, sunshine streaming in, when he first saw it.

She sat in the car, frowning, and trying to decide what to do. Should she unpack the trunk, go in and comb her hair etc., then go up the hill to Treetops? She couldn't see him around anywhere, so he was either up at the bunky, or down at the dock. Maybe she should run right up there now, and apologize for arriving after her guest. She didn't feel like apologizing though. After all, he wasn't supposed to be here till noon. Still, she wanted to be gracious. Heaving a sigh, and glancing in the car mirror, to be sure that she was presentable, she started up the path.

What if he was already hard at work, and was one of those authors who hated to be interrupted when the muse was whispering in his ear? No, she decided he wouldn't have had time to start working yet. Besides, who could stay inside and write on such a glorious sunny morning? He had likely just arrived moments before she had, and he would be enthusiastically exploring the little cottage, and unpacking.

Rounding the bend in the path, she gasped at her first sight of Mitchell Donaldson, famous author, standing buck naked on the deck, rubbing his hair with a big towel. He had obviously been swimming already, and was thoughtfully drying himself before going into the cottage.

Uttering an involuntary gasp of surprise, Kitty half turned to retreat back down the path. The naked man, however, whirled around to face her, and in so doing, gave her the full monty! "Wow" was her first impression.

Deftly wrapping the towel around his waist, he scowled at her, then lifted one eyebrow in a rather haughty manner. How could he act haughty when he was standing there in the nude, she wondered. Surely he was the one at a disadvantage. She noticed his strong jaw and brown eyes, before the rich deep voice dryly remarked, "Well, don't be shy now that you've had a good look. I didn't realize there were Peeping Toms in this area."

Was he laughing at her or being sarcastic? She wasn't sure, but it got her dander up. Was he actually accusing her of deliberately peeking at him? The nerve of the guy! She had to admit though that the one quick peek had been awfully good. He was a hunk, no doubt about it. He left all of her male friends far behind in the looks department.

Now feeling foolish, Kitty sputtered, "Excuse me. I'm so sorry. I didn't mean to startle you. I was just coming up to introduce myself. I'm Kitty Winfield. Dad couldn't come because he's hurt his back, so I'm here in his place. It's too bad you got here first, but we weren't expecting you till around noon." She was definitely babbling, as he continued to frown down at her. Now she was at a disadvantage, looking up at him from the path, plus she was getting a crick in her neck.

"Actually," he said slowly, with a deepening scowl, if that was possible, "the point was for me to be alone up here. I'm sure I made that quite clear to your father. I certainly wasn't expecting to have a baby sitter sneaking around."

Kitty couldn't believe her ears. This guy was pretty arrogant. What right did he have to talk to her like that, just because he was some two-bit writer. She felt like telling him to pack up and leave.

"Sneaking around!" she exclaimed in dismay and anger. "I certainly wasn't sneaking around. I rushed up here to say hello, and make sure that everything was in good shape for you. You weren't supposed to be here till noon." Oh shit, why did she keep harping on noon. Things were going all wrong. She needed to start again. Taking a big breath to calm herself, she twisted her pretty mouth into a phoney smile. "I'll leave you to get dressed now, and if there's anything you need, you can find me down in the main cottage. Believe me, I'm not here to spy on you. I have more interesting things to do. Actually I'm doing my dad a favour. I came all the way up here from Niagara Falls just because he wanted everything to be nice and fresh, and he wanted me to get the water going for you. You'll have all the privacy you want."

With that, she turned and stomped angrily down the path, her face flushed, and her heart thumping. She felt foolish, and knew that his first impression of her certainly would not be that she was interesting or charming or intelligent. She had reacted to his rudeness like a silly teenager, but he had really yanked her chain. She wasn't sure, but she thought she heard a deep chuckle, as she rounded the bend.

Shoot, why hadn't she said something more gracious, more saavy, more personable, than her foolish "I have more interesting things to do." He would think she was a total moron. She could have laughed and said, "I'm so sorry I startled you. I'm Kitty Winfield, and I'm delighted to meet you. You look great in the buff." Surely that would have made him laugh. Or she could have said, "Look, I'll meet you down in the cottage, and I'll show you around. Don't bother to put your clothes on." That would have caught his attention. She laughed at the nonsensical notion. Well, no point in worrying about it now. Kitty was determined not to let the unfortunate meeting ruin this sunny day. She would straighten things out with him later, after they had both calmed down.

She kept thinking of it, however, as she got the water turned on for both cottages, carefully following the instructions which her dad had written several years ago, when she first came up here on her own.

She then unpacked the car, opened the main cottage windows, and changed into the little pink bikini, which she had bought for that barbecue at Keith's cottage. Thinking of that party and of Drew, cheered her up somewhat. Compared to this arrogant, pompous jerk, Drew appeared pretty nice. Maybe she had been too critical of him. Still, she had to be honest. There was something about Mr. Mitchell Donaldson, "author extraordinaire", which had made her cheeks flush. He was extremely handsome, younger than he looked on his book covers, and what a body! With that one quick glance, she had been aware of long legs and tight buns. He had a lanky frame, and a sharply defined jaw line. When he turned to face her, she had seen a broad chest liberally covered with curly black hair, a flat stomach, and a, well, with a grin she told herself not to go any further.

While making fresh hummingbird food for the two feeders, she noticed the telltale signs that a mouse had been around. She washed the counters thoroughly before making her sandwich, and thought with satisfaction that at least the bunky had always been totally mouse-proof.

With fresh ham on a crusty bun, and an ice cold coke, she was headed down the steps to the dock, when she remembered the chipmunks. How could she possibly forget them, when they were scampering around in antici- pation of a treat. Going back into the cottage, she broke open a fresh bag of sunflower seeds, and put little piles of them in various places around the gazebo and picnic table. The chipmunks were right behind her, stuffing their fat little cheeks as fast as she could put down the seeds.

She had a quick swim, before eating her lunch. The cold clear water felt wonderfully refreshing on her hot body. Then she sat in one of the old com- fortable wooden Muskoka chairs, munching her sandwich, and enjoying the beauty and tranquility of the lake. The water was so clear, that she could see small fish zipping here and there. One large hairy dock spider dared to make an appearance between two boards, but one good stamp of her foot sent him racing away. She remembered how scared she was of them when she was a kid. Now they were just an interesting nuisance — not even that, really. She knew that they wouldn't bite, and were much more afraid of her, than she was of them.

A mother Merganser came floating by, followed by her six little ducklings. Kitty made a mental note to bring down some crackers for them, and watched, as they made their way slowly all around the shore of the bay. Not far out, she could see two loons, diving, then popping up, diving again and again. The fishing must be really good in that spot, she thought contentedly. She wished that the famous author was down here to see the wildlife, and to enjoy the beauty of Muskoka, but maybe he was too arrogant and full of him- self to appreciate nature.

She had promised to call her dad that night, to tell him how things were at the cottage, and she wondered idly what she would tell him about their cranky guest. She definitely would not go into detail about their first encoun- ter. She smiled, as she remembered those tight buns and the surprised look in his dark brown eyes, as he whirled to face her. She didn't know which one of them had been more surprised. Standing there in all his naked glory, he was even better endowed than Scott. This thought made her squirm a bit, and she chided herself for being so foolish. He was likely married, with a whole tribe of kids. Humming contentedly, as she added more suntan lotion to her arms and legs, she finally closed her eyes.

Lazily, her mind drifted to long ago summers spent right here, with so many other cottage kids. How privileged they had been, yet they had taken it all for granted. Her friend Josie Sheffield had lived three cottages away, around the curve of the bay, and they were able to wave to each other from their docks.

She and Josie had loved to canoe all over the lake, and every year they had entered the regatta, and usually won the teen pairs canoe races. Josie was a bit wild, but oh what great times they had water-skiing, swimming, singing around a campfire, fighting off the mosquitoes, which seemed to grow bigger and hungrier in cottage country than anywhere else.

As they grew into their teens, they all sat around the campfires drinking beer, and making plans for the future, their thoughts as light and bright as the sparks from the fire. They all felt as if they would live forever, young, beautiful, full of energy. How had those treasured days slipped by so quickly?

Josie had been the wildest of the group, and had found herself pregnant the summer before university. Undaunted, she had the baby, a perfect little boy named Steven, and after parking him with her parents, she went to university one year behind her friends. Now she was married to a terrific guy who was with the Ontario Provincial Police, and they came up to the family cottage as often as they could. Wouldn't it be great if they happened to come up this week! She hadn't seen Josie since last year.

It was getting hotter and hotter, with not even the whisper of a breeze. The air was so still, that Mother Nature seemed to be holding her breath, but for what? Kitty fancied that she could hear the wildflowers actually growing, stretching their stems and their petals toward the powdery blue sky. Suddenly the silence was broken by the ululating drone of the cicadas.

She dozed off for a while, the heat making her lethargic and somnolent. Eventually, she had another refreshing swim to cool off, before going up to the cottage to get dressed, and make herself a salad for dinner. There was no sign of the famous author. Maybe he was still sulking in the bunky. Well, it was his loss, if he had stayed in all day just to avoid her. The dock and the canoe and the wonderful lake were here for him to enjoy. She certainly wasn't stopping him, but she wasn't going to deprive herself of the pleasures of the cottage, just so as to keep out of his way. She wouldn't bother him, but she wouldn't hide from him either.

When Kitty called her dad after supper, she told him that Mitchell Donaldson had arrived before she had. She did not mention that when she first laid eyes on him, he was totally naked. She did say, however, that he seemed to be extremely rude, and full of his own importance. "Dad, he may be a celebrated author, but he certainly doesn't have the charm that Scott had." Damn, why had she thought of Scott? Wouldn't she ever get him out of her head? Dragons lurked back in that Scott era, and she didn't want to go down that road any more.

After a slight pause, he father replied, "Well, Kitty girl, maybe he has the integrity and decency which Scott didn't have."

"Touché," she laughed, just as she looked up, and saw with horror, that the author was standing at the screen door. The look on his face told her without a doubt that he had heard her nasty remarks. Oh Lord, she was stepping in doo doo every time she came in contact with this guy. It was going to be a long week! Hastily saying good-bye to her dad, she went to the door.

"I'm sorry to bother you," he said stiffly, "but the bulb is out in the desk lamp, and I need that light. I can't work with just a center light."

"Come on in, and I'll see if we have some extras." Kitty was as dry and formal as he was. She was so embarrassed that he had overheard her conversation. Should she mention it? No. It would be better to ignore it, and try to start all over again.

Handing him a pack of bulbs, she was surprised when they said simultaneously, "Look, I'm sorry about this morning." They both stopped, and laughed uncomfortably. Mitch was the first to speak. "It's just that I expected to be here alone. I need total peace and quiet when I write, and I can't have distractions. Your father led me to believe that I would have the place to myself. I know I was rude, but you did take me by surprise."

If this was an attempt at an apology, it wasn't working. Kitty felt her quick temper bubbling up again. "I assure you that you'll have all the peace and quiet you could possibly want. I'll do nothing but tiptoe all week, and I'll do my best to keep the loons quiet too," she added sarcastically, as she ushered him to the door.

Oh hell, now I've done it, she berated herself. Whatever had made her say that? She wasn't being very hospitable, and she regretted her smart-ass remarks. Should she run up the hill after him and apologize? Surely they could start all over again. If they didn't clear the air, it was going to be a very awkward week. She hesitated, then decided to let things go until the morning. Tonight she felt too cranky and ashamed of herself to be able to face him. They would straighten everything out in the morning, but tonight, well, "Frankly, my dear, I don't give a damn," she muttered under her breath, as she locked up the cottage and snuggled into bed.

CHAPTER 25

▼

Sunday morning, Kitty drove over to the little stone church in Windermere. It was very old, and as pretty as a postcard in a Victorian shop. She was disappointed that she wasn't going to have the chance to show it to Mr. High and Mighty Author. Maybe he could have worked it into his novel. Oh well, it's his loss, she told herself, as she settled in a pew near the front, beside an open window.

On this glorious Muskoka morning, the sun was shining, and the air was clear and fragrant. She enjoyed the gentle breezes wafting through the church. There was a visiting minister this morning, and as the sermon dragged on and on, Kitty gazed out the window, and focused on the tiny popcorn clouds scattered here and there throughout the bright blue sky. She thought that it was going to be a great afternoon for boating.

She stayed for tea and cookies after the service, and talked to some of the cottagers she had known all her life. She didn't, however, mention that there was a famous author renting their small cottage. He would likely throw a hissy fit, if any of her friends showed up to meet him.

Before heading back to the cottage, she walked down the little village street to Windermere House, the grand old lady of Muskoka resorts. So many of the old resorts had been lost to fire, and this one too had been burned in a dreadful fire one winter, when a Hollywood movie company was here shooting a film. Fortunately, with the help of the insurance and the locals, Windermere House had been totally rebuilt exactly as it had been, except, of course, with newer materials, and a topnotch sprinkler system. The large pictures of the original resort hotel in all its glory, then the same resort the night it burned, and then the newly rebuilt building, were fascinating to see. They were framed, and hanging side by side in the hotel lobby.

Kitty always liked to check out the delightful little gift shop for new ideas. She often found merchandise, which she knew would sell quickly in her boutique. She considered staying for lunch on the long front porch, which gazed out over the beautifully manicured lawns and flower gardens, and down to the sparkling waters of Lake Rosseau. Thinking about it for a few seconds, while she enjoyed the view, she decided against it. In the back of her mind was the idea that if she saw Mitch Donaldson back at the cottage, she would ask him to join her for lunch. She was feeling pretty silly about the way she had reacted yesterday, and wanted to make amends.

Driving the short distance back, she couldn't help musing about him. What made a handsome, intelligent, talented man so seemingly abrasive? Was he just hiding behind this rough exterior, in order to keep fans at arm's length? Did he think he was better than everyone else because he was a successful author, or was it simply his artistic temperament?

She wondered whether he had a wife or girlfriend. Who the heck would put up with his moodiness and rudeness? She shook her head in disbelief. He certainly wasn't what she had expected.

It would have been so nice to sit on the dock or in the gazebo, and share a glass of wine with him. She could have asked him a little about his writings, and given him a special insight into the world of cottage country. He was the first author she had ever met, but so far she wasn't too impressed. Actually, he was a big disappointment. Any personality he might have, had been kept well hidden yesterday.

Then, as she drove up the cottage road, she rebuked herself. After all, it was Sunday, and she had just come from church. She should give the guy another chance. He was likely very embarrassed at being caught naked like that, and he was disappointed that he was not all alone and private, the way he had expected to be. Also, hearing the things she was saying about him to her dad, wouldn't have endeared her to him. He must be thinking she was a mean spirited, sharp-tongued harridan.

Well, if she saw him, she would invite him to lunch. Kitty wasn't one to hold a grudge, and she was very intrigued with this handsome, taciturn author. She didn't want to go up to the bunky, however, in case she caught him in the nude again. She grinned as she drove slowly up the winding driveway. He had been quite a sight. Yes, maybe she would go up to invite him for lunch. They would make a fresh start.

"Shoot!" she exclaimed, when she realized that Mitch Donaldson's car was gone. She was amazed at how disappointed she felt, and the feelings nagged at her all day, as she listened and watched for the car, which didn't return until well after dark.

Monday morning dawned fresh and clear. Kitty packed her book, and a couple of soft drinks, and headed out in the big inboard bow rider. She flew at top speed all over the dark, sparkling water, enjoying the breeze in her face, and waving happily at other boaters.

There was nothing like being out in the boat, to make you feel totally at peace with yourself, she thought. Eventually she stopped the engine, and began reading her book, and sipping a coke. This was the life. She could stay here forever.

Somehow her mind drifted to the Black Sheep, and she wondered whether he could possibly be anyone she knew. She still couldn't remember who it was who had bought the little black sheep so many weeks ago, and it was always nipping at the back of her mind, like a pesky little dog.

She had such a good memory for details, so why wouldn't this memory show itself, so to speak? Was her subconscious deliberately hiding it from her? Who knew? Well, today, at this moment, who cared? She put the Black Sheep onto her mind's shelf for later, and looked around at the beautiful scenery.

Two young kids flew past on seadoos, a little too close for comfort. Those things were like giant buzzing bees, zipping here and there, and making such a racket. The turbulence rocked the boat, as they disappeared around an island. There didn't seem to be many regulations to control seadoos, which were just snowmobiles made for the water, and she was alarmed at how many young kids could be seen driving them, going way too fast and not wearing life jackets.

She wondered what the parents were thinking of, putting these potentially lethal watercraft in the hands of inexperienced children. She remembered how her parents had taught both her and her sister Lacey, to drive the boat with respect and skill, and they were never allowed out on the seadoos unless they were wearing their lifejackets.

The boat was rocking gently, and soon Kitty closed her eyes. In a moment she was dozing. She hadn't bothered to drop the anchor, preferring to just drift for a while. She really had not intended to doze, though.

She awoke with a start, and realized that she had drifted pretty close to shore. As she looked around, and prepared to start the engine, she noticed with surprise, that her red canoe was moving slowly along the shoreline. Mitch Donaldson was paddling, and looking with interest, at the cottages along this strip of the lake. Every once in a while he would stop, and make some notes in a little book. Without thinking, Kitty waved and called, "Hi there, how's the canoeing?"

The author barely paused. He glanced up, frowned, then gave her a half-hearted wave, and kept right on paddling.

What an insufferable, unfriendly man. What the heck was his problem? Well, that was the last friendly gesture she would make. She'd be sure to keep as far away from him as she could. This was becoming really embarrassing. What a shame though. She had to admit that he was very attractive, with that long lanky frame, and that concentrated look about him. If he would only loosen up and smile once in a while, he would be gorgeous.

Maybe he was just a different person while he was engrossed in his book. Her dad had seemed to like him, but as far as she was concerned, he was no Mr. Congeniality, more like Mr. Horse's Ass. Kitty wasn't used to being ignored by attractive men, and she was surprised that it hurt, as well as angered her. Starting the engine, she took off at full speed, hoping that her wake would tip him right out of the canoe. She didn't bother to look back, as she headed for the cottage.

On Tuesday and Wednesday, she heard the author's car starting up before she was even out of bed. Both days he was gone for hours. She figured he must be driving around the area, soaking up local colour. It would have been such fun if she could have gone with him. She knew so many interesting people and places in the area. There were some families who had lived and cottaged here for the last sixty years. They were the ones to whom he should be talking, if he wanted to absorb the rich and colourful history and feel of the place. He didn't know what he was missing by being so withdrawn.

Thursday morning Kitty was up very early, heading down to the dock, with her book and her mug of tea. It was one of Mitch's books, which she was re-reading. Somehow, she couldn't reconcile the wonderful dialogue, the insightful characterizations, the explicit love scenes, with this taciturn, somewhat glum man. She just couldn't wrap her mind around the tremendous difference in how he wrote and how he acted.

Well, in spite of the unfriendly author, she was having a marvellous rest, and enjoying her vacation. She just wished that Steffie could have come up with her, or even Cassie or Vickie. They were all good friends, and enjoyed their times together. That gave her a good idea. Sometime this summer, the four of them would come up for a couple of days. What a ball they would have! She felt quite excited, as she started making plans.

As she came down the stairs to the dock in her bare feet, she was surprised to see Mitch Donaldson sitting cross-legged on the dock, a tiny chipmunk in his hand. He was talking quietly, as he very gently petted it. The little fellow seemed to be hypnotized. He was certainly enjoying the attention, because he wasn't making any move to run away. Kitty could hardly believe it. She stood on the stairs, totally still, watching the author, who was oblivious to her presence.

Finally the chipmunk scampered away, and Mitch took off in the canoe. Kitty waited till he was around the point, before she came down the rest of the stairs. Somehow she felt that she had almost intruded on a very private moment.

This was a side of the aloof author, which she hadn't expected. She knew from experience, that it took a lot of patience and gentleness to coax a chipmunk to sit in your hand. She had been trying it for years, and had only occasionally succeeded. They were like little wind-up toys, and were perpetual motion. This guy couldn't be all bad, and she decided to try again with him. She was quite intrigued, and felt she just had to break through his cool exteriour. The picture of Mitch sitting on the dock, chipmunk in hand, took up permanent residence in her mind.

That afternoon Kitty called a friend, who now lived in Bracebridge, and went into town to meet her for coffee. Mitch's car was still gone when she returned. He was either deliberately avoiding her, or their paths were simply not crossing. Well, she had promised him that she would keep out of his way, and she had certainly kept her word. That didn't keep her from wondering about him though.

What kind of woman would appeal to him? It would have to be someone who was quiet, and faded into the wallpaper, yet she couldn't imagine him with anyone like that. With his looks, he might have a string of girlfriends, or maybe a wife. It was likely that he had a gloriously gorgeous redhead or brunette, with long legs and a perfect figure. Kitty had long legs and a pretty good figure, but she had these silly, unruly honey blond curls. She wasn't exactly elegant, and she was sure that the haughty Mr. Donaldson would demand an elegant woman. She sighed as she chided herself for even thinking such nonsense. He would be gone on Saturday, and that would be the end of it.

In the meantime, there sat the canoe, tied to the dock. She couldn't ask him for permission to use her own canoe, that would be ridiculous, but it annoyed her to see it sitting there. His deal had been that he was renting the bunky and the canoe, but oh, how she longed to get out for just one trip in it. Well, tomorrow morning she would get up at the crack of dawn, and go for just a little paddle around the bay. He'd never know. She would have it back and tied up, before he opened those big brown eyes.

CHAPTER 26

▼

Thursday evening Kitty sat in the gazebo, drinking her wine, and watching a flying squirrel at the bird feeder. They were fairly rare around here, so Kitty was delighted to watch this little guy with the big bush-baby eyes. She shone the flashlight right on him, and he stared back at her solemnly, his eyes reflecting the light.

She was thinking about Drew, and how unfortunate it was that their relationship had gone south so quickly. He could have been a great older brother type of friend. She felt a tad guilty about throwing the wine on him, but he had made her very angry, and she did have a temper, which she usually kept under control. She had always enjoyed Drew's company, when he wasn't sulking about something. He was likely dating someone else already, and might never forgive her for the restaurant incident, although he had called her a few times since then. She was really the one who was dumping the friendship. Oh well, she shrugged mentally. C'est la vie.

When she heard the noise on the path, she thought it was the author coming down from the bunky with another complaint. Her heart started pounding, however, when she realized that it was a full grown black bear. If he got between her and the cottage, she could be in real trouble. He could rip through the screened gazebo like a chainsaw through a curtain. His claws were like can openers. She had once watched a bear rip the lid off a can of sunflower seeds, which were meant for the chipmunks.

Knowing that bears were frightened by loud, unexpected noises, she jumped up, and stamping her feet like an Indian on the warpath, she began shouting and clapping her hands. Mostly she just scared herself. The startled bear, however, did stop in his tracks and peer at her, before taking off past the gazebo, and down the road behind the cottage. On some subconscious level, she was amazed at how fast it could run. A human would never be able to outrun a bear, if it was in a chasing mood.

Kitty shakily picked up the wineglass, which she had dropped in her mad dance, and was about to rush for the safety of the cottage, when Mitch Donaldson came flying down the path.

"What's wrong, are you okay?" he cried with concern. She smothered a giggle, as she saw that he was brandishing an axe.

"I'm fine," she gasped, feeling foolish now that the danger was passed. "It was a bear — a big one. I managed to scare him with my wild shouting and stomping. I scared myself too," she laughed shakily.

"Shit, I thought it was the Black Sheep," he replied with a laugh. "Where is he, which way did he go?" he asked with more interest than concern now. Maybe he would put this incident into his book, she thought sourly.

"He went down the road," she pointed. "I doubt that he'll be back this way too soon. Bears stay away from people unless they are really hungry. Luckily this one looked quite well fed." She thought that she must have sounded like a mad woman, with all her shouting and stomping. She felt extremely foolish now. She must have been awfully loud, to tear the author away from his writing.

"Thanks very much for coming to my rescue. I hope I didn't make you lose your train of thought." Then, smiling engagingly, and in an unexpected and offhand gesture, she opened the gazebo door, and asked him if he'd like to join her for a glass of wine. "I spilled mine all over myself," she added ruefully, "and I need something to calm my frazzled nerves. Besides, I'd appreciate the company, just in case he decides to come back."

He hesitated for a moment, and she instantly regretted the invitation. Here comes another put-down she thought, but to her surprise he replied, "Sure, that would be very nice. I need a break anyway. I've been writing for hours."

Kitty dashed into the cottage for the wine bottle, and two fresh glasses, and hastily poured some mixed nuts into a dish. Returning to the gazebo, she said, "Hope red is okay for you. I tend to drink white wine during the day, and switch to red at night." Oh Lord, she thought, I must sound like a real wino. "I do have white if you would prefer it." She knew that she was babbling a bit, but the combination of the bear and the author had her rattled.

"This is great, thanks. I like Cabernet Sauvignon," he added, glancing at the label. Actually, Mitch didn't like any kind of wine, and rarely drank it. He asked himself what he was doing here, drinking wine with this beautiful girl, who seemed to have a chip on her shoulder. He knew that she didn't like him, after hearing her talking to her father. I'll bet her boyfriend has his hands full with her, he told himself. Then he got the strange feeling that he would love to run his fingers through that thick mane of honey blond hair. The thought came unbidden to his mind, and he couldn't shake it.

They sat in awkward silence at first, but gradually began chatting. Finally, after his second glass of what he considered pure vinegar, he muttered, "Look, I'm really sorry if I've been rude. I'm working on a deadline with this book, and when you arrived so unexpectedly," here he chuckled and shook his head ruefully, "I just feared that you would totally disrupt my entire week. It made me angry, after I had come up here specifically looking for privacy. I thought you might be one of those ditsy fans who won't let go. Besides, I was embarrassed that you had caught me 'in flagrante delicto' as it were, and I didn't know how long you had been standing there. I tend to withdraw into a world of my own when I'm working on a book, but I know that's no excuse for rudeness. We've only got one day left. Could we start all over, do you think?"

This was the most conversation she had heard from him the entire week. Kitty was delighted to say, "Sure, why not?" as they sat chatting in a more comfortable way. She was happy to be able to answer all his questions about cottage country and cottage life. This was just the sort of thing she had pictured, before they got off to such a bad start.

"You know," he said, speaking slowly and deliberately, "I'm just realizing that no story about Muskoka would be complete without the wildlife. There's so much of it, and it's so varied."

She sat with her wineglass half-way to her mouth. "Well, if it's a murder mystery you're writing, how are you going to work in all the wildlife? Of course you could always have your heroine killed off by a big black bear." She looked at him as she said it, hoping to see him smiling too. He was one serious guy. She wondered whether he ever let down his defences, and had any fun.

"Actually, I'm thinking more of the back-ground for the over-all feeling of Muskoka. It seems to me that it's much more than perfect sunsets and sunrises, deep blue water, small rocky islands, cocktail parties on someone's deck, big old holiday resorts. That's only scratching the surface.

You've got the spoiled rich kids bombing around the lakes in daddy's big boat, there are the water-ski shows, the wonderful old style general stores, the artists' studios. I could go on and on. I love the way that the elegant birch and the majestic pines form canopies over the roads and the pink granite. This Precambrian shield is amazing. The whole picture is so mysterious and yet so peaceful."

Kitty nodded, but didn't say anything. She was contemplating what he had said, and silently agreeing with him.

Mitch seemed to be in a talking mood. Maybe it was the wine. "But then," he continued, "underlying all this, we have the animals. I get the impression from people with whom I've spoken this week, that cottagers spend half their time trying to keep the squirrels and the mice out, and don't forget the ever present chipmunks. Those red squirrels chew up the wires, and cause all kinds of trouble, the raccoons get into the garbage on a regular basis, the mosquitoes are a constant challenge, some areas have snakes, some have bears." Here he finally laughed, and raised his glass to her.

"Obviously I've been talking to a lot of the locals. You know, it seems to me that this constant give and take between the cottagers and the wildlife, is an integral part of the Muskoka mystique. You can't have one without the other. It must be a continuous learning experience, trying to live in harmony with the critters, big and small. Muskoka is nature at its finest, coupled with man at his craziest, yet somehow it works. There's an ambiance here that I'm not sure I'll be able to capture," he said, a little frown creasing his forehead.

Kitty suspected he had forgotten she was there. It seemed that he was talking to himself, working things out in his mind, before putting them on paper. She was amazed at his perception, and inordinately pleased that he had managed to savour and soak up so much of the essence of cottage country, in just a few short days. What a lovely experience, sitting here in the dark, with this handsome, mysterious man, discussing things which might appear later in his works. Wait till she told Steffie. She felt exhilarated and happy, and groaned inwardly at the time they had wasted.

"Oh, I'm sure you'll be able to do it justice," she replied. "You write so wonderfully." Damn, that sounded so fawning and fatuous, like a foolish fan.

As he asked her questions about herself, she poured them more wine, and told him about the boutique, and about Steffie and the shooting. They also talked about the Black Sheep, and about where he might be now. Mitch seemed very interested, when she said that the detectives felt there was a good chance that the strangler had bought at least one of the black sheep in her boutique.

She longed to ask him if he was married, but didn't dare. It was really none of her business, and she couldn't think of a casual way to lead up to it.

Eventually he stood up, and said it was time to head up to the bunky. Was it her imagination, or did he sound a bit regretful? Maybe he was sorry now for letting this entire week slip by without getting to know her. Good! She could have sat out here all night long, talking with this mysterious, attractive, sometimes taciturn, always interesting man.

With three glasses of wine under her belt, she had no qualms about asking him to sign her copies of his books. He seemed pleased at the request, and came into the cottage with her, while she brought them out of the bedroom. He graciously signed them, and it was only after he had gone up to the bunky, that she looked at what he had written. The first two books simply said, "To Kitty, Good Luck, Mitch Donaldson." The third, however, kept her awake for a long time. He had written in his big, bold stroke, "To Kitty, a beautiful girl, and a mystery waiting to be solved."

CHAPTER 27

▼

Steffie's day began as if she had a pebble in her shoe. By later that night, it had become a full-fledged boulder. It was a day which both women would remember for a long time, but for very different reasons. One would have a near fatal adventure, and one would have a heart-stopping, premonition-like nightmare.

When Steffie had wakened, it was barely light, and the birds were just beginning to sing. Miss Rosie was singing too. She was singing the weird, guttural moaning song which all cats do, just before they throw up a hair ball. In this case, she was sitting on the edge of the bed, and managed to barf into Steffie's slippers. That was the first pebble of the day.

With a sigh, Steffie managed to clean up the mess — retching a bit as she did so. What a way to start the day, she thought, as she examined the slippers, and decided that they were now destined for the garbage. Miss Rosie immediately ran out of the bedroom, as if offended by the bad smell.

Down in the kitchen, Steffie made a pot of coffee, but when she opened the cupboard to get herself a mug, she turned too quickly, and whacked herself on the side of the head with the cupboard door. After she stopped seeing stars, she drank her black coffee, which was so hot that it burned her tongue, ate a piece of toast very gingerly, and, glancing at the clock, decided she had time to do a small laundry, before leaving for work.

As she washed her face and brushed her teeth, she gave a startled little gasp. It couldn't be true, but yes, there they were. She had spotted two very grey hairs in amongst her lovely black curls. "Well, shit and damnation," she cried, staring in disbelief at the offending hairs. "How could I have grey hair when I'm only 32 years old?" Then she realized that it was likely all the trauma she had suffered with the shooting. "Guess I'm lucky my entire head hasn't turned white," she muttered to Petie Pie, who had come to the door when he heard her talking. He likely thought that Kitty was home.

Thinking of her hair turning white, made Steffie remember the story, old wive's tale, folklore, or urban legend, whatever it was, of the two men trapped overnight in the old scow on the upper Niagara River. This had happened back in the summer of 1918, and the men knew enough to scuttle the scow after the motor had died. This helped to slow down its inexorable journey toward the brink of the falls. By the time they were finally rescued nineteen hours later, — now this was the part which might by apocryphal — both men had hair which had turned totally white — or so the story goes. The old scow was rusting away, but it was still a real tourist attraction. People loved to look at it, picture the two men trapped on board, and imagine themselves in the same situation. If their hair could turn white over night, Steffie decided that two single grey hairs appearing after the shooting, were not cause for too much concern.

Dressing in her long navy skirt, topped with a pretty pink cotton sweater, she gathered all her whites, and headed for the laundry room. In a rush as usual, she accidentally splashed herself with the bleach. Suddenly, as if by black magic, her lovely outfit was covered with big grayish-white splotches. "Oh great," she muttered in disgust and disbelief. Maybe I can start a new trend — early ugly — she thought angrily, as she hurried upstairs again to change her clothes.

By the time she was ready to leave for work, she was all hot and bothered, but it was nothing to what she felt when she stepped out of the house. Would this heat wave never give up? The heat made everyone so cross, including herself. She wondered what it was doing to the Black Sheep. She also wondered whether the world was going to disappear in a spontaneous combustion pyrotechnic display, with no one left standing to watch it. It was definitely getting hotter every summer. Global warming was taking on new meaning. Walking to the car parked in the driveway, she felt as if she could hear droplets of sweat falling from her face, and sizzling on the pavement.

It didn't help her mood any when the neighbour from next door, Adrian the airline pilot, came hurrying over, waving his arms at her. She liked Adrian, because he was an interesting guy who had been to so many exotic places. Actually, he was a heck of a nice guy, lots of fun, and supposedly never married. Of course, these days you couldn't tell for sure. He might have two wives for all she knew. Flying the international routes gave him lots of opportunities. She sometimes wondered whether he and Kitty might eventually get together. It was always enjoyable talking to him, but now wasn't the time.

"Hi Adrian. I'm just about late for work. What's up?" she asked as graciously as possible, considering her bad mood.

"Well, I've seen you coming and going for the past few days, and I was just wondering what's happened to Kitty. You haven't done away with her have you?" He laughed as he gave her one of his thousand watt smiles. Steffie figured that he must have spent a fortune on his teeth. They were so white and so perfect.

"No. I'm just minding the cats for her. She had to go up to the cottage to do a few things for her father. She'll be back on the weekend."

"Oh good. I was getting a little worried about her. Well, I'm flying out tonight, but I'll be back in three days, so I'll catch up with her then. Talk to you later." He gave her another high powered smile, as she settled behind the driver's seat, and turned on the air full blast. Please God let the air conditioning be working at the boutique today, she thought, as she forgot all about Adrian and his nosy inquiries.

Driving down Morrison to Victoria Avenue, she thought of all the little problems she had already survived, and decided it was likely going to be one hell of a day. In the short space of time since getting out of bed, she had already given herself a good bonk on the head, burned her tongue, discovered some grey hairs, thrown out a favourite pair of slippers — thank you Rosie — and ruined a perfectly nice outfit — thank you bleach. By the time she had arrived at the boutique, she had used up her vocabulary of four letter words, and was making up some new ones.

Before Cleo arrived for work, Steffie decided to give Kitty a quick call. She missed her, and wished that she was at the cottage with her. None of these small mishaps would have happened, if she was lounging on the dock, or paddling around the bay in the canoe, with her friend.

When the phone rang at the cottage that Friday morning, Kitty assumed that it was her dad. Instead, however, it was Steffie, full of forced good cheer and enthusiasm. Actually, her chest and shoulder were aching, and she had already suffered through all the minor disasters. She was feeling a little nervous and ill at ease at this point, wondering what other calamities the day might bring, but she wasn't about to let Kitty know. Hopefully, her friend would be back in Niagara Falls tomorrow, and everything would return to normal.

"Hi Kitty. I called just to test your little pea sized brain this morning. Who played in 'Home before Dark?'"

Kitty laughed. "You stinker. Imagine calling just to try to get the best of me. Well, I know that Jean Simmons was in it, but I can't think who the gal in the gold dress was. Was it Eleanor Parker?"

"No. Guess again." Steffie was feeling better already.

"Okay, I think Efram Zimbalist Jr. was the husband, but who the heck was that gal?"

"Give up?"

"Yes, darn it. You've got me on this one," laughed Kitty.

"Well you were close. It was Rhonda Fleming."

"Oh of course. You old smarty. That was a good movie. We should try to rent it some night."

"Sure. Now tell me, how are things going with Mr. High and Mighty? Have you two kissed and made up yet?"

Kitty had told her about their first unfortunate meeting, when she had caught him in his birthday suit, and they had enjoyed a good laugh over the incident.

"If he's as good looking and well endowed as you say, you've wasted a lot of time, gal," Steffie kidded. "Are you still coming back tomorrow?"

"Either tomorrow or Sunday, I'm not sure. He's leaving on Saturday, though. We talked a bit last night, and he's much nicer than I first thought." Kitty glanced over her shoulder to be sure that Mitch wasn't at the screen door again, where he could overhear the conversation.

"Good. Keep working on him," said her friend. "I'm so mad at myself that I didn't send my copies of his books with you to be autographed. What a numbskull!"

"How are my babies?" asked Kitty, glad to change the subject.

"They're adorable. They've been sleeping with me, and we've played 'chase the ball' till my legs are ready to fall off. I'm three inches shorter than when you left. Guess who does all the chasing?" she added ruefully.

"Been there, done that," laughed Kitty. "Give them some hugs for me."

"Will do. Enjoy the rest of your vacation, and drive home safely. Give me a call if you decide to stay over till Sunday. Everything's great in the shop. Cleo and I are selling lots of stuff.

Oh, by the way, Josh has called twice, insisting that I tell him where you are. He wanted to know whether that 'so-called doctor' (his words, not mine), is with you. I'm not sure I like him, Kit. He's a bit off somehow. He seemed annoyed that I wouldn't tell him much about you, and I was a little afraid that he might come to the house and attack me." She was only half kidding.

"Damn, I'll have to talk to him when I get back. Oh well, I'll think about that tomorrow," Kitty drawled in her best Scarlett voice. "Okay pal, thanks for calling. I'll see you soon. Oh wait, no more murders?"

"No, nothing in the papers. Maybe the Black Sheep has left town or jumped over the falls."

"Let's hope so. Say hi to Cleo, and I'll see you tomorrow or Sunday. Bye-bye."

She had no way of knowing what fate had in store for her during those next two days.

CHAPTER 28

▼

Steffie felt much better after talking to her friend. Her little morning mishaps now seemed funny, rather than disastrous. She had forgotten to mention that Adrian had been asking about Kitty, but that wasn't really important. There always seemed to be a lot of men worrying about where Kitty was, and what she was doing. She certainly did attract them. It was surprising that Mitch Donaldson apparently hadn't fallen for her charms, not yet anyway.

As soon as she and Cleo opened for business, Cassandra Meredith and Vickie Craig walked in. They all chatted for a minute, then Cassie began browsing in the cat corner. Vickie and Steffie continued to chat.

Steffie couldn't help but notice the beautiful sapphire ring, which Vickie was wearing.

"Oh, Vickie, that is the most beautiful ring I've ever seen. It's so unique too in its design." Steffie was holding Vickie's finger to get a really good look at it.

Vickie beamed with delight. "There's a real history to this ring, and it's pretty funny. It's a long story, which I'll tell you some night over a glass of wine. The main part, however, is that, when Cassie inherited all her money, she very generously gave me a cheque for a million dollars. It was because we had been through so much together, and had helped each other out of some serious troubles. She's a wonderfully generous friend, and she wouldn't let me refuse it. Well, I told her right away that the first thing I was going to do, was to buy myself a big sapphire ring. You see, earlier on in the summer, I had pretended to have lost a nonexistent sapphire ring, and that silly story turned out to be the thing which likely saved our lives that night. We had broken into Jordan's house, and he came home early and caught us."

Steffie looked totally confused, but very intrigued.

"Oh, it's too complicated. As I said, I'll tell you all about it the next time we get together."

Just as she was saying this, the front door opened again, and they were both surprised to see Jack Willinger and Bud Lang stroll in. Those two never seemed to be in a hurry.

"Hi there," said Jack. Before Steffie could answer, Cassie looked up and smiled in delight. "Jack," she cried, walking toward him with a lovely smile on her face. Jack looked as pleased and surprised as she was, and he gave her a very affectionate hug. They hadn't seen each other since their somewhat clandestine lunch together at the Riverbend Inn, and each one had missed the other fiercely in the ensuing days.

When Jack eventually let her go, Cassie turned and hugged Bud, who was standing with a silly grin on his face, but a concerned look in his eyes. There was so much apparent electricity between the two of them, that Bud figured he would get a shock if he got too close. Something was going on, and he needed to know what it was all about. He was pretty sure he knew, and he didn't like it. Jack was a happily married man, and Cassie, nice as she was, could be trouble.

Steffie and Vickie watched this unfolding tableau with interest. All three seemed very chummy, but Jack and Cassandra seemed to have eyes only for each other. How intriguing! Steffie knew that they were both married to other people. The town heiress and a Niagara Regional detective, what a combination! She had recently learned that these were the two detectives involved in the big homicide case two years ago, and she also recalled that Cassie and Vickie had saved Jack's life somehow. She didn't recollect all the details, but she knew that there were lots of rumours about Jack and Cassie having been lovers at one time. Was that just gossip, or was there truth to it? She decided that it was likely true, judging by the way they looked at each other.

Steffie and Vickie continued to chat, and forgot about Cassandra and the two detectives. Finally, however, Cassandra and Vickie left, and Jack and Bud approached Steffie.

"Could we go in the office?" Jack asked quietly.

"Of course," said Steffie agreeably. "Cleo, keep an eye on things please, and call me if it gets hectic. I'll be back in a few minutes." Steffie said this over her shoulder, as she led them into the back room. "What's up? Have you found any more black sheep?"

"We haven't made much headway," admitted the usually sanguine Bud. Steffie noticed again that Bud was such a big guy, that he made the small room seem crowded.

"We've found distributors in Vancouver, Toronto and Montreal. That's just made it a lot more complicated, trying to track all the sheep. Have you had any luck remembering who bought them from you?" Jack looked so hopeful, that Steffie hated to burst his bubble.

"Kitty vaguely remembers selling one to someone she knows, but it's just there on the periphery of her mind. She can't get a handle on it yet. I think it will come to her though. She's got a good memory," she added loyally. "On the other hand, I have absolutely no idea how many I sold, or to whom. There were a lot of them around Christmas. I think that Kitty is our only hope, and even if she does remember who it was, he or she likely isn't the Black Sheep anyway."

At the request of the police, they had taken the remaining black sheep off the shelves, and put them aside. If anyone asked specifically for one, they were to take note of the customer, and call the detectives. The first few days after the information regarding the little black sheep had hit the news, the ceramic figurines had been very popular. They had sold several, but always tried to get the names of the customers. In some cases it hadn't worked. Some people were reluctant to give their names, and if they paid cash, there was nothing much Kitty or Steffie could do.

"Don't you have any clues at all?" she asked with surprise and sympathy.

Bud sighed as he shook his head. "We've got next to nothing. It's really a Catch-22 at this point. If he doesn't kill anyone else, we're almost dead in the water. It's a pretty cold trail. The guy is slick, and amazingly careful. You've got to give him credit, because he's left no clues so far. Of course we don't want him to strangle again, but it would likely help us if he did. He's bound to make a mistake sooner or later. It would be so helpful if you could only remember who bought those first bloody damn sheep."

This was the longest speech she had ever heard Bud make. It seemed apparent that the strain was getting to him. He looked harried, and his usually laughing eyes looked tired and bloodshot.

Jack was leaning against the desk, with his arms crossed in a casual attitude. He looked as if his mind was far away. He's likely thinking about Cassie, Steffie thought. Then when Bud stopped talking, Jack smiled at Steffie, as his deep blue eyes gazed at her. "I know either you or Kitty will remember eventually," he encouraged her.

"Maybe you should hypnotize us," Steffie joked.

"That's not a bad idea," said Bud, looking at Jack. "It's been known to work. Let's think about that, partner."

Bud was grasping at straws.

"I gather that Mrs. DeMarco from the church wasn't a good lead?"

Jack laughed ruefully, and straightened up. "No, she still has the little sheep in her bedroom. She says it's her good luck charm. Just about the only thing we are really sure of at this point, is that she is definitely not the killer."

"We're running down every damn clue we have from the public, but there haven't been too many. You know, even some small insignificant piece of info could be pivotal in the overall picture leading us to this guy. If you think of anything at all, or if anyone comes in just acting inquisitive about the ceramic sheep, give us a call. Don't be afraid that it's unimportant. We're beating our heads against a brick wall, here," said Bud, in disgust. "I like the idea of hypnotizing you. We'll give it some serious thought."

Steffie was enjoying talking to the two detectives, and hearing a bit about the case, but just then Cleo stuck her head in the door. "Steff, I need help right now. We've got a busload," she added, with panic in her voice.

"Be right there, Cleo. I'm sorry guys, but duty calls. Believe me, we'll phone you the minute we remember anything, or if anyone tries to buy one. And — I'll talk to Kitty about being hypnotized. If you think it could help, we'd be glad to do it."

"Great. We'll keep in touch."

Steffie thought being hypnotized would be really interesting, and she was sure that Kitty would feel the same way.

Cleo was consumed with curiosity, but they were run ragged with all the tourists, and Steffie never did have to explain or dodge the issue of what the detectives had wanted.

That night Peter Dunlop took Steffie out to dinner at Carpaccio's on Lundy's Lane. Peter talked a bit about real estate and what a fascinating job it could be at times. He liked the challenge, and he liked meeting people.

He hadn't found her the perfect condo yet, but he did seem to be trying, and she had looked at so many, that they were all blending together in her mind.

After a couple of glasses of wine, Steffie told him a bit about her ex and his philandering ways. "He hit me once, but I persuaded myself that everyone deserves a second chance. I don't hold a grudge, and I've always been able to see the other guy's point of view, so I was able to rationalize what he did. The second time, however, it was ballgame over. I'm not stupid, and I'm not a masochist.

I waited till he went out, then I packed a few things, and got the first plane out of Vancouver. We had just moved there from Toronto, and were barely unpacked. First though, I took scissors to all his clothes. That was fun," she added with a laugh. "I really did a hatchet job on his wardrobe. The good thing is that I don't miss him at all. He was just too charming, too glib, too much of an old smoothie." She shook her head in embarrassment at this point. "I'm so sorry. I'm treating you like a father confessor. End of story."

"No, I like listening to you talk. Do you know that those little curls around your face make you look like a painting by Cezanne? I forget what it's called, but I'll show it to you some time. And there's a tiny pulse in your throat, which is fascinating. You're very beautiful, Steffie," he whispered, as he took both her hands in his, and smiled into her eyes.

Oh brother! Steffie felt uncomfortable. Shoot. She liked Peter as a friend, but had no intention of getting involved with anyone for quite a while. Being free again was too much fun. Besides, that line about looking like a painting by Cezanne was baloney. This wasn't going to work if he was going to get all lovey-dovey. Why couldn't guys learn just to be friends first, and wait to see how things progressed?

Steffie knew that she was beautiful. She had known it all her life. Just like any woman, she was very grateful that she was attractive rather than ugly, but beauty definitely came with some drawbacks. The main one was that too many shallow people, specially men, only looked at the exterior package, and never bothered to learn about what was inside. She suspected that Peter might be that way.

She had dressed carefully for this date tonight, not to impress Peter, but just because she enjoyed looking her best. She was wearing a white top with little red roses on the sleeves. She had on a red gypsy skirt of some filmy material, and the uneven, flouncy hemline was accentuated by the high heeled red strappy shoes she was wearing. When she had walked in, she had drawn the attention of every man in the dining room.

Over their Spanish coffees, the subject of the Black Sheep came up. "Aren't you nervous in Kitty's big house all alone?" he queried.

"I am a little," she admitted, "but Kitty isn't scared living there, so why should I be? After being shot, and living to tell about it, I just figure that my time hasn't come yet."

It was hours later when Steffie sat up in bed and turned on the lamp, heart pounding, hands shaking, and tongue stuck to the roof of her mouth. It was likely the visit from the detectives and the discussion with Peter, which had brought on the nightmare.

She tried to recall the details of the awful dream. In it Kitty had been in a place where there were shelves of black sheep all around the room, and they were all glaring at her with malevolent eyes. Kitty was standing alone in the middle of the room, and Jack Willinger was there, but he was outside, looking through the screen door, which was locked. He was yelling at Kitty, trying to warn her, but she couldn't hear him. There was someone lurking in the shadows, and Kitty was trying to hand him one of the little black sheep, which was twisting and turning in her hand.

Steffie knew that whoever was hiding in the shadows, was grinning at Kitty, yet she couldn't see his face. He kept stepping further back into the shadows, as if the corner of the room was expanding outwards, and Kitty kept following him, going slowly into the dark. She was walking inexorably towards the unknown evil lurking so insidiously in the shadows. Steffie knew that if her friend went into that blackness, she would die. She yelled out in her sleep, and wakened in a cold sweat.

The dream made absolutely no sense, but it had left a gnawing fear in Steffie's heart. Should she call Kitty? Of course not. She really felt that her friend was in danger, but if it was all her imagination, Kitty would not appreciate being wakened at 3:30 in the morning. Steffie finally decided that there was absolutely nothing which she could do to protect Kitty at this point and from this distance, so, after making herself a mug of decaf tea, she went back up to bed.

The house seemed big and spooky, and she wished she was back in her own little apartment, where she felt much more secure. "Please God keep her safe," she mumbled, as, clutching Rosie in her arms, she tried to get back to sleep. The scary dream had seemed too real for comfort. Why was she dreaming about Kitty and the Black Sheep? This was the second nightmare she had experienced. Should she tell her friend about the bad dreams?

Steffie lay in the somewhat shaky comfort which follows a nightmare. She was relieved to be awake, and afraid to go back to sleep. She pictured Kitty all alone in that old cottage, with no one nearby except for that unfriendly author. What if he was the Black Sheep hiding out in Muskoka, looking for his next victim? No, that was ridiculous. Still, the normally imperturbable Stephanie Jeanne Chapman tossed and turned for a very long time that night. The nightmare refused to leave her mind, and sleep refused to come.

CHAPTER 29

▼

That same Friday morning, long before Steffie called her, Kitty was out of bed, and headed down to the dock, a cup of tea in one hand, a muffin in the other. The lake was calm and mirror-like, with a gentle mist hovering just above the surface. It was spooky, yet hauntingly beautiful. Soon the rising sun would burn the mist away. She wanted to take the canoe out for a nice paddle around the bays, and have it back in place before Mitch was even awake. She thought of him as "Mitch" now, rather than "that author" or "that arrogant snob."

As she descended the stairs to the dock, she wondered fleetingly whether the bear might be back. They loved to scavenge at this time of the morning, but there was no sign of him, and nothing was going to spoil her sense of well being today — in spite of the invasive, ubiquitous mosquitoes, which were already feasting on her arms and legs.

The morning serenity was broken only by the call of the loons, as they floated gracefully on the water. Kitty stopped on the landing partway down to the dock, to enjoy the view, and to listen to these strange prehistoric birds. She had learned a lot about them from a big book, which she had given her dad one Christmas. She knew, for instance, that although they were graceful on the water, they were cumbersome and ungainly on land. It was something to do with the way their feet were placed, perfect for swimming, but not so good for waddling.

A loon can only take off and become airborne from water. Apparently on the migration south for the winter, the long black stretches of highway look like water from the air. Unfortunately, once a loon lands on the highway, mistaking it for water, he is stuck. He is doomed to perish, unless some kind hearted motorist gives him a lift to the nearest body of water. That, of course, is easier said than done. Kitty often wondered whether she would have the courage to pick up a stranded loon, and whether he or she would fight ferociously, not understanding that it was being helped.

She loved the fact that loons mate for life. Strangely, however, they don't usually return together from their long trip down south. Whichever bird arrives back at the lake first, waits and calls for his mate, until he or she appears. Kitty remembered the summer when she was twelve. One lonely loon arrived back in the bay right in front of the cottage, but his mate never appeared. He called plaintively for weeks, and the haunting sound had made her cry.

Stepping onto the dock, she was amazed to see that the canoe was already gone. She couldn't believe that Mitch would be up at this ungodly hour, it was barely 5:30. She experienced a pang of disappointment, realizing that her early morning jaunt was not to be. Part of her, however, appreciated the fact that Mitch had made the effort to get up early, and experience the mystery and age-old tranquility of Muskoka in the early morning.

Then it occurred to her that maybe he had been up every morning, paddling around the lake, and enjoying its beauty. She didn't want to embarrass him or herself, by letting him know that she had planned to sneak out in the canoe, so she hurried back upstairs, and kept out of sight for a while. The one thought which kept intruding, was how happy she was that old Mr. Bear had come down that path last night, and had given her the opportunity to get to know Mitch a bit.

The rest of the day seemed to pass far too quickly, and Kitty was disappointed that there was no sign of Mitch. After her call from Steffie, she had a swim, lounged on the dock, and finally started packing for her departure the next morning. Later, when she returned to the dock, she saw that the canoe was back, but Mitch was nowhere in sight. Darn it, she had missed him again. Going back up to the cottage, she realized that his car was gone. Was he deliberately avoiding her? She felt inordinately disappointed.

Somehow she had felt that after their lovely visit last night, he might have made an effort to spend a little time with her. Wrong! She had pictured them having lunch together, maybe having a swim, possibly going for a nice boat ride. What a dunce you are, Kit Kat, she chided herself. Don't get any ideas, because he obviously doesn't want to see you. Finishing that book is all he cares about. She wondered though, what he had meant when he wrote that she was a "mystery waiting to be solved." That was a very provocative remark, but now she was totally puzzled and irritated by his seemingly cavalier attitude.

After an uninteresting dinner of leftovers, she went down to the dock with a glass of wine. She just wanted to sit and watch another breathtakingly beautiful Muskoka sunset. She and her family had been watching sunsets since she was a little girl, and they never disappointed her. They made her feel sad and joyful all at the same time. Tonight the sun was hovering there just above the horizon, a glowing, incandescent ball. It created a bold and bodacious sky around it, sending out tendrils of pink, orange and scarlet, and turning the navy water a royal purple. Kitty knew that, suddenly tired of hovering in the sky, the sun would plunge into the welcoming, dark water, and the show would be over, only to be repeated the following night.

On this particular evening, it was still hovering, teasing like a stripper does before disappearing behind the purple curtain. Some menacing dark clouds had suddenly appeared, and were swirling around in angry gyrations. When the wind dropped, there was a spooky stillness on the water. Kitty wondered whether they were in for a fierce summer storm, and made a mental note to close the windows before going to bed.

When she heard someone or something coming down the stairs to the dock, she took a quick glance over her shoulder, just to be sure that it wasn't the bear making a repeat appearance. To her delight, it was Mitch.

"Hi there," he said, in a surprisingly friendly tone. He had a great smile, which made his eyes crinkle. She hadn't seen it all week. The cleft in his chin looked deep enough to stick her tongue into it. This errant thought made her feel giddy.

"I had a lot of last minute things to do today for my book. I wish I had more time to explore. Anyway, do you feel like coming out in the canoe with me?"

Well, isn't that just great, she thought. He's waited all this time to ask me out in the canoe, and now it looks as if it's going to storm.

With real regret she said, "I don't think so. Look at those clouds. I think we're in for some serious weather."

"Nah" he scoffed, squinting up at the sky. "It's been too perfect a day. It wouldn't dare storm now." Then, taking an extra life jacket from the storage box at the bottom of the stairs, he untied the canoe. "Come on, you haven't been out in the canoe all week, and I have a feeling that you are a canoe kind of gal. Look how calm the water is. I'll do all the paddling, and you can just enjoy the rest of the sunset."

Kitty had on shorts and a tank top, and the temperature seemed to be dropping, even as they spoke. She thought it might be too cold out on the lake. Still, she would love to go paddling with him. She had wanted to go canoeing all week, and this would be her last chance. Last chance to what, she wondered. She just felt that she wanted and needed more time with him, before they went their separate ways tomorrow morning. "I don't know," she said doubtfully, gazing at the sky. Somehow, however, she sensed that he wasn't going to give up. This was a man accustomed to getting his own way, so, much against her better judgement, she agreed.

They rode in silence, Mitch paddling, and Kitty relaxing and drinking in the beauty of the night. She had despaired of having any quality time with this arrogant, handsome, intriguing stranger, and now here she was having a lovely canoe ride with him. She hardly dared think about what might come next. How frustrating that this was their last night at the cottage. Would they see each other again? She sincerely hoped so. She had a funny feeling about Mitch Donaldson. Deep down, she had been very attracted to him right from the very first, even when they had started off so badly. Now, after their time in the gazebo last night, she sensed that he was attracted to her too.

Shaking herself out of her daydreaming, she was abruptly aware that they were no longer hugging the shore, but were in fact heading out across an open stretch of water. Turning to look at Mitch over her shoulder, she asked in dismay, "Where are you going?"

"I thought we'd go out around that little island, and then head back," he answered calmly, giving her a half grin.

"But Mitch, it's much rougher out here, and the wind is coming up. Believe me, I know this lake, and I don't think we should go that far." Damn, she sounded like a nagging wife. She loved canoes, and was totally at ease in them, but tonight there was something weird in the air, an electric sort of feeling like the calm before the storm. She was much more familiar with the lake than he was, and she knew it could blow up quickly, but she hated to sound like a whining sissy.

"Relax and enjoy, and don't talk so much," he growled, paddling harder now to fight the increasing waves, which seemed to have come out of nowhere. One minute the water had an oily calm about it, and the next moment the wind was whipping it into a frenzy.

The waves seemed to be attacking the canoe with malicious intent. They were now past the point of no return. It would be closer to get to the island than to go back, but Kitty knew that they should be getting back to shelter as quickly as possible. It was getting colder by the second, and the clouds were turning the sky black. It seemed to have gone from the sunset to blackness without the usual twilight.

She could see that Mitch was handling the canoe expertly. Thank God for that. He had obviously had plenty of practice. She had no doubt that they could still get back safely, and if they got rained on, so what? She was alarmed though, at the thought of being caught out here in a lightning storm. Just as she thought it, a huge streak of chain lightning hit the lake with a zapping sound.

That prompted Mitch to say, "You know, you're absolutely right. This is getting way too rough. I should have listened to you. We're heading back right now."

As he began to turn the canoe, which was rocking wildly in the now turbulent water, two seadoos roared around the far side of the island, and swept past them at a great speed, causing a wake the size of a tsunami. The two young riders didn't seem to notice them, as they sped across the lake to safety.

"Dammit, you idiots," he shouted at them, as he valiantly tried to control the canoe. It was a losing battle. Kitty had already grabbed a paddle, but the wake hit them broadside before they had a chance. The canoe flipped over as if it was a plastic cup.

The sudden shock of the cold, hostile water was momentarily debilitating. As she surfaced from what seemed to have been a long way down, she gulped for air, and bonked her head on the canoe. She saw a kaleidoscope of stars and lights, as she choked on a mouthful of water, and sank like a stone. Although Kitty was usually very calm in a crisis, the second time she came up, she was flailing her arms and legs in the first stage of panic. All she accomplished was to hit her shinbone on the end of the canoe. The pain was breathtaking.

It had all happened so quickly. She was an excellent swimmer, and had spent many summers up here diving and cavorting in the water. Strange, though, how different things were in the pitch black, specially when you were taken by surprise, and dumped so unceremoniously into the cold, angry lake.

Up to this point, they had been battling in silence, but now she cried out "Mitch," as she went down again, gulping more water. This time when she came back up, the overturned canoe was well out of her reach, and barely discernible, as it bobbed along in the rough waves.

The wind was making a strange howling sound, and the sky was now as black as the water. There was no distinction between them. It was all one black cauldron. How could this have happened so quickly? Where was Mitch? Had he been knocked out by the canoe? Now she was truly floundering. Everything was so dark and so cold. She couldn't have seen him even if he was right beside her.

A pang of anger and disbelief ripped through her. No way was she going to let herself drown out here in some stupid useless accident. Thoughts of little Rosie and Petie flickered in her mind, as her head sank again beneath the angry waves. It was a real effort, almost impossible to stay afloat. Where were the damn life jackets? Who would take care of her dear little companions? Who would break the news to her parents? Her heart was bursting, as she took in more water through her mouth and nose. She couldn't believe that this usually calm, clear water, in which she had always had so much fun, had now turned into some cruel presence, grabbing at her with unfriendly arms.

She was so disoriented, that as she sank below the crashing waves, she wasn't sure which way was up. Was she struggling toward the bottom instead of the surface? She thrashed and flailed wildly, trying desperately to hold her breath. Her lungs were burning, and she was overcome with a feeling of despair.

As lethargy began to overwhelm her, and she knew how easy it would be to just relax and let it happen, she suddenly felt a strong arm grab her, and begin pulling her upwards. As they broke the surface, she coughed and greedily sucked in the cold night air, for which her lungs had been starving.

"Hold on, we'll make for the island," Mitch sputtered, as his warm arm held her firmly.

"Life jackets?" she croaked, through coughing paroxysms.

"Waves too high. Can't see. Floating flashlight gone too," he gasped, as he tried to tread water and hold on to her. She realized then that he was as worn out as she was. He must have been searching for her, as she had struggled in the malevolent turbulence.

It was obvious that Mitch was a strong swimmer, thank God for small mercies, she thought aimlessly, finding it difficult to focus. He waited and held her up, as she caught her breath, and spewed lake water out of her stomach and lungs. Eventually, they began to swim through the high waves toward the island. Mitch stayed right beside her, sometimes pushing, sometimes pulling, but always encouraging her.

The wind was actually blowing them away from the island, and between that and their fatigue, they made slow progress. She plodded along dizzily, her aching arms screaming at the effort. It would be so easy to just give up and sink to the bottom.

Then, sensing that Mitch was flagging, she took a big refreshing gulp of cold air and whispered, "Come on Mitch, we can make it, we're almost there." Of course it wasn't true, they still had a long way to go, but she was now getting that "second wind" about which she had often read. She tried to look on the positive side. At least there were no sharks, no barracuda, no piranha, just plain old deep, cold water. They were young and strong and they could do it. There was no way she was going to go down without a superhuman effort. She intended to see Steffie again, and her mom and dad, and little Rosie and Petie.

It seemed like forever before their anxious hands grasped at the slimy rocks, which heralded their arrival at the island. Oh great, she thought with dismay. There's no sandy beach, no dock, just this slippery, smooth rock surface. How were they going to haul themselves out? Kitty had always loved the Muskoka rocks, which were so picturesque and so primitive, but she hated this one, which kept rebuffing their efforts to climb out of the potentially deadly water. She couldn't remember for sure, but she decided that the dock must be on the other side of the island. Wouldn't that just be the final irony, if they had made it to the land, but couldn't climb out of the water.

As she struggled now with her few remaining bits of reserve, Mitch dragged and guided her along the rock face, searching in the dark for a way out. Finally he grasped a small bush determinedly growing out of a crack, and leaning out over the water at a precarious angle. Kitty remembered how often she had passed the island in her boat, and had thought how brave that little tree looked, growing right out of the rock. Perhaps now it was going to be their lifesaver.

Mitch lifted and pushed Kitty ahead of him, right up and out of the water, before he was able to clutch at the life-saving bush himself. Slowly he hawled his cold and aching body onto the rock. They lay there in silence, shivering and exhausted, scarcely daring to believe that they were safely out of that frigid, wind-whipped maelstrom.

It was raining so hard now, that the drops felt like stones hitting them. Jagged streaks of chain lightning pierced the blackness. Catching their breath, they realized that they were half frozen. "We need shelter," croaked Mitch, dragging her unwillingly to her feet. She would have been quite happy to lie there forever. Screw the lightning. She had survived the water, she could survive anything.

Just then a jagged streak of lightning hit a tree not 25 feet ahead of them. The tree lit up, sparks flew, and they could see that it was split right down the middle. That galvanized them. "We've got to get out of here Mitch. The lightning could strike again."

Heads down, peering into the blackness, they began to stumble and run, looking for the little cottage which she knew was here somewhere.

CHAPTER 30

▼

Ginny had been nervous now for the past week. She had the feeling that someone was following her, yet she had no proof — just this gut feeling. Since moving to Niagara Falls, she had been so happy. The job at "Cassandra's Cattery" was just what she needed to take her mind off her troubles. She loved those cats as if every one was her own, and Cassie was such a likeable, fun person for whom to work. She obviously loved the cats too, and was doing a remarkable bit of charity, spending so much money on a home for them.

Ginny had known that her brother-in-law was living here in Niagara Falls, but she really hadn't thought it would be a problem. He had moved here before she did. He had always been a nice guy — especially nice to her. She had liked him, but she loved Mike. After she married Mike though, his twin brother had changed in his attitude towards her. He had still flirted with her, and made her laugh, but she sensed a certain anger beneath the levity. He made her uncomfortable. After he had told that awful lie to Mike, and Mike had believed him, her whole world had shattered.

She had been so happy when she got the call from her kid brother Tommy, saying that he was in the city for a very short visit. He was on his way to Afghanistan with the peacekeeping forces, and he wanted to see her before he left. Unfortunately, Mike and Tommy, her husband and her brother, had never been able to get along, so she didn't even call Mike, to tell him that her brother was in town. She simply grabbed her purse, and rushed off to meet Tommy for lunch in the hotel restaurant. There would be plenty of time to tell Mike later, once Tommy was safely en route.

Mike had been the love of her life, but he had a short fuse, and a feeling of inferiority, in spite of being the spoiled twin. His brother was very obviously the dominant one.

It had just been a stroke of bad luck that Mike's twin had seen her going into the hotel with Tommy, holding onto his arm like a sweetheart, rather than a sister. Well, what was wrong with that? She loved Tommy, her big brother, and she didn't want him going off to Afghanistan. Of course she was clutching his arm, and looking up at him lovingly. Still, what gave Mike's twin the right to run to Mike, and tell him that he had seen her going into a hotel with her lover in the middle of the afternoon? What a horrible thing to say. Even worse than that, what right did Mike have to believe him, without giving her a chance to explain?

Mike hadn't said a word to her about it that day, but she had known that something was wrong. He had come home from work, and had barely spoken to her. He had said that he wasn't hungry, and was going out to the garage to work on the car, and to leave him alone. She had been too happy about seeing her darling brother Tommy, to pay much attention. She was used to Mike's moodiness.

It was her brother-in-law who had come over and found Mike in the garage. Her beloved Mike had written a note blaming her for his suicide, saying that his brother had seen her going into the hotel like a damn prostitute. That had nearly killed her, but she was putting it behind her now, and getting on with her life.

Her brother-in-law had tried to make amends in a half-hearted way, but she would have nothing to do with him. Oh yes, he was good looking and charming, and he reminded her of Mike in so many ways, but she hated him for what he had done. How could he have jumped to that ridiculous conclusion, and then run off to tattle to Mike.

In her mind, he was now a mean spirited, evil man, and she would never forgive him. He had taken to calling her lately though, asking her for a date, trying to sweet talk her, reminding her of how close they used to be. What did he mean by that? They had never been close — except in his imagination. He gave her the creeps, and she wondered whether he could be the one following her.

She had never told anyone that her brother-in-law lived right here in Niagara Falls, and she never intended to tell anyone. It was her business. If he came around again, or if he called, she would do her very best to discourage him. There was no way that she could ever marry or even date the man who had caused her husband's suicide. By jumping to that stupid conclusion, he had ruined two lives, Mike's and hers, and she would never forgive him.

She wondered again whether it had been a mistake to come here to Niagara Falls, knowing that her brother-in-law lived here now. Maybe she should have stayed in Toronto, or chosen some other nice city like London or Kitchener. She sighed as she got into the shower. Sometimes it was really tough to be alone, but there were times when it was wonderful to be able to make her own choices and decisions. She would deal with the brother-in-law if she had to, and in the meantime, she would continue to try to make herself a nice new life here, carve out a little niche for herself. Working at the Cattery was the first step to a new life. She had never had such a wonderful job. The work was easy, the pay was great, and the setting was beautiful. She loved everything about it, and there was no way that handsome, charming, snake-in-the-grass brother-in-law of hers, was going to spoil it for her.

Ginny had a shower, then made herself a toasted turkey sandwich and a big pot of tea. She was trying to make up her mind about adopting two kittens from the Cattery. The trouble was that they were all so adorable, and so needy. How would she ever be able to choose? She was lonely, though, and thought how great it would be to have two little furry friends waiting for her each night when she got home. She would definitely adopt two at the same time, so that they would have companionship while she was out all day. Watching them at the Cattery, she had learned that kittens needed someone with whom to rough and tumble and chase.

Taking her sandwich and tea, she went into the den of her little house, and turned on the television. There were no good movies to watch, so she turned to CNN. She was just nodding off, when the doorbell rang.

She sat there undecided. Should she answer it? There was no reason not to, except that it could be whoever had been following her. Making up her mind, she peeked out the blinds, and saw that it was Cassie standing there. Super! She could use the company.

"Hi Cassie. What a lovely surprise! Come on in," she said with genuine pleasure.

"Ginny, I hope you don't mind me barging in like this, but I had a great idea for the Cattery, and I wanted your opinion. I couldn't wait till tomorrow to talk to you about it. I'm just on my way home from a meeting, and this was on the way more or less, so here I am."

"Well, sit down and I'll make us a fresh pot of tea, or would you rather have wine?"

"Tea sounds terrific. Vickie will be wondering where I am though. May I call her?"

"Of course. The phone's in the kitchen. Come on in with me while I get the kettle boiling."

Actually, Cassie had made up this excuse to come around and visit Ginny. She liked this pretty young woman who was now working for her, but she could often feel the sad vibes coming from her. Ginny didn't talk much about herself, other than mentioning that she was a widow, and Cassie thought that it might do Ginny good to have someone with whom she could share her troubles. If there was any way to help, Cass would be there for her. Ginny was so excellent with the cats at the Cattery, that Cassie didn't want to lose her.

Cassie finished her call to Vickie, and looked around admiringly. Ginny was busy putting some home made chocolate chip cookies onto a delicate blue and white plate.

"You've done up your kitchen so prettily, Ginny. I love the blue and white décor. It looks so bright and clean."

"Thanks. I'm happy with it, but I'm not finished yet. Now I'm looking for a blue and white rug to put in front of the sink."

Taking their treats back into the den, the women chatted happily, sipping tea, nibbling the cookies, and just getting to know each other a little better. Cassie shared her new idea for the Cattery, and asked for Ginny's input. The idea, if put into practice, would mean more work for Ginny, and Cassie wanted to be sure she was willing to take it on.

Meanwhile, the Black Sheep had worked himself up into a frenzy again. He wondered whether he should give Ginny one more chance. Did he really have to kill her? He wasn't sure. He could pay her a visit, talk to her, try to soften her up. If she showed any signs of friendliness, he would make a date with her. In one moment he could picture them happily married, just as she and Mike had been. The next moment he could picture his hands around her pretty neck.

He really had no excuse for killing her now. She hadn't been unfaithful to Mike, and, although he hated to admit it, it was his fault that Mike had killed himself. Thinking about it reasonably, she really didn't deserve to die. He hadn't seen any evidence of her going out with anyone since she had moved here to Niagara. Why was she still on his list of victims anyway? He had put her on the list when he was sure that she had caused Mike's suicice. Now he was all mixed up.

He felt so confused as he paced up and down the hallway. He had a mother of a headache again. He wasn't really aware of the fact that this had become a pattern for him. Each time before he set out to kill some unsuspecting woman, he seemed to have a mind numbing headache. As a result, he always took a couple of pills and a drink of whiskey. He thought it was because of the headaches, which were becoming more frequent, but subconsciously he had become superstitious. He needed the pills and whiskey for courage, and he believed that somehow, the routine brought him luck. Headache, pills, whiskey, killing, it seemed to be a good ritual.

Tonight, however, he just couldn't make up his mind. What the hell should he do? Was he going to kill Ginny or not? If he was, then it would be tonight. He just couldn't stand the pressure in his head. A couple of times now, the pressure had started building up while he was working, and he was terrified that someone would notice. He was a good actor, and he didn't think anyone was aware of his problems, but it was becoming more difficult to keep up the charade.

He threw himself into a chair and sat staring blankly at a wall. He could sense his own disintegration. Viewing it dispassionately, it was an interesting downward spiral. He knew that he was drinking too much these days, and he noticed that his hands were shaking. Well that wouldn't be too good for his job. Funny how people needed their hands for just about everything they did. No time to start philosophizing. Was he going to kill her or not? If not Ginny, then who?

In his nervous state, he started to laugh. Was he the only serial killer on record who always tried to talk himself out of another killing? Most serial killers didn't care whether their victims deserved to die. They just did it for the selfish pleasure or the paranoid need. Here he was, sitting like a total loser, trying to decide whether or not Ginny deserved to be killed. It was ludicrous. He was definitely losing it.

Probably, some time in the future, when they wrote about him, and they certainly would write about him, they would likely refer to him as "the Black Sheep, aka the reluctant serial killer." It was more than ludicrous. It was ridiculous, and he wasn't going to let his conscience interfere any more. He would please himself, and forget about the rest of the world. They were mostly losers anyway. None of them had the guts or the imagination he had.

He started pacing again, trying to review what had been happening, and why. Why had he started this killing spree in the first place? Yes, of course. It was those darn fickle women who never gave a man a break. It was women like his wife, who had blindsided him when she took off like that. He had started by trying to teach them a lesson, but somewhere along the way, things had become confused. He hadn't expected to feel so guilty and so sad about what he was doing. When the powerful feelings came over him, however, he couldn't help himself. That might be a good defence — irresistible impulse. Of course, it could hardly be passed off as impulse, when he took such care to bring the black sheep and the camera with him.

There was one thing he knew for sure. He wasn't interested in killing any more prostitutes. They proliferated like cockroaches, kill one, and four more appeared. No, the killings had to have more meaning.

Well, he told himself, look at it this way. If Ginny hadn't been unfaithful to Mike while he was alive, and if she hadn't been unfaithful to his memory, she likely soon would be. She was too cute and too friendly not to have a boyfriend. Maybe she already had one, and he just hadn't caught them together. She was undoubtedly like all the rest. Maybe it wasn't exactly her fault that Mike was dead, but then, maybe it was. Maybe she had been going into that hotel to screw her brother. Who knew? Okay, that was it. Ginny was next.

A feeling of relief came over him, as soon as he had made up his mind. He didn't bother with the gym bag or briefcase this time. He simply took a pair of surgical gloves and a little black sheep, and stuffed them into his pocket. He wouldn't even bother with his disguise. He would be in and out so quickly that no one would have the chance to see him. He didn't want to admit to himself that he was getting a bit careless. He just had to get over there, get it done, and relieve the dreadful tension.

He knew where Ginny lived, because he had been following her off and on now for weeks. He had also been in her house a couple of times when she first moved to Niagara Falls. He had called on her to try to get friendly, and had a good idea of the layout of the house and yard. She had a big back yard, all fenced in, and quite private. He would go in the back way. No one would see him, and he recalled that the back door had looked like an easy access.

He parked in the lane behind her house, and, hunkering down, he ran across the lawn to the back door. Damn! There was a light on in the kitchen. He didn't like that. Well, no reason to panic. Maybe she always left a light on. Maybe she had fallen asleep watching TV. He could still sneak in and take her by surprise.

Picking the lock was easy. He did it in a quiet and quick fashion. Stealthily, he crept in and shut the door behind him. Then he felt his heart begin to pound. He could hear voices! Was it the television, or was it people? How could he tell?

He stood perfectly still in the kitchen, straining his ears to make out the voices. They were definitely women's voices, but how many of them were there? For all he knew, there could be several of them. He should leave and try again later, but he knew that what he should do and what he was going to do, were two different things. He was too hyped up now to turn back. His needs made him careless, an attitude he had always tried to avoid.

As he stood like a statue in that little blue and white kitchen, he berated himself for not cruising past the front of the house, to be sure that there was no extra car in the driveway. He wondered again why he was being so careless tonight. He had taken so many precautions with Eva. She had been his best one. He had felt so good after it was over, and he knew how careful he had been. Now he was getting sloppy. Sloppiness and carelessness could be very deleterious to his health. Did this mean that deep down he wanted to be caught? No, that wasn't it. It was just that he was in a hurry, and he had great confidence in his luck and superior abilities. This one would be a piece of cake.

He started down the hall toward the den, gliding along like a snake. The voices became clearer.

"I'm so glad you dropped around Cassie. We should do this more often." That was definitely Ginny's voice.

Someone named Cassie replied, "I enjoyed it too, Ginny. I had no intention of staying so late, though. You won't want to get up for work tomorrow, and you'll have me to blame. Anyway, thanks so much. I'll see you tomorrow. By the way, feel free to come in an hour later than usual. The other staff can keep things going till you get there."

"Cassie, that's nice of you, but I'll be there on time. You must know by now how much I love this job. It's been a real life-saver for me."

The Black Sheep heard that, and almost laughed. Poor Ginny really needed a life-saver just about now. She had no idea how close to the end of her life she was. If only she had been more receptive to his advances, he would be here tonight to make love to her, not to kill her.

Suddenly he realized that the women were walking out of the den.

There was no place to hide, and if he stayed in the hall, they would see him as they went to the front door. Shit and double shit. There was nothing he could do but retreat. He couldn't take on two of them at the same time, not unless he knocked one out first, while he strangled the other. No, whoever Cassie was, he had no interest in killing her.

These thoughts were slamming around in his head, as he turned and made his way to the back door. In his haste, scurrying down the dark hall like a frightened mouse, he wasn't as quiet as he should have been, and he heard someone behind him say, "What was that?"

He was in a true panic by the time he reached the kitchen door, and he didn't take time to close it behind him. He ran like a fool, like an idiotic scared little twit. As he headed towards the lane, he could hear them at the back door, and then the light came on. He wasn't wearing his disguise, and wondered in horror whether Ginny might have recognized him.

This was all so wrong. He was suave, funny, surrounded by people who liked and admired him, people who were impressed with the job he did. He wasn't meant to be scurrying across back yards and into alleys like some pathetic loser. He felt an unaccustomed heaviness in his wildly pounding heart.

It seemed years before he made it to his car, and peeled out of there. He had heard the one called Cassie say, "Call the police, Ginny. It might have been the strangler."

His heart continued to pound, and he couldn't get his breath. His tongue was stuck to the roof of his mouth, and he felt demented. He felt like a fool. If his friends could only see him now.

In spite of the unaccustomed fear, he kept precisely to the speed limit, and made it home safely. The good news was that he didn't think he had been followed. The bad news was, he was really distraught. The entire foray had been a near disaster, a total fiasco, and he was badly shaken. Was this the end of the Black Sheep? Just like the night he had killed Lana, he wondered whether his luck had finally run out.

CHAPTER 31

▼

Finally, thanks to another vicious streak of lightning, Kitty and Mitch saw the cabin hunkered down amongst the trees, like an animal hiding from its enemy. There were no lights on. Maybe old Mr. Jessop isn't even here, Kitty thought, or maybe it's just that the power is out, or he's already gone to bed. They had to have warmth and shelter, so they both pounded on the door. Kitty kept calling, "Mr. Jessop, it's Kitty Winfield from across the lake. We've had an accident. Please let us in." The silence was punctuated by more angry claps of thunder.

"Please be here, Mr. Jessop," she mumbled weakly, through chattering teeth.

Eventually Mitch stopped pounding, and, leaving her on the porch, he stumbled his way around the cottage, looking for an unlocked door or window.

He took such a long time, that Kitty began to despair of ever seeing him again. Then suddenly he appeared at her side. "We'll have to break in. We'll pay for the damages," he said tersely. He was now in a 'no nonsense' mood. Taking the rock over which he had stumbled in the dark, he heaved it through the window, which faced onto the porch. He carefully picked out the jagged pieces of glass, until there was a space through which he could crawl. Gingerly climbing over the windowsill, he made his way to the door, and opened it for Kitty. "Come into my parlour," he grinned, dragging her into the stuffy little cabin.

It was rudimentary to say the least, just a simple main room, but it did have a bathroom, and a small stone fireplace.

It was shelter from the storm, and that was all Kitty cared about at the moment. She knew that it belonged to old Mr. Jessop, who was well into his eighties. He usually spent his summers here, but the cabin had that empty, deserted feel, and there was a musty, mouse droppings sort of smell permeating the place. She wondered briefly whether the old boy was sick, or had died.

Mitch took charge right away, and began exploring their shelter. There were matches and a coal oil lamp on the table. There were also candles on the mantel. By the time the lamp and the candles were lit, the room, which had become their haven, seemed slightly more inviting. In one corner, Kitty noticed a single bed, which had been stripped of everything, except for a tired looking pillow, and a dirty old blanket.

Mitch proved to have a very practical streak, which seemed rather unusual for an author. He showed a stroke of brilliance, by using the plastic tablecloth to cover the broken window, through which the wind and rain were blowing. There was no way of securing it, so he simply hung it over the existing curtain rod. Kitty did her part by grabbing a couple of logs to hold it tight at the bottom.

There was glass all over the floor by the window, so Kitty found an old broom and dustpan, and soon got it cleaned up enough that they felt safe in taking off their soaking runners, and going barefoot.

The tiny washroom had one moderately clean looking towel, a small roll of toilet paper, and a couple of old Field and Stream magazines. It seemed obvious that Mr. Jessop had not been here this summer. This was all detritus left from another season. Kitty hoped that nothing had happened to the old fellow, who had a bit of a reputation on the lake as an old curmudgeon.

The cupboards and frig were empty, except for a couple of forgotten cans of peaches, and a can of sardines. Well, Mr. Jessop had certainly not been a gourmet cook, and who knew how old the cans were? They might not be safe to eat. Just realizing that there was no edible food around made Kitty feel ravenous. She could eat a Harvey's hamburger with fries and onion rings. She could eat a big bowl of spaghetti and meatballs. Shoot, who was she kidding? At this moment in time she could eat an entire chicken, and then look for dessert.

The find of the night was a half bottle of cheap whiskey, hidden behind the cups and plates. Grabbing the booze and the only two glasses in the cupboard, Mitch poured them both a generous amount.

"Yuk," this is pure rot-gut," complained Kitty, making a sour face. She didn't drink anything but wine, and this stuff tasted lethal.

"Drink up and don't complain. It's for medicinal purposes only. We're damn lucky to have found it. It'll warm us on the inside, then we can worry about the outside."

The other welcome discovery was a box full of wood, sitting beside the fireplace. Kitty had already used two pieces to hold the tablecloth in place over the window. It all looked nice and dry and very useable. "Thank you Lord," muttered Mitch, as his cold fingers built them a little fire.

The heat was wonderful. The warmth of the fire seemed to embrace them lovingly. Kitty surrendered herself to it gratefully. They stood in front of it as close as they could get, without actually climbing right into it. They sipped the whiskey in silence, each absorbed in his or her own thoughts.

When Mitch gently rubbed mud from her cheek, the touch of his hand sent shivers down her spine, but they were shivers of pleasure, not fear. He grinned, as he rubbed another spot on her nose. "You should see yourself. You look as if you have the measles or chicken pox, with mud spots all over you. When you slipped into that muddy patch, it must have splashed up onto your face."

Kitty could only imagine how bad she looked. She didn't realize that with her sodden shirt clinging to her body, her nipples were standing up hard and proud. It was a combination of the cold, the wet, and Mitch's proximity. She also didn't realize just how tantalizing she looked to Mitch, in spite of her muddy face.

Eventually he said, "You've got to get out of those wet clothes or you'll have pneumonia." Looking around the small room, he retrieved the old blanket. Shaking it well to get rid of any spiders or mouse droppings, he offered it to Kitty. "Here, wrap this around you, and give me your clothes. We'll try to dry them."

"What about you?" she asked through still chattering teeth. She remembered with relief that she was wearing her lacy blue bikini briefs and bra. Her penchant for filmy lingerie had been lucky this time. She would have been humiliated to have Mitch see her in some old droopy drawers, but that wouldn't have happened, because she always treated herself to lacy, filmy, provocative bras and panties. Gawd, what a jackass I am, she thought with a grin, as she began peeling off the wet shorts and shirt. Why should it matter whether he approves of my underwear? Still, she was happy that her undies were pretty and sexy. Modesty would get her nowhere now, except maybe a bed in the intensive care unit, so she boldly unfastened her bra and stepped out of her panties.

"What about you?" she repeated, as she very gingerly wound the repulsive blanket around herself. It was horribly rough, and she wouldn't let herself think about the possibility of spiders nesting in it.

Mitch grinned and said, "I'm as cold as you are, so I intend to share that blanket with you. Since you've already seen me in my birthday suit, it shouldn't be too shocking." He laughed at the chagrined look on her face.

"Not very likely, Mr. Donaldson. I hardly know you sir," she added in a silly southern accent. "I can hardly wrap myself up in a blanket with you." She shook her head as she took another sip of the whiskey, which was doing its job.

Was this Kitty talking? She couldn't believe herself. Here she'd been pining after this guy all week, well at least she'd been pretty interested, and now that this golden opportunity was staring her in the face, she was acting all coy and embarrassed. He would think she was a total nerd. Still, she couldn't quite see herself nude, wrapped in a blanket with an equally nude Mitch Donaldson. The thought was terrifying as well as titillating.

"Well, I'm taking off these wet clothes. If you won't share the blanket, I'll just have to stand here shivering in the buff. Suit yourself. I just hope that you'll have the decency to visit me in the hospital," he added, with a mock serious look. His eyes were flashing with amusement, as he challenged her.

This was another side of Mitch Donaldson, which she hadn't seen before. How many sides did this man have?

"Come on, Kitty-Kat," he whispered, as he turned his back and stepped out of his shorts and underwear. "Be a nice girl and share the blanket."

"This is ridiculous," laughed Kitty in spite of herself, as she gingerly opened one end of the blanket. "It smells and it's rough, and I hope it give you hives," she giggled, more from nervousness than gaiety.

They stood there in silence, gazing into the flames, wrapped together in the old dirty blanket.

"Hey, let's push that sofa over here, and we can be comfy. No sense standing if we could be sitting down," he suggested, dropping the blanket, and racing across the floor. He began pushing and pulling at the tattered sofa. "Come on, give me a hand. I'm just as tired as you are," he scolded. "This thing's as heavy as a cart full of coal."

Kitty hesitated, then dropping the blanket, she rushed over to the sofa, and helped him push it in front of the fireplace. Next, he placed the two chairs in front of the fire, and spread their clothes on them to dry. He held up the blue lace bikini briefs and said "very nice," with a lascivious leer, before placing them carefully on the chair. That little chore done, he wrapped himself in the other end of the blanket, and they sat there warm and cosy, in uneasy silence.

The whiskey bottle was right at their feet, and after replenishing their glasses, Kitty laughed, "You'll be able to put this adventure in your book. Be sure to write about how pretty my underwear was." The whiskey and the warmth of the fire were getting to her, and she was falling into a gentle, boozy comfort zone. She had stopped shaking, and her teeth were no longer chattering.

"I've already written it in my mind," he said, turning to grin at her.

This Mitch Donaldson was totally different from the cold, arrogant guy she'd seen most of the week. He had so many faces. Which one was the real Mitch? Her eyes were blurring now, and she felt totally exhausted, but she was aware that her heart was beginning to hammer, her stomach was doing flip-flops, and her toes were tingling. It must be the bad whiskey, she told herself, but she felt comfortable with him, at least more comfortable than she had all week. Then with a sigh, she closed her eyes, and warned herself to be careful. This one could really break your heart, Kitty girl, she cautioned herself. He's likely married or has a significant other. That was a very sobering thought.

"I'm wondering how we're going to get off this island tomorrow," mused Mitch, as he stretched his long legs out in front of him. He had perfectly shaped legs, with black curly hair on them. It made her dizzy to think of running her hand over that hair. Oh, get a grip, she groaned inwardly.

"I'm wondering whether there's a boat here that we could borrow. It's a shame we've lost the canoe."

"Getting off the island shouldn't be a problem," Kitty replied, as soberly as possible. Her lips were beginning to feel a bit numb, and so was her tongue. This really was rot-gut that they were drinking. "As soon as the storm ends, there'll be boats out. We'll just flag one down. That's one great thing about cottage country. People are always eager to help each other. Of course, if this darn storm lasts for another day, we'll be really screwed. There's no food, and I'm already hungry."

"I suspect that by morning, those old cans of peaches and sardines are going to look mighty appetizing," he chuckled. "By the way, I owe you a huge apology. I was a horse's ass to insist that we come out tonight. You were right about the impending storm, and I should have listened to you. I'm really sorry, Kitty. We could both be at the bottom of the lake right now."

He looked sincerely repentant and embarrassed, and any remaining feelings of anger towards him were gone. "Actually, I agree. You were a bit of a horse's ass, but I know this lake well, and I knew there was a storm coming. I'm an even worse idiot than you are. I should have talked you out of it, but I must confess that I really wanted to go in that canoe with you. Besides, we can't forget that you did save my life. When I came up and hit the canoe so hard, it really confused me. I hit it with my head the first time, then kicking out, I hit it with my shinbone. Look at the bruise and bump I'm getting." She held out her leg to show off her wound.

"When I went down again, I didn't know which way was up, and that was scary. If you hadn't got your arms around me and dragged me to the surface, I think I was headed for the bottom. I really do owe you my life, Mitch." She shivered as she thought of how close she had come to drowning. Now that she was warm and cosy, sitting here with this naked hunk beside her, the entire adventure seemed far away and unreal. All she could think about was Mitch, sitting naked so close to her. On a scale of one to ten, this guy was definitely a fifteen. Again she wondered whether all this was just fodder for his book.

The whiskey was loosening her tongue, and the warmth of the fire made her feel sleepy and contented. It was wonderful sitting here with Mitch so close, listening to the wind howling outside. When he casually asked if she was in a serious relationship, she should have told him "no" and let it go at that. Instead, because of the booze, she could barely believe her own ears, as she told him that there was no one important at the moment, and then started right in about Scott.

She had vowed never to tell a living soul, except for Steffie, about that awful sight of Scott and the unknown redhead in her very own bed, in her very own house. It still angered her when she thought about it. Somehow, however, she couldn't stop the words, which were cascading from her mouth like broken beads. She felt as if she was watching herself from a distance, as she blabbed on and on about Scott, and then started in about Drew. She even told him about throwing the wine at Drew, and marching out of the restaurant. She knew she would be sorry in the morning, but that didn't help to shut her up tonight.

Finally she was purged, and there was momentary silence, as they both stared at the fire. Then Mitch said tersely, "The first guy must be a fool and a total jerk. You're well rid of him. I don't know what to think about the second one. Doesn't he care that you've been up here all week with a total stranger, who could be the strangler for all he knows?"

Kitty's heart skipped a beat at that. Why would he bring up the strangler now? How bizarre! He must be on everyone's mind these days. What if Mitch was the strangler? What did she know about him anyway? Quelling these insidious thoughts as best she could, she blurted out, "Do you have a wife or someone who'll be worried about you?"

She held her breath in the ensuing silence. Darn, why had she asked such a stupid question. She really didn't want to know — weren't those the words to an old Eddy Arnold song? It was true though, she really didn't want to know, not tonight anyway.

There seemed to be an endless silence before he curtly replied, "There's a someone," and tugged the blanket tighter around his shoulders. That burst Kitty's little bubble in a hurry. She felt as if she had a mouthful of ashes. They sat there in a thick, uncomfortable vacuum. She had difficulty taking a breath. Why had she ever asked such a demented question? Why hadn't she just left well enough alone?

She could have chewed up her tongue and spit it out. She did not want to know that there was "someone" waiting for him. All her erotic flights of fancy had made him available and unattached. He had saved her life, and somehow they should be bound together. Didn't the Chinese say that once you saved a person's life, you were responsible for that person forever? Now she knew that there was some awful "someone" to rival her feelings for him. He was not available, so she just had to forget her romantic fancies, and go on about her dismal little way.

The booze was putting everything into a dramatic purple haze. Snuffling up the incipient tears, she finally closed her eyes. In her warm, boozy state, cuddled up within the scratchy old blanket, she eventually fell into an exhausted and troubled sleep.

CHAPTER 32

▼

When Kitty awoke the next morning, her head was on Mitch's shoulder, his arm was around her, and he was sound asleep. The fire was out, and the room was cold. The wind was still blowing, and rattling the windows, and she could hear the rain pelting down on the roof. Damn, the storm should have been over by now. As long as it kept raining this hard, there would be no boats out on the lake. They could be stuck here all day. Kitty didn't want to be stuck there with Mitch. She needed to get away from him, and she needed to clear her head. Besides, she was supposed to be home by tonight. People would start worrying.

It took her a few minutes to extricate herself from the blanket, and Mitch's arm. She realized that he was a very sound sleeper, because he didn't even stir. She stood looking down at him for a moment, before realizing how naked she was. Somehow, she didn't want Mitch to see her naked this morning. The magic, or whatever it had been last night for at least a few minutes, had totally disappeared in the light of day.

She felt slightly queasy from the cheap whiskey and her empty stomach. Pictures of eating sardines and peaches for breakfast, made her go rushing off to the little bathroom. She couldn't stand the thought of that dirty towel touching her face, so she washed it, and patted it dry with toilet tissue. There wasn't much of that, though, so she was very parsimonious with it.

Inevitably, her thoughts turned to the previous night. Her stomach lurched again as she remembered that one word "someone" which Mitch had uttered so solemnly. All week she had vacillated between being angry with his rudeness and unfriendliness, and being intrigued by his good looks and stand-offish manner. She had wasted the entire week, and now it was definitely too late. What an idiot she was!

Waking this morning, cuddled naked beside him, with his strong arm around her, she felt that she could have stayed right there forever, but that one word "someone" kept ringing in her ears. He belonged to someone else. Never mind that he passed her litmus test, which included making her heart pound, her stomach do flip-flops, and her toes tingle. He had a "someone" waiting for him, so he was off limits.

She tried to comfort herself by remembering that there were several men who were interested in her. Goodness, this summer alone, she had been invited on dates by Scott, Josh, Keith, Drew, Adrian. She mentally ticked them off. That was exactly the way it should be. She was good looking, she was young, she was unattached. She could have all the boyfriends she wanted. Unfortunately, right now, she wanted Mitch, and he was apparently taken. She sighed at the injustice of this, but would have been even more upset, if she had known that the Black Sheep was very interested in her, and was keeping a close watch on all her activities.

She peeked out of the bathroom, and saw that he was still sound asleep. Just then, a mouse ran across the back of the sofa. She watched in fascination, as it ran right down over the blanket and into a corner. Had it been running over them all night long? Probably. Tiptoeing around the room, she gathered up her now dry clothes, and took the whiskey bottle to use as a mouthwash for her furry-feeling teeth. The awful taste made her gag, so she took more toilet tissue, and rubbed it over her teeth as best she could. Her hair had dried curly as usual, but it looked alarmingly unruly, and there was no comb or brush to tame it.

She examined her right leg, which was sporting a long bruise where she had hit the canoe, or it had hit her. There was also a large bite on her thigh. It looked like a spider bite — unless Mitch had bitten her in a passionate frenzy during the night! She giggled at the thought. Then the idea of a big hairy spider running over her naked body made her wince. This was a vile little cabin, and she just wanted to get out of here as quickly as possible. She felt depressed and anxious, and just wanted to be home with the cats. She needed to be far from Mitch Donaldson. This entire week had been a disaster.

Get a grip, girl, she chided herself, as she came out of the bathroom. Some lucky woman is waiting for him, so just put him out of your mind. It wasn't meant to be, and the disappointment won't kill you. You may bend a bit, but you won't break. She often repeated this little mantra when she was feeling down, and it usually helped. This morning it didn't.

Mitch looked so handsome, yet somehow vulnerable, as he gradually stretched and opened his eyes. He stared at her for a moment, as if wondering who she was. Then, "Morning Miss Kitty," he drawled. Standing up, he kept the blanket wrapped carefully around his nakedness. Gone was the playfulness of last night. There was an awkward, tense feeling in the air.

"Breakfast ready?" he kidded, as he grabbed his clothes, and headed for the washroom.

"It will be as soon as I find a can opener." She tried a half-hearted laugh. No way was she going to let him know how uneasy and disappointed she felt. "What's your pleasure, peaches or sardines?"

"Peaches," he called over his shoulder, as he shut the bathroom door.

They spent the morning and afternoon in strained conversation, and uncomfortable silences. Mitch made another fire, and they sat in front of it on the old sofa, Kitty at one end, Mitch at the other. It was ridiculous and embarrassing.

They found a sticky old deck of cards, and a cribbage board, and played a few games, until they were bored. They were well matched, but it was stilted and overly polite. Where was that easy camaraderie they had achieved last night? He kept going to the window to gaze out at the storm, as if he couldn't wait to get away.

Kitty swept up more of the glass, and they pushed the old sofa back where it belonged. She said that she would contact Mr. Jessop or his family, and pay for the broken window and the whiskey.

By mid afternoon the rain had stopped, and the waves were calming down. The sun even began to shine, as if to say, "Here I am. What's all the fuss about?" The lake looked beautiful and enticing. It was now difficult to picture how ugly and menacing it had been last night. Birds were chirping again, and the sun glistened on the oh so innocent looking water.

Unfortunately, there was no sign of the canoe, so they were totally stranded until help came. They went out and sat on the damp rocks, watching in every direction for the first sign of a passing boat. They were extremely polite to each other, and both felt very uncomfortable.

It was interesting to see the slippery rocks, where they had come ashore in the dark. They looked so dangerous and unfriendly, that Kitty was amazed they had been able to climb out of that turbulent water at all. If she had been alone, she never would have made it. Of course, if she had been alone, she never would have come out in the canoe in the first place. When you got right down to it, it was really Mitch's fault that they were in this mess. That thought made her more grumpy than ever, and she flounced away to sit alone on a rock some distance from where Mitch was positioned.

It was almost five o'clock, and they were hungry and cross, before they spotted a young boy in a small aluminum craft. They waved and shouted frantically, as if they had been stranded for a couple of months. The youth was obviously excited at rescuing two people. He felt terribly important, and would have a great tale to tell his parents and friends when he got home.

Mitch suggested that the young lad should keep his eyes open for the canoe, which had disappeared in the storm. No telling where it was by now. It had been upside down the last time they saw it, so it might still be floating, or it might be at the very bottom of the lake, never to be seen again.

Arriving safely at the dock, Mitch asked their rescuer to wait for a moment. He returned quickly, with a twenty dollar bill. At first the young boy refused to take it, but his eyes were eager, as he looked at it. They assured him that it was to cover his gas and his time, so he allowed himself to be persuaded, and zoomed away, turning once to wave at them.

Mitch mumbled that he had to finish packing and be on his way, and he disappeared up the path. Kitty tidied the cottage quickly, threw her things into the car haphazardly, gathered the garbage, and was locking up, when Mitch appeared with his bags. He stowed them in his car, and they stood looking at each other for a moment. Kitty's heart was heavy. What she wanted to do was to throw her arms around him, and ask him to call her sometime. What she did do, was stand there like a cold fool, wishing him good luck with his book. He looked at her quizzically, then turned, got into his car, and sat there for a moment.

Kitty had turned her back on him, and was just opening her car door, when he leapt out of his vehicle, and rushed over to her. "Kitty, this is ridiculous. I don't want it to end this way. From the moment I saw you standing on the path, looking up at me, I've been hooked. I've had to stay as far away from you as possible. Last night could have been wonderful, but you reminded me that I have a commitment at home, with which I have to deal before I can get involved. I'm going to do it though, and I'm going to call you. Is that okay?"

He looked so earnest and rather desperate, that Kitty knew he was serious. "I feel the same Mitch. If you don't call me, I'm going to call you. I don't want this week to end, horrible as it was." She grinned at him, and he took her in his arms and kissed her. At last, she thought, this is it. She could feel the blood rushing to her head, her stomach was doing flip-flops, and her toes were tingling. She had finally found her prince, and this was all going to work out — somehow, some day.

They stood saying a thousand things to each other, then finally parted reluctantly. Mitch promised to call within the next few days, once he had dealt with his "someone."

She had a horrible sense of aloneness, as she stood watching his car drive slowly down the lane. He honked once before the car disappeared around the bend, and Kitty felt unwanted tears spring to her eyes. There were times when she could be such a fool, and she had wasted an entire week with her pigheadedness, but that was in the past now, and the future held great promise, at least she hoped it did.

CHAPTER 33

▼

Back in Niagara Falls, Steffie was looking forward to Kitty's return. She was surprised that Kitty hadn't been there at the house, when she got back from work. Oh well, it must have been a beautiful day at the cottage, she reasoned, and Kitty had likely spent it swimming and boating. She sincerely hoped that she would have a chance to get up there with Kitty before the summer was over. They always had a great time in Muskoka. Just thinking about the cottage, and the fun times they had experienced there, put her in a good mood.

She had fed the cats, and was just getting herself something to eat, when the doorbell rang. Kitty must have her arms full of luggage, and can't fish out her key, she thought, as she headed for the front door. It was a solid oak door with no window or peephole in it, so when Steffie flung it open, she could only gasp in surprise, and disbelief.

"Nick," she uttered. "Wh — what are you doing here? How did you find me?"

Nick grinned, as he pushed past her, and walked into the foyer, kicking the door shut behind him.

"Well, Steff, aren't you glad to see me," he leered at her.

Steffie was definitely not glad to see him. All of a sudden, she wasn't glad about anything. Her life had just taken a sickening downward spiral. Stephanie Jeanne Chapman, usually so calm, so cool, so in control, suddenly felt that a moment of hysteria would be appropriate.

"No, I'm not, Nick. I'm not at all happy to see you. You belong to my past, and I don't even want to know why you're here. Please, just go." Steffie sounded both defiant and desperate, as she stared at the ugly tattoo of two snakes intertwined on his neck. Yikes! What other changes had taken place since she last saw him?

She stared at his bald head, which had obviously been shaved. It was so different from the thick, curly hair she remembered. Eight years in Kingston penitentiary had changed him considerably. He had that jail house pallor, and a cocky sort of strut, which she didn't remember.

"Hey, pretty fancy digs you've got here," he said, ignoring her, and walking into the living room. "You must be doing well in that store of yours."

Her heart sank. How did he know about the boutique? How did he know that she was living in Niagara Falls? How had he found her here at Kitty's house?

"Nick, this isn't my place. I'm just cat sitting for a friend. Please don't touch anything," she begged, as she tried to take the Royal Doulton figurine from his careless hands.

"You mean this isn't your house?" he frowned.

"That's right. My friend lives here with her mother and **father**, and they'll be home any minute." She should have added that her **friend** had two big brothers too — both big enough to beat him up. Any lie would **do** if it got rid of Nick. Unfortunately, she was so shaken, that she couldn't **think** straight.

"Please go Nick. There's nothing here for you, and my friend doesn't know anything about you." Oh shit, maybe it was a mistake to tell him that. He'd be able to hold it over her head somehow. You never knew with Nick.

He didn't seem to be paying any attention to her. He had plumped himself down on the sofa, and had his legs stretched out on it, shoes included.

Steffie's heart sank as low as it could go. This was disaster. It was devastating. What if Kitty came home now? How would she ever explain? Would it be the end of the friendship, the partnership?

It took almost half an hour before she could persuade Nick that she would take him to her place, and find him some money, which seemed to be what he really wanted. He had already taken the fifty-one dollars from her purse. Steffie was so thankful that the cats had not appeared. They must have sensed that something was wrong, because they stayed hidden. Nick had always been fond of animals, but he seemed so different now.

When Kitty arrived home, she was surprised and disappointed that Steffie wasn't there. The plan had been that she would sleep over, and they would go to church together in the morning. She was very anxious to tell Steffie all about her latest adventures at the cottage. Mostly she wanted to talk about Mitch.

Petie and Rosie appeared from upstairs, and wound themselves ecstatically round and round her legs, purring like motor boats.

It was wonderful to be home again, but she had so much to tell Steffie. Why hadn't she been there to greet her as planned? Finally, after cuddling the cats, she called her friend. She knew right away that something was wrong. Steffie sounded strange, and somehow distant.

"What's wrong Steff? What's happened?"

"Kitty, I have to talk to you. It's so complicated that I don't know where to begin. I'm afraid to come back over there though. It might bring trouble for you."

"What in hell are you talking about? Steffie, is someone there with you?" Suddenly Kitty had the horrible picture of Steffie being held prisoner by the strangler. Was he there listening to the conversation? "Steff, should I call 911?"

"No, it's nothing like that. Look, I know you must be tired, but could you come over? I need help, and I don't know what to do." Steffie sounded distraught. What in the world could have happened?

When Kitty arrived at Steffie's condo, it looked suspiciously as if her friend had been crying. Her face was red, and her eyes were puffy. Kitty walked in warily. There might be someone hiding behind the door. She had a small kitchen knife in her hand, just in case.

Kitty noticed the wine bottle on the counter, so she poured a glass for each of them, as they sat down at the kitchen table. "Okay, take a big swig of this wine, and then tell me what's going on."

"I have no idea where to begin, because it's a long, involved story." Steffie took a big breath, and tried to smile at her friend. It came out an ugly little grimace. She was shaking like a malaria victim.

Kitty was scared now. Had Steffie just found out she was dying? Had their beloved boutique burned to the ground? Had there been a car accident, and maybe her parents were dead? "What the heck is it?" she almost shrieked at her friend.

"Kit, don't interrupt me. I've got to tell you everything before I lose my nerve. First, just let me say that I really love you. You are the dearest friend anyone could have, and I should have told you everything right up front." She sighed here, and shook her head in disgust at herself.

"I've lied to you right from the beginning. I told you that I had no living relatives, and that I was an only child. Well, that's not true. I have a younger brother, and he's, well, he's been in the penitentiary for armed robbery. He's out now, he's found me, and he's trouble. He followed me to your house tonight to get money from me. I brought him here, and gave him what I had, and he's gone off to the casino. He'll be back though. He needs a place to stay."

All the time she was giving this explanation, she was tearing a tissue into shreds. When she had finished, she looked at her friend with tears in her lovely dark eyes, and whispered, "I'm so sorry. I just couldn't tell you about him. He's turned into a bad person, and he's been in various kinds of trouble for years. I thought and prayed that he was out of my life forever."

Kitty was too shocked to say anything. At first she just sat there staring dumbly at Steffie. Then she said very slowly, "Wait a minute, kiddo. Are you saying that you didn't trust me enough to tell me about your brother? Are you implying that I wouldn't have been your friend, or your partner, that I would have freaked out? What do you mean you couldn't tell me?"

She was getting herself all riled up, and had to take a breath and calm down. She told herself that this was about Steffie and her problem. It was not about Kitty and her hurt feelings. She felt angry and betrayed, but some part of her knew that she had to be there for Steff. There was no time or place for petty pouting. She had to put her feelings aside, and help her friend. She could sort out the rest later.

Seeing how forlorn and beaten Steffie looked, she jumped up and hugged her, as if she would never let her go. She kept patting her on the back, and whispering, "It'll be okay. It's going to be fine. We'll work it out." What she was really thinking was "How could Steffie have lied to me all this time. I don't really know her. What other secrets does she have? What kind of friend is she? Why didn't she tell me?"

She felt hurt and shocked, but knew that Steffie felt even worse. Maybe she would have been exactly the same if the situations had been reversed. Would she have felt comfortable telling people that she had a brother in prison? Not very likely. Would she have hidden it from Steffie? She wasn't sure.

Steffie seemed hugely relieved to have shared her secret. Now she was ready to tell more. "His name is Nick, and he's been in trouble with the law since he was a kid. When he was about ten, he was diagnosed with a brain tumour. They operated, and everything seemed fine, but his whole personality changed. He became rebellious and mean, and he started hanging around with older boys who were always in trouble.

You know that my dad was a policeman, and he died in the line of duty, when Nick and I were both pretty young. My mom had to raise the two of us, and it was really hard for her when Nick started going wild." Steffie stopped here to finish her wine, and hold out her glass for more. Kitty refilled both glasses, and sat down again at the table, while her friend continued the tale.

"Kit, he was the dearest little fellow when he was young. We used to hang out together all the time. He was gentle and funny and smart — everything that he isn't now. After that damned surgery, he was just a totally different person. He got in with the wrong crowd, and they led him along. Because my dad had been killed in the line of duty, the police were all so good to Nick, and easy on him. It would have been better if they had been really tough, but they were trying to be so nice, mostly for my mom's sake.

He got away with too much, and he just kept doing more and more stupid stuff. He was caught in an armed robbery, and that's when his luck ran out. Two days after he was sentenced to prison, my mom died of a massive heart attack. I've always blamed him for killing her, because she really died of a broken heart.

I don't know how he found me, he wouldn't say, but he knew about the boutique, and he followed me back to your place today after work. He thought it was my house, and he was set to move right in. I was afraid he'd hurt the cats, so I brought him here. Now he knows where I live, he'll never leave me alone." There was genuine despair in her voice.

"Hey, we'll figure something out. We'll talk to Jack Willinger, and he'll help us. Maybe we can get a restraining order." Kitty didn't have any idea what she was saying, but she was sure that Jack would be able to help them. She had quickly pushed her hurt feelings aside, and was ready to do battle for Steffie. One thing was for sure. After the trauma of being shot, Steffie certainly didn't need this hassle. Kitty would do everything she could to help. It broke her heart to see her usually boisterous friend looking so whipped.

She finally persuaded Steffie to come back to her house with her, on the theory that there was safety in numbers. If Nick showed up, well, they would deal with him somehow. She helped Steffie pack a small bag, and they put all Steffie's jewellery into it. She didn't own very much, but some of the pieces were expensive. No point in taking any chances, and leaving them around for this Nick person to steal. Kitty already felt as if she hated him.

All the time they were packing, Steffie was telling her more about her brother Nick. She kept explaining that it wasn't his fault. He had been a wonderful brother right up until the time of the brain tumour, and after that damn operation, he had just never been the same. It was as if she was apologizing for him, or making excuses. Possibly she was trying to convince herself that he wasn't so bad.

"Steff, do you think that he would ever really hurt you?" Kitty didn't like to even ask the question, but she wanted to know just how dangerous this guy was.

"I doubt it. After all, he's my brother, and I'm sure there's still lots of good in him. He just made too many bad choices, and his luck ran out. He seems stupid and greedy now, but I can't imagine him actually hurting me. He was such a good brother when we were young." Steffie shook her head again, and wiped away a few more straggling tears.

"This is ridiculous. I can't let him frighten me this way. It's just that it was such a shock to open the door and see him standing there. He looks so different now. Gawd, Kitty, I feel like a bug on the windshield just waiting for the wipers to get me. First the shooting, and now this. What next?"

They both laughed at the ridiculous picture she had painted.

Kitty put the bag down on the bed, and gave Steffie another hug. "Don't worry, we'll sort it out. He'll likely be gone by tomorrow. Once he knows that there's nothing here for him, he'll just move on." She wasn't at all sure that this was the case, but it seemed to calm Steffie a bit.

They were almost back to Kitty's house, before she realized that she hadn't even had the chance to tell Steff about Mitch and the fateful canoe accident. Oh well, that could wait for another day. Somehow it all paled in comparison to Steffie's troubles. This was not the "welcome home" she had expected. Never mind, she told herself. We just have to make it through tonight, and then we'll get some advice.

CHAPTER 34

▼

Traffic was heavy on Highway 400 south, as Mitch made his way back to Toronto from the cottage. He had tried to call Sheridan as he drove along, but there was no answer. He knew that there wouldn't be, but he had to try. She would be so angry with him, that there would be sparks flying right out of her eyes. Damn, what a mess!

Sheridan Monteith was Mitch's girlfriend, lover, significant other, future bride, any and all of the above, or more likely none of them, he thought sourly. They had fought again before he left for Muskoka, and they sure as hell were going to fight when he got home so late. Her anger would know no bounds. She was the "someone" he had suddenly remembered, while cuddling on the dirty old couch with Kitty. He was amazed with himself, because he had thought so seldom of her all week long, while trying to get Kitty out of his head.

They were supposed to be going to a glittering social function tonight at the elegant old Royal York Hotel, and Mitch was about four hours late, maybe more. He hadn't wanted to go in the first place, but she would never believe that circumstances beyond his control, had kept him from returning on time. She would choose to believe that he had done it on purpose, and Sheridan could hold a grudge for weeks.

Mitch sighed, as he stared ahead at the highway. There was a long line of red tail lights for as far as he could see. How was he going to talk his way out of this one, and did he really care anymore? That was the big question. He was so tired of the quarrels they had been having in the past few months. They distracted him from his writing, and left him feeling frustrated and angry. It saddened him to realize that he just didn't care anymore. The girl he had loved since they were both university students, had changed dramatically, and he really didn't like the new Sheridan.

She was a tall, statuesque brunette, with slightly slanted green eyes, and high cheek bones, which gave her an exotic look. He had fallen in love with her, not just because of her looks, but because she had such an enthusiasm and intensity for life. She wanted to change the world, and Mitch had thought that she was just the one to do it.

In those early days, she had worshipped Mitch, proud to be associated with a budding author. He had already had a few short stories published, and enjoyed a certain measure of fame amongst his friends and fellow students.

Sheridan's father was a big Bay Street broker, and after graduation, she had joined his firm. She lived with him in their Rosedale mansion, and after her mother died, Sheridan became her dad's social partner, and chatelaine of the big house, hosting fancy dinner parties, and glittering soirées.

Gradually, under her father's influence, she had changed, become harder, more interested in the Toronto social scene, and less caring about the plight of the little people. She had forgotten all about changing the world, and making it a better place. She had changed towards Mitch too, always trying to drag him into her social world, which was anathema to him. He loathed the empty-headed, frantic paced life she seemed to have chosen, and they were pulling further and further apart.

Sheridan now hung around with people Mitch didn't like, and in return, she scorned his literary friends, most of whom were poor and struggling. He had a wonderful loft in a converted warehouse in downtown Toronto, within walking distance to the theatres, restaurants, libraries and parks. She had loved it at first, but would never move in with him because "daddy" needed her.

Under her father's aegis, she was appointed to several boards, did a certain amount of the requisite charity work, and filled her days with what appeared to Mitch to be meaningless activities. He suspected that she clung to him now, because he had become very successful, and it gave her a certain cachet to be associated with a well-known author.

He sometimes felt like a trained seal, when he accompanied her to one party after another, where it seemed that people all drank too much, gossiped constantly, and conducted tiresome business deals. These parties all had a feeling of desperation about them, and Mitch found that the best way to get through them, was by studying the guests as possible characters for his books. He often amused himself by picturing different ways of killing them off.

Recently, he had bought a sailboat, which was his solace. He had pictured them sailing out of Toronto harbour, headed for Niagara-on-the-Lake, for quiet, romantic weekends in one of the town's many quaint inns and hotels. In the old days, Sheridan would have loved it, and would have learned to sail right along with him. Now, however, she had sailed with him just once, and stated unequivocally that she would never be dragged out again. Her complaints ranged from — it had ruined her hairdo, she had broken a nail, and it had been colossally boring one minute, and too scary the next.

Granted, it had turned into a pretty rough ride that day, but Mitch thought it was exciting and challenging, and it disappointed him that she wasn't interested in sharing it with him. This was certainly not the Sheridan he had loved all these years. Hell, he couldn't even kiss her impulsively, for fear that he might smudge her lipstick. It was as if an alien had gradually taken over her body.

As he drove along, he thought about Kitty, and how different she was to Sheridan. He thought of that determined little frown which sometimes appeared on her forehead, and he liked the way her nose wrinkled when she laughed. She was beautiful in an outdoorsy sort of way, and seemed totally unaware of her looks. Her lips were delectable, and she had touched something deep inside Mitch. She was a warm, funny girl, who seemed to see the world in brilliant colours, while Sheridan was now a tough, take-no-prisoners type of woman, who saw the world in black and white, like the tile foyer in her father's mansion.

Mitch realized that he wanted to tell Sheridan their relationship was over, and he wanted to tell Kitty that their relationship was just beginning. He also wanted to talk to his best friend Steve. Steve Manning was a great piano player, a tall, lanky, funny, irreverent studio musician.

Unfortunately, Steve and Sheridan had never liked each other. One night not long ago, after drinking too much, Steve had apologized first, then told Mitch regretfully that he suspected Sheridan had a pineapple stuck up her ass. At the time, it had seemed hilarious. They were sailing and drinking buddies, and Mitch had realized just recently, that he would give up Sheridan, before he would lose his friend Steve. That was not the way he ever wanted to think of any woman in his life. The woman he chose to love forever, had to be the woman for whom he would choose to die. He was enough of a romantic, to know that this had to be true.

He was so damn hungry that his stomach was howling, as he turned into the Harvey's near Barrie. He watched in drooling anticipation, as the young girl behind the counter — likely a summer student — deftly piled the lettuce, onions and hot peppers onto his cheeseburger, adding a tomato and pickle, before quickly wrapping it in waxed paper, and putting it on his tray. Along with that, came a carton of crispy French fries, and a cup of scalding coffee.

If he hadn't been so late, he would have been eating filet mignon and lobster tails with Sheridan tonight at the Royal York, but the cheeseburger was pure ambrosia. He realized that he had eaten nothing since the canned peaches that morning. No wonder this tasted so good.

As he ate, Mitch looked around with interest at the other travellers. He loved to "people watch," and he often made up stories in his mind, as to what these people did for a living, and what kind of lives they had. One young couple in their early twenties looked to be madly in love, or perhaps they were merely lustful. He noticed that they kept touching their feet and legs together under the table, and the fellow ran his hand slowly along her arm, in between bites of his burger. That was how he and Sheridan had been a lifetime ago, and it tweaked some bittersweet memories.

There was an old couple sitting with their two rambunctious grandchildren. The couple looked bewildered and tired, as if they couldn't understand how they had come to this point in their lives. The kids were whining, and carrying on in an undisciplined way, and the grandparents barely had time to eat their snacks. He guessed that they were bringing the kids back from the cottage, and would be happy to turn them back over to their parents.

Two bikers in Harley Davidson leather jackets and bandanas, came in just as he was getting a coffee refill. The woman had a limp, and looked as if life had been difficult, but she was still trying to be young and wild. The man was stocky and rough cut, with grey hair in a pony tail, and steely blue eyes. He seemed oddly gentle with her, and Mitch wondered whether her limp was the result of a motorcycle accident.

One man sitting alone, looked somehow furtive in his movements, and Mitch thought immediately of the Black Sheep. Was he still in Niagara Falls, or was he on the road looking for more victims? This guy could easily pass for a serial killer. He had a strange, weasily look about him.

Mitch finally told himself that he had more important things about which to worry, and as he drove along, his thoughts went again to the little cabin on the island, and to last night's events. When Kitty had asked if there was anyone waiting at home for him, it had jolted him back to reality, and he remembered the big party at the Royal York to which he was supposed to be going. That was why he had been so curt when he replied "someone." Up to that moment, he had basically forgotten about Sheridan. He was too busy enjoying being there with Kitty, in her frilly blue lingerie — and out of it! She, however, had dragged him back to reality with that one question.

He sighed, as he approached the outskirts of the city. There would be hell to pay about being late for the gala. It was to raise money for the Royal Ontario Museum, certainly a worthy cause.

What excuse was he going to give Sheridan? If he told her the truth about spending the night in the cabin with Kitty, she would likely cut off his nuts. Well, she'd have to catch him first. He realized that he just didn't care that much what she thought. He was going to tell her that it was all over, and that would be the end of it — he hoped. At the moment, all he could think about was Kitty, and how her hair curled around her face, and how she looked standing naked, before wrapping that tatty old blanket around herself. She was funny and smart and beautiful, and he wanted to get to know her much better. He kicked himself mentally for having wasted the entire week. There had been a spark there, no doubt about it.

As he rode the creaky old elevator up to his large and airy loft, he made up his mind that it was too late to bother getting into his tux, and heading to the hotel. The gala would be winding down, and Sheridan would be in a terrible mood. He would talk to her tomorrow, and tell her that they were finished.

Plunking himself down by the window, he looked out at the beautiful city, adorned with twinkling and flashing lights. As he stared out into the inky blackness, broken by the myriads of lights, he felt as if the blinkers had just come off. He had been clinging to a dream, a memory of Sheridan as she used to be. "Time to move on, Mitch," he muttered, but shit, it was going to be a mess. He hated confrontation, and he knew he was about to step into a pile of doo-doo right up to his armpits. He sighed as he poured himself a drink. He wasn't going to call Kitty until he had broken things off with Sheridan. That would be the honest, fair, and gentlemanly thing to do. He owed Sheridan that much, after all their good years together. Still, his faithfulness during the bad years should count for something.

He absently ran his fingers through his hair, as he thought glumly that there would be no peaceful time to concentrate on his book, until he worked things out with Sheridan. Knowing Sheridan as well as he did, he realized that he was heading into a week of emotional hell.

CHAPTER 35

▼

Two Japanese women, who couldn't speak any English, were keeping Steffie busy. Kitty grinned, as she watched her friend become more and more frustrated, trying to communicate with them. They had chosen their items, and were holding out Japanese money at the counter. Steffie, in turn, was shaking her head, and holding out both Canadian and American money, to show that's what they needed. Steff had started to laugh, realizing the futility of her situation. Kitty wondered how she was going to extricate herself from the confusion. She was enjoying Steff's predicament, when she looked up and saw Scott Matheson stride in.

Damnation! A confrontation with Scott had not been on the agenda for this Monday morning. He looked cool and glamorous in his navy chinos, light blue shirt, and designer sunglasses. Kitty could understand now why she had fallen for him just on first impressions. Any red blooded woman under ninety would have done the same. Somehow, though, now that Mitch filled every waking moment, Scott had lost his luster. Thank goodness for small mercies.

"Well, Kitty Kat, how're you doing? Man, you look great in that lime green. That colour really suits you. It makes your eyes look turquoise. You've got a great tan too. Have you been away on vacation, or just sunning in your own backyard?" He sauntered over, and attempted to give her a hug.

Kitty side-stepped him nicely, and backed behind a display case, putting it between them. Her first impulse was to head for the office and shut the door in his face, but she stood her ground. He wasn't going to get the best of her this time. "Hello, Scott," she said coolly, ignoring his flattery. He seemed totally at ease, as if they were just two very close old friends who had been apart for a while. What a nerve he had!

"Now Kit-Kat, don't be unfriendly," he replied good-naturedly. "You made entirely too much of that situation. All guys cheat once in a while. It doesn't mean a damn thing. You were always the one, and deep down, I think you know it. Actually, I came to take you out for a coffee. We've got a lot of catching up to do." He grinned seductively at her, as if they had no bad history between them. Reaching across the counter, he took one of her hands, and began kissing each finger.

Kitty snatched her hand away quickly, as if she had been burned. She couldn't quite believe what she was hearing. This guy was something else. He was as oily as a jar of olives. What had she ever seen in him? She glanced over at Steffie, but her friend was still involved with the Japanese tourists.

"That situation?" she repeated incredulously. "Scott, the truly sad thing is that you don't even realize just how wrong that was. You don't get it that any woman would be disgusted and hurt at what you did. I'll give you a little word of advice. If you're going to cheat, don't bring her into your girlfriend's home, and into her bed. That's not only crude and insensitive, but it's a definite 'no-no.'"

He had never been one to take kindly to rejection, and he wasn't about to start now. "Come on baby," he cajoled in his deep, sexy voice. That voice used to thrill her, but now she thought sourly that he likely practised it in front of the mirror, dropping it an octave when he wanted to sound seductive. "Being nasty doesn't suit you. I could make a gallon of wine just from your sour grapes attitude. What's the point of not being friends? Remember the fun we had? I've really missed you, Kit-Kat. You know how good we were together. The fact that you're so angry, tells me that you still care. I say we should start all over."

Before Kitty could get a word in, Scott continued laying on the charm, like a kid lathering butter on his toast.

"Damn, I'd almost forgotten how adorable you are when you get all riled up. Your eyes sparkle, and your cheeks get all pink. Let's have dinner tonight. I've waited long enough for you to get over it." He was speaking quickly, not giving her a chance to answer. Strangely, he had made this little speech sound very sincere.

It didn't impress Kitty, however. While he was talking, all she could think about was that embarrassing, and infuriating moment, when she had walked in and seen the two of them rolling around on her bed. She was afraid that picture might be imprinted on her eyeballs for life.

"What part of 'no' don't you understand? I'm busy tonight, and as far as you're concerned, I'm busy every night right on into eternity. We're finished, Scott. Now, please stop calling me, and coming into the shop. Go back to your redhead, or has she smartened up and dumped you?" She couldn't resist that little zinger, childish as it was.

"Hardly," he laughed easily, taking off his sunglasses and twirling them around. "She was just a passing fancy. You know you're the only girl for me, and, as I've told you before, no woman ever leaves me. It isn't allowed." He smiled as he said this, but Kitty could tell by his eyes that he was deadly serious. She could feel the bad vibes radiating across the counter. "You're my girl, and you damn well know it," he added grimly.

"This is ridiculous, and I really don't have the time. Stop trying to be seductive one minute and sinister the next, Scott. It makes you look foolish." She laughed as she said this, and added, "Just get over yourself."

Kitty remembered that Scott couldn't stand to have anyone laugh at him. He was very sensitive in that respect, so her words had been a perfect put-down.

She heard Steffie give a little snort at this, and she had to smile. She was immediately sorry though, that she had become embroiled in this war of words. She should have shown more class, and simply walked away.

In a flash, Scott's powerful hand reached across the display case, and caught Kitty by the wrist. "No one leaves me, Kitty-Kat," he hissed through clenched teeth. "I've given you plenty of time to get over being mad, so just remember what I said, no one leaves me." Each word was hissed slowly. "You'd better rethink this relationship, and I'll be calling you."

Kitty tried to pull away, just as Cleo appeared from the storage room. Seeing Scott, and not properly assessing the situation, she waltzed right over to him. Immediately, his scowl disappeared, and was replaced by one of his poster-boy smiles. He let go of Kitty's wrist, and turned to Cleo.

"Hi Scott, good to see you again. How've you been?" She was all flirtatious and giggly, and Kitty was totally surprised. How the heck did Cleo know Scott? Were there any pretty women in town he didn't know? And were there any available men in town whom Cleo didn't know? She was glad of the interruption though, as she had nothing more to say to him. The old charm just didn't work on her any more. Compared to Mitch, he was a big zero.

Excusing herself, she approached a customer, who was picking up one fancy perfume bottle after another. She looked like a klutz, and the big purse hanging open on her arm, was either going to knock half the delicate little bottles off the shelf, or the woman might just accidentally on purpose, drop a few of the fancy items into it. Kitty wasn't taking any chances. Besides, she was grateful for an excuse to walk away from Scott. She might have been very uneasy, if she had seen the black look he gave her, as she turned her back and walked away.

He didn't stay long after that, although Cleo did her best to keep him chatting. By now the tour guide had arrived, looking for her two missing Japanese ladies. She got the money problems all sorted out, and they left, happily clutching their purchases, and talking excitedly in their own language.

Steffie enjoyed hearing the different languages of their summer patrons, and she and Kitty tried to keep track of how many different nationalities they served in a day. There were always Germans and Japanese on the tour buses, and they were seeing more and more East Indians and South Americans. Between the two of them, they could get by with rudimentary French, Spanish and German, but Steffie decided ruefully that she had better learn a few Japanese words too.

Steffie had heard bits and pieces of the exchange between Kitty and Scott, but she wanted to know everything. She listened with a frown on her face, as Kitty gave her a run down of the conversation.

"He gave you a very menacing look when he left," Steffie reported. "I thought the choo-choo was going to jump the track. He looked really wigged out."

"Oh, I don't give a hoot how he looked. He doesn't scare me," said Kitty crossly. "He's too full of himself to waste any more time on me. He's likely bedding three or four other foolish women by now. He's just an ordinary guy with too much testosterone. I think it's in the mist from the falls. Every man I've met in this damn town is full of the same macho horseshit."

"I don't think I'd call Scott an ordinary guy. As a matter of fact, he's about as ordinary as a cannibal at a vegetarian buffet," laughed Steffie, but she looked concerned.

Kitty grinned. "It was a bit of a debacle, wasn't it? I wish I had simply gone into the office and shut the door. I shouldn't have talked to him at all.

You know, I'm thinking I'm going to swear off men for at least a year. I'll be celibate, and avoid all these macho morons."

Steffie looked at her, and grinned. "Oh, sure. That will happen just about the same time that we see a bright star in the sky, and three wisemen come to call."

Kitty laughed and took a playful swipe at her friend. "Anyway, I didn't realize that Cleo knew Scott, did you?" She glanced over at Cleo, who was busy with a customer. "Should I warn her, or let her find out about him for herself?"

"You'd better mention it to her. She's so flighty she won't see it coming till it's too late, and I suspect she may be setting her sights on Scott as the boy-toy flavour of the month."

"Yah, just like someone else once did," said Kitty ruefully. As soon as she was free, she would ask Cleo where and when she had met Scott, and whether they had dated yet. This summer was turning into a little Peyton Place melodrama, with the Black Sheep thrown in for added excitement.

Cleo eventually finished with her customer, and turned to Kitty. "Did you have a nice time up at your cottage?" she asked with interest.

"Yes, it was wonderful. I hated to come back so soon," Kitty replied, as she tidied the miniature teapots. "Cleo, I didn't realize that you knew Scott Matheson. How did that come about?"

Cleo looked a bit embarrassed. "Can you believe it, I met him in the Canadian Tire Store up on Montrose. We started talking, and then he asked me out. We went out a couple of times and had fun, but then I had to turn him down twice, because I already had plans, and he stopped calling me. Maybe I shouldn't have told him that I was dating Keith too, but I like to be honest and up front with my dates. He didn't take it well. Then Keith was annoyed when I told him about Scott, so I got myself into a lot of trouble just for trying to be honest. Now I've met another guy, but I'm not even going to mention his name until I see how it works out. My problem is that when I'm with one man, someone else looks irresistible. There are so many wonderful men in the world. I'd like to date them all." She laughed at her own foolishness, and went off to help another customer.

Kitty and Steffie just looked at each other and shrugged. Cleo was young and silly, but she was a good little worker, and had been an asset to the boutique. Her love life was her own business.

It was at that point that one of their long-time customers walked in, and they both groaned. Niagara Falls was full of characters, and Donald Kirkwood was certainly one of them. He was a fatuous old fool, but his saving grace was that he had a lot of money. He spoke in funereal tones, which set the women giggling. They always wanted to ask him who had died. He was well into his 70's, but wore his hair, what was left of it, in a ridiculous, straggly, greyish-white ponytail. Actually, it was more like a rat's tail. He also sported three earrings in one ear.

In years gone by, Donald and his wife had run a very successful and elegant bed and breakfast down on River Road. After his wife died, however, Donald lost it. He bought himself a motorcycle, and he discontinued the B&B, but continued to live there by himself. Rumour had it that he had closed off the entire house, except for one bedroom, a bathroom, and the kitchen. Several entrepreneurs were interested in buying the gracious old three story home, which was sitting on prime property, overlooking the Niagara River. Donald, however, wouldn't let anyone in to see it. He had every intention of dying there.

The best thing about Donald, was that he loved to spend money. The worst thing was, well there were so many 'worst' things about him. He had become obstreperous in his old age, and was a difficult man with whom to deal. He was a regular customer, however, and always left with bags full of trinkets and treasures. Kitty and Steffie pictured him storing them in the unused bedrooms. What a waste! They hated to think of some of the beautiful articles from their boutique, being hidden away in a closet or a spare bedroom, where no one could see them, or enjoy them.

He was such a silly little man, who had just gone a bit crazy after losing his beloved wife of so many happy years. There was always a peculiar smell about him, like cabbage or dirty sox. They suspected that he didn't shower more than once a month.

Since Steffie really got along well with seniors, she was usually the one who got stuck waiting on him. Steffie felt that unkindness was the ultimate sin, so she always tried to be nice to old Donald, but at times it was difficult. In spite of all his faults, though, they both felt a bit sorry for him, and made a real effort to be friendly and helpful whenever he appeared.

Today, however, they couldn't help comparing the arrival of Scott, looking clean and attractive, with this smelly, ponytailed little fool. Each man was awful in his own way, but they decided that in the long run, maybe Scott was worse. Life was full of such unexpected inconsistencies, and people were the most inconsistent of all.

CHAPTER 36

▼

Steffie was having a difficult time adjusting to Nick and his chicanery. She kept trying to tell herself that he would soon move on to greener pastures, but she didn't really believe it. He came and went as he pleased, and he was taking every bit of cash from her. She had tried just saying "no" to him, but he had threatened to go over to Kitty's, and get money from her. Steffie couldn't let that happen. His moods were like quicksilver, and that kept Steffie off balance.

The pressure was making her feel as if her nerves were on the outside of her skin. She was suffering from an overwhelming sense of malaise. All fun had gone out of her life. She was having trouble sleeping, and she was cross with everyone in the boutique — not only the customers, but Kitty and Cleo as well.

She and Kitty had called Jack, and had a meeting with him and Bud. She explained the situation with her brother, and begged them to help her. Of course, until Nick did something outside the law, there was very little they could do. He had done his time in prison, had paid his debt to society, and was now a free man.

They did pull him over, however, when they followed him one night. He was driving Steffie's car. That was a golden opportunity, which she missed. All she had to do was say that he had stolen her car, and they could have arrested him. Two things stopped her, however. First of all, he was her brother, like it or not, and maybe he couldn't help himself. Maybe he had another tumour. Secondly, she had to admit that she was afraid of him, and of what he might do to her or to Kitty. So, the golden opportunity to have him arrested, came and went without anything being done.

He seemed to be spending all his time at the casino, and judging by his foul moods when he came back to the apartment, he was losing. She feared that he might be getting involved with loan sharks. What would happen if he got in way over his head? Steffie was afraid to go and stay at Kitty's, for fear that he would just follow her there, and cause trouble, or for fear that he would steal anything in her apartment which could be pawned, in his quest for cash. It seemed to be a catch-22 situation, and her heart was heavy. She really didn't know what to do.

It didn't help her mood any, when she looked up to see Cleo talking to Josh, of all people. What in the world was he doing here? Kitty was back in the office, and hadn't yet seen him.

Cleo was flirting outrageously, and smiling up at him. When Josh whispered something in a low voice, Cleo giggled, and nodded her head coquettishly. When Kitty walked back out into the boutique, Josh put his hand on Cleo's arm, said something quietly to her, then walked over to greet Kitty.

"I just thought it was about time I came to see where you spend your days," he said in a friendly way. "You've got a great shop here. I had no idea it was so big."

Kitty wasn't pleased to see him here, but she was coldly polite. Josh apparently got the message, because he didn't stay long. He spoke to Cleo again, and whatever he said, made her smile up at him and nod her head.

"Boy, she really does get around, doesn't she?" muttered Steffie to Kitty. She was giving Cleo one of her death-ray glares.

"I think she's asking for trouble. It's nice to be popular, but this is getting ridiculous. She's been dating Keith and that Barry, the male nurse, and I know she really has the hots for Drew. I think she may have been out with Scott, and now she's making goo-goo eyes at Josh. She's going to end up with a lot of angry men all mad at her. Talk about bees to a honey pot."

When Cassie and Vickie dropped into the boutique that day, they could see that something was wrong with Steffie. She just wasn't her usual fun-loving, sociable, sparkling self. Kitty had already told Cassie about her own near brush with death in the canoe, and Cassie, of course, knew about Steffie being shot earlier in the summer. She didn't know anything about Nick, but she did know that these two friends needed a vacation, and she had a brilliant idea.

Browsing around until the shop was empty, Cassie came right to the point. "I have a huge favour to ask you two, and in return, I can do you a favour. It will work well for everyone." This sounded intriguing, and caught their interest at once.

"What nefarious little schemes have you cooked up now?" laughed Kitty, glad to have the distraction. She was worried about Steffie, who seemed so on edge these days.

"First of all, let me tell you a little bit about my condo in Panama City Beach. It's a two bedroom, deluxe condo at a very elegant and fun-filled place called Edgewater Beach Resort. Honestly, this place has everything you could possibly want. The beach is about 18 miles long, and it's pure white sugary sand. Each condo tower has its own heated pool and hot tub, and there's a gorgeous lagoon pool for everyone to enjoy.

There are tennis courts, and a great gym. The towers are right on the beach, but the villas are built around the most difficult little par three course you would ever want to play. Best of all, there's a great restaurant called 'Oceans' which is also on the beach. You can sit on the deck and have breakfast. It's lovely just watching the swimmers, and the kids building sand castles, and the busy little sandpipers running here and there.

Cassie paused for a breath, and Vickie jumped in. "I've been there, and everything that Cassie says is true. It's a real paradise. You can sit out on your own balcony, drinking margaritas every night, watching the sunset. It's a kaleidoscope of colours. No two sunsets are the same in Florida. Then at bedtime, you can have your windows open, and let the sound of the surf lull you to sleep."

By now Steffie was getting restless. This was a nice little travelogue, but really, who cared? Why were Cassie and Vickie telling them all this junk?

"You can go seadooing or parasailing, or take the glass bottomed boat over to Shell Island," continued Cassie. "There are dozens of great little bars, and right across the street there's a mall with movie theatres, a state of the art bowling alley and lots of boutiques and restaurants.

Now comes the good part. I'm having new Mexican tile put in the foyer and bathrooms of my condo, and I'm supposed to be there next week to supervise. Unfortunately, my darling son Mark broke his leg yesterday water skiing, and —."

Here both Kitty and Steffie interrupted her. "What? How is he? Is it a bad break? Was it up at the resort where he's working for the summer?"

"He's doing fine, and it's a nice clean break, and yes, it was while he was working. He runs the water ski school there — at least he did," she added ruefully.

"Now, here's the point of all this info. You two really need a vacation. You've both been through a lot this summer. I need someone to supervise the laying of the tile, which will only take one day. I can't get away just now, with Mark in the hospital, so I would like to fly you two down for the week. You can stay in my condo, and you just need to dedicate the one day to seeing that the tile is finished properly. The rest of the time will be yours to do as you please. How about it?"

Kitty and Steffie simply stared at her, then looked at each other and grinned. "It sounds great," said Kitty slowly, but we couldn't possibly do it. What about our boutique, and what about my cats?"

"I've got that covered I think. Cleo will be here, and either Vickie or I will come in each day to help her. We should be able to manage, and I can learn a lot, since I'm planning to open a gift shop at The Cattery. As far as your cats are concerned, we have a couple of choices. I was wondering whether your mom and dad would come over from Toronto to mind them. If that isn't possible, either Vickie or I will move in to your house for the week. With both our husbands over in Europe again, we're free as birds. We can do whatever we like, and at the moment, this is what we like. There's just no way to say 'no', ladies. I need you and you need me. How about it?"

"You are one crazy lady," grinned Steffie, giving her a hug.

It was the first time Vickie had seen her smile for days.

"You're likely right about that," laughed Cassie, "but you love me anyway. It's a perfect place for you to do some sketching and painting, Steff. Be sure to bring the supplies you need."

There was absolutely nothing else to be said, except for a resounding 'yes,' and that was how, three days later, the two friends found themselves on a plane heading to Panama City Beach.

They had taken an early flight, had an hour in Atlanta, switched to a small jet, and found themselves landing at the comfortable little Panama City airport before noon. The temperature was in the high 80's, there was a balmy breeze causing the palm trees to sway gently, as if listening to music only they could hear, and the skies were a clear, vivid blue. Kitty and Steffie felt as if they had landed in paradise. "It's cooler here than it is at home," smiled Steffie with delight. Niagara Falls had been suffering under a heat wave for several days now, and the humidity had been really debilitating.

Following Cassie's careful directions, and driving the rental car, which they had picked up at the airport, they crossed the Hathaway Bridge. En route, they marvelled at how the sun twinkled and glistened on the aquamarine waters of the Gulf of Mexico.

"Kitty, look at those darling little pineapple palms. Oh, I wish we could take some home with us. They're just perfect."

They were thrilled with the deluxe, very elegantly decorated condo. They headed right for the balcony, which overlooked the turquoise water of the lagoon pool, the white sandy beach, which stretched as far as they could see in either direction, and the sparkling Gulf of Mexico. It was almost more than they could take in.

After exploring the condo, deciding who got which bedroom, and changing into shorts and tops, they elected to have lunch at the resort restaurant, "Oceans," which was right beside the lagoon pool. The place was full, but they arrived just as a family was leaving, so they got a prime table on the deck. Over deliciously tart margaritas, they discussed Cassie's generosity, and their great good fortune. Because Cassie had inherited so much money, which she really felt that she didn't deserve, she was extremely generous with it. It gave her pleasure to do nice things for her friends, but she never made a big thing of it. Kitty and Steffie just happened to be the latest recipients of her largesse.

The friends didn't know where to start first. After having two margaritas each, they were both feeling lethargic, relaxed, and totally incapable of doing anything but sit there and soak up the atmosphere. They had already forgotten about the shooting, the Black Sheep, and Nick. Life was good!

Eventually, they strolled around the resort, familiarizing themselves with all that it offered. The beautiful Convention Center really impressed them, although there were no entertainers scheduled for that week. When they saw how well equipped the exercise room was, they told themselves that they would use it every morning. Joke!!! There were far too many wonderful things to see and do. There would never be time to do them all in one short week, and exercising was far down the list.

By the time they had checked out the golf course and the tennis courts, and had a swim in the heated pool, they were ready for a short nap. They hated to waste a minute sleeping, but they had been up at 4am to catch their early flight out of Buffalo, and neither friend could keep her eyes open.

CHAPTER 37

▼

While Kitty and Steffie were getting used to the luxuries of Edgewater Beach Resort, back in Niagara Falls, the city residents were sweltering in the unusually hot, humid days. With the temperatures reaching the high 90's, and the humidex making it feel more like 120 degrees, city residents were becoming cranky. One person in particular, was really bothered by the heat. The Black Sheep was finding himself more and more nervous and antsy. He felt cross and angry with the world. The headaches were increasing, so that he was popping pills all day long, which was not conducive to carrying out his job in an efficient way. Wisely, he had taken two weeks vacation time, so that no one was likely to be aware of his deteriorating condition.

Tonight he was looking at his pictures in the Black Sheep box. One of these days he was going to put them in an album, but he wasn't quite ready yet. He liked the pictures well enough, but an idea had occurred to him, which was really annoying. Why hadn't he placed each body beside a trash can or dumpster? That would have been so perfect. The women he had strangled were nothing but trash, and it would have made such a great statement. Of course, he still would have put the little black sheep in each dead woman's hand, but they should have been sitting beside a trash can. Damn it anyway. Why hadn't he thought of it sooner? It was too late now. He didn't want to change his modus operandi. It might be unlucky.

He was now full of pent up rage at Kitty, who was to be his next and possibly last victim. He had pretty well decided to forget about killing Ginny. The near miss at her place had been a warning. There was no way he was going to try that again, so Ginny was off the hook, at least for the moment.

Anyway, he told himself that he really loved Ginny, and that sometime soon he was going to start trying to win her affections.

For now he had to concentrate on Kitty. Unfortunately, she had gone away very suddenly, and this had added to his anger and frustration. He simply could not wait for her to come back. He was so full of contradictory emotions and painful feelings, that he had to find release. He had to find a substitute victim within the next few days, or he might lose complete control, and make some incriminating mistake.

While the Black Sheep was struggling with his feelings, Kitty and Steffie were enjoying every moment. Edgewater Beach Resort was all that Cassie had promised. There weren't enough hours in the day to fit in all the fun activities. The tilers had come and gone, and had done an excellent job. They knew that Cassie would be pleased about that.

Steffie had taken the time to do some sketching, and was disappointed that she hadn't brought her watercolours with her. There were some incredible scenes here, and she wished she could recreate at least some of them. The next best thing would be to take pictures of them, and then try to paint them when she got home.

Walking the white sugary sands was a priority, and the friends were trying to do that each morning before it got too hot. They liked to walk from Edgewater right down to Pineapple Willy's and back. They figured that would be about four kilometres, which was a good way to start the day.

They loved to watch the busy little sandpipers running to the edge of the water, pecking at insects, then scurrying back, just ahead of the advancing waves. It was a ritual which they repeated over and over. They looked like tiny wind-up toys, endlessly running here and there in a pattern which only they could understand.

Steffie noted that the beach was relatively free of shells, and Kitty was happy that there were no jellyfish to be seen. It seemed quite safe to walk along the water's edge in their bare feet.

The beach was teeming with young children and families having fun. Frisbees flew everywhere, and there were often young teens playing football or volleyball. One morning they stopped and joined two young girls who were making a sand castle, and they spent some time talking with an old fellow who was standing in the water, fishing. He said that he never caught anything, but it gave him time to do a lot of thinking. Beach walking was definitely one of their greatest pleasures.

One evening early in the week, they had been sitting at the bar in the on-site restaurant "Oceans." It was a happening place, and there were always interesting people with whom to chat.

That particular evening, they met a handsome old fellow with a shock of white hair. He must have been in his 80's, but he was full of fun, and very witty. He told them that he was an Air Force full colonel, and liked to play golf at the Tyndall Air Force Base golf club, which was called Pelican Point. He told the friends just how beautiful the course was, as many of the holes ran right along the gulf.

Kitty and Steffie were interested to hear Colonel Jake's stories. He told them that Clark Gable had been at Tyndall for five weeks way back in 1942, while he was earning his silver wings. The story might have been apocryphal, but they were pretty sure that it was true. According to the colonel, the arrival of Gable put Panama City and Tyndall into the national spotlight for a short while.

He also told them some of the history of the area. According to him, there had been a proposal at one time to sell the Florida panhandle to Alabama. The Florida residents, however, had objected so strenuously, that the idea was finally scrapped.

General Andrew Jackson had apparently marched through the panhandle with his troups, on his way to New Orleans in 1818. The story goes that he was infuriated and horrified at the lawless nature of the place at that time. It had become a no-man's land for runaway slaves and Indians.

According to Colonel Jake, who was just getting warmed up to the subject, the Conquistadors liked to name places after catholic saints. St. Andrews Bay got its name because it was discovered on St. Andrews day.

Colonel Jake kept them entertained for a long time, but the best part of the evening was when he invited them to play a round of golf with him and his wife at Tyndall. It sounded exciting, but they had no idea just how exciting it would be.

True to his word, the colonel was there to meet them at the guardhouse when they arrived. It was another sunny day with vibrant blue skies, and even as they drove toward the golf club, they could hear the planes overhead. "Those must be the young pilots up there practising," remarked Steffie, sticking her head out the window, to look up at the sky.

Steffie and Kitty were not good golfers, but they were steady, and both could hit a pretty long, if slightly erratic, ball. Colonel Jake was an excellent golfer, but he couldn't see where his ball went, so Maybelle, his adoring wife, stood behind him on each tee, and kept her eyes on the ball. It seemed to be a system which worked well for them.

They were impressed with the signs which were posted at intervals all along the golf course. The warning was "Do not disturb the wildlife, and beware of alligators and snakes."

"Yikes," remarked Kitty. "Don't you dare go looking in the bushes for any of your balls. If you hit one in there, just let it go. I don't want you getting bitten by a rattler, and me having to suck the poison out of your leg."

"You don't need to tell me that," laughed Steffie. "I may be a daredevil, but I'm not stupid."

"Just look at those feathery clumps of pampas grass," said Kitty, pointing to a clump right ahead. "They look like ornamental native huts for pygmies."

"They look to me like perfect hiding places for snakes," replied Steffie pragmatically. Kitty did like to become a bit too poetic and imaginative at times. "Don't go looking in there for your balls. A snake might jump right out at you and bite you on the face." They both grimaced at that unpleasant thought.

The course was indeed very scenic, and Kitty had more fun enjoying the scenery than playing golf. On the sixth hole they noticed a perfectly symmetrical palm tree portal where two palms grew in a curved way. It was very picturesque, and Kitty had to get out the camera and take a few quick shots.

After the first nine holes, Kitty had lost three balls, and Steffie only one. They hadn't been in any serious trouble, and were really enjoying the game. They all dashed in to the clubhouse to buy hot dogs, bags of chips, and cans of pop, then they were off again.

The back nine proved to be much more exciting than they had expected. They were in their cart, riding beside the pond on the eleventh hole, when they saw the alligator. He looked to be about ten feet long, and he was sunning himself on the bank of the pond. They got as close as they thought would be safe, and had a good look at the old fellow. He seemed huge. He turned his head, and stared at them with unblinking eyes. It was a very scary moment. They stayed right in the cart, and Steffie had her foot on the gas, in case he decided to lunge at them. They assumed that the cart could outdistance an alligator, but wondered what would happen if it were to stall. Finally, because they couldn't hold up the game, they had to move on.

Neither woman could believe how beautiful the course was. So many of the holes ran right along the gulf. There were palm trees everywhere, and Spanish moss grew on many of the old oak trees. It hung from the branches like lacy shawls.

On the fifteenth hole, Steffie barely missed stepping on a large black snake, which was lying sunning itself just off the green. Kitty couldn't tell which one was more scared, Steffie or the snake. Steffie let out a small squeak of surprise, and the snake slithered away quickly across the path, and into the rocks on the beach. They couldn't tell what kind of snake it was, but the colonel, who had just seen it from a distance, thought it might have been a water moccasin.

All afternoon the F22's flew above them, sometimes just two, flying in perfect formation, and sometimes four or five. The colonel explained that they were practising precision flying and interceptions, and all kinds of clever things. He was a great source of information, and seemed delighted to have an interested audience.

Over the course of the game, they spotted several small deer, some raccoons, two small alligators in one of the ponds, a great blue heron, and a red-winged hawk. The wildlife was actually more fun than the golf. It was a long and tiring course.

The entire event blew apart on the seventeenth hole. Kitty and Steffie were getting tired, and had had just about enough. The three ladies were waiting for Colonel Jake to take his shot. As usual, Maybelle was standing directly behind him, in order to get a good line on his ball.

All morning they had been annoyed by hornets and smaller flying insects. Maybelle in particular, seemed quite nervous about them. Just as Colonel Jake brought his club back to take his drive, Maybelle ran directly toward him, swinging her arms wildly, as a hornet buzzed around her head. She was thinking of nothing but the hornet. Colonel Jake was thinking of nothing but his back swing.

The accident was inevitable, and both Steffie and Kitty saw it in slow motion. The club came back in the colonel's strong hands, Maybelle stumbled forward, intent on the hornet, and the club and Maybelle's face connected. There was a dreadful pulpy and cracking sound, as club met flesh and teeth. Maybelle dropped like a stone, blood spurting everywhere.

The colonel looked so stunned, that he just stood there, wondering what had happened. Both Kitty and Steffie ran to Maybelle, thinking she must be dead. They could see that almost all her front teeth were gone, both lips were split, and bleeding profusely, and her nose looked to be mashed and broken. She was breathing, but making a dreadful gurgling sound, as she choked on her own blood.

Colonel Jake was shouting at Maybelle, asking why she had done such a dumb thing, all the while trying to lift her. Steffie ran back to her golf bag, and retrieved her cell phone, quickly calling 911. Everything had happened so quickly, yet it seemed forever before help arrived. By then a crowd of golfers had gathered.

Poor Maybelle was taken away, her loving husband, Colonel Jake at her side. He looked as if he had aged twenty years in the past twenty minutes. He still didn't understand what had happened, or why it had happened. He hadn't known anything about the hornet, and had no idea why his wife would suddenly run right at him, as he was taking his swing.

He asked Steffie to call a very good friend of his, and when the fellow arrived, it was time for Kitty and Steff to leave. They weren't needed, and felt that they would just be in the way. It had been a harrowing experience for everyone — especially Maybelle.

CHAPTER 38

▼

The next day, the two women took a trip in to Panama City to do some shopping, to see Maybelle at the hospital, and to visit the beautiful Bay County library. The shopping was good, Maybelle was so bandaged up that she couldn't talk, and they fell in love with the library. It was located right on the gulf, and they discovered that people using the computer room, could sit there and gaze out at the water. What an incredible setting for a library. It seemed to be well supplied with all the latest books, and had a very good selection of audios.

The staff were friendly and helpful, and some of them were quite talkative. Kitty and Steffie were disappointed to learn that a new library was being built in the middle of the city, far away from this gorgeous site. This library was to be torn down, and likely replaced by a highrise condo. It seemed a shame. So-called progress was not always good.

On their way back to Edgewater, they stopped to take some pictures of The Treasure Ship, and to investigate its little gift shop. They discovered The Treasure Ship to be a very popular restaurant in Panama City Beach. It had been built as a two hundred foot long replica of an actual seventeenth century Spanish galleon. It was so intriguing, that they came back for an early dinner that same night.

Later that evening they were sitting in the hot tub, plastic glasses of wine in their hands. Life goes on, and Maybelle was going to be fine, although she would require extensive facial repairs.

It was a sultry, black evening, with a myriad of stars overhead. There had been people in the tub earlier, but now the friends had it to themselves. They enjoyed looking up at their condo building, in which every unit seemed to have lights blazing, doors open, and sounds of laughter floating through the air.

Kitty was thinking about Mitch. They talked on the phone every night, but had seen each other only three times since their wild adventure in Muskoka. They packed a lot into those three times though. It was quality time, and the relationship was going well. He had broken off with Sheridan, but had said little about it, except that she had taken it very hard, and was quite angry.

Kitty would have been horrified if she had realized the actual situation. Mitch had tried to break things off with Sheridan in a kind and gentle fashion. After all, they had been lovers since university days. Unfortunately it wasn't going well. Sheridan refused to take Mitch seriously, and had become much more loving and attentive. For Mitch it was a case of too much too late. For Sheridan, the thought of losing him had given her a real jolt, and she was using all her feminine wiles to hold him. There was no way that he could explain all this to Kitty.

Kitty, on the other hand, was looking forward to getting home and seeing him again. She was blythely unaware of any possible problems. He was a man of few words, quite taciturn at times, which seemed strange for such a prolific writer, but he was special, and things just felt right between them.

"This really is paradise," said Kitty softly. "I wonder whether people who live here all year round know how lucky they are? Do they appreciate it, or do they long to be up north where the seasons change regularly?"

"I'll bet most of them just take it for granted, if they've never known anything else. The constant heat might get really tiresome though. I remember reading one time that someone had called Florida 'a giant petri dish,' because its hot, humid climate is so hospitable and conducive to growth of weird things. I think I like our part of the world better," proclaimed Steffie, taking another sip of her nearly empty glass. She had been feeling so relaxed and more like her old self this week, but tonight there was a strange frisson of fear crawling down her spine. Why? She had no idea. She kept telling herself that they were in a beautiful part of the country, having a super time. Why was she suddenly so apprehensive?

What could be more peaceful than sitting in the hot tub with her friend at midnight? They had been listening to the sounds of the night — the music of the night as it were. There was the gentle, constant lapping of the waves rolling in from distant shores. That was enough to lull anyone to sleep. Then there were the certain persistent and inescapable background noises — the occasional car honking, short bursts of laughter, cries of a child waking from sleep. The night was alive with mystery and romance, yet here sat Steffie, wrinkling up like a prune in the hot tub, and feeling anxious. She felt as if she was unravelling again, and it wasn't a good feeling.

Could she be suffering from post traumatic stress syndrome? Everyone seemed to expect that she might develop it after the shooting. If that's all it was, she could fight it. She was a strong person both emotionally and mentally.

The almost constant ache in her chest and shoulder was gradually disappearing, thanks to all the swimming she had been doing, although the golfing certainly hadn't helped it. She didn't think much about the shooting now, so possibly her returning anxiety was just caused by her worries about Nick. She was very quiet, as they dried themselves and headed back up to their condo balcony. Nick's reappearance in her life, had been a dreadful shock. She still loved him — after all, he was her brother, and there was that strong family tie. Unfortunately, there was no doubt that she feared and resented him too. Something had to be done about Nick, but what?

"Hey, it's about time we had a round of our movie game. Who's turn is it?"

"I don't remember for sure, but I've got one for you," said Steffie, happy to get her mind off her brother for a while. "Name three of the actors in 'The Carpetbaggers.'"

Kitty stared up at the sky, as if hoping to find the answer there, written in the stars. "I liked that movie, but I liked the book even better. You'd think I'd be able to remember all the players, but I'm drawing a blank. Just give me a minute."

Steffie was quite content to shut her eyes and wait for her friend to come up with an answer.

"Okay, I think I've got it now. I know that George Peppard played Jonas Cord. That's the only character name I can remember. Alan Ladd was in it too. There were lots of women, but I think that Elizabeth Ashley and Carroll Baker were in it for sure."

"That's really good, Kit. I'd forgotten all about Elizabeth Ashley, but I remember that Martha Hyer was in it too, and maybe Lew Ayres, but I'm not sure about him. I'm going to have to go way way back to stump you. You saw too many movies in your youth, or you're watching too many replays on TV."

"You're right," laughed Kitty. "I've always loved movies, as you well know." Then adroitly changing the subject, she sighed, and, looking up at the stars, she murmured, "With that gentle breeze on our faces, and the gulf water lapping so rhythmically on that white sugar sand, I feel as if I could stay right here to sleep tonight."

"Oh, let's not get carried away," laughed Steffie. "You can stay out here if you like, but I'm getting into my lovely bed. I'll see you in the morning."

The par three golf course at Edgewater had been beckoning ever since their arrival. After the dreadful accident at Tyndall, however, they weren't sure whether they ever wanted to golf again. Maybelle was going to recover, but it would take a long time. They could both still shut their eyes and hear the sound of that club hitting her face. They had gone to visit her, had taken her flowers, and had invited the Colonel out to lunch. That was really all they could do. His family had arrived from various parts of the country, and he and Maybelle were now in good hands. There was no reason to let the unfortunate accident ruin their lovely holiday, so off they went to challenge the Edgewater course.

It was much more difficult than they had expected. The first hole, however, was relatively easy, and they both managed to get a par on it. The second hole was much more challenging, and they both lost a ball in the water. Each hole seemed to get harder, but they were having fun.

The course was busy, and they had to keep up the pace, so they couldn't stop to look for any errant balls, which flew into the woods or splashed into the water, or in one case, which banged off the roof of a villa. Kitty was embarrassed about that one, and wouldn't stop to look for it in the surrounding bushes. They were both tired by the time they finished the ninth, and headed back to the condo for a shower, then a swim in the lagoon pool.

They decided to have a late lunch at a funky little place called Bayou Joe's. They had met two fellows at the pool, who had mentioned that it was a rather unique spot to eat, and had given them directions. Driving down the short road on Massalina Bayou, their first impression of the restaurant was not a good one. Undaunted, however, they decided to have a look.

Because it was late, the lunch crowd had pretty well dissipated, and they were able to nab a table on the deck right by the railing. It was wonderful, and indeed, quite unique. Old as it was, it had character and appeal. As they sat there, waiting for their drinks and trashburgers — a specialty of the house — a large inboard pulled up right along the deck by their table, and a very attractive family tied up and got out.

There was a tall, tanned husband with curly blond hair, a perky little red-headed wife, and two adorable little redheaded kids, a boy and a girl, who looked to be about three and four. There was also a big golden retriever named Buddy, who looked quite at ease waiting for them. He seemed to know that if he behaved well, he would get a burger as a treat.

Kitty and Steffie struck up a conversation with the family, who sat at the next table to them. They were native Floridians, and said that they came to Bayou Joe's once a week for lunch. Both women tried to imagine what it would be like to live here all year round, but they just couldn't picture it. Nice as it was here, home was still the best place to be.

During the leisurely lunch, one of the patrons stood up and pointed out to the bay. "Look, there are two dolphins playing out there," he said excitedly. Sure enough, the diners were treated to a great display of diving and leaping by the two dolphins, who swam quite close to the deck. Buddy, the retriever, was so excited, they were afraid that he might jump into the water to join them, but a few stern words from his owner seemed to calm him.

The food was good, and the dolphin show was even better.

"What a wonderful way to spend an afternoon," exclaimed Kitty, as they paid the bill. The Black Sheep and the shooting incident seemed far away, and somehow unimportant.

Earlier in the week, they had lunched at Uncle Ernie's, which was a lovely restaurant in St. Andrews Bay. Again, they had sat out on the deck, and the big attraction that time had been the beautiful cats, which wandered around and visited with the patrons. They were very well behaved, never begging, but sometimes sitting looking up hopefully, as the enticing aroma of shrimp stuffed grouper wafted along the balmy air. Kitty and Steffie would have liked to take the cats home with them. They were all adorable, and obviously well fed.

Before heading back to Panama City Beach, they had driven along the very scenic Beach Road, which ran right along the gulf. Most of the houses were actually mansions, and they were magnificent. Many were in the tradition of the old South, with their wrought iron balconies and tall white pillars.

There were two in particular which caught their eyes. They actually had to stop the car and take some pictures. Both of the houses they liked were huge.

One had six white pillars and one had ten! They were landscaped beautifully, and the friends could picture lovely young Southern belles in hoop skirts, sitting on the front porches, sipping mint juleps. Many of the old oak and cypress trees were adorned with the lacy Spanish moss, which grows so plentifully in the south. Kitty knew that although it was romantic and mysterious looking, actually the moss was alive with tiny bugs which fed off it, and which, in turn, fed the birds.

They would have loved the opportunity to do a tour through one of these mansions, just to see how they were decorated, and how big the rooms were. They had already been told by one of the native Floridians, that in March, when the azaleas were in full bloom, many of the young high school girls did dress up in the romantic old ante-bellum dresses. They sat on the lawns of these magnificent homes, and people drove the "Azalea Trail" to enjoy not only the flowers, but the re-creation of gentler times long gone.

That night, sitting in the hot tub, they reviewed all the fun things they had been doing.

"This is absolutely hedonistic and dissolute. You know that, don't you," sighed Steffie, with a self-satisfied grin on her face.

"Oh ya," agreed Kitty. "I don't know how we'll ever be able to thank Cassie for letting us have her condo. This has been so good for us."

"I've hardly thought about the Black Sheep or Nick," sighed Steffie, swirling her wine in the plastic glass. No real glass was allowed near the pool or the hot tubs for obvious reasons.

"Oh, I agree. I haven't even thought about the boutique. Of course, I have thought a lot about Mitch," Kitty grinned, "and I do miss Petie and Rosie. They must wonder where I've gone."

"You know, you should think about putting one of these tubs on your new deck. It's big enough. Can't you just see us sitting, boozing it up, and soaking, on a beautiful moonlit night. We could invite Adrian over, and we could listen to his adventures as a pilot, and —"

"On no," cut in Kitty. "I see enough of Adrian. He's a nice guy, but he wouldn't need much encouragement to be hanging around all the time. He comes over too much as it is. He's a bit like Josh in that respect. Every time I turn around, one or the other of them seems to be there. I agree that Adrian is a lot of fun, though."

"Well, don't you think that a hot tub would be great on your deck?"

"I guess so, but I don't know how much work they entail. I wouldn't use it enough to make it worthwhile. We'll wait till you buy yourself a condo, and then you can put one on your deck."

Changing the subject, Steffie said, "Okay, are we going to go parasailing tomorrow? I can't believe we've only got two days left to this wonderful holiday. Tempus fugit, and carpe diem, and all that. Where the heck has the week gone?"

"Who knows. I guess it's true that time flies when you're having fun, and we should seize the day, as it were. Of course we're going to go parasailing. Are you sure it won't be deleterious to our health?" she added with a grin.

"Whether it is or not, that's not going to stop us. We'll kick ourselves if we miss this opportunity. We'll be sitting on the plane going home, and hating ourselves for being a couple of wussies. We have to do it if the weather's okay."

"You're absolutely right. We'll do it tomorrow for sure," said Kitty.

"Hey, we haven't played our game tonight, and I've got a great one. Looking up at all those windows in all those condos gave me the idea. Can you tell me who played in that great old suspense thriller 'The Window'?"

"Whew, that's a toughie. Let's see. I'm sure the kid was Bobby Driscoll, but I don't remember any of the others. Who the heck was the bad guy?"

"Shoot, I was hoping you could tell me. I'm pretty sure Ruth Roman was in it, or maybe it was Barbara Hale, or maybe they both were, but I can't picture the guy."

"Not fair. You have to know the answer before you ask the question."

"Okay, I'm going to guess that it was Raymond Burr. He was always the bad guy until he became Perry Mason."

"You're likely right, but we'll have to check that one out. I think I remember Arthur Kennedy in it, but I'm not sure."

They were about to play another round of "who starred in?" when the same two fellows they had met at the pool, appeared, and got into the hot tub with them. They were friendly and interesting. George was a dentist from Michigan, and Jim was a lawyer from Maine. They had been in the same fraternity at university, and had remained close friends. Apparently their two wives had gone on a week's cruise in the Caribbean, and, preferring a golfing holiday, George and Jim had opted for a week at Edgewater. They were going to meet in Fort Lauderdale at the end of the cruise, and spend a few days at Disneyworld before heading home.

The four of them chatted amiably for a short while, as they enjoyed the hot tub and the beautiful, starry night. George was a man of about fifty, and was good looking, with greying hair, big brown eyes, and an infectious grin. Nature had not been as good to Jim. He was the same age, but he was balding, had big ears, which stuck out, and his Roman nose was pock marked and red. He looked like a serious drinker, but he was a funny fellow, and he and George obviously were close friends.

Jim regaled them with one joke after another. They couldn't imagine how he could remember all of them. He laughed at them himself as he was telling them, and that seemed to make them funnier. Kitty and Steffie were exhausted from laughing so hard, but were reluctant to leave. They told Jim and George about their plans for parasailing the next morning, and the men said that they would come down to watch. They might even try it if the women got back safely!

Quickly drying themselves, they were both aware of the appreciative glances their new friends were giving them. Both women did look great in their bikinis, and these weren't the first men who had been attracted to them, since their arrival at Edgewater.

Thanking George and Jim once again for the tip about Bayou Joe's, Steffie and Kitty headed back up to their condo, saying silent thanks to Cassie, for her generosity in making this wonderful vacation possible.

CHAPTER 39

▼

The usual Florida blue sky, radiant sun, and balmy breezes, made the next morning the perfect day to be sailing high above the calm warm waters. Parasailing was definitely a go.

As the two friends had breakfast on the Oceans deck, they chatted about other things, but both were thinking about the exciting adventure to come. They were watching people who were already up there parasailing far above them, and seeing how easy it looked.

"Kitty, remember when we first came to Niagara Falls, and we took that ride on the Spanish Aerocar? Wasn't that a terrific time?"

"Oh, it was wonderful, after it was all over and we were safely back on terra firma. I didn't want to admit it, but I was scared that day," sighed Kitty. "Funny, I'm not the least bit scared today. I'm just really looking forward to our adventure.

We were both daredevils when we went on the Maid of the Mist too. Remember how rough it got as we came closer to the Canadian Falls? That little boat was just rocking and rolling."

"We were brave because the boat was loaded with tourists, and we didn't want to show any weakness. Actually, come to think of it, we weren't really brave, we just weren't too scared. I think there's a difference. It was great though, from start to finish. If this parasailing is half as much fun, it will be worth every penny."

Changing the subject as she took another sip of her coffee, Steffie said, "Cassie told me that in the winter months, this place is full of snowbirds from Canada and the northern states. Wonder what the old folk do down here all winter. They couldn't, or likely wouldn't do the parasailing or the seadoos, but I suppose they would do lots of golfing, and walking the beach."

"It must be really dull here then, with all the old people," replied Kitty, shaking her head.

"No way. I'll bet they have a great time," laughed Steffie. She loved seniors, and missed the people in the Niagara General Hospital, where she did her twice monthly volunteer work. "They likely play bridge, and cribbage, and go dancing, and have cocktail parties. There's so much stuff they could do. I read somewhere that these winter retreats for seniors offer line dancing and ballroom dancing, and things like chef's creations and art lessons. Also, it's a great place for widows and widowers to hook up. I'll bet it's a regular Peyton Place for the geritol set."

"You're likely right," conceded Kitty. "It certainly would be a totally different vibe from the summer people, but I'm sure they have fun in their own way. As a matter of fact, if you couldn't have fun in this gorgeous place, then you're likely already dead."

As they shared a breakfast of "heavenly hash" with bacon, and sipped their Starbucks coffee, their thoughts turned again to the matter at hand.

"I really want to do this, but part of me is telling me not to," Kitty laughed, frowning at Steffie. "How do we know we can trust the boat driver? What if the rope breaks and we plunge into the gulf, or even worse, sail away to Mexico or parts unknown? Whose dumb idea was this anyway?" She was only half kidding.

"Hey, I can't wait. Everyone says it's a marvelous experience. We'll kick ourselves forever if we don't do it. I'll be right behind you in that harness thing. Now remember, we are not going to scream like all those silly women in scary movies. We'll show a certain amount of decorum and courage, and act quite calm about it all, as if we've done it before. I refuse to be classified as some stupid, moronic, screaming ninny. Come on, let's sign up before we change our minds."

"Oh look, here come George and Jim. I'll bet they're going to do it too."

"Morning ladies," said the two men they had met at the pool, and again in the hot tub. "Are you really going to do this crazy thing?"

"Of course," replied Steffie quickly. She loved adventure.

"Well, if you do it, we'll do it too. That is, if you come back all in one piece," laughed George.

The young man who took their money, seemed far too blasé and uninterested. Steffie immediately got his attention. Giving him her most charming smile, she said, "You've got two neophytes here. We've never done this, and we need to know that it's totally safe." He just nodded in a bored way. He had no idea what "neophyte" meant, but he did notice that she was a real babe.

Steffie was not to be ignored. "I understand that the harnesses you use now, are much safer than the old bucket seats. Is it true that those tended to tip, and could dump the unsuspecting victim right into the water?"

The young man looked puzzled, and simply shrugged his shoulders. He didn't know, and he didn't care. His demeanor did not instill a lot of confidence. The chap who gave them their instructions, however, and who strapped them into the harness, was excellent. He was calm and careful, and assured them that they would love it so much that they wouldn't want to come back to earth.

It turned out that he was absolutely correct. First of all, the ride out to the boat on the seadoos was a real thrill. That would have been enough for them. The parasailing turned out to be the icing on the cake.

They both suppressed their squeals of anticipation, as the boat took off, and they found themselves going up and up and up. They had that wonderful anticipatory squiggle of fear in their stomachs, just like the butterflies they got when riding the ferris wheel or roller coaster. The harnesses were positioned so that Kitty was in front, with Steffie behind her.

The actual take-off, when their feet left the safety of something solid beneath them, was a bit hair-raising, but it was so quiet up there, so unbelievably peaceful. All they could hear was the wind whistling through the parasail. At first they were both absolutely silent, as they gawked around them.

It was such a smooth ride, that they felt totally relaxed. It was a beautiful, clear morning, and it seemed as if they could see all the way to Mexico. They had expected to be able to look down and see rocks and fish under the water, but, apparently it was so deep, that they could see nothing but the gently rippling surface. That was a bit of a disappointment, but everything else was a total plus. They decided that they wanted to stay up there forever. It was a magnificent, almost religious feeling.

"This must be what a bird feels like," said Steffie, dreamily.

"I think humans were meant to fly, but we just haven't figured out how yet," replied Kitty, turning to look back at her friend.

They had to shout to be heard above the noise of the wind whistling in the parasail.

"I think your parents left you out in the sun too long," laughed Steffie, as they gazed down at the greenish blue water below. "There's no way we were ever meant to fly, but I wish you were right. It's the most fabulous feeling."

The fifteen minutes went way too quickly, and Kitty couldn't get the grin off her face. It was so much more than she had expected. They could have floated on and on, but reality kicked in, and it was time to concentrate on getting back down safely. Suddenly it wasn't quite as much fun. What if they missed the boat, what if the tether line broke, what if they plunged into that mysterious and now unfriendly looking water?

Neither friend wanted to admit to the other just how fast her heart was beating.

There were some very anxious moments on the descent, when they seemed to be travelling too fast, but somehow they landed safely on the platform, which jutted out from the stern of the boat.

When they finally arrived back at the beach, George and Jim were very impressed. They were putting on a good show of bravado, but that attempted insouciant attitude seemed bogus to Kitty and Steffie.

"Let's do it again tomorrow," said Kitty.

"Sounds like a plan," laughed Steffie, as they watched the fellows being taken by seadoo out to the waiting boat. Jim looked as if he was going to be sick, but George was quite jaunty. They had agreed to meet the men back at the Oceans restaurant for a drink on the deck, so they headed back along the beach to wait for them. It had been scary at first, but every moment was worth it. Tomorrow they wanted to do it again. It would be a fabulous experience — even better than today.

They had a good laugh when they realized that their hair looked as if it had been styled by a weed wacker. The wind had really gotten to their heads in a rather unfriendly way.

George and Jim finally returned, full of machismo and good cheer. They were very boastful about what a "piece of cake" it had been, and what a tame ride it was. The women, however, weren't fooled. George and Jim had found it just as exciting as they had.

When they finally went back to the condo, they showered and headed out to the balcony to relax. Kitty got there first, and suddenly shouted for Steffie to come quickly.

Steffie had been painting her toenails, and had just finished one foot, when Kitty called. She rushed to the balcony, doing a strange little hip-hop from one foot to the other heel, trying to hold her freshly painted toes up off the carpet.

A whole cluster of dolphins had appeared. They were heading west, jumping and playing like children. It was a wonderful sight.

The friends had had quite enough excitement for a while, and were content to spend the rest of the day quietly. Steffie went back and finished painting her other toes, then returned to the balcony. They laughed and talked, rehashing all the fun they had been having, and sharing their feelings about what it was like to soar so high above the water.

Eventually they had discussed every aspect of the parasailing experience, and moved on to other topics. They were very pleased with two lovely coffee table books, which they had bought for Cassie. They were going to leave them here in the condo as a surprise for her.

They knew her well enough now to know that books to Cassie were like art to other people. She often said that they warmed her heart, and gave her a feeling of security. She was a true bibliophile. They had also bought her a couple of small gifts, and were planning to take her out for dinner when they got home. They had shopped in the big Panama City mall, and had gifts for Cleo and Vickie, and, of course, Kitty's parents, who were always there when she needed them.

That night, as they finished dinner, Steffie sighed and said, "I've been having the greatest time, but I feel as nervous and twitchy as a squirrel's tale tonight. There's something wrong. I can feel it, but I don't know what it is. You know how Cassie always says that her scalp starts to tingle when something bad is going to happen? Well, I've got these weird little maggots of fear crawling around in my stomach."

"Oh, spare me, please. It's likely something you ate. Don't be like Cassie. She gets these feelings that something is wrong, but I doubt that they ever turn out to mean anything. All she does is scare herself, and Vickie too. Don't spoil the rest of our time by being gloomy. Just leave the spooky stuff to her." Then, as an afterthought, she laughed and said, "Maybe you inhaled too much pure oxygen up there today."

"I'm sorry, Kitty. I can't help it. Things aren't right at home. Either something bad has happened, or it's going to happen."

"Cut it out, you're ruining a lovely night." Kitty had no interest in any bad vibes or premonitions tonight. The vacation had been too perfect. Then, feeling sorry for being so abrupt with her friend, she said, "Look, we'll call my mom, and we'll call Cleo, and then you can relax."

Kitty's mom was delighted to hear from her. "Everything is fine, dear. Don't worry about a thing. The cats are happy, and being very good. Little Rosy got up on the counter and helped herself to a few shrimp off the tray. She was plucking them up one at a time with those clever little paws of hers. It was so darn cute that I couldn't scold her.

That fellow Josh came around, supposedly to tighten one of the railings, and he kept asking where you had gone, and whether you had gone alone, and when you would be home. I just told him that it was none of his business," she added indignantly. "You shouldn't encourage him, Kitty, he's too pushy.

Let's see now, what else happened? Oh yes, Dr. Spenser called, wanting to know when you are returning. He said something about going up to his home on the lake to go through some old trunks or whatever. He sounds very interesting, and, of course, he's a doctor." Kitty groaned, because she knew that her mom would love her to marry a doctor.

"Oh, and that handsome fellow Adrian, the pilot from next door, came over and asked about you. He brought you a lovely silk scarf, which he said he picked up in Paris. He's very nice, dear," she said hopefully. "You certainly do seem to have a lot of men interested in you."

Kitty couldn't tell for sure from this last comment, whether her mother was happy for her, or indignant that these men were calling her, but she figured it was the former. Her mom was on a crusade to get her safely married.

The call to Cleo was also reassuring. Cleo said that they had been very busy in the boutique all week. Vickie had sold two old Mexican pots, which had sat there for months, so they were very pleased to be rid of them. She couldn't talk long because she was getting ready for a date. She didn't say with whom, and Kitty didn't like to ask. This oversight would prove to be a huge mistake, but there was no way of knowing that at the time.

Kitty felt good after the two calls. There was definitely nothing wrong at home. Steffie, however, was not to be put off. Finally she decided to call her own apartment, just in case Nick might answer. The phone rang and rang, until finally she heard her own voice telling her that she wasn't available. So much for that bright idea.

Not wanting to spoil their evening, however, she made no more mention of scary forebodings. It was likely Nick who was causing the bad vibes. She wondered what he was up to, and how soon he would leave Niagara Falls. Hopefully, when he realized that he couldn't get any more money out of her, he would move on.

She wondered whether anyone had checked Nick's head when he was in prison. If the tumour had grown back, that would definitely explain why he was so changed. Of course, he could be so changed now, so rough and tough, just from what he had learned in prison. It must have been a dreadful experience for him. How had he survived?

Her feelings about her brother were very ambivalent. She resented him for all the money he had squeezed out of her, yet when she thought of him the way he used to be, she felt so sorry for him. She longed to have the old Nick back, but knew that wasn't likely to happen.

Kitty could feel that Steffie was still upset, and the bad vibes were beginning to affect her too. She tried to cheer them both up by talking about the wonderful time they would have parasailing again the next day.

Unfortunately it was not to be. The following day it rained. The weatherman had called for sunshine and blue skies, but he couldn't have been more wrong. The rain came down in buckets, and it was quite windy. There was no chance to parasail. Later that same day, the friends would receive a call, which would drag them rudely back to reality, would prove Steffie's forebodings to be legitimate, and would bring their lovely vacation to a screeching halt.

CHAPTER 40

▼

His anxiety was growing by leaps and bounds. The madness was creeping up on him now like a stalking tiger. He felt that it might pounce and devour him at any moment. He had tried so hard to keep it at bay, but it was gaining on him in an inexorable fashion.

It was becoming more difficult to function on a daily basis. He knew he was in serious trouble, losing control, loosening his grasp on reality. He was drifting in and out of a hazy cloud of memories and dreams, and was having difficulty discerning the difference. It had been a good idea to take some time off just now. He had locked himself in, pacing and sweating and muttering for two days, drinking, popping pills and trying to reason with himself. The attempt on Ginny's life had been a fiasco, and he didn't want a repeat.

It seemed that gradually a dark curtain of hate, envy, and frustration had settled between him and reality. It had actually become his reality. As he sat there, staring into space, he could feel the anger boiling up in waves. He had to do something. Now was the time to take action.

There were times when he couldn't really remember why he had killed those women. Had they deserved to die? Was there any sense to what he had done? Then there were times when he relived those climactic moments, thrilling to the remembrance of the feel of their necks, the terror in their eyes, the surge of power which flowed through him.

The killings should stop, they had to stop, but the Black Sheep wasn't yet quite through with his crusade. Did it really matter whether the women had harmed him personally? No, of course not. Basically all women had the potential for evil. If they hadn't hurt him, they had likely hurt some other poor guy. Anyway, now he was killing as much for the thrill of it as for any social need. He was like a tiger which becomes a man-eater after its first taste of blood. He was like an addict who needs just one more fix. He knew it was wrong, he knew it was dangerous, but he also knew it was thrilling.

As he pawed through his pictures, he realized that the world would say he was a very sick individual, but he just didn't care. He was planning now for his next attack, savouring all the possibilities and intricacies of the act, and he knew exactly who his next victim would be. Actually, he knew who his next two victims would be. Maybe after those two were dead, the Black Sheep would retire. He promised himself that might be the end of it, but he wasn't really certain.

The boutique had been even busier than usual, and Cleo hurried home to shower and change for her date. It was fun working with Vickie, who had a real gift for selling. Things just seemed to fly off the shelves, as she chatted up the customers.

Life was good, and Cleo grinned at how adept she was becoming at juggling several men at the same time. Who would want to get married, when the dating scene was so alive and well in Niagara Falls?

She smiled at herself in the mirror, as she thickened her already thick lashes with mascara, and stepped into the lacy lavender bikini panties and bra. Staring at herself critically in the full length bathroom mirror, she turned this way and that, finally deciding that maybe tomorrow she would start a crash diet, and take off five pounds. She was slim and trim, but a girl could never be too slim. She would eat salads with lemon juice all week, and drink gallons of water. As soon as she took off the five pounds, she would treat herself to that funky little scarlet top with the frilly sleeves. It would be sensational with her white jeans.

Taking her time, she put together a small but very enticing hors d'oeuvres plate. She had seen it in a magazine, and thought it looked very elegant. He was sure to be impressed.

When the phone rang, Cleo debated whether to answer it or not. She still had a few things to do before her date arrived. Oh well, it might be important, so she wiped her hands and grabbed the receiver. It was Kitty calling from Panama City Beach, and just wondering how things were going in the shop. They chatted a few minutes, and Cleo assured her that business was great, and she and Vickie were having a lot of fun. Then she said that she had to run and get ready for her date, but she was careful not to mention who it was. She had overheard Kitty and Steffie talking about her, and speculating about all the men she dated, so she had made up her mind to be much more tight-lipped about her romances.

She carefully chose a couple of good cds to put on the player, then, glancing at the clock, decided it was time to light the several candles scattered around the room. When the doorbell rang, she was ready. They would sit and enjoy a couple of drinks in this enticing setting, before heading out for a night on the town. He hadn't told her where they were going, but she was sure that it would be a fun evening.

Opening the door, she frowned in surprise, when she saw that he was carrying a gym bag, and was dressed very casually in black jeans and a dark sweater.

"I thought we were going dancing," she pouted prettily, looking down in dismay at her spike heels and frilly skirt. "Did I misunderstand about the plans?"

"Don't you worry, my pet. We're going to dance up a storm," he laughed, as he took her in his arms and whirled her around.

She thought she smelled alcohol on his breath, and hoped he hadn't had too much to drink. His eyes seemed awfully bright, and there seemed to be an underlying current of excitement in his every move. It occurred to her that he might be on some drug, and she felt a little clutch of anxiety in her stomach.

"This is a very charming little nest you have here, Cleo," he said, strolling casually around the room. "I like your colour scheme. Colours say a lot about a person, don't they?"

"I suppose they do," she replied with relief. He seemed more calm now, and she put her nervousness aside. They sat down for a few moments, just talking casually, and she decided that she wouldn't mention the fact that he was in jeans, while she was all dressed up. If he wanted her to change, he would likely mention it. She felt disappointed, though. She had been looking forward all day to going dancing, and wearing this new outfit. Oh well, these days people could get away with wearing just about anything, so she wouldn't think any more about it. They would still go out and have a great time.

She was in the kitchen pouring their wine, when he came up behind her on silent feet, and put his arms around her waist. She liked that, and liked it even more when he nuzzled her neck. Then, however, he whispered, "Have you been a bad girl, Cleo? Have you been a bitch and a bimbo?"

"What?" she cried indignantly, turning to face him. "What do you mean?"

"I mean, you're all dressed up to catch the eye of every available man, aren't you? I think maybe little Miss Cleo needs to be punished."

"What in the world are you talking about?" she asked indignantly. "Don't tell me you're into any of that S&M crap."

"No," he laughed. "I'm just teasing."

He accepted a glass of wine from her, and they walked back into the living room. They chatted amiably for a while. He really was a handsome guy, she thought, congratulating herself on her good taste.

When it came time for refills, he followed her back into the kitchen. She had just topped up the glasses, when his hands went around her waist again.

"No wonder you have so many boyfriends, Cleo. You're a delectable little morsel."

"Why, thank you sir," she replied, fluttering her eyelashes at him.

"I really like your apartment. Could I have a tour, and see the bedroom?"

"Sure," she replied, setting down her wine. Maybe they wouldn't make it out dancing after all. Unfortunately she didn't know just how right she was.

In the bedroom, which was decorated in pink and burgundy tones, he placed his glass on the dresser, and once again took her in his arms.

"How many men have you entertained here, you sleazy tramp?"

"What?" Cleo's face turned crimson, as she tried to disengage his hands. "Let me go. You're disgusting. I won't be talked to like that."

"Don't be bad now, Cleo" he said in a menacing tone. "You know what happens to bad girls."

"Don't be silly," she replied, again trying to get free. "I don't like you when you talk like that. Come on, let's forget about the wine, and go dancing like you promised." All she really wanted now was to be rid of him. The evening had been totally spoiled, with his strange behaviour and crude language. Maybe she could get him out the door first, and then slam it and lock it. These thoughts were flickering like candle flames, and she couldn't quite grasp one. She was becoming seriously uneasy.

"No, I think we'll skip the dancing tonight, you bitch. You don't deserve to go dancing. Do you seriously think I want to be seen in public with you? You're just like all the rest of them. You're easy, flirting with every guy you see. Did you think I didn't realize what you are? It's time for you to take your medicine. You have to take what you deserve, what you've brought on yourself."

He was hurting her now, and Cleo's heart was pounding. Pushing at his face with her hand, she cried, "You'd better go now. You're acting like a total jerk. Go home and sober up, and don't bother calling me tomorrow."

She realized immediately that she had made a mistake. This little bit of bravado seemed to enrage him, and suddenly his hands were around her throat. Cleo was so surprised, that she lost precious seconds by not fighting back immediately. She stared unbelievingly into his face, as his fingers slowly closed tighter and tighter. Then the adrenaline kicked in, and with every bit of strength she had, she made a futile attempt to loosen those fingers, but they were like steel clamps.

As if from a distance, she noticed the sweat on his face, and the grim set of his mouth. What had she ever seen in this guy? What was the matter with him? Surely he wouldn't really hurt her, would he? Then she remembered what she had read about the Black Sheep, and her brain nearly exploded with fear. Tears sprang to her eyes, causing the carefully applied mascara to slowly run down her cheeks, like little black rivulets.

Cleo was now gasping for breath, pleading with him in her mind and with her eyes. An incipient scream died in her throat.

It didn't take as long as he had expected. Her scrawny little neck was as thin as a bird's. He felt so powerful that he thought he could have twisted her head right off her shoulders, just like those Barbie dolls in the prostitute's room. Her eyes bugged out, and her lips were turning an interesting shade of purple. Strange how they all looked the same in death.

When she went totally limp, he picked her up and carried her over to the bed. He jumped and nearly dropped her when she took a rattling breath. She was still alive! Dumping her on the pretty flowered duvet, he knelt over her, and once again put his hands around her neck. Her hands fluttered and lifted slightly, before falling back in defeat. Taking no chances, he knelt there, squeezing and whispering to her, till he was sure that she was dead.

He sat there on the edge of the bed with a bewildered and disappointed look on his face. Where was the thrill? Where was that exquisite rush of power and pleasure? This time there was nothing — just a feeling of emptiness.

He sat staring into space for at least five minutes, waiting for the climactic rush of energy, but it just wasn't there. He had been cheated. He had killed her for nothing. Turning, he glared at the corpse, feeling the desire to slap her, to punch those bulging eyes. Somehow it was all her fault.

Finally, heaving a sigh, he stood up like an old man. Gravely he went about his little ritual. He straightened her clothes and arranged her body. He got a cloth from the bathroom and wiped the trails of mascara off her cheeks. He placed the little black ceramic sheep in her hand, and took his three pictures, but there was no joy in the taking. He barely glanced at them, as he stuck them in his pocket, and went about the task of cleaning up any clues he might have left. There was no humming this time, no sense of a job well done.

He couldn't believe he had killed this bubbly, happy-go-lucky girl who wanted everyone to like her. Sure, she was a bimbo who had dated half the men in town. Still, so what? She hadn't meant anything to him. What did he care how many men she dated? Why was he doing this? Was he crazy, insane, totally mad? The words tumbled in his head like tiny acrobats.

Suddenly his mood shifted, and he became very angry at Cleo. It was all her fault. She had spoiled everything. Giving her arm a vicious pinch, he had the wild impulse to bite her as hard as he could. It took a great effort of will to stop himself. He actually had to grind his teeth together and hold them that way. He knew that a bite mark was easily traceable through dental records and DNA. It would have felt good though, he thought, as he dumped the hors d'oeuvres into a plastic baggie, and put it into his gym bag. He would dispose of them on the way home, along with the candles and cocktail napkins.

He washed the two wine glasses and the plate, and returned them to the cupboard. Then he carefully wiped down every surface he had touched. He didn't want the police to suspect that she had been waiting for her killer, or that she had known him well enough to be having drinks and nibblers with him. By the time he had cleaned up, there would be no way of knowing that Cleo had been entertaining someone she knew and trusted. As usual, he felt confident that he was several steps ahead of the homicide detectives.

CHAPTER 41

▼

Next morning, the day couldn't make up its mind what it wanted to do. One moment the sun was shining brilliantly, as if wanting to envelop Niagara Falls in its golden beauty. The next minute, dark sullen clouds were blowing right over the sun, and leaving in their wake a feeling of gloom.

Vickie had come in a bit early, because she wanted to rearrange a display of music boxes. She was having a wonderful week working in the boutique with Cleo. The days had flown by, and she had learned a lot. She and Cassie went out to dinner, and did fun things each evening, and she was quite content to play shopkeeper during the days, while Kitty and Steffie were enjoying their holiday in Florida.

Cleo was late this morning, but Vickie was quite comfortable being on her own, as long as no tour buses arrived to spit out forty or fifty customers all at once. That would definitely be panic time.

She groaned inwardly when the door opened, and a stumpy little man who looked a bit like Rumplestiltskin, entered the shop. She had heard Steffie and Kitty talking about this fellow. He apparently came in periodically to inspect things, and was always offering to buy the business from them. They simply looked on him as a bit of a loony, and kidded him along.

Vickie watched as he wandered up and down between the showcases, touching this, replacing that, and all the while muttering to himself. This guy was definitely one doughnut short of a dozen. She headed toward the phone, just in case he decided to attack her, but he really did look quite harmless.

Finally, he completed his inspection, and walked over to Vickie. "Well, have they decided to sell?" he asked brusquely.

Vickie smiled sweetly at him. "No, I'm quite sure they haven't. They love this boutique, and are quite happy running it."

"That's too bad. They're making a big mistake. I'd give them a good price," he said, good-naturedly, as if he had been quite prepared for Vickie's answer. "Tell them that I was in, and I'll be back." With that, he tipped his hat at her, and walked jauntily out the door.

Cocky little twerp, she thought to herself. She was glad they had warned her that he might make an appearance.

Glancing at her watch, Vickie realized with a start that it was after ten, and Cleo had still not appeared. Strange she hadn't called if she was going to be this late.

Vickie got quite busy with a stream of customers, and it was after eleven before she looked at her watch again. Still no sign of Cleo. Vickie was worried now, and called Cassie to see what she thought should be done. Cass said that she was on her way down to the Cattery, but would drive around to Cleo's place, and see if she was there. "Maybe she's run off with one of her many boyfriends," she suggested facetiously.

Cassie's trip to Cleo's apartment didn't accomplish much, except to frighten her. No one answered the door, so she spoke with the building superintendent, and asked if he could check to see whether Cleo's car was gone from the parking garage. To her dismay, Cleo's car was parked right where it should be. Had Cleo fallen and hit her head? Was she lying unconscious on the apartment floor? Another thought crossed Cassie's mind, but it was too ridiculous and far-fetched to give it head room. Still, she began to feel very uneasy, and her scalp was tingling, always a bad sign.

The uncooperative superintendent refused to use his key to check out Cleo's apartment, muttering that it was none of his business, so Cassie went back to her car, and sat thinking what to do. First she called Vickie at the boutique, to be sure that Cleo hadn't turned up. Then her heart began to beat faster, as she decided to call Jack Willinger. To her surprise, he was actually at his desk.

Every time she thought of him, she thought of the infamous luncheon at the Riverbend Inn. It could have turned out so differently. Because of that, she felt both excited and embarrassed calling him.

"Jack, it's Cassie. Have you got a minute?"

"Cass, what a great surprise. Is everything okay?"

He sounded wonderful, as always, and she could picture him sitting at his desk, legs stretched out, one hand behind his head, chair turned to look out on Morrison Street.

"I'm not sure. I may be getting all upset over nothing, but Cleo, the woman who works in Kitty Winfield's boutique, hasn't shown up for work today, and she's not answering her phone or the door, and her car is still in her underground parking space. The superintendent won't let me in to check on her, and I'm not sure what to do."

"Has she ever skipped work before without calling?" asked Jack in a reasonable tone.

"I don't really know. Steffie and Kitty are away on vacation in Florida, and Vickie and Cleo have been working in the shop all week. Vickie's there alone, and she's worried too."

"Where are you now, Cass?"

"I'm sitting in my car outside her apartment on Drummond Road."

"Okay, give me her address, and Bud and I will be there in a few minutes."

Jack always sounded so totally in charge and cool about things, that Cassie felt a great sense of relief. She had been right to call him, even though she had certain guilty feelings about her motives. Every time she saw Jack or talked with him, she felt like a schoolgirl again with her first crush. The chemistry between them was powerful, and it was almost painful trying to keep away from him. She was half-heartedly glad that he was bringing Bud along as a buffer.

As she sat there in the car, waiting for Jack and Bud to arrive, she noticed the little house next door to Cleo's apartment building. It was very dilapitated, and looked as if no one cared for it. Arrogant little weeds were poking their heads out of the cracks in the patchy, buckled driveway. Flakes of paint were peeling off the windows. The screen door was hanging slightly askew. What an eyesore to have right next to a decent looking apartment building. She wondered idly how long Cleo had lived here.

Cassie got out of the car, as soon as she saw Jack and Bud pulling up to the front of the building. She and Jack locked eyes, and smiled at each other, as if they were the only two people in the world. Then Jack became all business, and asked her to wait there rather than following them inside.

It didn't take long to find the superintendent, and get him to open up Cleo's door. The apartment was quiet and dark. The blinds were drawn, and there was no radio or television playing. They left the door open, but told the superintendent to wait in the hall, while they checked the rooms. They were very careful not to touch anything, as they went through the living room to the kitchen, then down the hall to the bathroom, and finally the bedroom.

Cleo was lying on her back on the bed, and Jack's heart gave a despondent leap, as he saw the little black sheep in her hand.

"Shit and damnation," Bud uttered, as they stood staring at the corpse. There was no need to touch her or to take her pulse. It was obvious that she was dead, and had been for several hours. Jack used his cell phone to call the station and the medical examiner's office.

Bud went out to speak with the super, giving him instructions to keep people off this floor, while Jack went down to tell Cassie.

Never for the rest of her life would she forget the grim look on his handsome face, as he approached her. She knew instantly that Cleo was dead.

"Was it the Black Sheep?" cried Cassie, putting her hand to her mouth in a gesture of fright and horror.

Jack sighed. "Looks like it. It's either the real guy or a copycat, but there's a little black sheep in her hand."

"Oh no," cried Cassie, as Jack put his arms around her, and smelled the sweet fragrance of her hair. He held her for a long time, silently thanking the Almighty that it was Cleo and not Cassie lying dead upstairs.

"I'm so sorry, Cass. I know she was a friend of yours. I'm just thankful that it wasn't you. Maybe this time he's left some clues. I have to get back up there with Bud, but you should go home."

"Oh, I can't go home. I'll go to the shop and tell Vickie. Then we'll have to call Kitty and Steffie in Florida. Luckily they're due home tomorrow night anyway. This is the last thing they need after the summer those two have had."

Jack still had his arms around her, and was patting her gently on the back. He always seemed to be there for her when she needed him. He dropped his arms, however, and stepped back a bit, when the first police car turned the corner, followed by the forensic experts.

"Are you sure you're okay to drive?" Jack was looking at her as if he didn't want to let her out of his sight.

"Oh you know me. I'm pretty tough. I'll be fine, but if you have the time, maybe you could call me tonight?" She asked this hesitantly, and looked up at him, as her big blue eyes filled with tears. "She was so full of fun, Jack. She loved men, and she loved to party. She was so full of life. Do you think it was someone she knew?"

"Can't tell yet, but I'll call you later. Just take it easy, Cass, and don't open your door to any men, even if you know them — except for me of course," he added with a grin.

Cassie would have liked to stay right there, or better yet, to go up to Cleo's apartment, and see for herself that she was really dead. She couldn't believe it, it just didn't seem possible. After all the killings two years ago, Cassie thought that she would never again know anyone who was murdered. After all, this was Niagara Falls, a lovely, quiet, safe city. The most exciting thing that ever happened here was someone jumping over the falls to commit suicide, or someone winning a huge pot at the casino. It was not a town which was accustomed to murders.

She felt faint at the thought of Cleo lying up there with a little black sheep in her hand. Who was this killer? How was it that he could come and go like a shadow? No one seemed to see him. No one ever heard anything. The victims never seemed to put up a fight. How did he do this black magic?

She had to get to the boutique to tell Vickie. Maybe it was all a huge mistake, and fun-loving Cleo would be there, innocently working and flirting with the male customers.

She knew in her heart, though, that Jack would not have made a mistake. Cleo was lying cold and forlorn upstairs in her own little apartment. This summer was becoming the summer from hell, not so much for Cassie, but for her friends.

CHAPTER 42

▼

Steffie and Kitty were devastated when they got the call from Cassie. It seemed impossible to wrap their minds around the terrifying thought that someone they knew and liked, and with whom they worked every day, could possibly have been the victim of the Black Sheep. How could it have happened? Did she know her killer? Was it a random killing? They preferred to think that it was. No one they knew or whom Cleo knew, could be guilty of such a heinous crime. Or could they?

The flight home seemed tedious and never-ending. There was no question of being able to read, or even to talk. They were traumatized, and sat staring into space like two zombies, trying to make sense out of the senseless news.

As they waited to change planes in Atlanta, they finally started talking, and kept going over and over the list of people they thought Cleo had dated. The list included Keith Spenser and Barry Johnson. Then there was Drew Carson. She had the hots for him, but had she dated him? Josh Tuttle was a possibility, and so was Scott Matheson. The list seemed endless. She had said she was going out with a new guy the night she was killed, but she hadn't mentioned his name. Either Josh or Scott could have been that "new guy." She had talked and flirted with both of them in the boutique. Of course the question became, was her new date the killer, or had she been killed by a stranger, after her date ended?

Cassie and Vickie met them at the Buffalo airport, and all four had a good cry and a circle hug, before setting out to cross the border for home.

The next day, Kitty and Steffie had to go down to the police station, and give their statements. Because they had worked with Cleo, it was assumed that they knew a lot about her personal life. That wasn't really the case, but they gave what help they could. They had convinced themselves that it was a total stranger who was doing the strangling, and were very reluctant to give the police the names of some of Cleo's dates. After all, these were respectable men in the community. There were two doctors, a male nurse, a fireman, and a contractor. None of these men could possibly be a killer, but who knew how many other men she had been dating? The Black Sheep had to be a stranger. He just could not be anyone Kitty and Steffie knew.

Jack and Bud were very interested in the fact that Cleo had a date the night she was killed. Kitty could have strangled herself for not asking Cleo the date's name. Of course the detectives realized that the date could have been a totally innocent fellow, who had left her apartment long before the Black Sheep arrived, but then, how would he have managed to get into her apartment? Cleo had been too smart to open the door to a stranger at night. Or was she? She was an inveterate flirt, and viewed all men as possible dates. If the Black Sheep was charming enough, he might very well have been able to talk himself into her apartment.

The women were quite drained by the time they left the police station. Neither wanted to be alone. They were sick at heart, and full of disbelief. Murder just didn't happen to anyone you knew. It was the stuff of mystery books and television dramas.

The next few days were a total blur. Steffie stayed with Kitty, and they clung to each other emotionally, as they tried to assimilate and accept the unacceptable. The boutique was closed, out of respect for Cleo.

Drew called in a fury that Kitty had given the police his name. He denied adamantly ever having dated Cleo, and was so angry with Kitty, that it was obvious the friendship was really over. He had been willing to forgive the glass of wine thrown in his face, but he wasn't going to forgive her possibly besmirching his reputation. Scott was also very angry that Kitty had mentioned his name. He admitted dating Cleo, but was annoyed at being interrogated. She didn't hear from Josh or Keith, or Barry, so maybe they didn't know that she was the one who had given the police the list of Cleo's friends.

Kitty kept picturing Josh that day in the shop. Had he made a date with Cleo? He had certainly been whispering and flirting with her, and Cleo had looked very happy.

The funeral was to be held back in Winnipeg, which was Cleo's home-town, so there was no visitation and no service in Niagara. The women felt badly about that, but Cleo's family wanted it that way.

Steffie felt totally helpless and at loose ends. She felt guilty that she had been rather mean and curt with Cleo the last time she had seen her. Damn, this had been a bad summer. The shooting had set her back a bit, but at least it had turned out all right. She wasn't dead. Nick's sudden arrival had been a different kind of shock, and she had no idea how that would turn out. Cleo's death was in a class all by itself. She still couldn't believe that pretty, vivacious girl was gone. Maybe those nightmares she had in which Kitty was threatened by the killer, were really premonitions about Cleo. She wondered about that, as she sat sipping her third cup of coffee in her sunny kitchen.

This entire summer had been so full of unexpected, unpleasant and unplanned events, that Steffie wondered what was coming next. She was a basically cheerful person though, couldn't be bothered with the "poor me" vibe, and told herself sharply that she was no crybaby. Everyone had some bumps along the road of life, and she wasn't going to be defeated by hers. The bad tidings were all behind her now. She had had her share, but the road ahead was going to be straight and clear. She would do that 'power of positive thinking' thing, and just get on with her life. The good thing was that it wasn't Kitty who had been killed. Those nightmares hadn't meant a thing, at least that's what she told herself.

Washing and drying her coffee mug, she put it back in the cupboard. Then, taking a pretty little watering can from the counter, she filled it, and watered the three plants in the living room.

Replacing the watering can on the counter, she stood looking out the win-dow, trying to make up her mind. Finally, nodding to herself, she rushed off to her bedroom, to pull on a pair of white slacks and a red turtleneck top. She had come to a decision. She wanted to do something to help, and she had a brilliant idea. She would go over to Cleo's apartment building, and try to interview some of the people who might have known her. She could pretend she was a roving reporter or a freelance journalist. What was the difference, she wondered. People were gullible. They would believe anything if you said it with conviction.

She grinned to herself, as she drove the short distance to the apartments on Drummond Rd. She could picture herself wearing a Sherlock Holmes peaked cap and carrying a spy glass. What an idiot I am, she thought, as she pulled into the parking lot.

Of course the crime scene van and the television cameras were gone, but the door to Cleo's apartment was still sealed by the heavy yellow tape.

She took a deep breath, and knocked on the door right across from Cleo's place. It was opened almost immediately by a cherubic looking fellow, with a corona of curly blond hair and fat rosy cheeks. A sprinkling of dandruff casually decorated his shoulders. Steffie could imagine him doing baby powder commercials, or ads for heavenly cream cheese. She had to stifle a giggle, when she noticed a little moustache of powdered sugar around his mouth. The paper coffee cup in his hand, told her that he had made a recent visit to the local Tim Horton's. She wondered absently why he wasn't at work in the middle of the day.

He eyed Steffie with surprise, and obviously liked what he saw.

"What can I do for you, pretty lady?" he asked hopefully.

"Well, I'm Jillian Chadwick, (she loved that name), and I'm doing an investigative report on your neighbour's death. Could I come in and talk to you?"

"Sure thing. Come on in. I'm Danny Greenaway, but I don't know squat about the murder. I was up camping in Algonquin Park, and I didn't get home till late the night she was killed. I didn't know a thing about it till they came to take her body away."

He said this regretfully, as if he was sorry that he had missed most of the excitement.

It suddenly occurred to Steffie that he could be the Black Sheep, and she wondered how smart it was for her to be here alone with this odd guy. No one knew where she was. Dumb move!

As he was talking, he ushered her into a typical bachelor-type apartment — more utilitarian than attractive. There was an ugly faux leather brown couch, with a long rip on one arm. The matching oversized ottoman also had a tear in it. A small scatter rug lay wrinkled and forlorn on the parquet floor. The coffee table was littered with the detritus of one who lives on junk food.

"Did you know Cleo well?" began Steffie, taking out a pad and pencil to make herself look more legitimate. It hadn't occurred to her that people might ask for identification. She had nothing which said that she was Jillian Chadwick. Another dumb move.

He hesitated. "Yes and no. We often talked, but we hadn't dated yet," he added softly.

And you never would have, thought Steffie uncharitably. He was definitely not Cleo's type, but then, how did she know that for sure? Cleo had seemed to like men in general — all shapes, all sizes.

"Did you ever see any of her dates?" Steffie asked hopefully.

"Nope," he answered quickly — maybe too quickly. He looked uncomfortable, and Steffie wondered whether he had looked out the peek hole a few times, when he heard knocking at Cleo's door.

"I think she was the architect of her own misfortune. You know what I mean?"

"Yes, maybe I do, but tell me please, exactly what do you mean?" Steffie was intrigued by the comment.

"Well, she went out with all kinds of guys. She likely had five dates a week, and it was rarely more than twice with the same guy. That's asking for trouble big-time, especially this summer, with the Black Sheep roaming around. Don't you think so?"

Steffie did think so, but she wasn't about to badmouth her friend and employee. She asked a few more questions, none of which gave her any useful info. This was hard work, and likely a huge mistake. When Danny Greenaway tried to coax her into having a drink with him, she knew it was time to leave. The fatuous fool had been no help at all.

No one answered at the next two apartments, but she got lucky at one further down the hall. After knocking a couple of times, she had the feeling she was being appraised through the peek hole. She had the crazy desire to cross her eyes and pick her teeth, but she pulled herself together, and said through the door, "I'm a free lance reporter, may I talk to you?"

After a few seconds, she heard the sound of a chain being disengaged, and several bolts being unlocked. This was one careful or paranoid person.

The old lady who opened the door must have been in her 80's. She was short and plump in a sleeveless, flowered dress. Her flyaway white hair was supposed to be contained in a little bun, but seemed to have a mind of its own. She had inquisitive, bright eyes behind little gold rimmed granny glasses. Once she decided that Steffie didn't look like a murderer, she seemed quite willing to talk.

She did not, however, invite Steffie in. Instead she stood at the door, ready to shut it quickly if she felt threatened.

"I'm Gladys, and this is my husband Fred," she said, pointing to an old codger who had shuffled up behind her. Fred didn't smile, but just stared at Steffie. It was rather disconcerting. She noticed that he had several dark bumps up and down his arms. How ugly. Guess they're just barnacles of old age, Steffie thought to herself. Then again, maybe Gladys kept him in line by abusing him.

"Did you hear anything suspicious the night Cleo was killed?" Steffie figured she might as well plunge right in.

"Oh no, we certainly didn't," said Gladys, shaking her head. "We take our hearing aids out at night, don't we Fred?" Fred nodded in agreement. "We didn't see anything either, did we dear?" Fred shook his head. He was obviously the silent type, quietly content to let Gladys do all the talking.

"Did she have a lot of visitors?" asked Steffie hopefully.

"Well, how should we know?" retorted Gladys, turning to give Fred a look. "We wouldn't know, would we dear?" she asked the man of few words. Again Fred shook his head.

Steffie had the wild desire to laugh. Was the old guy a mute, or had years of listening to Gladys's constant chatter encouraged him to give up the spoken language?

She realized that she was getting nowhere with these two, so after a few more non-productive questions, she thanked them and moved on.

The next door was answered by a tired looking woman of about forty, with two dirty looking kids clinging to her legs like a pair of frig magnets. Behind her stood a fat slob of a guy in a greyish sweat shirt and baggy pants. He had stringy hair, and leered at Steffie with interest. She asked her questions, but got no interesting answers.

As she was turning to leave, the slob volunteered wittily that Cleo had been quite a babe, but she had more boyfriends than a dog has fleas. He laughed at his own humour, and Steffie forced a smile, as she went on down the hall.

She was going to quit and go home, having been demoralized by the last idiot, but decided to try one more apartment. Surprisingly, she struck gold. A woman opened the door to the apartment second on the right to Cleo's. Actually it was the corner apartment. She was grey haired, well dressed, and obviously nervous.

Again introducing herself as Jillian Chadwick, Steffie was ushered into a charming apartment, with all the class and comfort lacking in Danny Greenaway's dump.

"I've been expecting the police, but you are the first person to contact me. I've been so frightened that the killer might come back." She sighed as she sat down on a ladder backed chair, with a beautiful petit point covering on the seat. "Oh, by the way, my name is Florence Thompson, and I've lived in these apartments for sixteen years."

"Did you see the killer, Mrs. Thompson?" asked Steffie in surprise. She really hadn't expected any success in this little venture, but she had hoped.

"I'm pretty sure that I saw him," the woman shuddered. "You must have noticed that the apartments on this side face the street, and being a corner one, I also face the side street."

Steffie nodded encouragement.

"Well, it was around eleven o'clock I guess. I wish I could be sure of the time, but I had been reading, and I lose all track of time when I read. Anyway, I was getting ready for bed. I always look out into the hall through the peek hole, as well as looking out on the street before I retire. It's just a little habit I've acquired since my husband died."

She stopped suddenly, and stared sharply at Steffie. "You don't think the police will be angry with me for talking to a reporter, do you?"

That made Steffie gulp. She certainly didn't want to get anyone in trouble. Shaking her head, she said, "That's no problem. They should have been around to see you by now, and we won't print anything without checking with them." Did that sound professional, she wondered. Likely not.

"Well, you mustn't print my name or tell where I live, because that Black Sheep could come after me."

"You have my promise," said Steffie guiltily. She was pretty sure that Jack Willinger and Bud would not be amused if they found out she had been here.

"Alright, this is what happened. Just as I looked out the peek hole, a man came past my door. He kept on going down the hall, but first he stopped almost right in front of my door, and looked back over his shoulder. The odd thing is that he was going away from the elevators, and heading for the stairs. I thought that was strange, so I went right to the window and watched for him. Sure enough, in a couple of minutes, he came out the side door, not the front one. He walked really fast down the street and out of sight. Now, he obviously hadn't parked in the back lot, so why didn't he come out the front door, and why did he use the stairs instead of the elevator? It was as if he just didn't want to be seen, or to meet anyone."

Steffie was on the edge of her seat. "Did you see him well enough to describe him?"

"Not really. He was about six feet tall, and had on a black jacket and dark jeans, and he wore big glasses with dark frames. His hair was really black and curly, and it stuck out from under his black baseball cap. That's all. I didn't really see his face clearly except for the glasses."

Steffie was thrilled. This woman was likely the first person to have seen the strangler, and she could certainly be in danger if he realized he had been seen. Steffie didn't know that the so-called good samaritan had also seen him, because the police had kept that quiet.

She decided that she had done enough sleuthing for one day. She now felt guilty at pretending to be a reporter. What a hair-brained idea. It was just that she had really wanted to do something to help find Cleo's killer.

Driving home, she decided that she would talk to Kitty, then call Jack Willinger. She knew for certain that he would not be pleased with her, when he found out what she had been doing. She sighed at how angry he was going to be. Sometimes life was very complicated. Still, she was only trying to help, and at this point, it looked as if the poor cops could use all the help available.

CHAPTER 43

▼

The boutique had reopened the following Monday, and it was extremely busy. The local newspaper had made much of the latest murder, and there were many customers who came in just to talk about Cleo. She had been well liked.

The shop was enjoying a certain twisted glamour or attraction, because of being the spot where the shooting had taken place earlier in the summer. Now one of the clerks had been murdered. Also, the rumour was spreading, that the strangler had bought his first little black sheep there. It was a notoriety which Steffie and Kitty did not appreciate, but they had to admit it was certainly bringing in the customers.

The entire city was now in a panic about the killings, and the police department was under a lot of pressure. The special task force, headed by detectives Willinger and Lang, was working twenty-four hours a day.

It made Kitty sick and angry to think that the Black Sheep was virtually holding her lovely city hostage. People were so nervous, so suspicious of each other. It was dreadful.

Co-workers looked at each other with mistrust, female tenants were afraid to use the elevators, home deliveries were almost non-existent, and it was as if the city was holding its breath, waiting for the next murder. The extreme heat didn't help. Niagara Falls was experiencing a heat wave, with temperatures soaring into the 90's, and tempers were ragged.

Kitty was in a philosophical mood today. She was thinking of the old saying "life goes on," and she was thinking what a stupid expression it was. Of course life goes on. The entire world doesn't stop because one woman gets herself killed. Still, it seemed an insult, somehow, that the world kept revolving as if nothing had happened. Life shouldn't go on that readily when someone dies.

They had kept the boutique closed for a few days, out of respect for Cleo, but they had to reopen it eventually. After all, it was their livelihood. Besides, they both agreed that it was better to keep working. When they weren't working, they couldn't get Cleo out of their heads. They missed her cheery, hopeful smile, and her energetic enthusiasm. She had really loved this boutique, but now she was gone, and in a short while, they knew that it would be as if she had never existed. They would laugh and cry and work and play, and really, their lives wouldn't change significantly. Somehow, that was wrong.

Kitty mused morosely that it was rather like scooping a cup of water out of Lake Ontario. It wouldn't be noticed at all. It would make no difference to the lake. How sad! How stinkingly sad. She felt like crying again for her poor lost friend.

Vickie had extended her visit with Cassie. There was just too much going on here in Niagara Falls, and she felt that she could be of help in the boutique. With her husband Brian still in Scotland, and her kids away working at summer jobs, her time was her own. She worked the afternoons, when either Kitty or Steffie had to be at the hospital for their volunteering services, and she would have enjoyed working a lot more. The boutique was fun. It reminded her of the times she and Cassie used to play "store" when they were young. When they weren't playing "library," they were playing "store," in the attic of Vickie's childhood home.

The first afternoon Kitty was back at the hospital, she ran into Keith Spenser. He looked awful. He and Cleo had enjoyed several dates, before she began juggling various men all at the same time. Kitty wondered whether he had been really serious about her. Cleo at one point had been imagining herself as Mrs. Keith Spenser. Could Keith have killed her in a fit of rage, because she was so fickle? No, of course not. What would have been his reason for killing all those other women? Still, his eyes looked a bit glassy, and Kitty noticed that there was sweat on his forehead. Was that because he was mourning Cleo, or was he doing drugs, or was he just hot like everyone else?

"How are you doing, Keith?" she asked solicitously, when they ran into each other in the hospital corridor.

"I'm still in shock," he answered. "It just can't be true. Who could have done such a thing? Cleo never set out to hurt anyone, she just liked a good time. She was a real party girl, and she couldn't help herself. Dammit, who would want to hurt her?"

Kitty wondered whether this was a good acting job, or whether he really was hurting. He certainly seemed sincere, and he didn't look his usual well put together self. He must have liked Cleo more than anyone suspected.

"Did she tell you who she was dating that last night?" Keith asked, his eyes studying Kitty's face.

"No, she didn't. I called her from Florida that evening, and she just said that she was in a hurry because she was getting ready for her date. I'm kicking myself for not asking who it was."

Keith sighed, then suddenly changed the subject and said, "I've been talking to Drew. He's really angry with you for giving his name to the police. I know you had to do it though. I also understand that you've met someone else already. That didn't take you long. What is it with you women? Can't you stick with one guy for a while?"

He was laughing when he said this, but Kitty was not amused. What possible business was it of Keith's? Moreover, how did the news of Mitch get around so fast? This darn hospital was a hotbed of rumour and intrigue. When did the staff ever have time to work?

"Come on, let's grab a coffee, and you can tell me all about the new man in your life."

"Sorry, Keith, I'm in a bit of a rush. They're expecting me in pediatrics. We'll do it next time for sure, though."

"Wait a minute. I have a favour I want to ask of you. Do you remember when you were up at my beach house, you promised that you would come back and help me go through all the trunks and boxes in the basement?"

This was news to Kitty. She hadn't promised any such thing. As she recalled, Keith had suggested that Steffie go up to help him, and she had tried to put him off, not wanting to be up there alone with him.

"I didn't really promise, Keith" she said, hesitantly. "I'm awfully busy now in the shop with Cleo gone, and,"

Keith interrupted before she could say more. "Come on, Kitty. I could really use your help. I won't be able to tell what stuff is valuable and what stuff isn't. Wouldn't you enjoy a nice afternoon up at the beach? It would do you good, and it would be a huge help to me."

He looked so forlorn when he said this, that Kitty didn't know how she could refuse. She didn't want to be up there alone with Keith. He was too much of a flirt, but she felt sorry for him. He really seemed upset about Cleo, and he was a very nice man. She hesitated, but couldn't think of any plausible excuse.

"Okay, Keith," she said reluctantly. "I'll only be able to go for a couple of hours, and it will have to be Sunday after church. I'll try to bring Steffie along. She's really good at organizing and sorting."

This was only partially true, but she would be much more comfortable with Steffie by her side. Keith didn't look too happy with the suggestion, but he agreed in his affable manner, and arranged to pick them up at around two o'clock. He gave her a little hug, and strolled off down the hall, leaving Kitty to wonder whether there was more to Keith than anyone knew or suspected. He was a lot of fun, and had a good reputation as a doctor. It was just that he was known as a big flirt, and she didn't feel up to fighting off his advances, if he got her up there alone and became romantic. She didn't like to admit to herself that there was also that little niggling doubt as to whether he could possibly have killed Cleo.

She sighed, and silently scolded herself for getting into this situation. She should have just said 'no'. Hopefully Steffie would be able to come, and they would enjoy going through the old trunks. They might find some real treasures.

Her afternoon duties in the children's ward went quickly. She spent the first hour rocking and hugging a chubby little fellow with asthma. He had been in twice before, and was one of her favourites. His parents worked during the day, and couldn't get in to visit him until evening. Another little fellow had broken his arm, when he fell out of a tree, while trying to catch a squirrel. He was uncomfortable and cranky, and Kitty read a couple of stories to him until he fell asleep. A little girl recovering from pneumonia, insisted that Kitty colour with her. Finally it was time to tidy up the books and toys, and to say goodbye to the kids.

As she walked up the hall of the hospital, towards the front door, she was thinking about Mitch, and the date they had for Friday night. He was coming over from Toronto, and they were going to the Blue Mermaid for dinner in St. Catharines. Unfortunately, he had to head back to Toronto on Saturday. Their relationship had been heating up, but mostly by telephone. Mitch had been on the road doing readings and book signings, and then Kitty had gone to Florida, so this coming weekend was important to both of them. The vibes were great, but she was taking it slowly. He wasn't at all like any of the other men she knew, Drew or Scott, or Josh or Keith or even Adrian. He was very quiet and intense, yet they had a lot in common, and the chemistry seemed right. Time would tell.

Kitty was trying to hold back a bit on her emotions, but she secretly felt that this was it — the big romance, the one which should last a lifetime. She liked Mitch more than she wanted to admit, but she was frightened of getting hurt again. Of necessity, it was going to be a long-distance romance, and they could be tricky, so she was willing to take her time.

The hospital was inordinately quiet this afternoon. Usually the corridors were full of visitors, technicians, cleaning people, nurses, and even a few doctors. There were always people sitting in the main waiting room, drinking coffee, and looking over the good supply of pocket books and magazines available there. There were always customers in the gift shop, which was packed with interesting items. Today, though, it was quiet and rather gloomy, and Kitty was glad to be heading home.

She would never know what it was that tweaked her memory. She was thinking of Cleo, and wondering for the umpteenth time whether she had been victim of a random killing, or whether it had been one of her many boyfriends who had done her in. Had it been that new date, or had he been an innocent player, long gone before the killer arrived. She was thinking about the Black Sheep, and the little talisman he left behind with each victim, when suddenly she gave a little gasp, and stopped in her tracks.

She stared off into space, seeing herself that first day that she and Scott had met. She was standing at the cash register, wrapping three items, and putting them in a pretty little gift bag. There was the braided silver bracelet, there was a small mirrored trinket box, and, yes, there was a little black ceramic sheep!!! The sudden memory and realization of what it could mean, nearly knocked her off her feet. Gasping, she leaned against the wall and thought about it.

A nurse hurrying past, stopped and asked if she was all right. "Do you need to sit down? You look very pale."

With a weak smile, and shaking her head, she replied, "No, I'm fine, thanks." With that, she pushed into the washroom, and splashed cold water on her face. Staring at herself in the mirror, with water dribbling off her chin, she took a few deep breaths and waited for her heart beat to slow down.

Just because Scott had bought a little black sheep, didn't make him a killer. Of course it didn't. Still, it all seemed to fit rather nicely. The killer was obviously clever and charming. Scott was clever and charming. The killer seemed to be pretty lucky. Scott had always claimed that he was a lucky person. The killer had known Cleo. Scott knew Cleo. The killer always left a black sheep. Scott had bought a black sheep.

What was that old saying that if you have enough feathers you can sink a boat? Well, it looked as if there might be enough clues to sink Scott.

Stop it, she hissed to her reflection. Those things are totally coincidental. There's no way that Scott could be the killer. Still, was that why he had tried to restart their romance? Was he planning to kill her when he got the chance? She thought of all the times he had stayed over at her place, of all the times they had slept cuddled together. Had she been sleeping with a killer? The very idea was disturbing, disheartening, disillusioning. Her thoughts were whirling like leaves in an autumn wind. There was a strange buzzing sound in her head, as she remembered how he had so angrily declared that no woman ever left him.

The idea that she might have slept with a killer, made her feel lightheaded and nauseated. It was a disgusting and terrifying thought. She was just an ordinary woman living an ordinary life. Things like this weren't meant to happen to ordinary people. She kept telling herself that Scott couldn't possibly be the Black Sheep. He was too charming, too much fun, too normal. Or was he? Hadn't Ted Bundy appeared totally normal to his co-workers? Hadn't he been charming and likeable? Hadn't someone said that Ted was the kind of man every mother wants her daughter to bring home? Was Scott like Ted Bundy or that awful Paul Bernardo?

These frightening questions were scraping Kitty's mind like fingers on a blackboard. She stood there, staring into the mirror, trying to put all the facts and suppositions into focus.

Just then two women walked into the washroom, one of them crying, the other trying to comfort her. Kitty took her time drying her face, and applying some lipstick. Her hand was shaking a bit. Thinking you might have slept with a killer could do that to you, she thought grimly. She had to laugh when her mouth ended up looking like a clown's. Quickly, she wiped the lipstick off, and started again. She needed to get home and sort things out. Dammit, she'd have to tell the police. At least she knew a couple of detectives. She would call Jack or Bud right away. They would know what to do, and the onus would be off her shoulders.

CHAPTER 44

▼

The task force, consisting of fifteen of Niagara's finest, had been at it for four hours. They were going over every scrap of information, every clue, all the bits and pieces, anything which could conceivably relate to the Black Sheep. In spite of all their efforts, they had "piss-all in a snowbank," as Bud Lang had so aptly put it.

They had been discussing the pros and cons of hypnotizing Steffie and Vickie, to see whether they could get any seriously helpful information out of them. The women had agreed to do it, and it was an ace in the hole, which they had on the back burner. If things didn't turn around in the next couple of days, the hypnotizing would take place.

They had finally given up for the day, and all had left except for Jack and Bud. These two were wearily sitting in the so-called conference room, in the police station on Morrison Street, both with their feet up on the table. At the moment, that table was littered with the detritus left from hours of "brainstorming," — Harvey's hamburger bags, McDonald's napkins, a half-eaten box of doughnuts, and the ubiquitous Tim Horton's coffee cups. Police always seemed to find it easier to think, when they were eating.

The so-called "good samaritan," had come forward, and told his tale of stopping to help the drunk out by Gibson Lake. He wouldn't have said anything, except that the body had been found exactly where he had stopped and talked to that strange guy. He knew that the man had been tall, with very curly hair, and he might possibly have had a moustache, but he wasn't sure. He had not noticed the make of car or its license, and he hadn't seen enough of the man's face, to have any success looking at mug shots. He was sure that he could never identify him, except maybe by his voice.

The small amount of information was basically useless, except that, as far as the police knew, he was the first person who had actually not only laid eyes on the Black Sheep, but had also heard him speak. Florence Thompson, the woman Steffie had found on her fishing expedition, had also seen him, but just through the peek hole in her door. At least they both agreed that he was tall, with very curly black hair. Both Florence and the young samaritan had begged them to keep their names out of the paper, for fear of retribution.

"Let's go over this one more time, Jack," said Bud, wearily running his fingers through his hair, then reaching for just one more doughnut. His wife Amanda would kill him, if she could see the junk he had eaten today. There seemed to be more lines around his eyes and mouth since taking on this case, as well as a few rolls around his middle.

"We know the perp is smart — likely well educated. He is without a doubt the most careful, thorough killer we've ever encountered. This guy leaves no clues. He takes the time to wipe away all fingerprints, seems to leave everything in perfect order, and obviously plans the killings thoughtfully, carefully, maybe obsessively." Bud was ticking off these traits on his fingers.

Jack stood up, stretched, and began pacing back and forth. "We know that he's got to be both charming and disarming. He has great people skills. His victims don't see it coming. There's no sign of a struggle. There hasn't been any trace of blood or flesh scrapings under the fingernails, nothing scattered or knocked over. The murder site is always pristine. His victims are totally at ease with him. That tells me it has to be someone they know. No woman would be that relaxed with some stranger who had just come to her door."

"Yep, everything you say is true," mumbled Bud, stuffing the last piece of doughnut into his mouth, and wiping away the crumbs. "I'm pretty sure that it's someone they know, likely someone they're expecting."

Jack absent-mindedly ran his finger along the scar on his cheek. It was a habit he had when he was concentrating. "This creep doesn't feel any of the normal human emotions, except maybe anger. He has a lack of empathy and sympathy, and he likely doesn't feel any guilt or remorse, although we can't be sure about that. According to the books, if he's a true sociopath, once his victim is dead, she becomes uninteresting and unimportant. The trouble with this guy is that, the way he arranges them so nicely, makes me think he feels sorry for them. Maybe he isn't a real sociopath or psychopath. Maybe he's just a mixed up son of a bitch who doesn't know or care why he's doing it."

He sighed and shook his head as he continued. "You know, I picture him as being genial and polite, and we know for sure that he's intelligent and manipulative. I can't wait to meet this guy. He's a really interesting specimen, but dammit, I feel as if we're trying to do a jig-saw puzzle, and half of the pieces are missing." He arched his back, and stretched his arms, as he said this. He'd been cooped up in this room for too long. He needed some fresh air to clear his head.

Bud was looking longingly at his empty coffee cup. He'd be up for three weeks straight if he took in any more caffeine, but it was tempting. "If he's a true sociopath, he'll be self-centered, and he'll be able to mimic normal responses. He's likely an affable, charming, witty 'guy-next-door' type. He could be your dentist or your lawyer or a doctor, or, God help us, he could even be a cop, although not too many of us are charming and witty," he added with a grin. "He's just someone who's really ticked off with women, but that's likely three quarters of the male population in Niagara Falls," he shrugged and raised his hands in a 'what are you going to do' sort of gesture.

"Okay, given all that, why do you suppose he leaves the bodies arranged so nicely? It's almost as if he respects them, and regrets killing them. I get the feeling that he likes women, or he wants to like them, so why is he doing this? Is he making a statement? If so, what is it? And, does he always choose his victim according to some pattern?" Jack was staring out the window as he asked these last questions. "You know, maybe it's just independent women he hates. Perhaps his wife left him for a good job."

"Or a good man," interrupted Bud.

Jack laughed at that.

"Anyway, who the bloody hell knows?" continued Bud, standing up, flexing his broad shoulders, and brushing the telltale crumbs from his shirt. "What we do know, is that he isn't obsessing on any one type of woman. They have all had different hairstyles and colours, and the women don't seem to have any links between them. They didn't know each other, as far as we can figure, so what's the connection? Does he pick them randomly out of the phone book? Does he see them someplace like at the library, or at the corner gas station, or at the local 7-11?"

"I wonder whether he picks them out at the casino?" mused Jack, pursing his lips, and staring at Bud. "The first one, Eva, worked there. Have we checked to see whether the others liked to gamble? You know, that would be a perfect place to wander around and check out women. No one would notice. If we could prove that all the victims had visited the casino on occasion, then we could check out the videos the casino makes. Those "eyes in the sky" are constantly monitoring everything that goes on in the casino. I wonder how long they keep those videos. We might be able to spot some guy who wanders around, just looking at women, and not playing."

Jack was excited now. He liked this idea, even though he knew he was clutching at straws.

"Yes, but remember, if he's picking them out randomly at the casino, he still has to meet them, and get to know them, and make them feel comfortable enough that they invite him back to their homes. That's a tall order. It wouldn't likely happen in just one night. I think it's more likely that he already knows these women, but how, and from where?"

At this point, Jack slammed a file folder down on the table so hard that one of the coffee cups jumped and spilled over. Luckily there wasn't much left in it.

The whole case was so damn frustrating. This guy was always two steps ahead of them. He had to screw up sometime, but when? Eva's home had been very neat. It didn't appear that she had been expecting company, except that she was dressed very nicely. Most women changed into jeans and tops, or sweat suits, or a long, loose dress, when they got home from work. They didn't stay in their dresses, high heels and pearls like June Cleaver in "Leave it to Beaver." Maybe she was dressed to go out for the evening. Maybe he had come to pick her up.

The prostitute, Lovey Darnell, had been dressed in her titillating street uniform, and her place was really messy, but it was obviously her messiness, not something done by the strangler. There seemed to be a couple of Barbie dolls missing from her collection, but they couldn't be sure, and if they were missing, what did that mean?

The girl, Pat Danvers, aka "Lana," who had been found in the bushes, was a different matter. She was the only one who hadn't been left stretched out on her bed, with the sheep in her hand. Pat Danvers had been placed, sitting up against a tree in the middle of some bushes. Her skirt was straightened properly though, and she had the little sheep in her right hand, otherwise the police likely wouldn't have made the connection. They would have thought it was just a random killing. The strangler had obviously wanted them to know he had done it. That was why he always left his unique calling card, the little black ceramic sheep. He was cocky, and sure of himself, and maybe that was good. It meant that he was more likely to make a mistake.

The fact that this murder had been different, led them to believe that it had not been planned. They knew she had left the bar with someone, but descriptions varied greatly. No one had paid much attention. Bars were places where people were supposed to pick up or be picked up. There was nothing notable about that. Two or three people did remember, however, that he had strange curly black hair. Somehow it looked phony, and was noticeable. They disagreed, however, on his height, and his clothes.

Was he getting careless, allowing himself to be seen picking up someone in a bar? Why didn't he fear being recognized? Perhaps he was from another city, and just came over to the Niagara area to choose his victims. Had he picked up Pat Danvers with the idea of killing her, or had something happened to trigger his anger? They still hadn't made the connection with the prostitute found strangled in the Don Valley in Toronto. She had not had a black sheep in her hand, so they didn't realize that she was one of the strangler's victims.

Cleo's rooms had been pristine. There was nothing out of place. She had been all dressed up as if she was planning to go out, but there was no sign of any company. Could the strangler have gone to the trouble of washing up any glasses or dishes they had used? It was very possible, and just served to point out how careful he was.

That little episode with Ginny hadn't fit the pattern at all. Ginny wasn't expecting any company, and she didn't have a date with anyone. That time, the guy had broken in through the back door. The police figured it was just a random burglary gone awry. They weren't considering it with regard to the strangler.

In three of the murders, however, because there was no forced entry, and because these women were dressed for company, it seemed that they must have known their killer. This meant that he wasn't likely picking them randomly. He was making dates with them. He was charming enough that women trusted him, in spite of all the hype and warnings about the Black Sheep. He was clever and resourceful, and he was likely laughing his ass off at the police, who were going around in circles, chasing their tails.

The Pat Danvers case was considered an anomaly. The big question was motive. What was it? Had each of these women done him some harm, hurt him in some way? Was he paying them back by strangling them? There was no way of telling. Was there something about each woman which triggered something in him? What the hell could it be? Was it a perfume they all wore? Jack made a note to check that out.

As far as they knew, the women had not all come from the same town, they hadn't gone to the same school. As far as the detectives knew, they had not all taken the same course such as a computer course or a language course, or dancing or singing. The lists went on and on, but no connections could be found. The most difficult type of murders to solve were the ones done by a serial killer, whose motives were known only to him, in his sick, twisted mind. It was a daunting and discouraging task.

"Maybe he kills women with whom he has had a relationship for a while. Maybe if his inamorata lets him down, or disappoints him in some way, he kills her, and moves on." Bud suggested this without much conviction.

"His inamorata?" laughed Jack. "That's a pretty big word for a tired old detective. Can you spell it?"

"Hell no, I'm not even sure what it means, but I like the sound of it," grinned Bud.

"Well, I've had enough for now," said Jack. "Speaking of inamoratas, let's go home and give our wives a thrill."

"Speaking of wives," said Bud slowly, wondering how to go about this, "What's up with you and Cassie?"

Jack just stared at him. "What do you mean?" he asked cautiously.

"Look, if you don't want to talk about it, it's okay, but when you two are in a room together you can see the sparks flying. What's going on?"

Jack sighed and sat down again. "Shit, I didn't realize it was so obvious. There's really nothing going on between us, but part of me wishes that there was. I can't get her out of my head, Bud. I think up reasons to drive past her house, just in case she's outside. I've been out to the Cattery twice, pretending I'm going to adopt a cat, but she hasn't been there either time. I took her to lunch one day, and we were so hot for each other that we could have set the tablecloth on fire.

The crazy thing is that I love Darla, and I wouldn't hurt her for anything. Still, if she wasn't around, and if Cassie was free, I'd run off with her in a minute. You know the story, Bud. I've told you before. I've loved her since we were kids. In high school we couldn't get enough of each other. If her mother hadn't interfered, we would have been married by the time we were eighteen.

When we broke up, she went on to university, and I went to Europe. I chased after every reddish-blond, blue-eyed doll I saw, but I couldn't get Cassie out of my mind or my heart. I came back, went to university, became a cop, and didn't even know we were living in the same city, until you and I met her that fateful day two years ago.

Then of course, she and Vickie saved my life when Willie the Weasel came after me. That seems a long time ago." He shook his head sadly and sighed again. "There's no future in it for either one of us, but I just can't leave it alone. I keep thinking that some day, somehow —," His voice trailed off, as he smiled ruefully at his old friend and partner.

He turned and stared out the window. Bud was quiet, and just waited for him to continue.

Jack feared that his marriage was disintegrating. He loved Darla, or did he? He wasn't sure anymore. Was it just habit? How did one tell? It certainly wasn't the way he felt about Cassie. Cass set a wildfire ablaze in his heart, in his very core. She always had. Sometimes he couldn't breathe, just thinking about her.

What hurt him so much was that Darla had become a silent drinker. Nothing had ever been said, but they both knew it, and they skirted around it, as if it was a pile of dung in the middle of the floor. There were times when he got home from work when she was overly welcoming, overly loving. Her beautiful eyes were just a little bit off, just a little bit glazed. Her smile was too wide, too forced. How much of the drinking was his fault? He wasn't sure, and it was cutting him up inside.

Darla wanted babies, and he was doing his best to make that happen for her. He was at an age when he really didn't care about having kids, but he kept dutifully getting her pregnant, and she kept miscarrying. How many times had it been now, four or five? He had lost count, as one miscarriage after another blurred together. The doctors were telling them absolutely no more, it was too dangerous to her health, but Darla was desperate and determined.

Jack sighed deeply as he turned again to his old friend.

"Don't worry, I'm not going to let my feelings for Cassie interfere with my work, and I'm not going to let them hurt my marriage. I came close, though, the other night. I was thinking about Cass, and out of the blue, Darla said she was planning on going out to see Cassandra's Cattery, because she's heard so much about it. Bud, I dropped the damn plate of steaks I was about to put on the barbecue. It really shook me to think of Darla and Cassie coming face to face. Darla looked at me very strangely, but didn't say anything. I've got a good wife, and I love her."

Bud thought Jack was trying too hard to convince himself, but before he could say anything, Jack continued.

"The fact that Cassie inherited all that money really screws everything up. She might always wonder whether I had gone after her because of her millions. It makes things much more complicated."

Jack himself had money from a book he had written. It was a handbook for detectives, and was now used in most police forces across the country. It was nothing, however, compared to the millions which Cassie had inherited.

"Anyway, there's no use talking about it," Jack continued, "because nothing is going to come of it. Darla and I are going to keep right on trying to have a baby, and I'm going to keep right on trying to put Cassie out of my head. You have to help me. Don't ever let me get carried away and do anything stupid."

Bud snorted at that. "Friend, the day I could stop you from doing anything you wanted to do, would be the day the Black Sheep would walk through those doors and give himself up."

They were both laughing when the phone rang.

Jack grabbed it, and was surprised to hear Kitty's voice. What she had to say surprised him even more.

Bud sat watching him, and listening to his side of the conversation with interest.

"Well, well, well," said Jack, after hanging up. "Kitty has finally remembered who bought the little ceramic sheep in her shop, and you'll never guess who it was."

"I don't feel like guessing," said Bud grumpily.

"It was none other than Scott Matheson, the fireman. Now that's a great connection. We know that he dated Cleo."

"Let's get him in here, pal. Maybe this is the break we've been looking for."

Scott was at home entertaining a long legged redhead with a ring in her tongue. He was furious at being dragged down to the station, and was very uncooperative.

"You know damn well that I didn't kill those women," he protested for at least the fourth time. "Just because I bought a black sheep doesn't make me a killer. Look, just call my niece Becky. She lives in Halifax. I've got her number at home, and she'll tell you, or at least my sister will tell you. It was just an extra little gift I bought for Becky, because she has a toy barn full of animals, and she wanted a little lamb. When I saw it in Kitty's store, I just bought it on impulse, and sent it with the books I had bought her.

You'll have to come home with me to get my sister's number, because I don't have it memorized. I hardly ever call her, but PLEASE, call and straighten this out. Yes, I dated Cleo, and yes, I bought a black sheep, but NO, I am not a murderer. Kitty must have told you about the sheep, and you know damn well that she's just trying to get back at me because I dumped her. Well, no, actually I didn't dump her. I really liked her, but she caught me with Danielle, and she threw a fit. Now she's trying to get even. Give me a break, guys. I'm not a killer, and I can prove where that black sheep went."

Scott was very upset now, and was pacing back and forth in front of the two detectives.

He seemed so sincere, though, that Jack and Bud felt their hopes flying away like feathers on the wind. Of course, he could have sent the black sheep to his little niece, and still bought more to use in his killing spree, but that didn't seem likely. When in hell were they going to catch a break on this case? They would check out Scott's story, but they both had a sinking feeling that he was telling the truth, and that once again they were back to square one.

CHAPTER 45

▼

Sunday afternoon was another glorious day in Niagara. It was still hot as Hades, but Kitty figured that it would be cooler up at the beach house. She and Keith chatted amiably all the way up. Unfortunately, Steffie had not been able to go along with them, but Kitty was looking forward to getting into those trunks and boxes, now that Keith owned the old mansion. No telling what treasures they might find.

Kitty had been wise enough to wear a pair of long cotton slacks and a long-sleeved cotton shirt. She brought a little bandana for her hair too. She wasn't about to have spiders running up her legs or arms, or burrowing in her hair. She had given up the idea of wearing her comfy sandals, and instead was wearing her running shoes and socks. She might be warm, but she would feel more protected. That spooky basement would be a haven for spiders.

There was a good breeze blowing in off Lake Erie, when they finally arrived at their destination. Kitty could see that Keith had already started doing some work around the place. A few of the front windows were proudly sporting a new coat of paint, and the difference was remarkable. She realized that the place would be magnificent by the time Keith was finished with it. She just hoped he had enough money to do all that needed to be done.

They sat out on the deck first, enjoying a cool drink. There were several pleasure boats out on the lake, and off in the distance, they could see a big freighter.

It was so relaxing, sitting there in the rocking chairs, and feeling the breeze on their faces, that Kitty laughingly told Keith she had decided to stay right there, while he went down into that dark, spidery basement to work. Just to postpone the inevitable, she asked him if they could go upstairs for another look around. She was fascinated with this old house, and wanted to see it again in the daylight, after their experience on that stormy night.

Keith was delighted that she took such an interest in his new home. He hadn't moved in yet permanently, but he was gradually getting things moved up from Niagara.

"I'm planning to have a big party as soon as I get moved in," he said, as they climbed the stairs to the third floor. "You'll have to come and maybe be my hostess, since you're helping me this way," he said hopefully.

Kitty knew that wasn't going to happen, but just murmured something noncommittal, and adroitly changed the subject.

The third floor didn't look nearly as scary as it had that rainy night, and she took a good look around. There was certainly no sign that any homeless man or serial killer had been living there. She laughed at her silly imagination, and at Steffie's.

The linen closet on the second floor still fascinated her, and she had to stop and take another peek. Keith waited agreeably, as she poked around in the bedrooms, specially the one in which she and Steffie had tried to sleep. Nothing looked scary or spooky today, and she wondered whether it really had just been the fatigue and wine, which had caused them to feel so threatened.

"Thanks, Keith. I really wanted to see everything again in the daylight. This house fascinates me."

"That's great. You're welcome to come up as often as you want. I'd love to have you," he added this double entendre with a leer."

Knowing what a flirt he was, Kitty just laughed.

As they looked out at the water again, before starting their work, Keith said, "I'm sorry, Kitty. I thought we could carry some of the boxes and trunks upstairs, but they're way too heavy. I've brought a couple of masks for us in case the dust gets too bad. I don't want to be responsible for you having an asthma attack from breathing all that stale, dusty air."

"Well, if I do, at least I'll have a doctor handy," she kidded.

She took a few deep breaths of the lovely clear air out on the deck, before following Keith downstairs. She didn't want to tell him just how frightened she was of spiders. There would be mice down there, and she could handle that, but spiders were a different story. They could be right on her head or back, and she wouldn't know it. She grimaced at the thought, and was thankful that she was well covered up.

The stairs were very steep, and the single light bulb hanging from the ceiling, didn't do much to illuminate the area below. Keith, however, had brought a couple of large flashlights, equipped with fresh batteries.

"You're like a boy scout, Keith. You're always prepared," Kitty grinned, as she adjusted the mask.

"I do like to organize things carefully ahead of time," he admitted. "Guess that comes with being a doctor. You have to look ahead, and be prepared for all eventualities."

It took the two of them to pull the first trunk out from the wall. The clasps on it were rusty, and Keith dug into his tool chest to get a hammer and chisel. When they finally got the clasps undone, and lifted the lid, a smell of dust and decay assailed them.

"We should have brought a fan," mumbled Kitty, trying not to breathe in the noxious smells.

"Great idea, I've got one in the kitchen. I'll be right back," said Keith enthusiastically.

There was no way that Kitty was going to stay down in that dank hell hole by herself, even for a few minutes, so she went partway up the stairs behind Keith, and stood waiting there for him. Back he came with a long extension cord plugged in somewhere in the kitchen, a big grin on his face. "This will make it much better. Good for you for thinking of it."

It was obvious that Keith was having a wonderful time. His brown eyes were sparkling with a strange intensity. He was as excited as a kid at Christmas, as they carefully removed a layer of old clothes, pants, heavy sweaters, and even shoes, from the trunk. Keith had brought a big box of green garbage bags, and they hastily threw the old clothes into these. Below the clothes were piles of papers. They looked like mostly receipts and miscellaneous papers, with nothing of much value. That was disappointing.

The second trunk was sturdier, and in better condition. It proved to be a treasure trove of diaries, pictures and scrapbooks.

"Keith, you'll need hours to go through these. They could be really valuable historically, and you shouldn't throw anything out, till you've had a good look at them upstairs in the daylight."

"You're right. We'll take all the paper stuff up to that little ante-room between the living room and the kitchen. That'll be a perfect place to keep stuff till we can go through it."

That sounded as if he was expecting her to come up with him again. Kitty sighed. What had she started here? Well, if there was a next time, she would definitely bring Steffie with her.

The afternoon went quickly, and they got a lot accomplished. They had just come up the basement stairs, and were washing their hands in the kitchen, when Keith suddenly grabbed Kitty from behind and began to nuzzle her neck. "You've been a great help, Kitty. You'll have to come back again, maybe a few more times, and we'll finish the job. It can be our summer project. I won't be able to do it without you."

Kitty was struggling to free herself when, looking up, she saw Drew standing in the kitchen doorway, glaring at them through his John Lennon glasses. She let out a little yelp of surprise, as she pushed away from Keith.

She remembered that one night so clearly, when Drew had taken her to dinner, and she had thrown the wine in his face. That had been the beginning of the end, and, of course, giving the police Drew's name as one of Cleo's friends, had really finished things. She regretted the loss of his friendship, but didn't really miss him. Her thoughts and time were taken up entirely with one Mitchell Donaldson, the latest, and hopefully the last, one true love of her life.

"Hey pal, I thought you said you couldn't make it," said Keith, with a big grin on his face. "You're a bit late, we've got all the work done for today." He didn't seem the least embarrassed at having been caught putting the hustle on Kitty.

Drew said truculently, "I got finished earlier than I expected, so I came up to lend a hand. Didn't know I would be interrupting anything."

"No, you're just in time. We were going to have a nice drink out on the deck. What'll you have?"

Kitty felt very uncomfortable. The last time she had spoken with Drew, was when he called her so angrily, after she had given his name to the police. She also felt embarrassed that he had seen her struggling with Keith. She wondered how long he had been standing there.

Putting on a pretty smile, however, she said, "Hi, Drew. It's good to see you. We could have used your help down there. It's dark and dirty, and there are still lots of boxes unopened. The best thing about it was that I wasn't bitten by any spiders."

Drew merely nodded, as if he wasn't really interested.

Carrying their drinks, they adjourned to the deck, where it was much cooler. Kitty carried one small box of old photos with her, and sat at the little deck table to go through them. They were wonderful old pictures, faded but still legible, showing the fashions right from the turn of the century up to the roaring twenties era. There were many boxes of photos, and this was just the first one.

Drew and Keith were talking about the Black Sheep, which was the favourite topic of conversation in and around Niagara these days. They all agreed that the police seemed baffled, and didn't have much to go on. Keith felt that the Black Sheep was much more clever than the entire police force put together, and Drew was of the same opinion.

Kitty didn't want to talk about it at all, for fear that Drew would get all riled up at her again. She engrossed herself in the pictures, trying to drown out what the fellows were saying. It was interesting to look at the old snapshots, and she was trying to determine which ones were the original owners of Stockton House, and which ones were their children, when she suddenly stopped in utter shock. She stared in disbelief at the picture of a very pretty young girl, who was obviously the maid. She had dark curly hair, big dark eyes, and a slight stature. She was the "Nora" Steffie had pictured so vividly up in the attic, and again the night of the storm, in the hall beside the linen closet.

"Keith," she interrupted excitedly, handing him the picture. "Does she look familiar?"

Keith stared at the picture for some time, then said in amazement, "She's just like the maid Steffie described up in the attic. I said that she had quite an imagination, but here she is. That's impossible. Had you seen this picture somewhere before?"

"No, absolutely not. Wait till I tell Steffie. The night we were up here in the storm, she saw this girl plain as day, standing in the hall by the big linen closet. Honestly Keith, she really saw her. She was standing staring at us with those big eyes, and she didn't exactly look friendly. At least that's what Steffie said."

"Sounds as if you two had a bit too much to drink," said Drew. He hadn't really said anything to Kitty since his unexpected arrival. It was obvious that he was still mad at her.

Kitty knew that she and Steffie had in fact, drunk quite a bit of wine that stormy night, but she knew what Steffie had seen. She was sure that it hadn't just been her imagination. "I think this place is haunted, Keith," she said with a laugh. "You'd better be careful that you don't do anything to hurt the old house. I think that little 'Nora' or 'Eileen' or whatever her name is, is guarding it.

"Well, she's a cute looking little lass. She can guard my bedroom any time she wants," he grinned, as he put the picture back in the box.

Kitty was hungry after their hard work, and was happy when Keith suggested that they stop somewhere on the way back to Niagara Falls, to get a bite to eat. Drew, however, said that he had to get back early, so he couldn't join them. Kitty assumed that he was still grumpy because she was there, so she didn't try to coax him to change his mind. Neither did Keith.

She had really enjoyed herself, and was glad that she had come to help Keith. She could hardly wait to get home to tell Steffie about the picture. She felt badly that Drew seemed so angry with her. She missed him as a friend. She also kept thinking about that awkward scene when Keith had begun to get amorous in the kitchen. What would have happened if Drew hadn't shown up at that precise moment? Would she have had trouble fending off Keith's advances? Did Drew think there was something going on between them now? Did she care anymore what Drew thought?

She was uncomfortable at first in the car going home with Keith, but neither of them mentioned the incident. Keith was as charming and flirty as ever, and he didn't seem concerned or annoyed that she had tried to rebuff his advances. Flirting seemed to come naturally to him, and he apparently expected a certain amount of rejection, or else he knew that the women understood he wasn't serious.

Whatever the situation, she had enjoyed her afternoon very much. She would tell Mitch about it, and she hoped that she would have the opportunity to go up there again to go through more boxes.

CHAPTER 46

▼

Steffie was taking a day off. Since Vickie had been in town, taking great pleasure in helping out in the boutique, both Kitty and Steff had been taking extra days off whenever they felt like it. They were careful to co-ordinate it so that they didn't both take a day at the same time, leaving Vickie to hold the fort.

This golden Niagara morning, Steffie was anxious to get back to her sketching. She had an idea for a set of three sketches, one of the Canadian Horseshoe Falls, one looking down the Niagara River, with the Rainbow bridge in the background, and possibly, one of the fearless little Maid of the Mist, between the American and Canadian Falls. She knew that they would be appealing to tourists, and would sell quickly.

She had already picked out the spot from which she would sketch the Horseshoe Falls, and had made the arrangements. She had met and liked the interesting fellow who operated the lights, which illuminated the falls at night. He likely should have been retired, but he obviously loved his work, and had so many stories to tell.

The lights were housed in an historic old stone building, which sat atop a hill directly across from the falls. It looked down on the multitude of tourists from all over the world, who had made the journey to see those wonders of nature for themselves.

Steffie had arranged to meet with Frank at 9:30 this bright and beautiful morning, and the obliging custodian of the lights was already there waiting for her. Carrying her artist's sketchbook, she walked around the crowded and damp stone room, looking at all the clippings and photos, which covered the walls. There was so much history here. A lot of important people, including political leaders, and movie and television stars, had visited this site, and operated the bank of switches, which focused a rainbow of coloured lights on the falls every night.

Steffie had been here a couple of times previously, but only at night, and she knew that this old stone building after dark gave new meaning to the term "spooky." She could even picture the Black Sheep hanging out here. Shaking her head at this nonsensical idea, she chatted a few minutes with the charming and fun-loving Frank, and then went out on the landing, and began sketching.

Previously, when she had been here at night with friends, they had delighted in the families of raccoons who came around faithfully looking for handouts. Frank always had treats for them, and they were so tame, that they brought their babies along. Baby raccoons were very cute, and Frank had let Steffie give them treats on one of her visits. From that time on, she and Frank had been friends.

It was a gorgeous day, and there were already crowds of tourists down below, gawking in amazement and delight at the rumbling, roaring, timeless cataracts. Steffie never looked at the falls without thinking of "The Miracle of Niagara." It had happened way back in the 50's, when a young boy around eight years of age, wearing a little orange life jacket, had been swept over the falls, bobbed up in front of the Maid of the Mist, was spotted by the captain and a boatload of tourists, was rescued, and lived to tell about it. A miracle indeed!

Frank kept himself busy putting up new pictures, and tidying his desk in a half-hearted way, while Steffie sketched, and pondered the majesty and ferocious nature of the water below.

Eventually, she had done all that she could. She stretched, and packed up her equipment. Thanking her host profusely for allowing her this wonderful opportunity, she presented him with a bottle of Crown Royal. She didn't even know whether he drank, but he had a lot of mischief in his eyes, and looked as if he might enjoy a nip now and again.

Going straight home, she hardly had time to put on the coffee pot, when Nick came through the door. Steffie's heart sank. Now what did he want? Would he never leave her alone?

Nick grinned at her, and gave her a hug. He was letting his hair grow back, and he already looked much better. She had hated that bald dome, which seemed to draw attention to the awful snake tattoo on his neck.

"Man, you are one good looking babe," he exclaimed, running his eyes up and down her curvaceous body, which was shown to best advantage in her tight jeans and bright yellow top. "If you weren't my sister I'd be all over you," he added, with a lecherous smile.

Ignoring this comment, she said, "What can I do for you this time, Nick?" as she got out two coffee mugs.

"No no, sister dearest. It's what can I do for you?" he answered jovially.

Steffie thought that he must have won at the casino, he was in such a good mood. Maybe he was going to pay her back some of the money he had been "borrowing."

No, that was too much to expect. Instead, Nick said, "You and I haven't done a damn thing together since I got here. Remember the fun times we had when we were kids? We were almost inseparable in those days." There was a wistful tone in his voice. What had happened to him? He seemed almost mellow, not at all like her tough, wisecracking, ex-con brother.

"Sure I remember," she said sarcastically. "I also remember you being brought home by the cops on more than one occasion, and mom sitting crying her heart out." Steff was upset that Nick was obviously going to spoil her lovely free day.

"Okay," he said gruffly. "Forget that shit. Don't try spoiling things just when I'm in such a good mood. Let's go to the Lion Safari this afternoon. It's a perfect day for it, and I want to spend some time with you. It's my treat. I'd like to try to make up for how nasty I've been."

Steffie couldn't believe her ears. Was this Nick, or some alien who had taken over his body? He sounded like the old Nick, loving and considerate and full of fun. Still, there must be a catch. Why did he want to take her away some place in the car? Was he planning to hurt her?

"Come on, sis, please. This is very important to me. I really want to spend some time with you. You told me that you've never been there, so let's go. What's the hold-up? We can talk on the way."

Steffie wondered whether the tumours had started growing again in his head. Maybe they were changing his personality back to the sweet, loveable person he had been years ago. She stared at him doubtfully, then made her decision. She would go with him and see what happened. She loved her brother, or at least she loved the person he had once been, and she wanted that person back. Maybe they could be like they used to be years ago.

"Let me call Kitty, and then we'll go," she said, heading for the phone.

"No way. Why do you have to call her? Don't you trust me?" He was angry now, and was wearing his menacing look.

"Of course not, and don't be nasty or I won't go." Unfortunately Nick was right on the button. He knew her so well. This was why she wanted to tell Kitty where she was going. If she disappeared, at least they would know where to start looking.

Picking up the phone, she quickly called Kitty at the boutique, and told her that she was going to the Lion Safari up in Rockton with Nick.

Kitty was surprised, and immediately apprehensive, but Steffie had no time to talk, not with Nick standing glowering at her.

Grabbing her jacket, her camera and her purse, she left with her brother, wondering whether she would ever return.

All her fears, however, were groundless. They had a wonderful, fun-filled day. Nick couldn't have been nicer, or more fun. He bought the tickets to get them into the park, even though Steffie offered to pay. The first thing they did was get on the bus to tour the many fenced and locked animal compounds.

The lions were disappointing, since they were all lounging around in the sun, doing nothing except chilling out. One of them lifted his head, shook his magnificent mane, and yawned, but that was the most action they saw from these beautiful beasts.

As usual, the monkeys were hugely entertaining. The visitors who had chosen to drive their cars, rather than taking the bus, soon realized the error of their ways. The fearless and mischievous monkeys leaped on the cars, pulling at the windshield wipers, pounding on the side mirrors, sitting on the car roofs, and trying to get their nimble fingers through the windows for treats. From the bus, Steffie and Nick had a great view of all the antics, and Steffie took a pile of pictures on her new digital camera.

One giraffe walked over to the bus, and peered in the window, as if looking for a friend. The bus driver/tour guide told them that the giraffe has a brain the same size as his eyeball, and the passengers laughed when they saw how small his eyes were.

After the excellent bus trip, they bought some cokes and pizza slices, and wandered over to see the elephant show. The elephants were dutifully going through their tricks, standing on their heads, carting logs around, holding tails and marching in circles. One baby pachyderm was the hit of the show. He tried so hard to do what the big boys were doing, but he failed so miserably. He was enthusiastic and very adorable.

Nick and Steffie laughed uproariously at the parrot who rode his bicycle on a tightrope, and the parrot who sang the first line of "Oh Canada."

Steffie couldn't remember when she had laughed so much. Nick seemed to be a totally different person today — a person she used to know and love. He laughed and joked with her, but at times she noticed that he became quiet, and seemed sad. What a mystery man he had become.

On the drive home they talked mostly about the animals, and they were both so full of the junk food they had consumed, that neither was interested in dinner.

Arriving back at Steffie's apartment, Nick hugged her, and thanked her for spending the afternoon with him. He told her that he loved her, and asked her to always remember this wonderful time they had shared, then he was gone. Steffie went to bed thinking that Nick wasn't as tough as he tried to pretend. Maybe things were going to work out after all.

CHAPTER 47

▼

In the days following Cleo's death, Kitty and Steffie had found themselves talking quietly, and almost afraid to laugh. It seemed somehow, to be a sacrilege to be alive and having fun, when poor Cleo had died such a dreadful death, at the hands of some unknown psycho.

The police seemed to have few clues, although they were certainly working hard. It was baffling the way the Black Sheep cleaned up the murder scenes so well. The police were following up on every man Cleo had dated or talked with in the past year. That in itself was an onerous task. They knew that they would get him, at least that's what they told each other, but it was a question of when. Could they stop him before he killed again?

Steffie felt as if all her feelings and nerves were tied in a barbed wire bundle. She couldn't even pick at them to separate them. They were a jumble of anger, fear and guilt. She thought that she might collapse like a house of cards. She was angry at the killer, fearful of what was going on with Nick, and guilty about how she and Kitty had laughed at Cleo and her many boyfriends.

Both women were determined to help catch the killer in any way they could, but what could they possibly do? Steffie had been soundly scolded for her trip to Cleo's apartment, even though she had found a witness who had actually seen the strangler. Kitty was sure that the killer was someone Cleo had known, and in her innermost mind she suspected that it might be Josh. She couldn't forget those big hands of his, and the way he had snuck into her house and her bathroom that one afternoon. Even though he owned a very respectable business in town, there was something about him that worried her, yet she had nothing to take to the police.

At least it was a relief that Scott had been telling the truth about buying the little black sheep for his niece. It still gave her the shivers, though, thinking that he could have been the killer, and she had actually slept with him. It also gave her the shivers that so many things seemed to point directly to Scott. What if he had bought some other black sheep somewhere else? Just because he could account for the one he had bought from her, didn't mean that he couldn't have bought other ones. He could have sent the one to his little niece as a perfect cover for the others he might have bought. She just hoped that the detectives weren't discounting him completely, yet she hoped that he was innocent. It was so confusing, and disturbing.

When Kitty got the call from her sister Lacey, she was delighted. Lacey and the baby Charlie, were flying down to Toronto from Thunder Bay, to spend a few days with their parents. She was leaving the two older children at home with her husband and the in-laws. After visiting in Toronto, Lacey wanted to come over to Niagara Falls for a few days, to spend some time with her sister. Although Lacey was two years older, they had always been very close. It was just the diversion Kitty needed.

The morning that Lacey arrived in a rental car, Kitty had stayed home to greet her. When they pulled into the driveway, Kitty ran out to hug her sister, and grab her little nephew from his car seat. She whirled him round and round, much to his delight.

Kitty was crazy about this adorable little cherub, who was the most placid, cuddly little kid she had ever encountered. At eighteen months he would sit seriously and quietly, amusing himself with anything within reach. He stared at books, and turned the pages as if he understood every word. Even a blade of grass could amuse him for ages, as he sniffed it, tasted it, wound it around his chubby fingers, and examined it, as if it were a rare jewel. He seldom cried, and had a goofy grin, which lit up his little face. The family had taken to calling him "Turnip," and Kitty was afraid that the awful name would stick. As far as she was concerned, he was smarter than any of them. He could fit round pegs and square blocks into the appropriate holes faster than any five year old. He would likely grow up to be a scientist, or maybe an engineer.

Little Charlie loved music, and waved his hands wildly, as he tried to dance on his chubby legs. When he looked at Kitty with those gorgeous greeny-blue eyes, edged by thick black lashes, her heart melted. She would steal him if she could.

As they dragged all the baby paraphernalia into the house, Lacey said, "I'm so sorry about Cleo. You must still be in shock. Have the police got any clues at all?" She agreed with her mom, that Kitty shouldn't be living in this big house all by herself, but she had to be careful what she said. She knew all too well that her little sister was not too good at taking advice.

Rosie and Petie took one look at the pint sized intruder, and took off for parts unknown. Charlie plumped himself down, and began examining a feathered toy on a stick — one of Petie's favourites. The sisters kept a close eye on him, as they sat chatting and catching up.

"Well, how's your love life?" asked Lacey after lunch. They had put Charlie down for a nap, and were sipping wine, as they lounged in the gazebo. Lacey looked very much like Kitty. She had the same curly blond hair, big blue eyes, and long shapely legs. After three children and ten years of marriage, however, she was a bit heavier than her sister. She had always loved giving advice to Kitty, and felt that she should definitely be married and settled down by now.

She would never have admitted that she felt a little jealous of Kitty's freedom. She loved her handsome dentist husband, and her adorable three kids, but they did demand attention twenty-four hours a day. There were occasions when she felt like running away, but most of the time she felt that marriage was wonderful, and she realized how lucky she was. She wanted Kitty to find a guy as nice as her husband, and she loved hearing about all Kitty's boyfriends, passing judgement on them from her venerable position as a married woman.

Kitty told Lacey all about Drew, and the fun they had enjoyed before they broke up. She explained that she couldn't stand his jealousy and his little sulking episodes, and his lack of understanding about her beloved cats.

"He'd be great to know, though, if you ever want a tummy tuck or to have your boobs lifted," laughed Lacey. "You might get a discount for the whole family."

They giggled about that, and then Kitty continued. She told about Scott trying to patch things up with her, and about how she just hadn't realized what a skunk he was. "Well, actually, I guess I did know, or at least I was coming to that conclusion just before I found him in my bed with the redhead." She shook her head in disgust at the memory.

"Had he done something to tip you off that he wasn't the perfect guy you thought he was?" asked Lacey with interest, holding out her wineglass for a refill.

"Well, yes, as a matter of fact, he had." Kitty was reluctant to tell the tale, because she knew it put her in a bad light, but it was so easy to talk to Lacey. "He had slept over the night before I was going to Toronto to see Mom and Dad, and I was just coming out of the shower. I saw him digging into my wallet, and it really ticked me off. Actually, he had borrowed money from me a few times, and had never paid it back, but at least he had always asked first. This time he was just helping himself. You know me, I saw red. I said something like 'What the hell are you doing in my wallet? If you need money you could at least have the courtesy to ask me for it, instead of sneaking around like a stupid kid.'

That's when all hell broke loose. Before I realized what he was doing, he dropped the wallet, bounded around the bed, and grabbed me by the upper arms. He was squeezing as hard as he could, and it really hurt. He had never raised a hand to me before, so I was absolutely stunned. I told him to let me go, and I called him a moron, but he just kept squeezing. He glared at me with the most malevolent look, and he snarled, 'Don't you ever talk to me like that again. I'll damn well look in your purse or anywhere else I want. You're lucky I don't knock you across the room.'"

"Oh, Kitty. You should have called the police on him." Lacey was truly horrified that this could have happened to her sister.

"Yes, maybe I should have, but I was too stunned to think clearly. He shoved me down on the bed, and stomped out. Before he got to the door, however, he came back all contrite, with a sheepish look on his face. He was really apologetic, and said that he had a fierce migraine, which was driving him crazy. His excuse for helping himself to the money, was that they were supposedly taking up a collection at the fire station for a widow and three kids, whose trailer had burned to the ground a few days before. I knew about the fire, because I had seen the article in the paper. Scott said that he was just a little short that month, and he didn't think I would mind helping out. It seemed logical at the time, so I didn't make a big scene about it.

I didn't care about the money. It was the fact that he grabbed my arms so hard, and then shoved me down on the bed. He was like a Jekyll and Hyde character. On the way to Toronto, I thought it over, and decided that I could do better than a fireman with a temper like that. When I got back to Niagara

Falls, I had pretty well made up my mind that I would tell him it was all over, but he beat me to it. When I found him with that girl in my bed, I was so angry and hurt and ashamed, that I've been angry with myself ever since. It was a case of very bad judgement, and I've learned my lesson. No man should ever treat a woman that way, and I was a total bird brain to let him get away with it." Kitty sighed and hugged herself. "Let's just say that it was not my finest hour."

Lacey commiserated with her, then turned the subject to the rugged carpenter her dad had mentioned. Her life with a husband and three children was so settled and predictable, that she loved hearing all Kitty's tales.

Kitty had now finished her glass of wine, and was pouring a second, so she didn't hesitate to tell her sister about Josh coming right into the bathroom when she was showering. As soon as she had mentioned that, however, she realized that she had made a bad mistake.

Lacey pounced on the information like a cat with a mouse. "You can't be serious. He actually came right into the bathroom while you were in the shower? Did you call the police? How did you get rid of him?" She was appalled at the thought of her sister alone in the house, with a possible psycho or serial killer.

Kitty made light of any possible danger from Josh, and made Lacey promise that she would not tell their parents. Quickly she brought the subject around to Mitch. She told all about the accident, when their canoe overturned in the stormy waters, and she described their night together in the cabin. Again she made Lacey promise "on fear of death" not to tell their folks about the canoe accident.

She tried to make it sound romantic and titillating, but Lacey was not to be deterred. She kept coming back to Josh, and the fact that he could be dangerous. Kitty wasn't going to admit that she suspected he could be the killer. Lacey would tell their parents, and they would try yanking her right out of her home, or worse still, they might descend upon her, and say that they were moving in to protect her.

Steffie dropped around after supper, and they spent a fun-filled evening talking about men, babies, boyfriends, and even killers. Adrian heard them laughing and talking, and he came over with a bottle of wine.

Lacey had met Adrian before, and thought that he was very interesting. She liked his rather exotic look, and he was a lot of fun. He had dark hair and a widow's peak, which was very romantic looking. Also he had one dimple on his left cheek, which gave him a rather loveable lopsided grin. His eyes were a dark brown, and he always had a nice tan. He looked marvellous in his pilot's uniform, and she wondered why Kitty wasn't more interested in him. She was anxious to meet the mysterious Mitch and see the comparison.

They all sat out in the gazebo till very late. It was one of those beautiful nights in Niagara, with a black velvet sky, and a myriad of diamond-like stars twinkling in a friendly fashion. Lacey loved this city, and was so glad that Kitty had inherited Grandma's house, while she herself had inherited the money. It had proved much more useful than the house, as she and Tom expected to live in Thunder Bay forever.

As usual, the conversation came around to the Black Sheep, and there were wild speculations as to whether it was someone they all knew, or a total stranger. Lacey put her two cents worth in, and wondered whether it could be a strong, ugly woman who was jealous of attractive females. After all the wine they had consumed, that idea seemed pretty funny, but it also had a shred of possibility to it, and they wondered whether they should suggest it to the police.

Changing the subject, Steffie said, "Mr. Mason was in the shop this afternoon."

"No kidding," cried Kitty in surprise. "He hasn't been back since he tried to date you, and you turned him down. Did he buy anything?"

"No, but he asked me out again," laughed Steffie.

Lacey and Adrian were looking from one to the other, sensing that there might be a story involved.

"What did you tell him this time?" asked Kitty.

"I put on a very serious face, and told him that I'm involved in a relationship at the moment, but that it was very kind of him to think of me. I didn't want him calling me names like last time," she grinned.

"Who is this guy?" asked Adrian.

"Oh, he's a charmer," giggled Kitty. "He's bald, but he has little clumps of hair, which Steffie thinks look like tarantulas clinging to his scalp. He has a bad temper and bad breath."

"To tell you the truth, his face looks like ten miles of bad road, and he's likely got carbuncles on his ass," interrupted Steffie, "but other than that, he's quite a catch." They all had a good laugh at that.

"Actually, at one point we thought he might be the Black Sheep," said Kitty. "He's pretty creepy. But then we decided that the Black Sheep is likely good looking and charming and romantic, or at least fun to be with. That's likely how he gets the women to trust him."

Everyone had something to say about the Black Sheep, but eventually Lacey changed the subject. "Adrian, what great adventures have you been having lately?"

"Not many these days. It's just the same old same old," he laughed. "I've been on the Mediterranean run for some time now, and I really like it. I'm in Spain or Italy or Portugal or Greece every few days, and they are all great countries. I get several days off in between, so it works out really well. Next I think I'll go back to the South American run. That's exciting in a different way."

They chatted about all the romantic places he had seen, till Lacey went back into the house to check on Charlie.

"Jack and Bud were in this afternoon," said Steffie, refusing any more wine. "They haven't been able to make any connection between the little black sheep and any of Cleo's boyfriends, at least not yet. They are really dedicated though, and are bound to discover something soon. Scott seemed like such a good lead, but I gather they aren't too interested in him now. This guy is just too damn smart, but he's bound to screw up eventually."

"What makes them so sure that he's one of Cleo's boyfriends?" asked Adrian. "Couldn't it just as easily be some guy picking them out at random? Maybe he saw Cleo, and something went off in his head, and he followed her home."

"But then, how did he get her to let him in?" shot back Kitty. "There was no sign of a forced entry — there never is, so obviously it was someone she knew and trusted."

"Well, I wish they would catch him soon. Women seem to be looking at all the men with fear and mistrust these days. It doesn't do anything for our egos," he grinned, showing the one lop-sided dimple.

Having exhausted the Black Sheep topic, Kitty and Steffie began telling Lacey and Adrian about the lovely old mansion on Lake Erie, and the scary night they had spent there. That led them to Keith Spenser, and how fond he had been of Cleo. Then they began speculating as to whether Keith could possibly be the killer.

"I think it could be the nurse Barry somebody or other," declared Steffie. He has a bad temper for sure, and he seemed to have a crush on Cleo. I wonder whether the other victims had been in the hospital recently. That would be a possible connection."

"That's a good idea, Steffie," said Kitty excitedly. "I wonder whether the task force has given that any thought. We should mention it to them."

"I'm sure the detectives don't appreciate you two amateur sleuths butting in," laughed Adrian, "but you know, you could be right. You should call them, even if they don't like the interference."

Eventually the party broke up, and Lacey went to bed, feeling lucky to be married to her darling husband, and to be living safely in Thunder Bay, far away from the dangers of being single in Niagara Falls. She just wished that Kitty could persuade Steffie to move in to this big house with her for a few months, or until the Black Sheep was caught and put away. She understood now why her parents were so worried about Kitty.

The next day, Kitty and Lacey and the baby went down to Queenston Park, and had a picnic. It was something which they used to do a lot when they were young, and came to Niagara Falls to visit their Grandma.

It was another sunny day, and little Charlie toddled around the grass, trying to kick a colourful beach ball, which Kitty had bought for him. The sisters had always loved to "people watch," and they laughed at the woman with the Farrah Fawcett hairdo framing a pitbull face. Her boobs in the tight top were pumped up like helium balloons.

They were sitting on a park bench, surrounded by lush green grass, stately old trees, and chirping birds. A gentle breeze coming off the river kept them comfortable.

The park was full of families, many of them setting out a picnic lunch. As they chatted, they noticed a beautiful little round-faced girl standing a few feet in front of them. She was lifting her skirt with one hand, and rubbing her tummy with the other. She was looking at Charlie, and he had stopped kicking his ball, and was now looking at her.

Kitty couldn't help wondering what kind of children she and Mitch might have. The thought startled her. She had never really thought seriously about having kids with any of the men she had dated, and thinking of them now in relation to Mitch was somehow scary. She mustn't let herself get too serious about Mitch, until they had spent more time together. There was so much about him that she didn't know. For all she knew, he could be the Black Sheep. He certainly had a dark side to him. She laughed at that absurdity, as they packed up the picnic basket and headed for home.

CHAPTER 48

▼

After her sister Lacey and baby Charlie had gone, Kitty found the house somehow too big and too quiet. They had been there a very short time, but it had been such fun, and Kitty hadn't expected to miss them so much.

She was ready for bed, and had just been talking to Mitch on the phone. She was really looking forward to his upcoming visit.

She felt so excited tonight, that she couldn't concentrate on television. She had read the paper cover to cover, and was interested in a short article about the Black Sheep. Unfortunately, there wasn't much new information in it. It was as if the entire city was holding its collective breath, waiting for the other shoe to drop, waiting for the next killing.

She played the piano for a while, because she was too excited for sleep. Mitch was coming for a short visit, and it was going to be such fun.

Tonight Petie didn't come to sit on the piano, as he usually did. Instead, he and little Rosie were curled up together in a big chair. They were snuggled so tightly, that there was no way of telling where one head began and another tail finished. They looked like a big fur pillow, and Kitty laughed fondly when she finally found them.

She called Steffie, but there was no answer. Next she tried Cassie, but again, no one was home. Where were all her friends tonight? She thought about calling her dad, just to say hello, but realized he would likely be in bed.

Finally she decided to have a nice hot shower. That was always soothing, and relaxing. She followed that by going back down to the kitchen to make a pot of tea. As she waited for the water to boil, she was thinking about Keith

Spenser, and what an interesting afternoon they had spent up at the lake house.

Keith had called again, trying to coax her back up there, but she had been a bit ambivalent. She definitely would like to go up again, and delve further into all those mysterious boxes and trunks. Also, the picture of the little maid was still on her mind. That had been so very strange. How could Steffie have imagined seeing that Irish maid standing in the hall, and then have her turn up in an old photo. It was too creepy to believe. Yes, she would definitely love to go back up to the old house, but, she didn't want to encourage Keith. She could never be sure when he was kidding, or when he was serious in his flirtations with her.

Sipping her tea at the kitchen table, she began making a list of groceries she would need for Mitch's upcoming visit. This time wouldn't be so rushed. He was staying for the entire weekend. They would be eating out one of the nights, but there would be a couple of breakfasts, and maybe even a romantic dinner by candlelight.

At first she wasn't sure of just what she had heard outside, so she sat very still and listened. There it was again! Someone was calling "Here kitty, kitty. Come out, kitty."

That was odd. As far as Kitty knew, there were no cats in the immediate neighbourhood. The only animal around was the little dog Maxie, next door. Her two cats were always in the house, so who was out looking for his cat at this hour?

She hurried to the sliding doors, and went out on the deck. It was a beautiful, black night. Although there was no moon at the moment, she could see a few stars here and there. She stood perfectly still and listened, but there was no sound in the backyard. "Is someone there? Can I help you?" she called into the darkness. If someone had lost his cat, she would be happy to help. The thought of a little cat being lost and far from home, filled her with dismay.

There was no answer to her call. Actually, there was no sound at all. She was sure that she hadn't imagined it, so she called again. Well, I guess he found his cat, she thought to herself, as she finally went back into the house, and carefully locked the sliding doors.

Petie and Rosie had come into the kitchen, and were sitting gazing out into the dark. Were they able to see something which she couldn't? Probably. They seemed very interested in something or someone out there, and Petie was beginning a long low growl from deep in his chest.

"It's okay, guys," she said, quietly. "It's just someone looking for his little lost cat. You two would want me to look for you, if you were lost, wouldn't you?"

The cats made no response.

Pouring herself a fresh cup of hot tea, she went back to her grocery list. There it was again, a little clearer this time. "Here kitty, kitty. Come on out, kitty."

Where the heck was that voice? It suddenly occurred to her that it could be someone playing a joke. Could they possibly be calling her, rather than a lost feline? She hurried to a kitchen drawer, and grabbed a flashlight. This time she stood on the deck, and flashed the light in all directions. There was definitely no one there, yet she thought she could feel someone's eyes on her. It was spooky, and she realized that she was being very stupid, standing out on the deck in her housecoat, late at night. She suddenly felt like a giant jackass, calling to some non-existent cat owner. People would think she had been into the loco weed. Shaking her head at her own foolishness, she returned to the house, locking the doors carefully behind her.

I must be hearing things, she chided herself, as she threw out the rest of her tea, which was now cold. She rinsed the mug, and put it in the dishwasher. She was sure that she hadn't imagined the sounds, yet there didn't seem to be anyone there. She thought about calling Adrian to come over and look in her backyard, but the lights were out in his house. Wasn't this the week he had said he would be away on the Rome, Madrid run? She couldn't remember. Oh well, it wasn't that important.

"Come on you two. Let's go up to bed and cuddle." The cats paid no attention to her, but now Rosie had joined in the strange growling.

Kitty was not the nervous type, so she turned out the kitchen light, and was about to head upstairs, when she heard it again. This time there was no doubt. The caller was not looking for any little cat. He was definitely calling to Kitty, and what he said made her knees almost buckle under her. It sounded as if he was right up at the patio door calling, "Soon, Kitty, so very soon now."

She flattened herself against the wall, trying to peek out the patio door without being seen. That didn't work. She couldn't see anything out there in the blackness. What to do? She would feel totally foolish calling the police. They would never believe that it was anyone other than a neighbourhood man looking for his cat. Had she really heard what she thought she had heard? The voice had been soft, and sounded very close, but what did he mean by "Soon, Kitty, so very soon now." It had been a crooning sort of sound, very creepy, and definitely threatening. She began to feel as if she was playing a part in one of those teen horror movies like "Halloween."

She wished fervently that Adrian was home. He was a 'take-charge' kind of guy, and he would willingly come to her rescue. Suddenly it occurred to her that it could have been Keith Spenser. He loved practical jokes, and maybe he meant that he was going to get her up to the beach house soon. He had been calling and trying to persuade her to come. Yes, that was it, it was probably Keith out there. What a dumb thing to do. Why would he try to scare her like that? He had teased her about the ghost at his summer place, and he likely thought he was being extremely funny and clever, teasing her some more.

Silently and carefully, she opened the sliding doors again, just a couple of inches, and yelled out, "Come on, Keith. Give it up. It isn't funny. Come on in, and we'll have a drink."

Silence. She was getting fed up now. Keith was an idiot. "Keith, this is your last chance. I'm locking up now, so if you're there, come out where I can see you." More silence.

Well, one way to find out would be to call him. If Keith wasn't at home at this hour, then he was likely out in her back yard, laughing at her. Lord save me from practical jokers, she thought, as she reached for the phone.

She had to turn on the light to look up his number, and that made her feel very vulnerable. The curtains over the sliding doors were sheer. Was he looking in at her right now?

To her surprise and dismay, Keith answered the phone. "Kitty, great to hear from you, but it's a little late. Is anything wrong?"

She felt like an utter fool, and knew that she would sound ridiculous if she tried to tell him what had happened. Instead, she blurted out that she would love to go back up to the beach house to help him go through the trunks and boxes. Could they do it next weekend? She suggested that she could bring Steffie too, so that they would have more help. Keith sounded a little disappointed at that, just as he had the first time she suggested bringing Steffie, but he agreed, and said they would decide on the day later. Right now he was on his way back to bed.

Kitty turned out the light, and, standing there in the dark, she tried to make up her mind what to do. If it wasn't Keith, then who the heck was it?

Surely it couldn't be Scott. As far as she knew, he wasn't a practical joker, and why in the world would he do such a stupid thing? No, for sure it couldn't be Scott, and Drew didn't have much of a sense of humour, although he could have been mean enough to do something like this.

Suddenly she knew who it was. It had to be Josh. This was just the kind of hair-brained thing he would do. He knew her backyard well, too.

Muttering to herself, she went right to her little phone book, and looked up his number. She let the phone ring several times before his answering machine picked up. That proved it, or at least, it lent credence to her suspicions. It had to be Josh Tuttle. But why? She knew he had always acted sulky when she went out with Drew. He hadn't liked Drew, but that was no reason to try scaring her. She had turned him down a few times when he tried to date her, but so what? That didn't give him reason to be nasty.

While she stood there, flat against the wall, trying to make some sense out of the situation, she heard him again. "Soon, Kitty-Kat. I'll see you soon." It was a horrible, sing-song voice now, not natural. It certainly didn't sound like Josh, but who else could it be?

The cats were still glued to the patio doors, and were meowing loudly.

An errant thought began bobbing in her head like a cork in the river. She hurriedly pushed it aside, not wanting to give it any space in her mind, but it kept popping up again. Surely it couldn't be the Black Sheep, or could it? Would the Black Sheep play silly games like this? She doubted it, but the thought persisted to the point that she decided she really should call the police.

The dispatcher didn't sound very interested or concerned, but promised that a squad car would be sent. Kitty suspected it would be too late. Whoever it was, would be long gone. Still, he might have dropped something, or left a footprint. She just couldn't go to bed and do nothing.

It seemed to take forever, but was likely around twenty minutes before she heard voices in the backyard. Peeking out, she saw two policemen with flashlights. At that point, she felt sufficiently safe to open the door, and go out onto the deck again.

"There's certainly no one here now," said the younger of the two officers. He had curly hair and a clean cut face, and he looked as if he was not even out of high school yet. How old did they have to be before they could join the force, she wondered. The other officer was older, and shorter. He seemed cross to have been dragged out on a wild goose chase, but they both came into the kitchen, and listened to what Kitty had to say.

Even to her ears it sounded ridiculous.

"There was definitely someone there, and he was trying to scare me. He did a good job too. My cats were even upset. You should have heard them growling. What if it was the Black Sheep?"

"Every woman in town thinks that the Black Sheep is after her. There's a lot of paranoia at the moment," said the older of the two officers, with a supercilious tone.

Kitty felt insulted. She was not paranoid, and she didn't appreciate this little twerp suggesting that she was.

"It was likely just some guy looking for his cat. That's what made your cats get all excited. They could likely see the cat out there around the bushes. Cats are pretty territorial, you know."

Kitty knew she wasn't going to get anywhere with these two morons. They had a mindset which didn't allow for any new or different ideas to penetrate. She was sorry that she had called them.

The younger one said, "That's a really neat gazebo you've got out there. Bet it cost a bundle."

Kitty couldn't believe her ears. The Black Sheep might be out there stalking her, and the police department had sent two imbeciles to check things out. Now they were discussing construction costs.

"It cost a great deal," she answered crossly, glaring at him. "Are you sure you didn't see any footprints or candy wrappers or cigarette butts out there? He was here quite a while, and he could have left something behind."

The two officers glanced at each other rather smugly. After all, they were the police. She was just a dumb taxpayer, although a mighty pretty one.

They assured her that there were no clues to be seen. "The guy found his friggin' cat and went home," affirmed shortie, trying unsuccessfully to stifle a belch. "Woops, scuse me. Musta been something I ate," he guffawed.

She was thoroughly ticked off, but there wasn't much she could do about it. Her story seemed so flimsy, and she had no proof. They likely thought she was just a lonely female looking for a little attention. Maybe tomorrow she would give Jack Willinger a call. He was always very approachable.

The policemen didn't seem to have any suggestions. They said that she should just be sure all the doors and windows were locked, and go back to bed. Whoever it was, wouldn't likely be back again tonight. They offered to drive past the house every hour or so until daylight, but Kitty told them not to bother.

She did try to keep them talking as long as possible, however, just to be sure that the intruder was gone, and to make the night a little shorter. "Are you sure you wouldn't like a nice hot cup of tea and some fresh brownies?" she asked hopefully. She reasoned that their company was somewhat better than no company at all.

The younger one looked as if he was about to say yes, but the older one refused.

She stood there dejectedly, as she watched them go. She had never felt so alone and so frustrated. There was nothing to be done but to take her cell phone to bed with her. She also brought the two cats into her bedroom, and the three of them settled down into an uncomfortable rest. Tomorrow she would check out the backyard herself and see what she could see.

CHAPTER 49

▼

Mitch's weekend visit with Kitty was wonderful. He was a great guy, no doubt about it. Kitty had worried so much about what she should wear, what she should say, what she should cook. It turned out that none of that mattered. Mitch was easy going, and fun to be with. He was interested in what she wanted to do or say or eat, and when she ran out of ideas, he had plenty of his own. He was entirely different to the morose man with whom she had spent the week at the cottage.

He had finally been able to make Sheridan understand that the relationship was really over, so he had a great sense of freedom on this very important weekend with Kitty. He was an honest man, and he hadn't felt quite right about being with Kitty, while Sheridan was trying so frantically to patch things up with him. Now, finally, he felt free to pursue these new feelings with this attractive and intriguing woman.

Friday night they played tourists, walking down Clifton Hill, inhaling the mist from the falls, gawking at the coloured lights, enjoying the fireworks, eating ice cream cones. They went in and out of several cheesy souvenir shops, laughing at the ridiculous shirts, the Mountie dolls, the maple leaf shaped coasters, and the tiny, overpriced bottles of genuine Canadian maple syrup. He bought her a silver and turquoise ring which Kitty had admired. It cost the grand sum of $5.00, and Kitty laughingly vowed to wear it forever.

They sat drinking beer at an outdoor café, watching the tourists strolling up and down the hill. They walked to Table Rock, and leaned over the railings, staring down into the steaming cauldron which was the Canadian Falls.

It was a magic night, and Kitty couldn't help but wonder whether Mitch was storing all this local colour for future use in a book.

Saturday dawned bright and clear. They slept in, then had bagels, bacon and coffee out on the deck. Mitch could hardly tear himself away from Petie and Miss Rosie. He lay on the floor, playing with them. He tickled Petie, which was pretty well unheard of. Usually Sir Petie was above tickling.

He cuddled little Miss Rosie as if she were a newborn. She purred loudly, and her little body vibrated with delight. The cats wound themselves round and round his legs, and seemed to have forgotten Kitty totally. She thought that if he was trying to ingratiate himself with her, he couldn't have chosen a better way to do it. She was delighted that her pets had taken to him so readily. Cats were very perceptive when it came to humans.

Eventually they dressed, and headed out to do some more sightseeing. They sat by Lock 3 at the Welland Canal, and watched a tanker and two freighters make their way through the system. Two were coming from Lake Erie, and had to be lowered into Lake Ontario, and one was coming the other direction, and had to be raised up into Lake Erie. Kitty had seen the procedure before, but it took on new interest when she was watching it with Mitch. He asked so many questions, and was so interested in everything around him. Again, she figured that was the author side of him. He just couldn't help taking in information like a sponge.

Lunch was a long leisurely affair at the Riverbend Inn. After that, they parked the car, and walked up and down the main street of Niagara-on-the-Lake. There were so many interesting little shops, which took on new lustre when seen with Mitch. He was so good at noticing things.

In one boutique, Mitch insisted on buying her a beautiful hand knit cotton sweater with two adorable cats on the sleeves. It was a lovely light gray, with a black cat on one sleeve and a white one on the other. Kitty knew it would look terrific with her black skirt.

The overly proud citizens of Niagara-on-the-Lake, claimed that it was the most beautiful little town in Canada, and possibly the entire world. That may have been an exaggeration, but it certainly was a delightful walk up and down the main street. The profusion of flowers around the Prince of Wales hotel and the Shaw Café, and the amazing variety of colours all up and down the street, were a form of eye candy. The soul just had to eat up the beauty.

Kitty loved this quaint and colourful little town, but she felt that the supposedly romantic horse-drawn carriages were a blight on the horizon. The horses always looked so tired and so despondent and hopeless. It broke her heart to see them plodding along the same routes day after day, heads hanging low. Other than that, they enjoyed everything about their afternoon in the picturesque little town, rubbing shoulders with the crowds of tourists who flocked there every summer.

Steffie had invited them to come for a drink around 4:30, so after doing every shop on the main street, they headed back to Niagara Falls.

Steffie had prepared some delicious hors d'oeuvres — hot cheese puffs, a hot vidalia dip with little crackers, and large succulent shrimp. They ate so much, that they decided they didn't need to go out for dinner, and they stayed at Steffie's till almost ten o'clock.

It was obvious that Mitch was very taken with Steffie. She was looking gorgeous in her long raspberry and cream skirt with a sleeveless raspberry cowl-necked top. Her wild black curls were tousled and untamed. Mitch couldn't believe that she hadn't been snapped up by a dozen men by now. She was a real knock-out, and he liked her spirited and genuine laugh.

His friend Steve Manning, the studio musician, would kill for a girl like Steffie, and he promised himself that he would get them together somehow. Steve played a great jazz piano. He was smart, witty, full of fun, and very sexy — or so the girls claimed. He always seemed to have women chasing him, but had never been caught. Mitch was sure that Steffie was the girl for his friend Steve.

Steffie, on the other hand, thought that Mitch was a real dream. He was definitely the right man for Kitty. She liked the way he spoke so quietly, the way he looked at Kitty, the self-assured way he lounged in the chair, and made himself at home. He seemed comfortable in his own skin. She couldn't believe that this was the guy Kitty had first thought was so arrogant and stand-offish. He stood head and shoulders above any of Kitty's other boy-friends, and Steffie hoped that this all worked out for her friend. Actually, she was a little sorry that she hadn't seen him first. He was a catch — no doubt about it.

It was such a beautiful night, that Kitty and Mitch sat out in the gazebo, having a glass of wine before heading up to bed.

"This reminds me of that night at the cottage," grinned Kitty, as they clinked glasses.

"Please, don't remind me. I was totally out of it that week. What a waste," laughed Mitch, shaking his head. "If it hadn't been for that wild canoe ride, it's unlikely that we would have gotten together at all. I think it was seeing you in that frilly blue underwear that did it for me," he added, with a leer.

"Well, it was my first glimpse of you standing naked on the bunky deck that did it for me," replied Kitty. "I just figured that anyone who looked that good in the nude couldn't be all bad."

Mitch threw his head back and laughed, then leaned over and kissed her lightly. "Naughty girl, Miss Kitty. Didn't your daddy ever tell you not to judge people by their outward appearance? I could have been the strangler for all you knew."

"Yes, I thought about that a couple of times that week. You were so cold and mysterious, that I began thinking you just very well could be the Black Sheep hiding out up there. Then I saw you with that little chipmunk in your hand, and you were actually petting it. I knew then that you couldn't be bad."

Mitch looked surprised. "I didn't realize that you had seen me that morning. I was so pleased to coax that little fellow into my hand. That's one of my favourite memories, except of course, snuggling under that scratchy blanket with you."

"Oh, that was vile," she shuddered. "My skin still crawls when I think about it. We were lucky we didn't pick up some dreadful disease from that filthy thing."

As they sat and enjoyed each other's company, they heard a loud caterwauling coming from the kitchen. Kitty had left the sliding glass door open, with just the screen to keep the cats inside. They were both standing howling at the screen door.

"I think they're calling you," she laughed. "They've forgotten all about me."

"Oh they're just trying to make me welcome. Let's go in and play with them."

Kitty couldn't believe it. She had finally found a man who loved animals the way she did. This was heaven.

It was almost midnight before Mitch suggested, "How do you feel about going down to the casino? We can sleep in tomorrow, and I'm not at all tired. How about you?"

"That's fine by me. I haven't been there for ages. Let's go."

As usual, the Niagara Fallsview Casino was humming with activity. There was a high octane ambiance which always made Kitty feel wild and crazy. It put her in a party mood right away. She stood and watched while Mitch played the roulette wheel, managing to pick up $70 in a short space of time. Then he sat down at the black jack table, and she wandered over to the slot machines.

A couple of men tried to hit on her as she wandered around, stopping here and there to try a machine which appealed to her. It pleased her that the men found her attractive. She felt beautiful and pampered and privileged, and she basked in the bright lights and clamour. The hysterical laughter, the moans of disappointment, the clanging bells, all contributed to a cacaphony, which was charged with excitement, and strangely intoxicating. The boutique, Steffie, the Black Sheep, all seemed far away.

She finally settled down at a dollar machine, which looked intriguing. She felt so good tonight, that she was absolutely confident that she was going to win something. Mitch made her feel wonderful. At first she just put in one dollar, but then she got bolder, and put in three at a time. It was some sort of progressive machine, which she didn't really understand. She was playing slowly to make her money last, and was just about to move on and find Mitch, when the unbelievable happened. The bells started clanging, and the light on her machine came on.

Kitty couldn't get the smile off her face. She had no idea what she had won, but knew that it was something really good. The attendant came quite quickly, as she was looking around hopefully for Mitch. Finally she saw him striding toward her, a big grin on his face. She realized that once again her heart was hammering, her stomach was doing flip-flops, and her toes were tingling. She knew without any doubt that this was the man for her. She just had to make sure that Mitch knew it too.

He stood and watched, as the attendant explained that she had won the progressive, which on this machine at the moment was a little over a thousand dollars. Kitty thought she would fall off the stool. She was sure that she had misunderstood. Thank goodness Mitch was there to calm her down.

She and Mitch kissed and hugged and laughed, when they realized what had happened. Kitty knew right away what she would do with some of the money. Mitch had seen a beautiful blue cashmere sweater in one of the expensive shops in the lobby, but had blanched at the outrageous price tag. Kitty would buy it for him in spite of all his protests. She also knew what she was going to buy for the cats. She had seen a carpet-covered cat tree in a pet store this week. It had two platforms like branches on it, and it looked to be about eight feet high. It would be perfect in the corner window of the rec room. They could perch there and happily look out at the world. She would buy it on Monday. Nothing was too good for her darling little pets.

Her parents were planning on doing a Mediterranean cruise this winter, so she would put a few hundred dollars in their Christmas stockings. Oh this was such fun!!! Found money was wonderful, because you had no qualms about spending it. She thought she might buy Steffie a cashmere sweater too — maybe shocking pink, to show off that lustrous black hair. This money was such a bonanza, and she intended to spend every penny of it on the people she loved.

Kitty didn't want to gamble any more in case she lost any of her money. Mitch, however, was in a gambling mood, and went back to the black jack table. Kitty stood quietly, and watched him play for half an hour. He picked up over two hundred dollars, and was quite content with that.

Gradually they made their way through the casino, and headed back to Kitty's. It was still such a lovely quiet night that they opened a bottle of champagne to celebrate, and sat out on the deck. This hot steamy summer made for beautiful nights to sit outside and count the stars. Kitty wondered, though, what the never-ending heat and humidity might be doing to the Black Sheep. If he was crazy, or even just slightly demented, this hot spell could push him right over the edge. It was not a happy thought.

The night was extremely calm. There wasn't even a hint of a breeze. There seemed to be a lot of fireflies enjoying the black night. These irridescent little insects hovered and fluttered like winged sequins decorating the velvet night. Eventually the two new lovers tumbled into bed, totally in tune with each other, and still excited about Kitty's big win. It had been quite a day, but the rest of the night was even better.

CHAPTER 50

▼

No one was more surprised than Steffie, when her brother appeared suddenly at her door that fateful night. She hadn't seen him since their wonderful day at the Lion Safari, and felt that things must be going better for him. He hadn't been pestering her for money. Actually, he hadn't been pestering her at all.

Steffie often sat thinking about what fun it would be to have Nick in her life again, if he could always be as sweet as he was that day they went to Rockton. They had connected again, just the way they had when they were younger. She thought maybe he could get a job here in Niagara Falls, and she could help him find a little place of his own. She would help him to get on his feet, even though he had pretty well cleaned her out.

She didn't hold a grudge, and if there was any way that she could help Nick, the sweet, fun-loving Nick she used to know, she would do it. She didn't want to think about the mean spirited bully who had come out of prison, and had been making her life miserable the past few weeks. Everyone deserved a second chance.

Steffie had always been pretty much in control of her life and her surroundings. When her husband had turned out to be so wrong for her, she had dumped him quickly and quietly, with no fuss. Well, of course, cutting up all his clothes before she left, had likely created quite a fuss, but that hadn't been her problem. This business with Nick, however, was very different. Try as she might, she just couldn't learn to hate this man who was her brother. True, he had been the cause of their mom's sudden heart attack and subsequent death, but she realized now that perhaps Nick couldn't really be blamed totally for that tragedy. It wasn't his fault that his brain had grown that tumour, and it wasn't his fault that it had changed his personality so radically.

The bottom line was that she would love to have her brother back in her life, if only he could be as gentle and kind as he had once been.

"Nick," she cried in delight when she saw him. I haven't heard from you for a few days, and I've been wondering what you were doing. Have you been job hunting?"

"Not exactly," he grumbled in a low, tired voice. "Steff, have you got money in any accounts you haven't told me about?" He felt that he might as well get right to the reason he had shown up here tonight.

Steffie looked shocked and disappointed. "Nick, I've given you everything I have, except for a few small investment certificates which are tied up for a few years. I can't help you that way. I'm all tapped out."

"Shit. Have you got anything else around here that we could pawn?" He looked desperate, and Steffie felt the familiar niggling cold twinges down her spine. Maggots of fear and despair came alive in her stomach.

"Nick, what's wrong? What have you got yourself into now? Please don't tell me that you've gambled away that last money I gave you. That was over three thousand dollars."

She didn't like the sound of her own voice. She sounded shrewish and bitchy.

Nick decided to tell her the truth. "Steff, I'm in a hell of a lot of trouble. I owe a loan shark over sixty thousand, and he won't wait any longer."

"What? You can't be serious. There's no way you could owe anyone that much money. If you're just saying this to tease me, then shame on you. Who is this supposed loan shark?" she added with distrust.

"Believe me, you don't want to know. At this point, I'm pretty sure that he doesn't have any idea that I have a sister, and I want to keep it that way. He doesn't fool around. It's a good thing that you kept your married name. He won't have any way of tracking you down."

"Oh, Nick. How could you have lost that much money? Why didn't you quit when you started losing? Are you nuts? Can't you just tell him the truth — that you don't have it and have no way of getting it?" She knew how foolish that sounded, but she felt frantic.

"Sis, don't be crazy. You know damn well that you can't just tell a loan shark that you're sorry because you can't pay him what you owe him. Haven't you ever watched 'The Sopranos'? They'll break your legs for a thousand, just guess what this guy would do for what I owe him. I don't know whether he's connected or not, but it's likely that he is." He sank down on the chesterfield, and put his head in his hands. "I'm a dead man. I've got to get out of town. Couldn't you borrow on your shop?" He looked up hopefully, and Steffie felt her heart thud. It was not a good feeling.

She sat down beside him and took his hand in hers. "Nick, you're my little brother, and I'll always love you, but I don't understand this awful gambling habit. You know that we don't have that kind of money, so how could you possibly get in so deep. How can you gamble with money you don't have?" She was frightened now, wondering whether the loan shark, or maybe even the mob, would come crashing through the door at any moment. She knew she sounded whiny and preachy, but she couldn't seem to stop herself.

"Shut up!" he moaned. "The last thing I need now is a lecture. It's done, I tell you. I owe them money, and if I don't pay up by the end of the week, he'll be coming for me. You didn't answer my question. Can you mortage the shop?"

"No I can't mortgage the shop. It's only half mine, and there's no way we could do it. It's already got a mortage on it." This wasn't exactly true. There was still a small amount left on the mortage, but one more payment, and the shop would be theirs free and clear. She didn't want Nick to know this though.

She couldn't ask Kitty to go into debt again, in order to pay a stinking loan shark. Besides, part of her didn't really believe Nick. She suspected that it was a ploy to get more money out of her. He had become very devious since his stay in the pen. She wouldn't be surprised if it turned out to be just some of Nick's chicanery. It was difficult to tell anymore. Much as she loved her brother, or the brother he used to be, she wasn't going to be a patsy any more.

They talked a while longer, but it was no use. Nick was adamant that he had to have the money or he would be killed, and Steffie was just as determined that she could not get any more money for him. At one point she did think of Cassie with all her millions. Cassie was such a lovely, generous person, but how could Steffie go to her, and ask for thousands of dollars, which she could never repay. She would be so ashamed, that she would have to leave town. No, that was definitely not the answer to the dilemma.

"Look, I can't help you tonight, and I just can't imagine where we could get that kind of money. Let me sleep on it, and maybe I'll get an idea. Come on over for breakfast, or better yet, sleep here tonight, and we'll talk some more in the morning. You'll be safe here." She wondered whether that was true.

Nick gave her a long look, then stood up. "It's okay, kiddo. Don't worry about it. I was just testing the water, so to speak. I was just hoping to get some money out of you, but it really isn't as bad as I said. Forget it." He tried to smile, but it seemed forced.

Steffie felt a great sense of relief, but still had some nagging doubts. What was Nick up to? Did he really owe money to a loan shark? Was he just being cruel and thoughtless, trying to scare her with a crazy made-up story? Had that brain tumour come back?

"Okay, I've got to go. Uh, you may not see me for a while. I'm going to be busy getting myself out of this jam. Don't worry though. Just keep in mind that I love you, and I do appreciate what you've done for me. I'm so sorry that I took your money. If I could pay it back, I would. I hope you know that."

He looked penitent and contrite, and Steffie's heart felt as if it would break. If only she could turn the years back to when they were both healthy little kids, and life was so easy and uncomplicated.

"Listen to me, Steffie. This is really important. Don't tell anyone I've been here, and if anyone comes and asks about me, you don't know anything. If he finds out that you're my sister, you can tell him that you and I had a big fight, and we haven't spoken for a long time. You could say that the last you heard, I was talking about heading to Mexico. I really don't think he knows about you, so I'm pretty sure you're safe. I'm so sorry, kiddo. I wish we could just go on having fun like we did that day at the Lion Safari. I'll always cherish that day, and I want you to remember it too."

He held her for a long time, then kissed her on the tip of her nose, and was gone.

Steffie paced back and forth long after Nick had left. She drank an entire pot of coffee, and knew that there would be no sleep for her. She kept thinking of all the money that Cassie had, yet there was no way she could ever ask for her help. Part of her was very ashamed of Nick. Prison had not been good for him, and he had become a low-life. Still, he was her brother, and part of her still loved him. What to do?

She finally decided that she would talk to Kitty tomorrow, and see if she had any bright ideas. Then she would wait to hear from Nick again. If he really was in serious trouble, maybe she would swallow her pride and go to see Cassie. Maybe Cassie could borrow the money from a bank for her, and maybe she could pay it back in dribs and drabs for the rest of her life. What a prospect! She was piling up the "maybes" on a shelf in her mind, and she didn't like the look of them.

The next day was quite busy in the boutique, and the two friends really didn't have a chance to talk. Kitty sensed that there was something wrong, because Steffie was so quiet and withdrawn. She guessed it was likely related to Nick, and knew that Steffie would eventually tell her.

Steffie invited her to come over for supper. That would give them a chance to talk, and also to go through some of the new gift catalogues which had come in.

Kitty went home to feed Petie and Rosie, and to visit with them for half an hour, before heading to Steffie's. She didn't like leaving them too long at a time. Cats were like people. They needed companionship and stimulation, and someone to talk to them in an intelligent way. They were great listeners, and she was convinced that they understood a good deal of what she said to them. Occasionally they even offered an opinion, such as a huge yawn, a flick of the ear, or squeezing their eyes shut in apparent agreement.

As usual, they wound themselves round and round her ankles, purring like two Cadillac motors. Then they headed to the kitchen, and waited patiently while she opened a can, and set out two plates, along with two bowls of fresh water.

By the time she was ready to leave for Steffie's apartment, Rosie was washing Petie behind his ears, and he had a dazed, far-away look in his beautiful green eyes.

Over their food, Steffie told her friend about the latest visit from Nick, and about the quandary in which she found herself. Kitty was a sympathetic and patient listener. She felt very badly for her friend and partner, but knew that there was no way she should agree to remortgaging the boutique. She thought it would be a dreadful mistake to ask Cassie for the money. It would be nothing for Cassie to come up with that amount. That would be like pocket change to her, but there was a principle involved, and she knew Steffie would do the right thing.

Kitty was still upset by the time she got home. She just couldn't figure out how best to help Steffie.

She had a nice long shower, and was just painting her nails when the phone rang. Thinking that it might be Mitch, she raced from the bathroom into her bedroom, blowing on her nails to dry them. Quickly she grabbed the phone, before her answering machine could pick up.

"Hello" she said in a friendly tone, picturing Mitch on the other end of the line.

"Hi Miss Kitty. It's Keith. How are you?"

She couldn't help feeling disappointed, but acted pleasantly surprised.

They chatted for a few minutes before Keith said, "Listen, the reason I called is that I've got two tickets for the Shaw on Saturday night, and I want you to go with me."

He said it as if there was no doubt that she would.

"Oh, Keith, I'm so sorry. You know that I'm in a relationship now, and it's pretty serious. There's no way I could go. We talked about it briefly when we met at the hospital not long ago. Surely you haven't forgotten. Anyway, it's lucky for you that you've got so many women in your little black book. I'm sure that any one of them would love to go with you."

"Don't tell me you're still wasting time with that author. He must be pretty dull. Even so, we're still friends, and he can't stop you from coming to the theatre with me." This last was said with a truculent tone.

The idea of Mitch being dull made Kitty laugh. He was the most exciting man she had ever known. "Sorry, Keith, I really can't. It's nice of you to think of me, but there's no way. I know you'll enjoy it though with whichever one of your many ladies you decide to invite." She was trying to get out of the situation without annoying Keith, but she knew how persistent he could be.

They spoke for another few minutes, and Keith finally seemed to realize that she was serious. "Well, I think you're making a big mistake. You and I could be great together. Does this mean that you won't come up to the summer house again with me? We have more boxes and trunks to unpack, you know."

Kitty was relieved to change the subject. "It's such a wonderful old place, Keith, and you'll have a great time living there. Will you be moving up there permanently any time soon?"

"I think so, once I fix it up a bit. I like the fact that it's so private. Anyway, you haven't answered me. Are you going to come up again, yes or no?"

"Well, at the moment I'm going to have to say 'no,' but I might change my mind. I would love another chance to get at those boxes and trunks. Let me think about it, and I'll call you back."

When she got off the phone, she just sat there looking at it for a moment. Keith was strange. He sounded almost threatening, and yet she knew that it was just his way. He was a doctor who was used to getting what he wanted. She wondered whether he talked to his patients in such a demanding way.

When Kitty was upset, she found it comforting and relaxing to play the piano, so that's what she did. She finished painting her nails, put on her housecoat, and sat down at the piano. Of course, Petie appeared like magic, and jumped up on top, where he could feel the vibrations. It was a soothing interlude for both of them, and Kitty felt much better by bedtime.

Steffie hadn't heard from Nick all day, and she didn't know whether that was good or bad. She didn't have a phone number for him, or have any idea how to reach him, so she just had to wait till he called or came to see her.

For weeks to come, she would wonder why she had no premonition that night. Actually, it had been a comfortable, relaxed evening. After Kitty left, she had snuggled into bed to read until just past midnight. Then, turning out the light, she had cuddled down into a dreamless sleep. She and Nick had once been very close, and he had been on her mind a lot these past few days, so, in retrospect, she wondered why she hadn't seen this dreadful night coming.

When she heard someone knocking at her door just before six in the morning, she assumed that it was Nick. She didn't even bother putting on her housecoat, since she was sure that it was just her brother.

Opening the door, it was as if an electric shock went through her body. One look at the faces of Jack Willinger and Bud Lang told her what she didn't want to know. What possible reason could they have to be here at this hour? Her whole center of gravity shifted ever so slightly. She invited them in unwillingly. In her heart of hearts, she already knew what they were going to tell her. Strangely, she didn't even consider that it might be some bad news about Kitty. It didn't occur to her that possibly her nightmares had come true, and Kitty had been the victim of the Black Sheep. She just seemed to know that it was about her brother, and she knew that he must be dead, or very badly hurt.

CHAPTER 51

▼

This was the worst type of call which Jack and Bud ever had to make. They avoided these visits as much as possible, although they were both very good at them. Years of experience had taught them how to show the proper amount of concern and empathy in a professional way.

They had been up for several hours now, ever since the call had come in from the Niagara Parks police. One of the policemen on patrol, had found a rental car parked down by Table Rock, and inside, there was a note from Nick. It wasn't addressed to anyone in particular. It simply said that he was sorry for doing this, but it was the only way out. He owed too much money, and had no way of paying it back. He was being hounded, and was going to be killed, if he didn't come up with the money.

Both detectives thought it was a strange note. Why wasn't it addressed to his sister Steffie? Then they realized that he must have been trying to protect her from the guy or guys who were after him. He had finally done something thoughtful for his sister, after all the grief he had caused.

A Niagara Parks policeman reported that he had spoken with a man answering Nick's description around midnight. The man had been standing staring into the water. He was standing at the place called "suicide corner." It was a relatively easy access place to jump in, if one was so inclined. The policeman felt there was something not quite right about the fellow, and was worried that indeed, he might be contemplating suicide. He had spoken to the chap, and had hung around in the area until he saw him get into his rental car and drive away. Obviously, and unfortunately, he must have come back later.

It hadn't taken too long to discover who had rented the car.

When she opened her apartment door, Steffie moaned softly, before the detectives had a chance to say anything to her. Bud put his big arms around her, and held her quietly. Then, pushing him away, she politely asked them to sit down, and she herself sat in a chair and gripped its arms as if she was in the dentist's office.

"He got him, didn't he? That horrible man got him. He didn't give him a chance. How did he do it — a bullet to the back of his head?" She was looking from one to the other, waiting to hear the terrible details.

Jack and Bud looked at each other. What horrible man did she mean? What did she know that they didn't?

"Look, Steffie, this is rough. We're so sorry to have to tell you. Nick wasn't murdered, if that's what you're thinking. He committed suicide."

The words hung there, polluting the room with their savagery. 'Suicide' was a word far worse than 'murder.' By its very nature, it put blame on other people — those closest to the suicide victim.

Steffie couldn't believe what they were saying. Nick had killed himself? Was it possible? She stared in disbelief. She hadn't realized just how desperate he had been. Why hadn't she understood? Why hadn't she promised to help? Why hadn't she given him even a tiny bit of hope to which he could cling? She had been cold and uncaring, and her little brother was dead. Her hopes for their future together lay broken at her feet like crumbled cookies.

Nick was dead. He was now just a suicide statistic. How much of it was her fault? She hadn't paid enough attention to him. She hadn't given him enough support and love and guidance. She had abrogated her responsibilities as the older sister, and had left him swinging in the wind.

She asked many questions then, but there weren't very many answers. Eventually, Bud went into the kitchen, and made a pot of strong coffee. Steffie clutched at the mug as a drowning man would clutch a lifesaver. She seemed to derive strength from its warmth.

Both Jack and Bud admired the quiet dignity with which she was handling the news.

Eventually she heaved a sigh, and put the mug down. "I need to see where he did it," she murmured, in a hollow but determined voice.

"That's not a good idea, Steff," replied Jack. "It will only make you feel worse. You know what the falls look like. You don't have to go down there."

"Yes, I do, Jack. Please wait while I throw on some clothes." She suddenly realized that she had been sitting in her lacy pink nightgown, but that didn't seem the least bit important.

Jack and Bud looked at each other, and sat back to wait. They knew that Steffie had made up her mind, and maybe it was a good idea after all. From where Nick had apparently taken his jump or dive, his body would likely come up in about two weeks, right down by the Maid of the Mist dock. If it didn't come up there, it would eventually be found down by the whirlpool. That seemed to be the pattern. If, however, it got caught among the rocks, it might never come up. They would have to explain that to Steffie later on, although she likely knew it already. Most residents of Niagara Falls knew the strange rhythms and patterns of the wild, tumbling waters, which weren't always willing to give up their dead.

It was a dull, dismal morning, quite in keeping with their moods, as they parked at Table Rock, and walked with Steffie to the brink of the falls.

As they approached the railing, they could see several police from both the Niagara Regional force and the Niagara Parks Commission, combing the rough, rocky, treed area between the upper landing and the river bank. There was always the chance that Nick had changed his mind about jumping, and had perhaps walked along the top, and fallen over the edge, into the trees and rocks below. He could be lying down there on the river bank with a broken leg, or unconscious. A thorough search had to be done, although they were all pretty sure it was an exercise in futility. They were certain that Nick had taken the tough way out, and had gone into those unforgiving waters.

Steffie seemed totally unaware of the men, as she stared with fascination into the foamy green waters below. The tumbling, roaring waters reminded her of an angry prehistoric beast. How had Nick ever had the courage to jump into that maelstrom? He must have been very desperate.

As she stood staring down into the cascading waters, she remembered Nick as a little boy. He had always loved jumping into the water when they went to the lake. He would never just walk in gradually, the way their mom did. Steffie liked to dive, and was good at it. Nick, on the other hand, always got on the dock, and, taking a run at it, would cannonball out, making a loud whooping noise as he hit the water. Had he done that last night? She had to smile at the picture in her mind.

She stayed there for possibly twenty minutes, just staring blankly into the water, seeing happy pictures from her childhood. She remembered sleeping out in a little tent in the backyard — just Steffie and Nick. They lay awake most of the night, telling each other ghost stories, until they were so scared that they made a run for the safety of the house.

She thought of the time two big boys chased her, and knocked the school-books out of her hand. Her little brother Nick had charged at them, trying to protect her, but getting a black eye and a bloody nose for his trouble.

Gradually Nick had changed, as the tumour grew. Slowly they drifted apart, without Steffie even realizing it. By the time he recovered from the surgery, he was a totally different person, someone she hadn't liked, or wanted to know.

As she stood there, gazing into the tumultuous waters, Jack and Bud tried to give her privacy, but they stayed as close as possible. They didn't want to take any chances that she might get the sudden wild desire to jump in as well. You never knew just how grief-stricken people were going to react.

Finally, she realized that she was becoming dizzy from staring at the water. It was a phenomenon which affected most people. The falls had a very hypnotic effect. Turning, she looked at Jack and Bud, and extended her hands to them. "Thank you so much for bringing me here. It was something I had to see for myself. I feel better now. Nick loved the water, so he wouldn't have been scared. I just pray that his body will come up, because I want to know for sure that the loan shark or his minions didn't get him. Do you think they could have shot him, and thrown him over?"

Steffie was more like her old self now, pragmatic and calm. She seemed to have come to terms with what had happened, and wasn't going to shed useless tears. If Nick had chosen that way out, in a way it was better than thinking he had been the unwilling victim of some two-bit mobster.

As they walked back to the car, Bud and Jack tried to pretend that the idea of murder had not already occurred to them. They were being pretty non-committal until they could retrieve Nick's body for an autopsy. At this point, however, suicide seemed to be almost too convenient an answer.

They took Steffie home, and then Jack called Kitty. She hadn't left yet for work, so she came right over. He also took the opportunity as an excuse to call Cassie. She was thrilled to hear his voice, but was appalled to hear his news. She promised that she and Vickie would be right over to Steffie's apartment. The detectives knew that Steffie would be in good hands, and they waited with her until her friends arrived.

Driving back to the station on Morrison Street, they kept going over the scenario. "You know, Nick didn't strike me as the type who would kill himself. He came out of the pen a pretty tough guy. What could have happened to suddenly make him decide he had no choice but to jump?" Bud was running his fingers through his curly hair, and frowning, as he stared straight ahead.

Jack was driving, and he turned to look briefly at his partner. "Do you think the loan shark got tired of waiting for his money?"

"Nope, I don't. Loan sharks and mobsters would rather break a couple of legs or arms, and put the fear of the devil into someone. They know they'll never get their money if they kill him."

"I wonder whether he or they, have any idea that Steffie is Nick's sister? We'd better put a tail on her for a while. Someone just might try squeezing the money out of her."

"Shit, I hope not. She's a nice lady, and she's had enough trouble this summer, what with getting herself shot in the store, and then losing her friend to the Black Sheep. Having her brother commit suicide is more than enough. She doesn't need anyone harassing her." Bud looked angry at the very thought of it.

Jack wheeled the car into the nearest Tim Horton's. Turning to his friend, he said, "I'm tired, and I need some quick energy. How about a cup of coffee and a couple of doughnuts before we get back to work?"

"You took the words right out of my mouth," grinned Bud. "I can always think better with a couple of extra pounds of sugar and cholesterol in my stomach."

CHAPTER 52

▼

He had all the pictures spread out before him. What a sight. They told a very interesting story. He had started out by just keeping them loose in the locked steel box, which sat in his closet. His one big regret was that he didn't have pictures of the first two. They had been his mother, and that prostitute in Toronto, with the pink boa around her neck. It bothered him that his collection wasn't complete, but it was too late now.

He also wished so much that he had put each body beside a dumpster. They still would have had the little black sheep clutched in the dead hand, but they would have been sitting by a dumpster, to show that they were just trash. That would have made such a clear statement. He sighed with regret at not having thought things out more carefully, before beginning this crusade. Of course, killing his mother had been spur of the moment. It was only after he found out how good it felt, that he had begun the crusade.

Tonight he was putting the pictures in an album, and was muttering to himself quietly, as he worked. A foolish thought struck him, and he laughed out loud. What if he left the finished album out on his coffee table? He could make it a game. If anyone picked it up and looked inside, he would have to kill him or her. If they weren't interested enough or curious enough to look inside the album, well then, they would go free. No, that was ridiculous. These killings were his little secret, and would remain so until the day he died. Then it wouldn't matter who saw the album.

He had been feeling better these days, much more calm. He wondered whether it was the calm before the storm. Maybe he would go on a rampage, and kill several women all within the space of a few days. No, that would be too tiring and too dangerous. He still intended to kill Kitty, but she might be his last victim. He got angry every time he thought about how she had rebuffed him.

Ginny was now off the hook for good. He told himself that he really did love Ginny. He always had. She should have been his from the start. If his twin brother Mike hadn't stepped in and stolen her away, things would have been very different. He would be married to Ginny, and Mike would still be alive. None of this bad stuff would have happened. Come to think of it, the entire killing spree was Mike's fault, starting right back with their mother. She had always favoured Mike. Yes, indeed, it was his mother and his twin brother who had caused him to become the Black Sheep. It felt good to have someone he could blame.

At that point, another errant thought intruded, and he stopped what he was doing, and stared off into space. What if both he and Mike had been serial killers? Man, wouldn't that have been something. They might have been the first twin serial killers in history. Imagine how confusing that would have been for the cops. He loved that idea, and played with it for quite a while.

Well, he couldn't erase the past, but he could rewrite the future. He would go slowly with Ginny, win back her trust, and then make her love him. He and Mike had been identical twins, even though their personalities were slightly different. Why had Ginny chosen Mike over him? It was a question he had never been able to answer, but he had confidence that he could win her love now.

Of course, he still had to kill Kitty, to punish her for being so flighty, hopping from one boyfriend to the next. Mostly he had to punish her for not taking him seriously. Yes indeed, he had a whole list of grievances against Miss Kitty. Once she was dead, though, it would be over for good. The Black Sheep would vanish into the night, never to be heard from again. He liked that idea. It was mysterious and poetic. Always leave them guessing, he laughed to himself, as he thought of the police running around in circles, while the killer was right under their noses all the time.

He replenished his drink, and sat back in the chair. Closing his eyes, he replayed each murder in his head. Sometimes he could reenact them so well that it was almost like the real thing. His imagination and memory were excellent. He often replayed the various murders, even when he was busy doing his job.

Strangely, although he remembered each murder quite clearly, he no longer had any feelings of guilt or remorse. It was as if a heavy metal curtain had come down and cut off any of the normal human emotions. The victims were no more important than bugs squished under his feet. He could think of them quite dispassionately.

Well, enough of looking backwards and inwards. Now was the time to look to the future. He had to make his plans for Kitty. There must be no possible way anyone could connect him with her death. That would be a bit tricky. It was so much easier when it was someone he didn't know, like the two prostitutes. That way, the police were totally baffled, and spent their time just chasing their tails.

Meanwhile, as the Black Sheep sat in seclusion, enjoying his reveries, Cassie was enjoying a delicious stolen hour with Jack. It was an unexpected pleasure, which she just hadn't been able to resist.

After calling Cassie to tell her about Nick's suicide, Jack had the irrepressible urge to see her again — just for a little while. Without giving himself a chance to think it through, he called and asked if she could meet him for a coffee. Cassie knew she should say 'no,' but she was quick to say 'yes.'

They met in St. Catharines, in a little coffee and pastry shop. Cassie had just washed her reddish blond hair when Jack called, and it had that bouncy freshness which made her look like a teenager. She was wearing her white jeans, and a red and white tank top. Her red sandals had high heels on them, accentuating her lovely long legs. She looks like a model, Jack thought, as he watched her come swinging through the door.

Oh, Cassie, my love, he thought to himself, as she grinned her mischievous grin, when she spotted him. They hugged, but in a strictly "friend meeting friend" sort of way. Then he couldn't help a quick nuzzle of her hair. "You smell so good," he whispered, looking into her blue eyes, which looked back at him trustingly. He would have liked to kiss her, or at least hold her in his arms a little longer, but he didn't dare. He was pretty sure that there was no one in the café who would know him or Cassie, but he had to be careful. He didn't want to cause either one of them any trouble.

"What's up?" asked Cass, as she slid into the high-backed booth.

"I just felt that I'd explode if I didn't see you," replied Jack. "Thinking about Nick's suicide made me realize just how short our time on this planet really is. I just had to touch you, hold your hand, see you smile," he said quietly.

"I know what you mean," she sighed. "I feel the same. It's really difficult, Jack. We shouldn't be seeing each other at all, but I can't help myself. You have a very hypnotic power over me, and it makes me feel guilty as hell. If Dave ever found out, he would be heart broken. He trusts me completely."

"Okay, let's just have a cup of coffee, and visit like two old friends, — nothing romantic, I promise."

"Ya, right," she laughed ruefully, as he rubbed his leg against hers under the table.

"Stop that or you'll be really sorry," she scolded, as the waitress approached.

They spent an hour just laughing, talking, and enjoying each other. Stolen moments were better than no moments at all, and Cassie was resigned to the fact that she would never really get Jack out of her system.

They talked about Steffie, and how well she was holding up.

"You know, Jack, it's almost as if she doesn't really believe he's dead. No, I don't mean that exactly. She knows he's dead, but I think she feels that he's happy now. She says that she doesn't think he would ever have changed. If she had borrowed the money for him, he would have paid off his debts, and then started gambling again. He was his own worst enemy. Talk about being the master of your own fate.

It seems as if Nick really did a number on himself, yet maybe he just couldn't help it. Steffie keeps wondering whether maybe the tumour had grown back. That could have accounted for all his strange behaviour. You know, just before he committed suicide, he and Steffie spent a wonderful day together at the African Lion Safari. She said he was just as sweet and thoughtful as he had been years ago. He was a bit of a Jekyll and Hyde."

"Well, surprisingly, there's been very little talk about it on the street. Our informants haven't heard any flack from the mob, or from any of the shylocks in town. So far, it looks as if they didn't have anything to do with his death. That's good news, plus the fact that there's no indication that they know anything about Steffie. We don't think they're looking for her."

"Thank heavens for that. She's a darling person, really funny and smart. She's getting on with her life one day at a time, and putting the past behind her. I just pray that nothing else bad happens to her. She's had a hell of a summer."

They only allowed themselves an hour, sitting over their coffee cups, enjoying every moment. When it was time to go, they made a date for lunch in two months. They promised they wouldn't see each other till then, unless, of course, they ran into each other by chance. Then it could be blamed on fate, and would be out of their hands. Both feeling guilty, but happy, they headed to their respective homes.

Cassie hadn't been at the Cattery for three days, so she decided to drive out there before going home. Everything seemed fine, and she chatted with Ginny for a few minutes. She cuddled a couple of the cats, and talked to the vet, before heading to her house.

Turning the corner onto her street, she was surprised to see what looked like a rental car in her driveway. She knew that Vickie was home, but couldn't imagine who would be driving the rental. Closing the front door behind her, she opened her mouth to call to Vickie, then stopped in shocked disbelief. She couldn't be seeing what she was seeing. Her husband Dave, who as far as she knew, was supposed to be still in Greece, was walking out of the sunroom towards her, arms outstretched.

CHAPTER 53

▼

"Well, where has my wandering wife been?" he grinned, as he took her in his arms, and buried his face in her hair. "Man, you smell good."

Cassie stifled a little gasp. Jack had said the same thing to her just an hour earlier. This was like a cheesy soap opera. She felt smaller than a gnat.

"Dave, I didn't expect you. I thought you were still in Greece." Cassie squeaked. She was so surprised, and so overwhelmed with feelings of guilt, that she could barely speak.

"I'm only home for a couple of days, then I'm off again. I've got a couple of important appointments in London. I just got lonesome for you, and decided to make a quick flight home. What's the use of having all that money, if we can't spend it in frivolous ways now and then?" He was nuzzling her neck, and running his hands over her behind as he spoke.

"Speaking of spending money in frivolous ways, come into the sunroom. I've got something for you."

Cassie walked like a zombie, hand in hand with her husband. What awful timing. She couldn't feel more guilty if she tried, and she was sure that her strained smile would give her away.

Dave looked wonderful. He was very tanned and seemed relaxed, and laid back. This trip had obviously been good for him. He must have been spending quite a few hours out in the sun, she thought briefly. He couldn't have been working all the time. He looked like a man who had just returned from a lovely vacation. Then she realized that she was trying to make herself feel resentful or angry with him, just to assuage her own guilt. That wasn't fair, and she knew it.

Dave was handing her a beautifully wrapped small parcel, and he was grinning like the old Cheshire cat.

"What is it?" she asked in surprise. Dave never brought her presents unless it was her birthday or Christmas.

"Well, darlin', I suggest you open it and find out," he laughed, obviously pleased with himself.

Cassie gasped as she opened the velvet box, and stared at the absolutely stunning diamond and ruby pendant. She was totally speechless.

"Here, let me put it on for you. Do you like it? It won't look so great with this top, but just picture it with that black strapless dress you bought when we were in New York. I just had to buy it for you, Cass. I missed you so damn much while I was away." He was fumbling with the catch of the pendant, and talking very quickly. Was he acting suspiciously guilty? She wasn't sure.

"I realized just how much I love you," Dave continued. "You've handled this money thing in your usual capable way, as well as all that shock about your mother and your grandmother. I'm proud of you, and I'm so happy that you're my wife. I know that I really haven't been there for you the way I should have been." He kissed her tenderly, and grinned that old familiar grin. "Next time you're coming with me."

He certainly could be an old smoothie when he put his mind to it. Cassie felt her heart sink right down to her shoes. She didn't deserve this gentle, loving man, who had always been so good to her. Sure, he went off on long trips without her, sure she wondered whether they were necessary, and what he was doing when he was so far away, but the bottom line was that he was her husband, and she loved him. This was the man with whom she had chosen to spend the rest of her life. This was the man who was the father of her children. He was her anchor, her friend, her lover. She would not, she must not, think of Jack. That part of her life was over, starting right now. Still, she couldn't get the thought out of her mind, that he was acting suspiciously like a guilty husband.

Just then Vickie walked into the room, rolling her eyes at Cassie. She knew where her friend had been, and she didn't approve. She worried that Cass was heading for trouble, and had tried to talk her out of meeting Jack for coffee, but Cass hadn't listened to her. It was a potentially volatile situation, and they both knew it.

As they sat having drinks in the sunroom, Cassie and Vickie told Dave all about the Black Sheep, and about Nick. He couldn't believe that they were having so much excitement again. It was almost as bad as two years ago, but at least this time he didn't think that they were the intended victims.

Cassie was grateful to have Vickie there as a buffer. She was excited about the extravagant gift, but frightened that Dave would sense something amiss. She felt as if she was trying to run through a mine field. It was difficult to know just what to say, and how to look. She suspected that the smile pasted on her face, probably looked more like a grimace.

Dave looked so terrific. She hadn't really paid much attention to him during the past two years, because there had been so much going on in her life. He was an attractive man, with dark wavy hair, brown eyes, a really nice nose, and a very strong jaw. He had a husky voice, which Cassie had always liked, and he looked at her with real love in his eyes. It was real love, wasn't it? They often fought, and there was a lot of resentment there because of all his travelling, but the bottom line was that they really loved each other. Cassie wondered again how she could possibly love two men at the same time. What was wrong with her?

Their two cats, Muffy and Sugar Plum, heard Dave's voice, and came sauntering in to greet him. He picked up each one in turn, and gave it a squeeze and a little scratch behind the ears. They were both purring by the time he put them down. Muffy immediately jumped back into his lap, ready to settle down for a nap, but Sugar began giving herself a thorough bath right at his feet.

"I've really missed these two spoiled little twerps," he laughed. "Greece is absolutely full of stray cats. It would break your heart, Cass. I'm never going to take you there, because it would drive you crazy. The tourists feed them, of course, but it's a sad situation."

"You're right, I wouldn't be able to stand it," agreed Cassie. "I'd want to bring them all home to the Cattery."

Dave just laughed, and shook his head. Turning to Vickie, he said, "I'm going to see Brian while I'm in London. Is there anything you want me to tell him?"

"Yes," said Vickie, nodding her head vigorously. "Tell him that I am not moving to Scotland under any circumstances, no matter how much he huffs and puffs."

Dave grinned. "I doubt that he's really serious about that, Vic. You don't need to worry. He's just yanking your chain a bit, pressing a few of your buttons." Then, changing the subject, and rubbing Muffy's ears again, he continued, "Now listen, you two. Tell me more about the Black Sheep. Do the police have any clues, or are they still running around in circles the way they did two years ago? And, please tell me that you are not doing your amateur sleuthing this time. This guy sounds very dangerous, and you don't want to get yourselves on his hit list."

Dave didn't think that the detectives and the police had done a very good job of protecting Cassie and Vickie, and they certainly had taken their time in solving the case two summers ago. He didn't realize, though, that he was stepping on Cassie's toes by casting aspersions on Jack's detective abilities. He knew that the three of them, Cassie, Vickie and Jack, were old school chums, but that was as far as it went. Cassie hadn't seen any need to tell him that Jack had been the love of her life before she met Dave.

They decided that they would go out somewhere nice for dinner, to celebrate Dave's unexpected return. Then Vickie said that, after dinner she was going over to Steffie's for a visit. This would give Dave and Cassie some private time, and Vickie could check on Steffie, and be sure that she wasn't sitting alone in her apartment, wallowing in sadness about Nick. Actually, Steffie seemed remarkably fine, and they were all proud of her.

Vickie and Dave got along very well. In fact, two years ago, there was one point at which Cassie began to wonder whether they might be having an affair. That, of course, was nonsense, but it had been such a crazy, mixed up summer, that just about anything was possible.

As Dave went up the stairs to shower and change, he called over his shoulder, "Aren't you coming up, Cass? You'll need to change too. Hurry up, I'm starving. We can shower together to save time." He raised his eyebrows and leered at her. "Sorry, Vickie," he laughed, "the shower isn't big enough for three. Oh, by the way, tomorrow I'm taking you two down to the Riverbend Inn for lunch. I love that place, and we haven't been there for ages. Boy, it's great to be home, even for a couple of days. And who could be luckier than I am to have two lovely gals to squire around town." He laughed happily as he disappeared into the master bedroom.

Cassie felt her knees go weak, and her breath caught in her throat. There was no way she could go to the Riverbend with Dave, after that romantic lunch with Jack. She pictured herself and Jack walking up those stairs to room 209, and she felt sick at heart.

She remembered that darling little desk, and the French doors opening out to the balcony. How many times had she pictured lying in that large sized bed, with Jack's arms around her. He had little black curly hair on his arms. She had always loved that about him. When she closed her eyes, she could see the fireplace, and the basket of fruit on the coffee table. Beside it was a bottle of champagne in an ice bucket.

She remembered dancing around the room with him, slowly and gently, her head on his chest. Oh what a tangled web we weave, she thought. I'll never be able to go to the Riverbend again. There are too many guilty memories, and that's so stupid, because we didn't do anything. Ah, said a little voice deep in her head, the point is that you intended to, and you wanted to. That's almost as bad. Cassie knew that somehow she would have to talk Dave out of going to the Riverbend, and she would have to do it in such a way that he wouldn't become suspicious.

Vickie shook her head at Cassie, and whispered, "I told you so. You, my dear friend, are playing with fire, and you know what happens when little girls play with fire."

"Oh, shut up," hissed Cass more crossly than she intended. She felt so ashamed of herself, that she had barely been able to look into her husband's trusting brown eyes. He loved her enough to make that long tiring flight home just to see her. He loved her enough to bring her that very expensive gift. How tawdry that this very day she had been out cavorting around, making goo-goo eyes at Jack, and rubbing legs under the table like a couple of grasshoppers. Cassie was now sailing on a sea of regret.

Vickie was so right. She was playing with fire, and it had to stop. She would never see Jack again. Well, let's not get crazy about this, she thought. "Never" was such a harsh word, it left no wiggle room. The trouble was that she wanted to see Jack again. She wouldn't be unfaithful to Dave in the true sense of the word, but she definitely wanted to see Jack again. She wanted to hear him laugh, feel the touch of his hand on her hand, talk about old times. At this point in her life, she wanted her cake and she wanted to eat it too. She just couldn't say that she would never see him again. She would really try, though, she told herself sadly and firmly, and that was the best anyone could do.

CHAPTER 54

▼

Way back in the spring, long before any of the bad events had happened in their lives, Kitty and Steffie had made arrangements to attend the big gift trade show at the Air Canada Centre in Toronto. This was where all the newest ideas in gifts would be on display, and it was where they would do a great deal of the buying or ordering of stock for their boutique for the next year. It was always a fun expedition.

They had made their reservations at the Holiday Inn on King Street, and finally the date had arrived. They were both looking forward to getting away for two whole days of fun, with a little bit of work thrown in.

As usual, Kitty's parents were coming over from Toronto to mind the cats. They had offered to have Kitty and Steffie stay in their home in Toronto to save the hotel money, but the answer to that was a resounding "no." The friends were looking forward very much to the fun of staying in a hotel, drinking in the bar, eating in a fancy restaurant, and just living it up.

It turned out that Mitch was away on a reading tour, so they would have the two days totally to themselves.

They drove over to Toronto on a sunny, slightly cooler day. The traffic was as heavy as it always was on that dreadful Queen Elizabeth Highway, but they were too excited to let it bother them. Steffie was driving, and Kitty always felt totally confident with Steff at the wheel.

They lucked out with the hotel room. It was a large corner room with two queen size beds, and it looked out onto Lake Ontario. It was perfect. They had driven up Wednesday afternoon, so that they could be up bright and early for the opening of the show on Thursday morning.

Hastily unpacking their bags, and hanging up the few clothes they had brought, they put on good walking shoes, and set out to do a little shopping and sight seeing. Both women had lived and worked in Toronto, before moving to Niagara Falls, so it was always a treat to come back for a visit.

Yonge Street was as interesting as ever. If you walked far enough on it you could see every nationality, every type of store, and every possible eating place. The variety was amazing. That one street was really a microcosm of the entire city.

Beautifully dressed women wearing the latest fashions, rubbed shoulders with the grungiest of punks, with green hair and droopy drawers. Mothers with babies hanging in chest huggers, and school kids with books and treasures in backpacks, walked side by side. Business men with briefcases walked behind pimps with their ladies. It was fascinating, and Kitty and Steffie walked right up north of Bloor Street, to Yorkville and beyond.

They didn't buy much, although Steffie found a great pair of espadrilles, which she loved, and Kitty found a pretty summer cotton sweater in aquas and blues.

By the time they made it back to the hotel, they were exhausted. It had been a very long walk, and had taken three hours. They dropped their purchases in the room, showered quickly, and headed back downstairs, to have a drink in the lounge, and decide where to have dinner.

After a leisurely dinner at Alice Fazooli's, they headed back to the hotel lounge to have a pre-bedtime drink. They had to be up early the next morning, but they hated to leave the lounge. There was an excellent piano player, who was playing some of the great old jazz standards, and they couldn't tear themselves away.

Sitting in the darkened lounge, sipping their drinks, and leaning back on the leather banquettes, they played a couple of rounds of their favourite "Who played in this movie?" quiz. Kitty stumped Steffie when she asked who had starred in "Body Heat."

Steffie groaned as she took another sip of her wine. "I'm sure it was Kathleen Turner," she finally muttered, but I can't think of the guy's name. I can see him clearly, but his name just won't come."

"Would it help if I gave you his initials?" asked Kitty smugly.

"Okay," agreed Steffie.

"The initials are 'W' and 'H'.

Steffie still couldn't get it, so Kitty had to tell her that it was William Hurt.

"Oh, poo. That was a hard one. Who else was in it?"

"I'm not really sure," admitted Kitty, "but I think that Richard Crenna played a part. Can't think of any others though."

They chatted some more, and then Steffie nudged her friend. "See those two guys over at that table?"

"Yes, I see them. One has his back to us, and the cute one is looking this way. What about them?"

"The one looking this way, wearing that light blue sweater, looks very much like my ex."

"You're kidding. He's gorgeous. If your ex husband was as cute as that guy, why did you ever let him get away?" As soon as she said it, she regretted it. She remembered with dismay that Steffie had once admitted her husband had been abusive, as well as a philanderer.

"Oh, I'm sorry, Steff. That was a stupid thing to say. I must have had too much wine. I know that you didn't just let him get away. You dumped him, and with good reason. I can see why you married him though, if he's as attractive as that guy."

Steffie laughed ruefully. "I was young, right out of university, and he swept me off my feet. I was totally taken in by his good looks and his charm, much like you with Scott. At least my guy didn't turn out to be a serial killer, which Scott might prove to be."

"Oh, don't even mention it. I really don't think the police believe that he's the Black Sheep, although they were hoping to pin it on him. I don't think there's any proof."

Steffie had drunk enough wine that it had loosened her tongue, and she was on the verge of telling Kitty about the two nightmares she had had. She decided against it, however. Why spoil their lovely little vacation? Finally, the piano player packed it in, good sense prevailed, and they headed up to bed.

They had both fallen asleep quickly, when the pounding on the door started. Steffie was the first to waken, but Kitty was the first to jump out of bed and turn on the lights.

"Who is it?" she asked sleepily, trying to peek out the peek hole in the door. It looked as if there were three men standing there, and two of them had wine bottles in their hands.

"Is this where the party is?" called out one, swaying a bit.

"No, it's on the next floor up," called Kitty crossly, realizing that they had been wakened out of their sound sleep by three drunks.

"Come on, baby, open up. I know the party's right here," called another one, pounding on the door again.

"Honestly, there's no party here. I'm taking care of my sick grandmother, and I thought you were the hotel doctor," answered Kitty earnestly.

"Oh, sorry lady," they all mumbled, as they staggered off down the hall.

"Am I the sick grandmother?" asked Steffie with a grin.

"Well it worked didn't it?" replied Kitty, as she fell back into bed.

It was close to five a.m. when the fire alarm went off.

"I don't believe this," grumbled Steffie, hurrying into her clothes. "Where the heck did I put my shoes?"

"Do you think it's a real fire? Let's call down to the front desk before we walk all the way down those stairs," suggested Kitty grimly. "Remember, we're on the seventeenth floor. After that walk we did this afternoon, I don't think I could make it."

Steffie put her hands on the door, and since it didn't feel hot, she opened it a crack. There wasn't any smoke, but people were coming out of their rooms and heading for the stairwell. The loud speakers were blaring requests that everyone head for the lobby.

Kitty was told the same thing when she called the front desk, so, reluctantly, they took their keys and purses, and set out. They also wet two towels to put over their faces, in case they encountered smoke.

Going down and down the stairs, making turns on each floor, had a dizzying effect, specially after the drinks they had consumed in the lounge. By the eighth floor, they realized that there was definitely smoke in the stairwell. That created a bit of panic. Maybe there really was a fire. Could they make it to the lobby before the smoke got too thick?

They couldn't really speed up their descent, as there were now too many people in the stairwell. One old couple must have been in their eighties, and they were holding onto each other, as they slowly made their way down. At one point the woman tripped, and would have fallen, if her husband hadn't had a good grip on her. Steffie and Kitty slowed up, and helped the two down the remaining stairs. It was difficult not to think about the people in the twin towers on that fateful September morning.

The smoke was much thicker on the fifth and sixth floors, and the two friends gave their wet towels to the two old folk, as they struggled through the smoke.

Finally they all reached the lobby, and watched as more firemen arrived, with extra hoses and hatchets.

Kitty and Steffie walked outside to get fresh air, and to watch all the excitement. They knew it would be quite a while before the elevators were back in service, so they walked along King Street a short distance, then came back. It seemed forever before the firemen returned to their trucks, and the hotel announced that the fire was out, and it was safe to return to their rooms. The hotel staff were very helpful and very apologetic. They said that the fire had apparently started in a guest's room, when the guest fell asleep smoking. Kitty and Steffie immediately wondered whether it was one of the drunks who had been pounding on their door, looking for a party.

The elevators were jammed, and it took another half hour before they made it back to their room. By now they were so tired that their eyes were hanging at half mast, and they would be getting their wake-up call in a little over an hour. Without saying a word, they fell into their separate beds, and were asleep almost instantaneously.

When the wake-up call came, it took several rings before either one stirred. They stumbled around, had breakfast downstairs in the café, and took a taxi to the Air Canada Centre. It was going to be a long day.

CHAPTER 55

▼

Daily routines are just that — daily routines. One can get out of bed in the morning, shower, brush her teeth and her hair, (hopefully not with the same brush), and choose a becoming outfit, all with no knowledge or warning of what life changing events are destined to occur before bedtime. That was how it was with Kitty on this clear, sunny morning.

She and Steffie were chatting during a quiet moment in the shop. They were having a little dinner party for Cassie and Vickie, that very night. It would be part of a "thank-you" to Cassie, for letting them use her lovely condo. The vacation had done them a lot of good, and had been such fun, until they received the dreadful news about Cleo. There would just be the four of them, although if Cleo had still been alive, they would have invited her too.

They were going over the menu one more time. "The jumbo shrimp and fancy cheese tray should be more than enough, while we're having drinks," said Steffie, who was really looking forward to the evening. "That crisp Greek salad you make, is terrific. Then you'll do the filets on the barbecue, and I'll do the lovely roasted potatoes, which only I can do so well," she added with a modest grin. "Those Italian green beans will be great too. I haven't had them all summer. Now, you still haven't told me what you've made for dessert."

"Oh last night I made that lemon ambrosia, which is so rich and delicious. Remember I made it last Christmas, and everyone seemed to like it. It will be cholesterol city, but who cares? I want to have a super duper meal for Cassie. She's been so generous to us."

They had considered having lobster tails as well, but decided that might be overkill. They would save those for another time. They agreed that the menu was perfect, and Steffie went off to help a customer reach down a large vase from a top shelf. When the store was quiet again, she came back to Kitty and said, "Who played in "Captain Newman M.D"? I need you to name at least three actors."

Kitty screwed her eyes shut, and began pulling at one bouncy little curl with her right hand. "I know that Gregory Peck was in it, and the nurse was Angie Dickinson, but who else? Let's see. I think that maybe Bobby Darin had a small part in it. Wasn't he the shell shocked one? I don't remember that movie well at all, but I'd love to see it again."

"That's pretty good. They were the three I remembered too, but I also think that maybe Robert Duvall was in it. Remind me to look it up on the computer."

Both friends realized that they were trying to keep each other amused and busy, so that they wouldn't have to think about Cleo, and how recently she had been the happy third member of the staff. Life just didn't make any sense these days.

The night was perfect for the party. It was warm and balmy, and there were a trillion stars in the sky, just hanging there, waiting to be counted. After dinner, they all trooped out to the gazebo, wine glasses in hand. They talked for a while about the Cattery, and what a wonderful job Cassie had made of it.

Steffie told Vickie how great she looked tonight in her new long beige skirt and fitted jacket, which she was wearing over a coral silk shirt. The coral was perfect with her auburn hair and peaches and cream complexion. She looked much younger than her "40 something" years.

Her big brown eyes were sparkling, as she told them about the trip she was thinking of taking to Tennessee to visit some friends from Vancouver who had just moved there. The silly thing was that she planned to drive all by herself.

Cassie wasn't sure that she could get away right now, or she would have been going with her. She hated to think of Vickie making that long drive to Tennessee on her own, so she was doing her best to rearrange her commitments, in order to go too. Actually, she didn't understand why Vickie was going at all. It didn't make sense to her, but Vickie had a mind of her own, and could be very stubborn at times. Cass just shook her head in disbelief.

Who would drive all the way to Tennessee by herself, when she could just as easily go with a friend, or, better still, when she could fly. The only person crazy enough to do it was Vickie.

They were all talking too much and too fast, just to insure that there were no long pauses in which they would all think about Cleo. It was still impossible to take in the fact that someone they knew so well, had been murdered by the Black Sheep. No one felt safe. In fact, the entire city of Niagara Falls was in a tizzy. Families were having extra locks put on their doors and windows. Women were cancelling or rearranging any nighttime meetings. Husbands who travelled on business, were cancelling their trips to stay home with their families.

People felt as if they were under siege. Handymen and servicemen were no longer allowed into homes. The bars, restaurants and strip clubs were basically empty, and even the casinos and the movies were suffering. No one wanted to be out in the dark. Even sitting out in the gazebo in the dark was a scary thing to do. It was only the "safety in numbers" mentality which allowed it.

Steffie had driven over with Cassie and Vickie, and was going to stay the night. She and Kitty knew that it would take quite a while to clean up all the mess after their guests left. The main reason, however, the one neither of them verbalized, was that they were glad to have each other for company. Daytime was okay, but once the dark set in, those old atavistic fears reared up, and made themselves known. Anything was possible in the blackness of the night.

Steffie was in a giddy mood, and started telling some of her blond jokes. She did this periodically, just to tease Kitty, who had such blond curly hair. "Okay, guys, listen up. How do you get a blond's eyes to sparkle?" she asked in a serious tone.

No one knew or cared, but she told them anyway. "You shine a flashlight in her ear."

They couldn't help but laugh, so this encouraged her.

"What does a blond say after her doctor tells her she's pregnant?"

This was answered by silence.

"She says 'Is it mine?'"

They laughed again, but now Kitty and Cassie were putting their hands over their ears so as not to listen. They were pretending annoyance at these bad jokes aimed at them.

"Okay, I've got one more for you, since you don't appreciate the humour," grinned Steffie. "What do you call a blond with half a brain?" Not expecting an answer, she continued, "You say she's gifted."

This was followed by squeals of laughter, as the champagne made the stale old jokes seem hilarious.

Vickie thought of one just as she and Cassie were about to leave. "How can you tell a blond has been using the computer? There's white-out on the screen."

This was followed with more peals of laughter, as the evening came to an end.

Cassie and Vickie finally left, after many thanks for the great dinner and the fun-filled evening. It was so good to laugh again, after the sadness of Cleo's death.

Kitty ran upstairs to change out of her party clothes — a long turquoise skirt with a cream and turquoise summer sweater. Steffie began to gather all the glasses and silverware which couldn't go into the dishwasher. When Kitty returned in her red shorts and navy top, Steffie realized that she should also change out of her emerald green patio pants and matching top. She didn't want to spill anything on the new outfit, which she had bought for their trip to Florida, and then never had a chance to wear.

Kitty went out to check that the propane tank was turned off, and all the barbecue tools had been brought in. She was just walking to the gazebo, to look for any forgotten wineglasses, when Adrian suddenly appeared out of the dark.

"Adrian, you scared me. What's up? Were we too loud tonight?"

"I'm sorry I scared you, Kitty. I knew you were having a party because of all the laughter, so I waited till I saw that the car was gone from the driveway, before I came over. I didn't want to interrupt. You women seemed to be having such a good time. I'm having a problem, and I wanted to ask for some advice, so I waited till you were alone."

Kitty was about to tell him that Steffie was still here, but he continued, "You look terrific in shorts, you know. You've got great legs."

Oh shit, Kitty thought. Here we go again. "Well, it's a bit late tonight, pal. Could it wait till tomorrow? I still have all the kitchen to clean up, unless you'd like to help me," she added with a grin.

"Come on now, darlin'. Don't brush me off like that. I really want your advice."

He chucked her under the chin, and made kissing motions with his lips.

He was staring right into her eyes, and Kitty suddenly had a queasy feeling in her stomach. Was it from all the food she had eaten, or was Adrian giving off strange vibes? If he was here to put the make on her again, she still wasn't interested. He had already asked her out several times, and she had always politely refused. Tonight she was just too tired to be bothered. He was getting to be a pest.

She wished that Steffie would hurry and come back downstairs to keep her company, and help with the clean-up. She liked Adrian a lot. He was a fun guy and a great neighbour, but Kitty was exhausted, and she had drunk too much wine. She just wanted to lay her head on her pillow, and sleep for hours.

"Okay, Adrian, what kind of advice could I possibly give you? You seem to have lots of lady friends, and you fly to all those exotic places, which most of us will never see. You've got a lovely home, and you've never had a wife to nag you. Seems to me that you've got it made. Now I, on the other hand, seem to go from one problem to another. I never know what I'm doing."

"Boy, when you put it that way, I guess you're right," he laughed. "Actually, I just wanted to pop over to see you for a minute. I haven't seen much of you lately, because you're always out with some guy. You can't seem to be faithful to anyone, can you?"

Kitty was totally taken aback at that remark, and annoyed as well. "Look, Adrian, I'm tired, and I've had too much wine, and I have a whole kitchen full of dirty dishes I have to do. I don't want to get into an argument with you, because you are a dear, funny friend, so why don't you go home, and I'll forget you said that." She turned and started toward the back door.

"Oh, Kitty, I'm sorry. I'm a bit distraught tonight. I heard you gals laughing and talking about all the men in your lives. You were laughing at how you treat us."

"We were no such thing," cried Kitty in astonishment. "What gave you that crazy idea?" But then she remembered guiltily that maybe they had been talking about men, and the intricacies of relationships.

"It's true. You women are all alike. You flit from guy to guy. You can't be trusted, and then you laugh about it. My wife was a perfect example."

"Your wife," cried Kitty. "I thought you weren't married."

"I'm not now," he laughed bitterly. "She got what she deserved though, the bitch."

Kitty was astounded, and suddenly she was afraid. Spikes of fear clawed at her chest. This was not the Adrian she thought she knew. Had he been drinking? She didn't want to hear any more. Somehow she had to get into the house and lock the doors. Where the heck was Steffie?

She made it up the four steps to the deck, and was just opening her mouth to call her friend, when Adrian's big hand clamped on her mouth, with the other hand grabbing her around the waist.

"Oh no you don't, you little tramp, you frivolous, flighty, fickle little tramp. You're like all the rest. You think you're too good for me, and yet you're running around with every other guy in town. Let's see, just this summer alone there's been Scott, then Drew. I don't know what went on with Josh while he was working here, but I can guess, and then of course there was Keith, and now you're all agog over the writer, the famous Mitch Donaldson," he said, with a sour look on his face. "That's way too many men for one gal in one summer. Don't you see how bad that makes you look? Don't you see what an ugly picture it paints? Don't you see how that hurts me when you flaunt them in my face?"

She was so taken aback at what he had said, and what he was doing, that she was momentarily immobilized. How in the world did he know all this about her private life? She hadn't told him anything about Mitch, or had she? Had he been listening at her kitchen door when she was on the phone? Oh yes, maybe they had talked about Mitch that night in the gazebo, when Lacey was here. Well, no matter. It certainly wasn't any of his business how many men she dated. This was Adrian, her friend and confidante. What was the matter with him? She tried to twist under his arm, and get close enough to the door so that she could yell for Steffie, but he was too quick for her. Suddenly his hands were around her throat, and he was squeezing.

Kitty tried to fight him off, but he seemed very strong. She couldn't believe it. This couldn't be happening. Was this the Black Sheep? No, not Adrian, never Adrian. Adrian was a great neighbour. Adrian was the one who had come over to fix the hose when it sprang a leak. Adrian had brought over the first tray of chocolate chip cookies he had ever baked, slightly burned and lopsided, but still pretty good for a first attempt. Adrian had played with the baby Charlie, and had bounced him on his lap right here on the deck. No way was Adrian the Black Sheep. There was some awful mistake. No way had that psycho killer who strangled Cleo, been living right next door to her.

Impossible. He must be fooling, acting silly, but the pressure on her throat, and the crazed look in his eyes made her discard that faint hope.

Who would have guessed? Obviously not the police! Life was so strange with its twists and turns. Her heart was pounding feverishly now, and there was a frightening ringing in her ears. Her thoughts jumped and crackled like popping corn.

Poor Scott had been so maligned. She had suspected him of being the killer at one point, when all he wanted to do was patch things up with her. How could she have been so wrong? She had always been a pretty good judge of character. She had to tell Jack, but Jack would know soon enough. But what if Jack and Bud jumped to the conclusion that Scott had killed her? She couldn't tap into that possibility. Was she really going to die on such a velvety soft evening? The sky was so beautiful, and the warm air seemed to wrap itself around her comfortingly, but there was no comfort to be found in what Adrian was doing.

Well, there was no way she was going to just give up and let the Black Sheep kill her, if that's who he thought he was. Maybe he had snapped, and was trying to be a copycat killer. She was certain that he couldn't have killed Cleo, and those other poor women.

Kitty was a fighter, and she would fight with her last breath. Unfortunately, that seemed to be just what was happening. She was slight, but she was in pretty good shape. Adrian, however, was much stronger than he appeared. The more he squeezed, the more panicky and breathless she became. She tried to knee him, but that was futile. She clawed at his face, and did manage a few good scratches, but that didn't stop him. He was glaring at her with such intensity, and something else — excitement maybe — that he seemed quite crazy. What could she possibly do to save herself?

CHAPTER 56

▼

Time was moving on two different levels for Kitty — her mind's time, and real time. In her mind, she was thinking of the almost fatal canoe trip, which she had survived. She had to cling to that thought. She had survived. God wouldn't have saved her in Muskoka, just so that she could be killed here at the hands of a psycho. Things were becoming a bit blurry now in real time. Her lungs were burning, and she was frantic for air.

Kitty's resolve came through just as it had in Muskoka in that treacherous water. She owed it to herself, and to the people and cats she loved, to fight with every ounce of strength and hope that she had. She struggled as if there was no tomorrow, and perhaps for her there wasn't.

She clawed at his face again, and she tried prying his hands open — anything to make him loosen his grip, anything to buy time. "Oh please God, let Steffie show up. I need help here." Her ears were ringing, and a kaleidoscope of lights danced before her eyes.

He was trying to drag her into the house. Was that good or bad? It was definitely bad. There was more privacy in the house, and no chance of anyone looking over the fence and seeing him. Also, Steffie was in the house, and he didn't know that yet. By the time Steffie realized what was happening, and called 911, Kitty would be dead. He would finish killing Kitty, and then go after Steffie, once he discovered she was there.

All these thoughts were whirling in her head, as she put up the second fight for her life within a period of a few weeks.

Adrian was panting now. She was not making it easy for him.

"I thought you were such a nice woman, Kitty. Why did you have to be such a tramp? Why couldn't you settle down with one man? You've left a trail of broken hearts behind you. Why wouldn't you go out with me? I would have been so good to you." All the time he was asking these rhetorical questions, he was squeezing tighter and tighter.

For some strange reason, she noticed the sweat on his forehead, and the mole he had on his cheek. She had never noticed that stupid mole before. Maybe it was cancerous. Well, if it was, it wouldn't do her any good. Her mind was playing hopscotch, and she thought that someone must have dimmed the patio lights, because her world was becoming a dark haze. Try as she might with her kicking and scratching, she knew that she was losing. She and Mitch would never make beautiful music together. She had run out of time.

None of his victims had ever fought the way Kitty did. He felt that he was struggling with a tiger. She was almost more than he could handle, but he could feel her weakening.

"Don't worry, Kitty, after you're dead I'm going to take three nice pictures of you. They'll go in my album — the Black Sheep's album. I have quite a collection already. Oh, and don't worry. I'll take you inside and lay you on the bed. I'll be sure that you look as good as can be expected under the circumstances." He made a strange little sound at this point, half giggle, half snort.

"You know, I've heard you and Steffie play that movie game — who starred in what movie? Well, here's one you should be able to guess. Who starred in that blockbuster 'The Black Sheep Strikes Again'? Well now, I think it just might be that little trollop, Kitty Winfield, and the avenger, Adrian Simpson." He apparently loved this little joke, and squeezed tighter, as he felt Kitty go limp in his hands.

Inside, Steffie was pulling her shirt over her head, as she ran downstairs to help Kitty finish tidying. It had been a really fun evening, and she was so glad that she had decided to sleep over. They had such good times together. She considered herself very lucky to have a friend and partner like Kitty Winfield. Life was so darn good these days, except for losing Nick and Cleo. She didn't want to ever lose anyone else in her lifetime. Friends and loved ones were just too precious.

Meanwhile, Cassie and Vickie had been almost home, when Cassie realized that her gold bracelet was gone. "It must have fallen off at Kitty's," she said in disgust, after Vickie assured her that it wasn't in the backseat or any-where in front. "I knew that the clasp was loose, and I shouldn't have worn it. Damn. I'm sorry Vickie. We'll have to go back. It's likely in the gazebo. I think I remember fiddling with it when we were all sitting out there. You know, my scalp has been tingling like crazy all evening. I guess it was because I was going to lose that bracelet. I should have paid attention and checked the clasp."

"Oh, God, save me from Cassandra and her tingling scalp," intoned Vickie facetiously. "How many times does that scalp of yours tingle?"

"Laugh all you want, oh ye of little faith. Remember how often it tingled two summers ago, and remember how many times bad things happened?

As they parked in the driveway, Cassie said "I'll just go round to the back and get it, and we won't even have to bother Kitty."

"I've got a better idea. I'll go with you. Maybe Kitty will ask us in for another glass of wine," grinned Vickie. It was a decision which would have huge repercussions for all of them.

As they rounded the corner to the back yard, they were surprised to see Kitty engaged in an awkward dance with a tall man.

"Who the heck is she dancing with now?" laughed Cassie. Then they real-ized that he had his hands around Kitty's neck, and that she wasn't dancing, but was struggling feebly with him.

"Hey, stop that," shrieked Cassie, as she dove at the man. He looked over his shoulder in utter astonishment, as this woman tried to grab his arms. Keeping his big left hand around Kitty's neck, he took his right hand away long enough to elbow Cassie right in the face. She staggered back against the barbecue, lost her balance, and fell down the four stairs to the grass.

At this point Kitty was barely aware of Cassie's arrival, but when her friend dove at the strangler, causing him to take one hand away from her throat, Kitty was able to suck in a few puffs of fresh air. This cleared her head momentarily, and gave her a little strength. A small squeak escaped from her mouth, like a fluttering bird. Then the big hand closed around her neck again.

Vickie, looking around frantically for a weapon of some kind, spotted a knife on the barbecue, along with tongs and a flipper. Of course, if she had realized that it was Adrian, she might have hesitated, thinking that he was just goofing around with Kitty. Seeing in disbelief what he had done to Cassie, however, and what he was trying to do to Kitty, she didn't have time to think. She simply grabbed up the knife, and sprang at him, driving it right into his neck.

Suddenly it was déjà vu. It was as if she was back in the woods outside the old burning house two years ago. She had brought a rock down on the head of Willy the Weasel, the night he had been about to plunge his knife into Jack Willinger. Now Vickie was the one with the knife, plunging it into someone she didn't even know. She hadn't seen his face, so she didn't realize that it was Adrian, the handsome pilot from next door.

That night two years ago had been horrific. She and Cassie had been locked in a burning house, and were saved at the last moment, just before the old house collapsed in on itself. Vickie had a concussion from being hit over the head with the handle of a gun, and she was in pretty bad shape when she attacked Willy with the rock. Cassie had been there to help, by stabbing him in the back of the hand with a pair of scissors.

Now here they were again, somehow caught up in a life and death situation. Seeing Kitty being strangled that way had left Vickie no time to think. She had simply reacted as anyone would. At least she hoped that was how the police would see it.

She had been having such a great time this summer, just as she always did when she and Cassie got together. Two years ago it had been fun, exciting and scary, as she and Cass had gone from one adventure to another. This time, however, they weren't the targets of any killer, and they weren't being stalked, so it was much more relaxing.

Of course, she and Brian were still feuding in a long-distance way. He really wanted to move the family to Scotland, and Vickie really wanted to talk him out of it. The idea of actually leaving Canada for another country was appalling. Vickie loved Scotland, it was a beautiful country full of friendly people, but the weather was less than perfect, and it just wasn't home, and never could be. She was avoiding even talking to Brian at the moment, and she was working on a list of reasons why they should not move. Now, however, she wanted that darling man here beside her.

These thoughts were flying through her mind like a video being fast-forwarded.

Adrian howled as the knife penetrated his neck, and he loosened his hold on Kitty's throat. Just then Steffie burst out the patio door, wondering who was making all the noise.

It was total chaos. The strangler was trying desperately to grab the knife, which was sticking out of his neck. He felt as if he was strangling on his own blood. Suddenly he realized how terrifying it was to be facing death. He had a clear picture of what his victims had gone through. Why had he created all this mayhem? He could be married now to Ginny, leading a good life, having fun with his friends, enjoying his wonderful job. Where had he jumped the track? What had happened to bring him to this place, with a knife sticking out of his throat?

Vickie had stabbed him with all her might, and the knife was embedded almost up to the hilt. As he loosened it slightly, blood started spurting everywhere. Cassie was weaving on her feet, and trying to staunch the flow of blood from her mouth and lip. When he had elbowed her so viciously, the Black Sheep had split her lip, and had caused her to bite her tongue.

"Oh, no, here we go again," was Cassie's first thought, as she tried valiantly to clear her head. She felt really woozy, and her tongue was bleeding all over the front of her pretty white sweater.

Her thoughts also turned to that wicked night two years ago, when she and Vickie had been locked in the burning house. They had been attacked, hit on their heads, and dragged down the stairs to the basement, before the house was set ablaze. Being freed by a relative, they had been shot at by one of the killers, and had barely managed to save Jack's life, by attacking Willy the Weasel. They had ended up in the hospital, suffering from smoke inhalation, concussion, and torn fingers. That night, she and Vickie had worked as a team. Tonight, however, it looked as if Vickie had taken care of things all on her own.

Steffie barely had time to assess the situation, before she got her arms around Kitty, and half dragged, half carried her to a chair. She was remembering the two nightmares she had experienced. In them she had somehow known that Kitty was in danger from the strangler, and now it had happened. Her friend had almost been killed by some maniac. Then she realized that the maniac was Adrian from next door.

Was he the Black Sheep? No, it wasn't possible. Adrian must have just flipped out. What if she hadn't been here? What if Cassie and Vickie hadn't returned? Why had they returned? All these questions were flapping around in her head like a torn sheet in the wind. She frantically tended to Kitty, who was now coughing and gagging, but looking more alert.

Vickie was standing, looking terrified at what she had done. With the sickening amount of blood pumping out of his neck, she knew that she must have sliced the strangler's carotid artery. Strange how blood looked so black in the moonlight, she thought vaguely.

Her frightened thoughts were somersaulting in her head. She had visions of prison bars, and pictured Brian and her kids coming to visit her. Thank God Brian wasn't here to see her in this mess. Oh, but how she wished that he could be here to comfort and reassure her. She suddenly felt very much alone.

Would they say that she had committed murder, or was it manslaughter, or was it self-defense? No, it couldn't be the latter. The strangler hadn't had his hands around HER neck. Surely, though, she would get some Brownie points for saving Kitty's life. On the other hand, the police might say that she had used "undue force" or whatever the term was. Maybe they would say she should have just tapped him on the shoulder and said "please stop killing my friend."

Vickie was on the point of hysteria, and began to giggle at this last thought. She was vaguely aware of someone's arms around her, and someone was telling her she had done the right thing. They would call Jack, and he would straighten things out. Jack was always there when they needed him. Of course it was Cassie who was trying to comfort her. Cass was always there for her.

Adrian was now on his knees, making strange gurgling noises. This was all wrong. He was the strangler, but now he was the one strangling on his own blood.

He was still trying to grab at the knife and pull it out, but his hands were too slippery from the blood, and the knife was in too far. He couldn't believe it. This wasn't the way it was supposed to happen. He was the Black Sheep. He was invincible. How had all these women suddenly appeared? He had seen the car leave just a few minutes ago, and he thought all three women had been in it. Now they were all back here. How could he have made such a mistake? Perhaps this was just a nightmare. Yes, that was it. It was just a horrible nightmare. It was a warning that he must stop the stranglings. If he could just waken up, everything would be all right.

Things were getting hazy now, but he could see Kitty holding her hands to her neck. He wished that he had had time to explain to her why he had to kill her. Somehow it wasn't the same if they didn't understand. But now he couldn't quite remember why he felt he had to kill her. Obviously he hadn't succeeded, because she was standing right there in front of him. If he could just get to his feet, maybe he could make a run for it before the police came.

In the excitement and its bloody aftermath, not one of the women had thought to call 911. They were all staring at Adrian, as he knelt amongst them, as if in supplication. It made a weird tableau, the four women surrounding the killer, as his dark life's blood pumped quietly and steadily onto the gleaming wood of the new deck.

Adrian had a terrified look on his face, as he saw not just the four women, Kitty, Steffie, Cassie and Vickie, all staring at him, but also, — no, it couldn't be. Yes, there she was — his scrawny old mother, and beside her were the two prostitutes. One had the pink boa around her neck, and the other was the Barbie doll bimbo. Beside them was that nice girl he had picked up in the bar and left by Lake Gibson. Her name had been Lana. Eva was there, looking at him reproachfully, and, oh God, there was Cleo, frowning at him. Five of them were holding out their hands toward him, and in each hand was a little black sheep. It was as if they were trying to give the sheep back to him. Only the woman with the pink boa didn't have one.

All of the ghastly, ghostly women had bulging eyes, red faces, reddish purple necks, blue lips, and signs of petechial hemorrhaging in the eyes, lids and lips. Their tongues were sticking out, and they were hideous and terrifying. Adrian tried to scream, but it came out sounding like a tiny little gurgle, as he toppled over onto the deck.

It was some time before anyone noticed the little black sheep which had fallen from Adrian's pocket, and which was lying broken in two pieces in a puddle of blood.

EPILOGUE

▼

Two weeks later.

The heat wave was finally over. The citizens of Niagara Falls breathed a collective sigh of relief, because the reign of terror was also over. The Black Sheep was dead. It was amazing how that news seemed to lighten the entire city. People laughed and patted each other on the back. Neighbours were neighbourly again. Friends were friendly. It was as if some undeclared war had been won.

Vickie had been questionned extensively by the police, as had the other three witnesses. There was no doubt in anyone's mind that Vickie had saved Kitty, by plunging that knife into Adrian's neck. She had been totally exonerated. There would be no charges pending.

She had called Brian in Scotland, and told him the whole story. He declared that he would come home immediately, but Vickie said it wasn't necessary. She was fine now with what she had done. She had had so much praise from so many people, that she was beginning to feel like quite the heroine.

Cassie was just glad that she had gone back that night to look for her gold bracelet. Her face had healed nicely, and luckily Adrian had not loosened any of her teeth, when he hit her so viciously, and knocked her down the stairs.

Steffie was still trying to understand the frightening nightmares she had experienced. She had never been clairvoyant, and yet twice she had dreamt that Kitty was going to be a victim of the Black Sheep. Those nightmares had very nearly come true. She hoped sincerely that she would never have night-mares like that again.

Kitty had bounced right back. The first few nights had been bad, but Steffie had stayed right with her. Her parents had also come over from Toronto. Her mother kept saying "I told you so," and wringing her hands at how close she had come to losing her beloved daughter.

Kitty kept dreaming that she could feel Adrian's hands around her neck, and she would waken up in a sweat. Everytime she looked at herself in the mirror, she saw those deep purple bruises on her neck, and relived the experience. Now, however, she was fine. She had put it behind her, and was enjoying the fuss that everyone, especially Mitch, was making over her. She was apparently the first of Adrian's would-be victims who had fought so hard, and the police had commended her on her bravery, and fight for survival.

True, for a little while there, her whole world had tilted slightly, and she had been in danger of falling right off, but it had righted itself, and things were now crystal clear. The very air she breathed seemed fresh and sweet. Things and people had sharply delineated edges, and colours were brighter and more exciting. Adrian had not succeeded in strangling her. The Muskoka lake had not managed to drown her when her canoe flipped over. Steffie had not been killed by that crazy robber. Best of all, she and Mitch had found each other. Life was impossibly good!

The police had found Adrian's album, with pictures of some of the victims. Of course the police assumed and hoped that these were the only women he had killed. They had no way of knowing about his mother and the Toronto prostitute. He hadn't had a camera to take pictures of those first two victims.

In that locked metal box from the Black Sheep's closet, they also found a long, rambling love letter to Ginny, who, it turned out, was Adrian's sister-in-law. She had been married to his twin brother Mike. Jack blanched when he realized that it was no doubt Adrian who had broken into Ginny's house that night earlier in the summer. Apparently, at one point, Ginny was to be his next victim. Jack knew that Cassie had been there, visiting Ginny, when the break-in occurred. Cassie could have been one of his victims too. His heart beat wildly at the very thought.

On this particular Sunday evening, Kitty was having her three close friends over for a barbecue. Now that the heat wave was over, the weather was beautiful again, and they were sitting out in the gazebo, talking about the summer, and all the strange things which had happened. Somehow, they couldn't bring themselves to sit on the deck where Adrian had been killed. It was even surreal looking over the fence at Adrian's empty house. They still could barely believe that their charming friend had been the much sought after strangler. They had known he was intelligent, they had known he was a flirt, they just hadn't known he was a killer.

Before heading over to Kitty's house, Steffie had taken a shower, and was drying herself, when the phone rang. Hastily wrapping a towel around her body, she hurried to answer it, thinking it would be Kitty asking her to bring some forgotten item.

"Hello," she said, standing in the kitchen, and looking at the wet footprints she had made on her shiny kitchen floor.

"Hi, Steffie," came a voice she had never expected to hear again, at least not in this lifetime.

She gasped, and gave an involuntary shudder. "Who, who is this?" she asked, frowning in confusion. Was someone playing a macabre trick on her?

"You know who it is, little sister. It's Nick, back from the dead."

She knew immediately that it really was Nick. She could tell his voice anywhere. "I don't understand," she whispered, falling back onto a kitchen chair.

"Well, I hate to shock you like this, but I needed to talk to you. You see, that loan shark was after me, and I was afraid that he might go after you too. I decided the only way out was to plan my own suicide. It wasn't hard to do. I'm sorry I had to put you through all that, but I couldn't let you know, or you might not have been able to fake surprise or sorrow or whatever."

"But where are you now?"

"Sis, I can't tell you, just in case he's still looking for me, although I'm pretty sure he believes I'm dead. As a matter of fact, I am almost dead. That damn brain tumour is back, and the docs have given me six months to a year. They told me just before I got out of prison. I'm so sorry that I treated you so shabbily. It's just that, well, my head is really screwed up, and there are times when I can't help myself. I do awful and crazy things. Then I have days when I'm fine."

"But Nick, can't they operate? Are they doing radiation or anything?" Steffie was now very calm. Nick was alive, and somehow they could get through this.

"No, there's nothing to be done. I've had it, as they say. But, honestly, I'm okay. I'm in a beautiful, warm, safe place, and it's far enough away, that I don't think anyone will ever find me. You can't tell a soul, sis. It's got to be our little secret. I want to live out the rest of my days in peace on this island, and I need to know that you are safe."

"Oh, Nick, please let me come and meet you. I could stay with you till, well, — I could stay with you. I could take care of you."

"No, listen, Steff. I'm fine, really. This is one of my good days. I just had to talk to you, and say how sorry I am for all the trouble I caused you. I want you to have a great life. Find yourself a nice guy and get married again. I'll always remember what a good sister you were to me, and what a great time we had together at the Lion Safari that day. I wish things could have been different for us."

Before Steffie could even reply to him, he continued, "Gotta go now. Take care, and keep my secret for me. I love you, sis," and the line went dead.

Steffie hung up the phone, and just sat there for a long time. Nick was alive. What wonderfully incredible news that was. It was terrible about his tumour, but maybe the doctors were wrong about that. Maybe he would live longer than a year.

No matter how it turned out, a huge weight had been lifted from her heart. Nick had not committed suicide, so she could live with at least some relief, picturing him in Hawaii or Tahiti, or some other beautiful tropical island. He sounded happy, and that was enough for Steffie. He had acted mean and tough at times, but that was caused by the tumour. There had been a lot of good in Nick, and she prayed that no one would ever find out that he was still alive. That was a secret she would be happy to keep, although it would be difficult to keep it from her friends. She wanted to shout it to the skies. Nick was alive!

The barbecue at Kitty's was a huge success. The four women had bonded in a very special way. What they had experienced that night on the deck with Adrian, had left a lasting mark on each of them, and they knew that their friendship would endure. Life was good, and they all intended to enjoy every moment of it.

Cassie had been very quiet, not really taking part in the conversation. Suddenly she started to grin.

"What's with you?" asked Vickie. "You look as if you've just had a brilliant idea. I think I saw a little light bulb go off over your head."

"You bet I've had a brilliant idea," said Cassie, jumping up and looking from one to the other of her friends. "This has been a very exciting and scary summer for all of us, in one way or another. Actually, it has been one helluva summer," she added. In reality, her bad summer had been two years ago, when she had survived several attempts on her life, had learned a shocking secret about her parentage, and had inherited what she liked to call "a whole shitload of money." It was déjà vu, sitting there, thinking about it, and remembering how she and Vickie had sat together in her little library just this way, talking about what had transpired. She had a big surprise for Vickie that day two years ago, and tonight she had a big surprise for not only Vickie, but Kitty and Steffie as well.

This summer had been a piece of cake for her, in comparison to two years ago. Getting Cassandra's Cattery up and running had been a lot of work, but it had been fun and rewarding. Her personal moral dilemma concerning Jack was wearing her down a bit, but she was a resilient and positive thinking person. Her three friends, however, had suffered one trauma after another.

She thought about Steffie being shot, coming so close to death, recovering from that shock, and then losing her brother. At one point she remembered Steffie declaring that she felt like a human piñata.

Vickie's summer hadn't been too bad, except that she had been fighting Brian for months about moving to Scotland, and then she had the worries of having killed a man, and possibly being charged with murder. Cassie knew and understood that she was still struggling with the feelings of guilt. The very thought of having taken a human life, even though, in doing so, she had saved another human, was pretty devastating.

Kitty had almost been drowned in a frightening canoe accident, and then had come close to being the strangling victim of the crazy Black Sheep, someone she had liked and trusted. Above all that, lurked the dreadful and pathetic picture of poor Cleo, a friend to all of them. There had certainly been enough terror and excitement to go around, and now Cassie was about to give them a bit more excitement. Hopefully, however, the terror was all behind them, and the excitement would be a welcome diversion.

"You know, ladies, we've all been through a lot this summer, and we deserve a holiday, so here's what we're going to do." She looked from one to another as she spoke, trying to draw out the suspense as long as possible. "Kitty, if you can arrange for your mom and dad to come and look after the boutique and the cats, then, well, let me put it this way." She was laughing now, delighted with her brilliant idea.

"You all know that I inherited all that money which I didn't deserve, and there's plenty to go around. Money is only fun if you can share it with friends, so-o-o," here she paused to smile at each of them, and to keep the suspense going. Her three friends were all looking at her with curious expressions.

"We four are going on a cruise, and the best part is that — the cruise is on me." She beamed at them happily, as they all stared at her.

Of course, everyone started talking at once. Each one of them had a reason or reasons why she couldn't possibly accept such a generous gift. After a few minutes, however, knowing Cassie the way they did, they realized that it was useless to argue. If she said that she was taking them on a cruise, then that's exactly what they would be doing. Shootings and stranglings and suicides were now far in the past.

It took Vickie about ten seconds to discard her silly notion of driving to Tennessee on her own. All of a sudden, she couldn't remember why in the world she had wanted to do that.

Realizing that a cruise was really going to happen, all three friends suddenly launched themselves from their chairs like pop tarts springing from a toaster. They surrounded Cassie, laughing and hugging.

They were all ready for a change of scenery, for new sights and new sounds. The more they thought about a cruise, the happier they became. Cassie was totally serious about treating them, and she would be dreadfully hurt if they turned her down.

Fifteen minutes later, they had all agreed that a cruise was exactly what they needed to finish off the summer with a bang. Kitty broke out the champagne, which she always had on hand.

They had suffered their ups and downs, but after a couple of glasses of champagne, the future looked pretty rosy. The Black Sheep was dead, and there was a wonderfully carefree attitude of relief and freedom in the air. A weight had been lifted from their shoulders, and their laughter and happy voices could be heard all up and down the street that evening, as they planned their next adventure.

The End

978-0-595-44879-
0-595-44879-8

Printed in the United States
79950LV00003B/4-36

9 780595 448791